COURTSHIP

What Reviewers Say About Carsen Taite's Work

It Should be a Crime

"Taite also practices criminal law and she weaves her insider knowledge of the criminal justice system into the love story seamlessly and with excellent timing."—*Curve Magazine*

"This [*It Should be a Crime*] is just Taite's second novel…, but it's as if she has bookshelves full of bestsellers under her belt."—*Gay List Daily*

Do Not Disturb

"Taite's tale of sexual tension is entertaining in itself, but a number of secondary characters…add substantial color to romantic inevitability"—Richard Labonte, *Book Marks*

Nothing but the Truth

Author Taite is really a Dallas defense attorney herself, and it's obvious her viewpoint adds considerable realism to her story, making it especially riveting as a mystery. I give it four stars out of five."
—Bob Lind, *Echo Magazine*

"As a criminal defense attorney in Dallas, Texas, Carsen Taite knows her way around the court house. …*Nothing But the Truth* is an enjoyable mystery with some hot romance thrown in."—*Just About Write*

"Taite has written an excellent courtroom drama with two interesting women leading the cast of characters. Taite herself is a practicing defense attorney, and her courtroom scenes are clearly based on real knowledge. This should be another winner for Taite."—*Lambda Literary*

The Best Defense

"Real Life defense attorney Carsen Taite polishes her fifth work of lesbian fiction, *The Best Defense*, with the realism she daily encounters in the office and in the courts. And that polish is something that makes *The Best Defense* shine as an excellent read."—*Out & About Newspaper*

Slingshot

"The mean streets of lesbian literature finally have the hard boiled bounty hunter they deserve. It's a slingshot of a ride, bad guys and hot women rolled into one page turning package. I'm looking forward to Luca Bennett's next adventure."—J. M. Redmann, author of the Micky Knight mystery series

Battle Axe

"This second book is satisfying, substantial, and slick. Plus, it has heart and love coupled with Luca's array of weapons and a bad-ass verbal repertoire...I cannot imagine anyone not having a great time riding shotgun through all of Luca's escapades. I recommend hopping on Luca's band wagon and having a blast."—*Rainbow Book Reviews*

Beyond Innocence

"Taite keeps you guessing with delicious delay until the very last minute...Taite's time in the courtroom lends *Beyond Innocence*, a terrific verisimilitude someone not in the profession couldn't impart. And damned if she doesn't make practicing law interesting."—*Out in Print*

"As you would expect, sparks and legal writs fly. What I liked about this book were the shades of grey (no, not the smutty Shades of Grey)—both in the relationship as well as the cases."—*C-spot Reviews*

Rush

"A simply beautiful interplay of police procedural magic, murder, FBI presence, misguided protective cover-ups, and a superheated love affair…a Gold Star from me and major encouragement for all readers to dive right in and consume this story with gusto!"—*Rainbow Book Reviews*

Switchblade

"I enjoyed the book and it was a fun read—mystery, action, humour, and a bit of romance. Who could ask for more? If you've read and enjoyed Taite's legal novels, you'll like this. If you've read and enjoyed the two other books in this series, this one will definitely satisfy your Luca fix and I highly recommend picking it up. Highly recommended."—*C Spot Reviews*

Visit us at www.boldstrokesbooks.com

By the Author

Truelesbianlove.com

It Should be a Crime

Do Not Disturb

Nothing but the Truth

The Best Defense

Beyond Innocence

Rush

Courtship

The Luca Bennett Mystery Series:

Slingshot

Battle Axe

Switchblade

COURTSHIP

by

Carsen Taite

2014

COURTSHIP

ISBN 13: 978-1-62639-210-6

THIS TRADE PAPERBACK ORIGINAL IS PUBLISHED BY
BOLD STROKES BOOKS, INC.
P.O. BOX 249
VALLEY FALLS, NY 12185

FIRST EDITION: NOVEMBER 2014

CREDITS
EDITOR: CINDY CRESAP
PRODUCTION DESIGN: SUSAN RAMUNDO
COVER DESIGN BY SHERI (GRAPHICARTIST2020@HOTMAIL.COM)

Acknowledgments

I owe big thanks to the usual suspects. Len Barot aka Radclyffe—you continue to raise the bar when it comes to expanding the horizons of GLBTQ publishing, and I count myself lucky to be along for the ride. My editor, Cindy Cresap—this is our tenth book together! I can't thank you enough for your guidance, always delivered with a touch of humor. To my author pals, Ashley Bartlett and VK Powell, thanks for your insights, your critiques, and your support—the finished product is always better because of your help. Ruth Sternglantz—thanks for the perfect title. And to Sandy Lowe and all the associates at BSB who make the process seamless—you're the best!

The nomination process for a Supreme Court justice is a careful and deliberate process, and I'll be the first to admit I've taken a great deal of liberties in order to condense the details into what I hope is a compelling story. I did, however, read several volumes of nonfiction as part of my research, and I owe thanks to Jeffrey Toobin, *The Nine: Inside the Secret World of the Supreme Court*; Edward Lazarus, *Closed Chambers*; and Todd C. Peppers and Artemus Ward, editors of *In Chambers*, for their frank tales about the inner workings of the court.

Thanks to my best friend, Tony Vedda, who helped me with a last-minute trip to D.C. so that I could get a feel for the location and lend some extra authenticity to this story.

My wife, Lainey, makes it possible for me to write. She takes on extra tasks around the house, tiptoes around when she knows that quiet fuels my inspiration, and cheers me on like no one else. Thanks, L., I love you.

To all the readers—I write these stories because you keep reading them and asking for more. Every e-mail, every tweet, every Facebook post, keeps me motivated. Thank you!

Dedication

To Lainey and the best courtship ever.

CHAPTER ONE

A nyone ever tell you you're too hot to be a dean?"

"Can't say that's ever been a topic of conversation." Addison Riley ushered Eva Monroe into her apartment and took her coat. "Maybe I should start the next regents meeting by posing the question: Dean Riley, hot or not?"

"Just don't tell anyone I started the poll."

They were joking, but the comment still stung. She and Eva had engaged in an on and off relationship ever since Eva had taken over the Rondel Fellowship at Jefferson University's law school, but even their on had been a bit off since Eva insisted on keeping their relationship private. Eva said it would cause problems with the rest of the faculty if everyone knew she was sleeping with the dean. And she was probably right. The law school was a tight-knit community, and the faculty lounge was a den of gossip. Addison didn't care who knew she was seeing Eva, but she had agreed to be circumspect even when she didn't agree with the need for so much privacy.

Safest maneuver was to change the subject. She pointed to the TV remote on the coffee table. "I put several movies in the queue. Your choice. Glass of wine?"

"Wine would be perfect."

Addison poured two glasses of red and settled onto the couch, unable to stop pondering Eva's opening salvo. She knew she was attractive, but hot? Eva was one to talk about off the charts good looks. When she'd transferred in, students scrambled to sign up for her class, and Addison suspected it wasn't just for her keen insights into women and gender in the law. Her flawless dark skin and deep brown bedroom eyes definitely keep the law from being dry. She imagined the Socratic method wasn't as punishing when administered from her gorgeous lips. Eva may think she was hot, but next to her, Addison felt plain. Fair skin, brown eyes, and brunette hair in a nondescript style. No, she was nothing like the woman nestled next to her.

Eva flipped through the movie selections and then set the remote back on the coffee table. "You know, I've seen these. Should we check cable and see if there's anything we both haven't seen?"

"Sure." If this night went like most others, they'd wind up in bed before they finished the movie anyway. Their dates tended to consist of one glass of wine, an hour of film, and enough nice sex to leave them both satisfied.

Most people would probably think they had the perfect arrangement, but Addison craved more. More companionship, more conversation, more than a series of one-night stands. Not for the first time, she pondered how two smart women in their late thirties had settled for so little. Since becoming dean, her teaching load had decreased, which meant she spent most of her time doing monotonous paperwork. When she and Eva talked, they usually agreed on the issues, so no debate there. Their sex was reliable, but definitely not spark-inducing. Was her life really this boring? Was she?

Rather than dwell on it, Addison picked up the remote and slipped into the ease of the usual. As she flipped her way to the movie channels, she couldn't help but stall as she went through the major news outlets.

Eva nudged her. "Are you trying to cheat on me with Rachel Maddow?"

"Celebrity pass?"

"Deal."

They'd discussed the good-looking brainiac who hosted a news show on MSNBC many times before, and they'd both agreed there was nothing more attractive than beauty and brains in the same package. Addison put the remote down and stared at the object of affection. Rachel was in the middle of one of her well-written, excellently delivered diatribes about the antics of the Republican party. Because it was an election year, the prose was even more pointed than usual and her monologue enthralling. When it was over, Addison reached for the remote again, but Eva stopped her.

"Wait, something's happening."

Addison looked at the screen and watched while Maddow read from a tablet someone off screen had handed to her. Her face became drawn and pale and, when she started to speak, her speech was stiff and she fumbled for words. Addison turned up the volume and leaned forward to hear the news.

"I've just been informed that Chief Justice Weir was involved in a car accident. Details are still coming in, but our sources say the accident was extremely serious. He was pulled from his burning car and is in an ambulance en route to the George Washington University Hospital. He wasn't conscious, and he had severe burns over a good portion of his body. We have a reporter in the field and we're going to them now for more details."

Addison started to stand, but a wave of nausea swept her and she sat back down.

"Are you okay? Can I get you anything?"

Eva's voice sounded faint, like she was very far away, but Addison managed to reply, "Water. Please."

When Eva returned, she took a few small swallows, scared she wouldn't keep it down as she focused on the television. Rachel was firing questions at some other woman, a local affiliate reporter who happened to be in the area where Judge Weir's car crashed.

"Rachel, we're still getting details from witnesses to the accident. It appears he just lost control of his car and careened into that dividing wall over there." The reporter pointed toward a tall cement divider with chunks missing. "The car flipped and rolled and then caught fire." She turned to interview the Good Samaritan who pulled the judge from the car, but Rachel stopped her before they could proceed.

"Hold on, Shelia. We're getting some additional information now."

Rachel consulted the screen in front of her. Addison watched, completely focused, as she waited for the update. When Rachel touched the corner of her eye, Addison saw the tear, and she braced for the news.

"We've just received word that Chief Justice Harrison Weir has died. To confirm, the Chief Justice of the United States Supreme

Court, Harrison Weir, has died." Rachel started to say more, but wound up shaking her head instead, appearing to struggle with the emotion of the news.

Addison didn't even try to hold her feelings in check. She clutched her sides as she sobbed with uncontrollable grief. Eva held her, stroked her back, murmured words of comfort, but none of it mattered. Addison hadn't felt a greater loss since her mother lost her battle with cancer, and she didn't think the pain would ever go away.

"If you interrupt me one more time, I swear..." Julia didn't bother finishing the sentence. Her authoritative tone was usually enough to scare most of the junior staffers into doing her bidding. But this one stuck around. John or Joe, she couldn't remember all their names. If things kept going like they had been, she wouldn't have to. Election day would come and go and they'd be looking for new jobs.

She looked up from the crappy poll results, but whatever his name was still stood in the doorway. "It had better be important."

He looked like he wanted to be anywhere but here as he tentatively handed her a folded sheet of paper. "Brad asked me to give this to you. Said you'd need it right away."

Julia took the paper from him, and he scurried off while she unfolded the note and skimmed the contents. Holy shit. Chief Justice Weir was dead. In a fluke car accident no less. No judge had been more influential on the court than he had in the past ten years, and he had been a colorful personality to boot. A legend, gone in an instant. What an incredible waste.

Julia shook her head as the implications sunk in. There were several justices on the court that everyone figured would retire in the next couple of years, but Weir wasn't one of them. A liberal giant, he'd been expected to stick around for a number of years, especially if, as expected, their opposing candidate won the upcoming election. Well, it looked like the Republicans were going to get a double win in a few weeks: president-elect and the opportunity to appoint a new chief justice of the United States, right out of the gate. She had no doubt they'd appoint the youngest, most conservative man they could find.

Looks like I'm going to be delivering two pieces of bad news tonight. Julia tucked the bad poll results under her arm along with the news she'd just received, and headed down the hall. The president's room was only two doors down, but she lingered during the walk, wishing her news could wait until morning, but knowing it couldn't. Any moment now, the press would be calling her wanting to know whether President Garrett had any comment on the news of Weir's death. She had to have a statement ready. Her only comfort was that the death of a Supreme Court justice would steal the news cycle away from the latest poll results. For a few hours anyway.

She knocked at the door and waited. First Lady Veronica Garrett answered the door and sighed when she saw Julia.

"Seriously? He just agreed to turn the TV off. He could use a good night's sleep.

"Sorry, it can't wait."

The First Lady pointed at the folder under her arm. "Are those the poll results?"

"Yes, but—"

"No buts. It can wait." She started to shut the door, but Julia stuck her hand in the opening and forced it open. This late in the campaign, any pretense at deference was a waste of time. Someone had to be the bad guy, and more often than not, that someone was her.

The Garretts were exhausted, worn-out, and Veronica Garrett, who'd always reluctantly assumed the role of political wife, was ready for the constant campaigning to stop. She had enough of a microscope on her life during their first term in office, but elections had a way of raising the bar on invasion of privacy. Julia got it. She really did. For a brief moment, she considered walking away, but she had a job to do, and since that was all she had, she was going to do it right. "I'm sorry, ma'am, but it can't wait."

Veronica swung the door wide, and as Julia entered, she left, trailed by a duo of Secret Service agents. She was pissed, but she'd be back. Once Julia delivered the news, especially about the new drop in the polls, her husband would need her by his side more than ever. Must be nice to have someone be there for you. No matter what.

CHAPTER TWO

The morning of the day before the funeral, Addison rolled over and was surprised to find Eva still in her bed. Eva met her curious look and said, "I figured this would be a hard day for you."

Not wanting to scare her away, Addison nodded a silent thanks. "Coffee?"

"Sure, I'll even get it."

Before Addison could protest, Eva stood and walked across the room to the chair where she'd left her silk robe the night before. Addison watched as she drew the shimmering fabric over her well-toned shoulders. Addison wished she was back in bed, naked. She started to say so, but Eva called out from the next room.

"Looks like we both have a really busy day ahead. I promised the moot court team I'd listen to a run-through of their arguments this morning. Maybe one day before the competition, you can join me. Bryan Campbell thinks he's God's gift to advocacy, and you're just the person to take him down a peg or two. He needs a good kick in the teeth before competition or he's going to blow it for everyone else. And Megan, don't even get me started about the way she flips her hair, like the judges are going to fall for..."

Addison tuned out the rest, her desire for sex fading as Eva's rambling conversation reminded her that despite her personal loss, life went on. She reached over the nightstand and picked up her journal. When Justice Weir's son Larry had called with the details about the funeral, she'd written down every detail, committed it to memory, but seeing the words in her own handwriting made it real.

Today she would meet a cadre of Justice Weir's former law clerks, an elite group of which she was proud to be a member. They would have lunch with Larry Weir and discuss the roles outlined for them at the funeral to take place at Saint Matthew's church the next day. She'd cleared her calendar and would be present for all the events. It was her duty as a former clerk, as the dean of one of the top law schools in the country, and as a woman who'd lost her most treasured mentor. She only wished she didn't have to go alone.

When Eva reappeared with a steaming cup of coffee, she didn't wait for a break in conversation, instead blurting out, "Come with me. Tomorrow. To the funeral, I mean. I'd like it if you would."

Eva's cheery smile faded quickly, and Addison watched as she struggled for an excuse. She could almost choose the words herself. Too public. Too intimate. It was a state funeral. Tons of dignitaries would be there, not to mention the press. The event was invitation only. Partners of those in mourning were welcome, but Eva wouldn't want to be labeled as such, certainly not for the world to see. Addison wished she'd never brought it up.

"Never mind." She stood up, no longer wanting to feel the vulnerability of being in bed, the one place where she usually gave in to her needs. She slipped on her robe. "I have to leave soon. You should go."

"Addison, wait—"

"No, it's fine. I'm fine. I appreciate you being here last night, this morning. But this is something I need to do on my own." She softened her tone and added the smile that Eva expected, the one that would let her know she was off the hook. "Thank you. Really. I'm going to get in the shower. Go give Bryan Campbell hell."

An hour later, showered and dressed in her most somber black suit, Addison took a cab to the Supreme Court building. The ride gave her time to think, and she wondered who among Weir's chosen would show up for this event.

Event. An odd word for a final good-bye. Weir would have hated all the pomp and circumstance. During his tenure on the court, he'd had little patience for the formal trappings of the job. He'd been a workhorse, and his clerks spent their year at the court on call twenty-four seven and loving every minute of it.

At twenty-five, she'd been well prepared for whatever the high court clerkship had to offer. The Ninth Circuit judge she'd clerked for just out of law school had initiated her to long hours, and even at the lower court, judicial eccentricities were considered the norm. Weir had plenty, which many of his clerks made fun of when they retired to their private dining room for a rare moment of relaxation. He started every day with a hard-boiled egg, which he peeled himself, leaving remnants of eggshells all over his desk. He would salt the egg liberally while he solicited opinions about the drafts of opinions circulating around the court. Later in the day, he would commandeer a clerk to walk with him through the halls of the building for what he called his afternoon constitutional.

Many clerks, past and present, had joked about the ritualistic habits, but Addison knew Weir valued routine as a way to tune out the things that shouldn't matter, like the politics within and without the high court. During the walks she shared with him, she learned lessons she carried with her to this day, lessons about temperament, compassion, and balance. Harrison Weir had been an amazing mentor, and he had continued to be an important figure in her life throughout her professional career, long after the year she spent at the court. He'd told the board of trustees of Jefferson University they'd be fools not to hire her as dean. She imagined she'd been hired as much because of the advice of their most famous alumni as for her own reputation as an accomplished appellate attorney.

When the cab pulled up to the corner of Independence and First Street, Addison spotted the Supreme Court building and told the driver to let her out there. As she stepped from the cab, she shivered. She had argued many cases here since her remarkable year as a clerk, but the weight of the work that emanated from this building never failed to leave her awestruck. *Brown v. Board of Education*, *Roe v. Wade*, *Citizens United*. Landmark decisions that affected every American were made here, by nine justices. History. And she'd been a part of it.

"Addison! Great to see you."

The tall, lanky man walking toward her held out his arms and pulled her into a hug. Jeff Burrows, another former clerk, now a United States senator. She hugged him back and blinked back tears.

They'd grown close during the year they worked together despite their distinct ideological differences. "It's great to see you too."

When they stepped apart, she took a minute to appraise her old friend. She hadn't seen him in years. All the promises they'd made after their year in service together had fallen by the wayside after they'd scattered to various parts of the country, wielding their time at the court into high profile jobs at various firms and agencies. They'd kept up via the occasional e-mail, but more often than not, the communications were quick announcements of address changes, promotions, and transfers rather than the close confidences they'd shared when they'd spent a year in servitude. She knew Jeff was the senior United States senator from Montana, that he was married and had two children. But she didn't know much else about her old friend. She fumbled for small talk. "Did you come by yourself or is Helen with you?"

"Just me today. Helen's in town with the kids, but she won't join us until tomorrow morning. She figured all of us would want today to catch up with each other. And you? You bring anyone special along?"

He danced around the subject like he had the first time they'd had the discussion. He knew she was a lesbian, as did everyone in her close circle of friends. A circle that was pretty damn small. But, like most people, when she never showed up at events with a woman in tow, they wondered if she'd changed her mind. She set him straight to keep him from speculating. "No special woman in my life at the moment."

Mostly true. Eva was special, but her status as a part-time lover didn't really constitute a mention, especially since she wasn't sure how to describe their relationship. Addison could almost hear Judge Weir scolding her for being too damn literal, and she smiled at the memory. Before Jeff could ask any more questions, she took his arm. "Let's go in. I want to see who else is here."

The Supreme Court dining hall was lined with clerks. During his twenty-year tenure, Justice Weir had amassed a large group of alumnae. Because each clerk only served a year with the justice, they didn't all know each other, but the fellowship was small enough and prestigious enough that they all knew of each other, and Addison recognized many familiar faces. She scoured the room for Sasha Easton, the final member of the trio that had served with her and Jeff.

"Sasha couldn't make it," Jeff said. "She called me last night. Her daughter went into labor yesterday, and she had to fly to Seattle. Can you believe Sasha's going to be a grandmother?"

"Not even." Sasha had been older than most clerks and the only one of them who'd had children at the time of clerkship. Addison had been amazed at Sasha's ability, as a single mother, to handle the heavy load of the clerkship. She'd left the court and garnered a position with a prestigious Wall Street law firm. Addison wondered if she was still there, wondered if she'd ever married. She wished she'd kept in touch, especially now that the person who had been their common link was gone.

"Do you see Larry?" she asked Jeff.

"Over there. Looks like he's been cornered by the terrible twosome." Jeff referred to a pair of clerks who'd served a couple of years after they had. Jake Jeffries and Evan Spence. She'd met them at the judge's seventieth birthday party and had never understood why the gentle-tempered justice had ever chosen these smug know-it-alls as clerks.

"Let's save him." Addison strode across the room with Jeff on her heels. Larry looked up as she approached, obviously relieved.

"Addison, how good to see you. Dad would be so happy that you came." He trailed off, and Addison figured the silence meant he realized his father's happiness would never be a tangible thing again. With a pointed look at Jake and Evan, Larry motioned to the door. "Excuse me, everyone, but I need to speak to Addison privately. We'll be back in just a moment."

Addison followed him out the door to an alcove. She started to ask him if everything was okay, but quickly realized the stupidity of the question. Larry was an only son and his mother had died several years ago. In the wake of his father's death, Larry's world had likely been thrown into disarray.

"I wanted to talk to you. First. Before the others. About the funeral."

"Whatever you need. I'm here for you."

"You realize Dad considered you part of his family, don't you?"

Addison felt the tears gather in the corner of her eyes once again. If she wasn't able to keep her emotions in check, it was going to be a very long two days. "He meant the world to me. I'm so sorry I haven't seen him more in the last few years. I guess I always thought there would be time…"

"Don't even go there. He was proud of you, and he, of all people, would have wanted you to be happy with your work. We all thought he would live forever."

She nodded. Words weren't enough to express her sorrow.

"He left notes about his funeral. He wanted his favored clerks to be pallbearers. I have a list, and you're at the top of it. I'd also like you to say a few words at the service if you feel up to it."

"Of course."

"They'll have a reserved section at the church for the clerks. Let's go back in and I'll announce the pallbearers and then the court administrator will go over the arrangements for this afternoon." He started to walk back toward the dining hall, but stopped when Addison touched his arm.

"Larry, I was serious. Anything you need."

"Dad loved that about you. You challenged his ideas, but you never debated his work ethic. He always said he'd never had a more hard-working, more devoted clerk. Thank you, Addison, for everything you were to him."

Addison squeezed his hand and then watched as he headed back to the dining room. Several deep breaths later, she felt composed enough to join him and ready to face whatever the next two days might bring.

❖

"Brad, we'll be at the ellipse in five minutes. While we're gone, I need you to…" Julia drilled through a mile-long to-do list as she jogged down the hall in the West Wing with Brad running along behind her. Both sides had suspended campaigning after the news of Justice Weir's death, but behind the scenes, the election machinery chugged on. They'd arrived back in D.C. the night before last. While the Garretts visited the Supreme Court building to pay their respects to Justice Weir as he lay in state, she'd never stopped working. Today, Wesley had insisted that she attend the funeral with them, and she was already cursing the loss of valuable time. If she was going to go, she was determined to be there on time, since nothing would begin until the president arrived.

When she reached the Oval Office, she nodded at the president's secretary, Sue Marks, and knocked on the door. "Sir, the car is waiting."

Veronica Garrett opened the door, and Julia sucked in a breath. She was Jackie Kennedy reincarnated. No woman had any business looking drop-dead gorgeous in funeral black. If she were smiling, she'd be too gorgeous for words. Her somber expression was probably more about her disgust with politics than sorrow for Justice Weir's passing. Although he was a liberal, President Garrett had spent the second half of his term moving as close to the middle as he could without completely alienating his base, which included distancing himself from some of the justice's leftist leanings. If he and his wife weren't a public couple, they'd probably be enjoying a morning of reading the paper over eggs and coffee instead of attending this funeral.

Well, before long, leisurely mornings out of the public eye might be open to them once again. The polls had them trailing Governor Delbert Briscoe by a deadly seven points across the board. While a former president was never completely out of the public eye, Wesley Garrett was about to be relegated to back page news.

Julia shook her head. She couldn't think about that right now. Her job was to get him elected. That job didn't stop until all the votes were counted, and there were two weeks to go. She wasn't being negative; she was only being realistic. Right now, she'd take things one step at a time. Today, a funeral. Day after tomorrow, a four-state whirlwind of events. She'd keep pushing until it was over. And then she'd take a month off. Go to Tahiti and lay on the beach. Until it was time to find another candidate and begin again. This was her life and she'd learned to love it.

"Julia, you should ride with us."

She nodded and joined the Secret Service detail that escorted the Garretts out of the West Wing. She planned on riding with several of her staffers so they could review the week's schedule, but the president's statement wasn't a suggestion. As they pulled out of the gates, throngs of people lined the streets. Some appeared somber, as if to express mourning, and some held placards. Protect Our Right to Bear Arms. Life is Sacred. And so on. The crazies were already out, and they'd keep up their vigil of protest until the Senate confirmed a new Supreme Court justice.

Once they passed the crowd, President Garrett leaned back in the seat and unbuttoned his jacket. The first lady made a show of playing with the hem of her dress, while Julia wondered why she'd been asked to ride with them. Finally, the president spoke.

"I know what the polls say, but I want to know what you think. You've always been straight with me. We're two weeks out. Can we win?"

He was right. She'd run his campaign twice in the House and once before for the office he held now, and she'd always told him the truth, even if it was painful. It was a policy she had with all the candidates she worked with. The key was when to deliver bad news. Sometimes elections really were too close to call until hours after the polls had closed, but most of the time the outcome was clear weeks in advance, even if the candidate and his inner circle didn't want to face the truth.

But this time was different. After a rough four years as an incumbent, President Garrett had to pivot away from some of his own policies to try to win back the base that had lost faith in him. He walked a fine line between consistent and unfocused. The up and down they'd experienced in the polls was evidence their audience wasn't certain about the message. If the election were a few months away, the problem might be fixable, but at two weeks out, there was no cure. As Julia fished for a way to balance the hard truth against the fact that candidates usually wanted a pep talk about how they could pull out a victory, true or not. Truth, in this case, wasn't very motivating.

"We've upped the ad buys in key states and we're reconfiguring the electoral math. It's not over until it's over, sir. I promise you your entire team is behind you."

Veronica Garrett delivered a mirthless laugh. "You should get back into running politics from the inside, Julia. You've got the doublespeak down. Noah says there's no way we can win. At least he's got the balls to tell it like it is."

Julia winced inwardly at the reference to the president's chief of staff and resisted pointing out that if Wesley trusted Noah to get him elected, she wouldn't be here. "With all due respect, ma'am, anything could happen, and I've seen plenty of strange comebacks. But if you want some hard truth, I'll give it to you."

"I think that's exactly what we want." Veronica glanced at her husband, but Julia noted he continued to stare out the window. If he was going to let his wife ask the tough questions, then she'd let him handle the fallout when she delivered the tough answers.

"It's almost impossible to make the kind of gains we need with the election this close. We will do everything we can to make it happen. That's all I can promise you."

The partition between the passenger compartment lowered and the driver called out, "We're a block away from Saint Matthew's, sir. We should be there in just a minute."

The president nodded, and Julia was glad for the interruption. When he turned back to her, she cleared her throat. "I can tell you one thing. If you believe you will lose, you will lose. If you believe you will win, you can win. I will do everything in my power to make sure when this election is over, that whatever happens, you know you did everything you could. It's not always about the best man for the job. Sometimes, it's just a matter of timing. Even if you don't win this election, you've accomplished a lot. You'll always be known as a statesman."

"Fair enough." Wesley took his wife's hand. "We'll do whatever you ask us to do for the next two weeks, right, dear?" Veronica nodded, but her eyes were full of fire.

"Great. Day after tomorrow, we'll start up again in Ohio. Right after the funeral, you're hosting a wake at the White House." In response to Wesley's surprised look, she said, "Elections are all about capitalizing on opportunity. Justice Weir's mourners represent your base. You know, the ones you don't want to stay home because they can read polls too. It's important for you to be visible to them, every opportunity you can get." She didn't bother mentioning as the gap in the polls widened, money was starting to dry up. She'd take every bit of free press they could get. "Don't worry. Governor Briscoe is not on the guest list."

Later, seated in the pew at Saint Matthew's, Julia glanced around at the sea of people who'd come to pay their respects, some driven by duty, some spurred by real emotion. The pallbearers, Justice Weir's most treasured clerks, each of them with a hand on the casket, walked as if they had all the time in the world when it was apparent by their very load they did not. Seven men, one woman. Julia checked the program. Addison Riley. Even if she weren't the only woman in the bunch, she'd stand out. Her tall carriage spoke of pride to be included in this elite group while her eyes glistened with sorrow. Half a room away, Julia could tell her emotion was raw, deep. Watching her, Julia was swallowed up with loneliness. If she died, would anyone come to the funeral? The only people she knew were the ones who paid for her services. If she were gone, they would be released of further obligation. No one would cry, carry her casket, or eulogize her good deeds. They'd merely shell out a few bucks for someone else to take her place.

CHAPTER THREE

As Addison entered the White House, a flood of memories settled over her. She hadn't been here often, but each time she'd been on the job, as solicitor general, here to brief the president or his chief of staff on her thoughts about the position the administration should take on a number of cases pending before the Supreme Court. Usually accompanied by an assistant from the justice department, she would lay out her reasoning as to why the administration should appeal a loss in a lower court or intervene when Congress enacted a new law that ran afoul of the constitution. She'd been issued a badge and escorted through the West Wing, but her trips had stopped years ago, and even then she'd never been here, in the ornate and spacious East Room. She wouldn't even be here now, but all Weir's clerks had been invited to attend the private reception, and Larry had insisted she come along.

The room was full of Washington power players. She looked around the room until she found Jeff standing near the bar. When she joined him, he ordered drinks for both of them and passed her a heavy crystal tumbler full of scotch.

"Drink up. Jake and Evan are headed our way."

She didn't have time to respond before she heard Jake's voice.

"If it isn't the wonder clerks. Tell me something. Does your arm hurt? I heard they use a fake casket that's made of balsa wood so no one drops the box. Can you imagine if the body fell out and skittered down the steps in front of all the press?"

"Jake, you're an ass," Jeff said.

"Don't be so prissy, Senator. I'm just proof that you can be smart and funny all in the same package." Jake ribbed Evan, and they both snorted with laughter. Addison looked around the room and watched the guests shoot them indulgent looks. Everyone expressed their grief differently, but these two were just what Jeff said, asses. She started to walk away, but stopped at Jake's next words.

"I wonder if the wreck was really an accident."

She whirled around and got in his face. "What's that supposed to mean?"

"You heard me. I heard the judge was driving home from dinner. Maybe he had a few too many." Jake cupped his hand and mimicked drinking while making gulping sounds. Evan laughed while Jeff looked like he'd rather be anywhere else.

The pressure of the last two days bubbled over, and Addison shoved a pointed finger into Jake's chest. In a low, but steely voice, she said, "If I hear you offer that opinion anywhere else, ever, I'll see that your legal career is finished. Nod if you understand."

Jake's eyes widened and he nodded. Addison wasn't surprised at his reaction. Very few people ever got a glimpse of her temper, which gave it added effect when unleashed. She lowered her hand, and Jake and Evan took off.

"Wow, Riley. Don't think I've ever seen you so pissed off."

Addison let the anger slide away and she smiled. "It doesn't happen often."

"I think he was just joking around."

"He needs to find something to joke about that's actually funny."

"Agreed. Another drink?"

Addison looked down at her glass, surprised to find most of the amber liquid gone. "Another scotch and lives might be in danger. Club soda for me, but I'll get it. You need anything?"

Jeff shook his head, and Addison walked back over to the bar where a line had formed. The woman in front of her tapped her foot and then her fingers against her thigh, obviously impatient at the wait. She looked at her watch several times and sighed. After a brief interval, she pulled out her phone and composed a brief text, tapping the screen until it buzzed with a response. A heavier sigh followed, but it was accompanied with resignation. No more tapping, no more glances at the time.

"I'd offer to let you in front of me, but you already are." Addison wasn't sure what had spurred her to speak, but once the words were out, she decided to add a smile. The woman's head jerked up, and she looked like she was about to offer a smart remark, but then her entire expression relaxed, and she smiled back, a dazzling, beautiful smile.

"I'm not good at waiting."

"I could tell."

"You, on the other hand, seem to be a glutton for it."

"What?" Addison followed the woman's glance to her hand, which held the now empty glass. "If it makes you feel any better, there wasn't a wait the first time."

"Nope. Doesn't make me feel better at all." The woman cocked her head. "I recognize you." The tapping started again. "From the service. You were one of the pallbearers, right?"

"I was." She reached out her hand. "Addison Riley, nice to meet you."

"Julia Scott."

Her hand was soft, but her shake was firm, and neither one of them seemed interested in letting go. Julia Scott was captivating with wavy red hair, sharp green eyes, and a strong jaw. She wasn't classically beautiful, but definitely eye-catching. The bustle of the room fell away as she lost moments in Julia's strong gaze. When a tray-bearing waiter bumped her arm, she shook off the trance and looked down to see that they were still holding hands. As she released her grasp, Julia said, "So, you were one of Justice Weir's clerks?"

"I was."

"How did they decide which of you would carry the casket?"

"What?" The question seemed to come out of left field, but it served to cut through the haze of attraction. Trivia. That's all this woman wanted to know. Probably a reporter, which might explain why she recognized her. Although she couldn't imagine how a reporter had gained entry to this private event. Suddenly, Addison was the impatient one, and she willed the bartender to move faster, but Julia pressed on.

"Sorry if that's too personal. Although considering how long we're likely to stand here waiting, I'll probably find out everything about you before we ever get served."

"Are you a reporter?"

Julia laughed, a hearty laugh as if she hadn't heard anything funny in days. "You're kidding, right?"

"No. I mean it would be strange for a reporter to be here, but then again, it might be normal to have members of the White House press corps attend social events."

Julia started to reply, but was suddenly distracted by something behind Addison. Addison turned around and found herself standing face-to-face with the president of the United States.

"Sorry to interrupt, ladies. Julia, I was hoping to get a moment with you."

Addison watched while Julia looked completely unflappable in the face of such a request.

"Sure. Mr. President, I'd like to introduce Addison Riley. She was one of Justice Weir's clerks."

He shook her hand and smiled warmly. "Of course. I apologize for not recognizing you at first. Please accept my condolences. I understand you were close to the justice."

Addison was impressed he knew who she was, considering they'd never met. "Thank you, sir. And thanks for this invitation."

"Please visit anytime. And forgive me for stealing your companion. Julia?" He motioned to the door and started walking with two men in suits following at a discreet distance. Julia took Addison's hand, pulled her close, and whispered in her ear. "I'm only following because I know he's got a private bar. Good luck with the line."

Addison watched her go, confused, aroused, and more than a little curious. She was still staring when she saw Jeff across the room. He waved and made his way to her.

"I saw you talking to the president. If you're looking for a job, I don't think he's in a good place to help since he'll be looking for one himself in the next few weeks."

This wasn't the time or place to talk politics, and she refused to take the bait. "I'm perfectly happy with the job I have, thanks. Do you know the woman he left with? Julia Scott?"

"She's his campaign manager. If you're a Democrat, she's the person you want on your side, despite her personal baggage. Although I don't think even a miracle worker could save this president from his lack of a cohesive domestic agenda and inept foreign policy. She's definitely got her work cut out for her. Garrett just doesn't have…"

Addison tuned out the rest of his right wing rhetoric while she reflected on her short conversation with Julia. She'd just insulted one of the most powerful women in the country. No wonder Julia had been so impatient. She probably had a thousand places to be, a thousand people who commanded her time and attention. Julia Scott had certainly caught her eye. Would their banter over drinks have led to something more if she hadn't mistaken Julia for a reporter?

Doubtful. But Addison couldn't help but let her mind wander to the possibilities.

❖

As Julia followed Wesley into the Oval Office, her thoughts lingered on Addison Riley. Beautiful, accomplished, painstakingly polite. She'd been instantly attracted to her charm and, as much as she knew the president wouldn't have interrupted if it weren't important, she wished she could have had another moment with Addison.

"Have a seat." Wesley directed his lead agent to shut the door. "Drink?"

Finally. "Bourbon. Double. Neat." While he poured from a crystal decanter on a cart, she offered what she hoped he would mistake for small talk. "That woman, Addison Riley. Who is she?"

"If I didn't know better, I'd think you live under a rock. How is it that you know the name of every national and state elected politician, but you don't know the dean of the most prestigious law school in the region?"

"I know who I need to know. I'm not big on local folks."

"True. She's the dean of Jefferson University Law School in Virginia," Wesley said. "I would've thought you might have heard of her. She's quite the scholar, one of the youngest Supreme Court clerks of modern day. Former solicitor general. Jefferson was lucky to get her."

"Well, not all of us lawyers are scholars are we, sir?"

"Good point. Sometimes I forget you're a lawyer. I think of you more as a—"

"I think the word you're looking for is player."

"I was going to say marketing specialist."

"You're one to talk, using your law degree for political gain."

They both laughed and clinked glasses in a toast before settling into the chairs arranged around the large rug emblazoned with the presidential seal. He spoke first. "Are you dead set on us starting back up in Ohio?"

"Who wants to know?" Julia asked. "You or the DNC?"

"I won't lie. I'm getting pressure from every angle. Everyone has an opinion about where we should focus our efforts."

Julia set her glass down. She should've seen this coming. "If you want someone else to call the shots, tell me now. There's still time for me to book a flight to an island and watch the returns from a bar in the middle of nowhere."

Garrett sat forward on the edge of his chair. "Now, hold on. I tell everyone who calls the same thing. There's no one I'd want running this campaign but you. Hell, you got me elected. Twice. If it can be done, you're the one to do it."

"But?"

Julia looked on while the leader of the free world squirmed in his chair. Someone very close to him must have questioned her strategy to put him in such an uncomfortable position. The president and the Democratic national chair had never been close, so it had to be someone else. She took a stab. "Is the first lady displeased with my work?"

"What? No, Veronica may not care for the life I've chosen, but she doesn't get in the middle of business."

"Who then?"

He sighed. "Noah. He thinks we should spend more time in California. Shore up the base."

Julia silently counted to ten. This wasn't the first time she and Noah had butted heads over campaign strategy, but at least in the past he had come directly to her instead of going over her head. "Mr. President, if you don't take a commanding lead on election day in key states like Ohio and Pennsylvania, by the time the polls close on the East Coast your base in California won't even bother to vote."

He started to respond, but she cut him short. "Noah is an excellent politician, but campaigning for public office is not the same thing as pushing a bill through congress. I don't try to do his job, and he shouldn't try to do mine. If you think I'm not doing a good enough job, then by all means bring someone else in to replace me, but make sure it's someone with a proven track record as a campaign manager, not your chief of staff."

"I have no intention of replacing you."

"Maybe you should. We're way down in the polls. I keep thinking I must have missed something."

"You didn't. Not your style. If I lose, it's my own fault. I had so much I wanted to get done, but I couldn't seem to get my message across."

"Bullshit. If the election doesn't go your way, you'll still be leaving this place in better shape than when you got it. Now enough talk about losing. It's bad luck. Throw your drink over your shoulder or something."

"Salt. It's salt you throw over your shoulder, but only if you spill it first."

Julia raised her glass. "Then here's to never spilling anything."

Garrett stood. "For the next two weeks, I'm completely in your hands. You decide where we go, what we say. Agreed?"

"Agreed."

"What are you going to do when this is over?"

"I was thinking about that earlier today. Tahiti was all I'd come up with for now."

"Sounds great, but if you ever decide you want something more, let me know. If I win…" He paused and then amended, "*When* we win, there will always be a place for you here."

She smiled, but all she could think about was a cushy chair on a white sandy beach and a tall, fruity drink, maybe a beautiful woman in the chair beside her. She briefly closed her eyes and imagined it were true. In her dream, an imaginary companion turned to toast their trip to paradise, but her face was familiar, and suddenly, she wasn't imaginary at all. Her companion in paradise was Addison Riley.

Time to get back to work.

CHAPTER FOUR

A week later, Julia stepped off the plane, not entirely sure where they were. It was the third stop of the day, and at this point, every place they landed looked the same. Seven more days.

She glanced at the schedule on her phone. Los Angeles. First up was a meeting with the governor of California who was in town for a benefit. He'd graciously offered a few minutes of speaking time to the hometown candidate. Another rubber chicken dinner. Garrett would get to preach to the choir and hope the press gave them enough free publicity to save them from having to shell out for another ad buy. She hadn't wanted to stop here again until the end, but the president didn't want to risk a bad showing in his home state, so she'd agreed to a quick hop through on their way to Nevada.

Money was getting really tight, and she didn't have a clue how they were going to survive the last week. Governor Briscoe and his band of corporate PACs with their endless fountain of wealth were slaughtering them with TV and online ads. She'd already scheduled a meeting with her team to decide where they would need to go black in order to stay on the air in the places still in contention.

Already compiling a list in her head, she called out to her number two. "Brad, write a short meeting into the president's schedule after the dinner. I want to have a revised ad plan in place, work up something to show me before the dinner's over."

"Great. Hey, did you know Governor Briscoe is just across town at the Hilton?"

"I thought he was headed back to Ohio. Any idea what's going on?"

"Not a clue, but I'll see what I can find out. Any changes to the schedule tomorrow I should know about?"

"No, but keep it fluid. Definitely Nevada, then Florida, but beyond that, there may be some last-minute changes. Let me know what you find out about Briscoe."

"Will do." He made some notes on his phone and then held open the door to her waiting car. She slipped in and gave the driver the name of the hotel where the Garrett campaign had reservations. She should be riding with the president to go over campaign details, but his family was with him, and she figured another business discussion in front of the first lady might get her slapped.

Julia dictated notes while shrugging into another of the endless supply of little black dresses that made up her appearance wardrobe. She should be able to deduct the cost of these garments as a uniform expense. Looking at herself in the mirror, she was happy to find that a steady diet of coffee and hamburgers hadn't impeded her ability to look good in evening wear. But a closer look at the circles under her eyes and the wrinkles at the corners of her mouth, told her the undeniable. This campaign had aged her more than the others.

Seven more days. Tahiti. Umbrella on the beach, umbrella in her drink. She repeated the mantra as she left the room. In the elevator, she switched gears and started planning for the staff meeting later that evening. By the time she reached the Garrett's room, she was fully immersed in her job and ready for action.

"Mr. President, we need to leave for the event in ten minutes. Mrs. Garrett, you look beautiful as always."

The first lady smiled and offered her a drink. Julia declined, but noted that she was in much better spirits today. Must be the fact the kids were with them. She couldn't really blame her for being grouchy. All this time spent traveling would be hell on most people.

Forty minutes later, when they reached the event venue, Julia waited backstage with the president. She couldn't help but notice he was in an exceptionally good mood and she said as much.

"No sense being tense on the downhill stretch. I guess I figure that whatever's going to happen is going to happen, and the best I can do is enjoy the ride."

She started to say something about not writing things off until the end, but decided against it. His decision not to stress out might be the best thing he'd done. Besides, it was really her job from here on out. The strategic decisions she made about where to appear, what to have him say, all of that were what could make the difference on Election Day. As long as he didn't do anything stupid, his good mood was a benefit, and she decided not to burst his bubble. "No matter what happens, sir. It's been a helluva ride."

"And now, President of the United States Wesley Garrett!"

"That's me." He shook her hand. "I'll give it everything I got."

She knew that he would. She only wished his best would be good enough.

Addison poured another glass of wine and handed it to Eva who lounged on the couch, flipping through the channels on TV. "Let's go out to dinner."

Eva yawned and stretched. "I was hoping we could stay in."

"We can watch TV anytime. I'm feeling restless."

"You've been that way ever since the funeral. Would you like to talk about it?"

"There's nothing to talk about. Having the desire to leave one's home is not a mental condition. It's actually pretty normal." Addison knew she sounded crabby. Eva was right. Her restlessness had started when she'd returned home after the funeral. Suddenly, spending evenings alone with Eva in the confines of her apartment felt more claustrophobic than something to look forward to. She wanted fresh air, a variety of restaurants. She wanted to be in the world. Be a part of it.

She imagined part of her change in mood had to do with grief and the realization that life is fleeting. She didn't have time to waste living her life in secret, with a woman who didn't want to be seen in public with her. Her patience for Eva's desire for privacy was wearing thin.

As if she sensed Addison's growing agitation, Eva said, "Let's plan a night out. We can take the train to Manhattan. See a show, have a decadent dinner, and stay the night at the Peninsula. I'll make all the reservations."

Eva punctuated her offer with a wicked smile that promised extra entertainment. Any other time, Addison would have compromised to keep the peace, but she wasn't in the mood for compromise. She knew exactly what she wanted, and she wasn't going to take a train ride to get it.

"I'll do you one better. *Book of Mormon* is playing at the Kennedy. I'll make the reservations and treat you to dinner before. Tomorrow night?"

Eva shifted on the couch, and Addison could feel the air between them chill as she braced for the answer that wouldn't be a surprise. "Tomorrow's not good for me. I have that meeting with the moot court team."

Addison persisted. "Reschedule. You're volunteering to help them. They're students. They'll meet with you whenever."

Eva shook her head. "It's not a good time."

"What you mean is it's not a good place. Too close to home. Too likely you'll be seen with me."

"Addison, don't."

Keeping her frustration in check no longer seemed worthwhile. "Don't what? Don't ask for more than you're willing to give? Even if what you're willing to give is no longer enough?"

"Is that how you really feel?"

Was it? A week ago she wouldn't be pushing this, but now she couldn't stop. She was tired of settling. The eulogies for Justice Weir rang in her ears, all with a common theme. He had never compromised. He'd gone toe-to-toe with his adversaries, and he'd made enemies along the way, but he'd lived his life to the fullest, and that included standing up for his beliefs and being true to himself.

Addison looked at the woman seated next to her. She cared for Eva, was definitely attracted to her, but she couldn't completely give all of herself to her because she knew Eva wouldn't return the favor. Their relationship was confined to chance glances on campus, the occasional phone call, and secret dates mostly taking place here at her apartment. She didn't have a clue if she and Eva could have or would have more, but this fraction of a relationship wasn't enough. Only one way to find out if Eva was willing to risk losing her. "I want more."

Eva sighed and hung her head. "I was afraid you would say that."

"I don't understand why you don't."

"I'm happy with the way things are between us. Can't you be happy too?"

"Not anymore."

"Something's changed. You used to be satisfied with what we have."

"I don't know. Maybe Justice Weir's death affected me more than I realized, but it's not a temporary thing. I want to live large and I want the woman I care about to live large with me."

Sidestepping the last part of her declaration, Eva said, "You're not going to start doing things like bungee-jumping are you?"

Addison couldn't help but laugh. "I can see the headline now. Dean Riley jumps off the Washington Monument. Middle-age crisis suspected."

Eva joined in her laughter. "Maybe you should start with something more tame, like kayaking the Potomac."

Addison's laughter faded into something else. Something wistful. "Maybe I'll start by going out in public with a woman who doesn't mind being seen with me."

Eva reached for her hand. "It's not you."

"I know. And that's precisely the problem."

"I'm not ready to be who you want me to be." Eva sighed. "I guess I should go."

As much as she wanted more, Addison wasn't ready to lose what she had. Not yet. She wasn't going to get what she wanted, but she needed to ease away from her expectations. Searching for levity, she said, "Right, and leave me with all this food? Nice try. Stay. Tonight, anyway."

Eva met her eyes, and they both knew this was good-bye, even if a prolonged one. Before the conversation could devolve, Addison grabbed the remote. "I'll find a movie. We'll eat too much, and drink too much, and then you can stumble back to your place." She started flipping through the channels.

"Stop. Right there." Eva pointed at the TV screen, and Addison's heart stopped as she saw the banner, *Breaking News*. This couldn't be happening again. Paralyzed, she stared at the screen.

"Governor Briscoe is about to take the podium, and I think he's going to address the accusations. That's his wife next to him."

"Can you give us a summary of what's known so far?"

"Sources say a number of women have come forward saying that he sent them revealing texts. Upon further investigation, we found out one of the individuals who received these sexts was not a woman at all, but an underage girl. Obviously, we're not releasing her identity, but the police have confirmed that they have opened an investigation. This isn't the usual situation of a candidate caught with his pants down. The governor could be facing serious felony charges."

"Holy shit." Eva stared at the screen, and Addison joined her, relieved that the bad news wasn't reminiscent of the last time she'd seen the breaking news banner onscreen. "I thought he was a sure bet to win."

"Me too. I wonder if they even saw this one coming."

"Judging by the look on his face, I don't think so. And check out his wife. She looks positively shell-shocked."

Addison looked at the ostensibly perfect couple that filled her TV screen. Governor Briscoe and his lovely wife. Neither of their two perfect children were present for this occasion, probably because the subject matter was R-rated. The crowd of reporters shouted out questions while the governor tried to make his way through what sounded like a hastily prepared presentation. It didn't really matter what he said at this point. Merely being accused would leave his reputation in tatters, and with only a week until the election, it'd be a miracle if he bounced back.

"Let's see what Maddow has to say." Eva switched the channel, and they both settled in to watch the fray. Addison marveled at how quickly they'd slipped into different roles, from lovers to friends. Was this easier?

She could overanalyze the issue later. Now, she turned her attention to the screen and watched while Rachel Maddow offered a few crisp comments about the governor's statement.

"That man needs a lawyer before he says another word. Following Governor Briscoe's statement, the Garrett campaign was quick to react. Let's go live to California where the candidate just gave a rousing speech at the Keystone dinner."

"Rachel, President Garrett didn't make a statement himself, but his campaign manager is about to address the press corps. Here she is now."

As the tall, beautiful redhead stepped up to the microphone, Addison gasped.

"What?" Eva asked. "Are you okay?"

Addison took a deep breath. "I'm fine. I know her." She pointed at the screen. "I mean, I don't know her, but I met her at the funeral. At a reception at the White House. After the funeral." Realizing how stupid her rambling sounded, she abruptly shut up.

Eva looked back and forth from the screen to Addison. "She seems to have made quite an impression."

Truer words had never been spoken.

As Julia watched her candidate charm the audience, she almost forgot she'd already heard this speech or a variation of it about dozen times in the past two days. The delivery was the difference. The president had a renewed spirit of optimism she hadn't seen in months.

She was so engrossed in his words, she almost didn't notice Brad tapping on her shoulder. When she finally turned his way, his face lit up with excitement.

"What is it?" she whispered.

He signaled for her to follow him back into the hotel kitchen, far away from the stage, and then he handed her a piece of paper. She read it through three times while he watched, practically frothing at the mouth. When she was satisfied she'd thought it through, she said, "Who else has this?"

"On our side? Only Diane. Cary Beyer from the *Post* gave her the tip. Governor Briscoe is going to have a press conference in about ten minutes."

She looked at her watch. Normally, Diane Rollins, the White House press secretary, would coordinate a response to this kind of bombshell, but she wasn't with them on this leg of the trip, and this wasn't a job that could be left to a deputy. The dinner would last another half hour. The press corps would be waiting like wolves for the president as he left, ready to pepper him with questions. There was no time to go through channels. She'd have to take charge and she'd need to act fast. She began firing off instructions.

"Tell the agents to bring the president back here before he leaves. They'll like that he's not mingling in the crowd. I need five minutes to brief him before he leaves the building, but then I want him to exit the front entrance. He'll have one sound bite, something that makes him sound above the fray, but appearing to be on top of things. Give me three options in the next ten minutes. Call Diane and get her to tell her reporter friend we'll have a full statement as soon as the dinner is over. I'll give the statement right there in the ballroom. You'll stick with the president on the way to his car, and he will not take a single question. You can tell the press to head back into the room if they want to hear what we have to say. Understood?"

Brad nodded and then sprinted out of the room to set things in motion. Julia read the note in her hand one more time, unable to believe their opposition had been so overwhelmingly stupid, not only to let this happen, but to let the press surprise them.

She walked back across the room and stood in the curtains, listening to Garrett deliver the rote words and relishing his renewed sense of energy. For the first time in months, she felt hopeful.

Thirty minutes later, she stood in the well of the ballroom, dozens of microphones pointed her way, unable to see the crowd for the flash of cameras. Her carefully crafted statement was short and to the point.

"We are astonished at the accusations leveled against Governor Briscoe. As much as we would like to offer comfort and guidance to the American people as they form their decision about what to do in the upcoming election, all we can say at this time is that we are confident that justice will be done in the courts. In the meantime, we will continue to address the issues facing regular, law-abiding citizens: the economy, healthcare, and equal rights for all. Our thoughts and prayers are with the Briscoes as they turn their attention to their personal crisis."

Like the president, she didn't take any questions. When she was done with her statement, she walked away from the shouting crowd, her face fixed into a serious expression. Not until she reached her room at the hotel did she burst into a smile and down the best bottle of scotch in the hotel mini-bar. Maybe her trip to Tahiti would be a celebration rather than a respite.

CHAPTER FIVE

Addison waited patiently in the long line. She could've voted early, but there was something about casting her vote on the very day it would be counted that seemed special. As she looked around at the crowd, she was happy to see so many people had turned out, and she wondered how much the recent revelations from Governor Briscoe's camp had to do with the renewed interest in the election.

When she finally reached the front of the line, she took the ballot the volunteer handed her and stepped into the booth. The entire process only took a few minutes since she'd carefully researched the candidates and issues before she'd arrived.

A few minutes later, she was back outside, shivering against the chill of the morning air. She spotted a coffee shop on the corner and ducked in for something warm to drink, surprised to see a familiar face standing in line.

"Julia?"

"Yes?" She turned, and her expression morphed from confused to comfortable.

Addison stuck out a hand. "Hi, I'm Addison Riley. We met at—"

"At the White House. A pleasure to see you again, Dean Riley."

Addison cocked her head. They hadn't discussed her employment, so Julia must have asked around about her, or at the very least Googled her. Flattering. "Please, just call me Addison. May I buy you a cup of coffee?"

Julia glanced at her watch and Addison caught the hint. "Sorry. Don't know what I was thinking. You probably have a thousand things to do today."

Julia pointed at her watch. "No, I'm sorry. Occupational hazard. You know, I do have a long to-do list, but I don't think anything on it will make a difference at this point. I'm pretty sure the well-oiled machine won't miss me for a few minutes."

They placed their orders and then snagged a table near the back of the room. Julia was more beautiful in person than on TV. The tired, haggard look she'd sported when Addison first met her had been replaced by a fresh smile and bright eyes.

"You seem to be in an awfully good mood. Guess that's because your work is essentially over."

At Julia's raised eyebrows, Addison admitted, "I've seen you on the news. Your occupation isn't exactly a secret."

"True. You'd think we could relax, wouldn't you? But voting on the West Coast isn't even open yet. So many things could happen today that could change the course of the election, most of them completely out of my control. What if, God forbid, my candidate had a revelation like the one we heard a week ago? Wouldn't matter for all the early voters, but there's a whole half of the country that hasn't voted yet. We have several events scheduled even today. Carefully planned and well scripted. I guess I'm in a good mood because we're up in the polls for the first time since we started."

"I don't know how you do it. Spend two years running, then after two years in office, start running again."

"Well, I don't do the middle part and that makes it a hell of a lot easier."

"I'm not following."

"I only work on the election. After today, I'm out of a job. No matter what happens."

"Interesting. I thought all you groupies were ideologues, in it for the long haul."

"I'm a realist. Every campaign is full of the other folks. They need people like me for the practical aspects. Raising money, planning strategy. We make sure the candidate wins and then bow out to let the rest of the team govern."

"Did you even vote for Garrett?"

"There you go, asking personal questions."

"Sorry, that was kind of rude."

"No, it's okay. And I did. Did you think I voted for the perv on the other ticket?"

Addison laughed. "I voted for Garrett too, lest you think I voted for the perv. But I would've voted for him no matter what."

"What convinced you?"

"Excuse me?"

"Guess I'm trying to learn what worked. For next time."

"Are you starting another campaign right away?"

"Not a chance. I bought a one-way ticket to Tahiti. I'll be on a plane by the end of the week."

Addison's heart sank, and she wasn't sure why. Had she really expected this chance meeting to lead to something more? Silly, really. Julia bounced from place to place, running campaigns. She might not even live in the area, which led Addison to wonder how they'd run into each other this morning. "What brings you to this part of town?"

"Sentimental reasons, I guess. I have an apartment here, and I have a thing about voting in person. I'm not always able to do it, but obviously since my candidate lives down the street..." She glanced at her watch. "Speaking of which, I should head back. Thanks for the coffee. I can't think of a better way to start this day."

"It was great seeing you again." Addison stopped herself from offering another invitation. Julia was headed to Tahiti, and it was clear her sights were set on boarding a plane. "I hope your guy wins and that you have a splendid trip." She paused and then plunged in. "If you decide not to go, give me a call. I'll buy you dinner."

"Too bad, I already bought the ticket." Julia sounded reluctant, but seconds later, she was gone.

Addison sighed. At least she'd asked.

Julia stood in front of the map on the wall, a red marker in one hand and a blue one in the other. Only five states were still in play, and the entire room was fixed in front of a bank of televisions, holding their collective breath for the results.

Her impromptu breakfast with Addison seemed like an eternity ago. When she'd returned to the West Wing, a dozen issues needed her attention, and she'd spent most of the day on the phone with pollsters, giving television interviews, and ciphering electoral math.

She was focused, but her intensity didn't change the fact that in the back of her mind, she wondered what Addison was doing. Had she gone back to work? Was she teaching a class? Dealing with faculty issues? Doing whatever law school deans do?

Despite the craziness of the day, she'd almost placed a call to Addison, told her she could make time for that dinner before she left town. She'd gone as far as looking up the phone number for the law school, but each time she'd started to punch in the numbers, she'd been interrupted with a new problem to solve, another decision to make.

Just as well. Her desire to call was probably just a symptom of the loneliness she always felt as the manic pace of an election spun up fast and then dwindled down. This time tomorrow, barring a *Bush v. Gore* fiasco, she'd wake up with absolutely nothing left to do.

"Turn it up. They're about to call California."

Julia shrugged off her melancholy and turned to the bank of televisions in time to see three more states turn blue. As the rest of the room cheered, she walked to the board and colored in California, Nevada, and Colorado. When she turned around, President Garrett stood right behind her, wearing a huge grin.

"I owe this all to you."

"Me and Governor Briscoe's poor judgment. You're the best candidate for the job. I'm just glad the best man's going to win."

"Whatever happened to not calling it until it's over?"

She looked back at the map. "I suppose he could still beat you, but he'd have to take two states you've had wrapped up from the start. Not going to happen. We'll wait until they call it to break out the champagne, but it's over, sir."

His expression became serious. "We need to talk."

"Now?"

"No. Day after tomorrow. I think we should all take tomorrow off, don't you?"

She didn't bother reminding him that he didn't take days off. But she did, and she wasn't ready to give it up. "My work here is done, and the only suit I'll be wearing for the foreseeable future is a swimsuit."

"I know you deserve a vacation, but if tonight is indeed the miracle it's shaping up to be, I need one more thing from you. Come by Thursday for lunch."

She scanned his face and decided it wasn't a request. That shouldn't matter since she worked for him of her own free will, and tomorrow she wouldn't work for him at all. But something about his tone told her she really didn't have a choice. Besides, she wasn't leaving until Friday. Plenty of time to show up at a meeting and get her packing done.

"Thursday, it is." She started to ask for more details, but before she could get the words out, the room erupted in cheers and the popping of corks. She looked up at the map board and watched Brad scribble enough blue onto the final two states to show the win. She spun around and watched the celebration as the realization that they'd won sunk in. People hugged, some kissed. Giddy campaign workers slapped each other on the back and toasted everyone in sight.

As she watched the surreal display of camaraderie, she realized she'd never felt more alone.

CHAPTER SIX

Wednesday morning, Addison was in her office with Eva, discussing an issue with the moot court team's funding, when her secretary buzzed in with the call.

Eva raised her eyebrows. "Julia Scott? Isn't that Garrett's campaign manager? The one you met at the White House?"

Addison lifted her shoulders. "That's her. Did I mention I ran into her the morning of the election? At Starbucks of all places. We actually shared a piece of banana bread. Crazy, right?"

Eva stood. "I should go so you can answer that. Maybe she wants to recruit you to run for public office."

"Hardly." Addison started to tell Eva to wait during the call, but she stopped mid-breath. Whatever Julia wanted probably wouldn't take very long. Of course, she couldn't imagine why she was even calling in the first place, but whatever it was, she wanted to hear it in private. "I'll call you later."

If Eva minded the brush-off, she didn't let it show. Addison watched her go, and mixed messages trailed in her wake. They'd been in a weird place ever since Addison had pressed for more. She should've cut off ties when she hadn't gotten the commitment she'd asked for, but...she didn't really know what the "but" was. She only knew small comforts with Eva were better than nothing.

Addison picked up the phone. "Congratulations. I thought you'd be on an island by now, sipping something sweet out of one of those curvy glasses with an umbrella sticking out the top."

"Friday. I leave Friday."

"That's only two days away. Better start packing."

"Oh, I've been packed for weeks. So now I need to find something else to occupy my time."

Addison waited, not really sure how to read the conversation. She wasn't sure why Julia was calling in the first place. They'd met twice and talked for a total of twenty minutes, tops. But the quantity of the time they'd spent together wasn't a factor. She'd felt an instant attraction, strong and stirring. Had Julia felt the same?

Didn't matter if she did. Julia was headed out of town, make that out of the country, and when she returned, she'd be working on the next full course run-up to mid-term elections. Her schedule was likely impossible, and she was probably out of town most of the time. The realization cooled her reaction. "I'm sure you'll find something to do."

"Actually, I've already thought of something. Join me for dinner?"

And just like that, her resolve to hold out flew out the window. "I'd love to."

Later that evening, in her apartment, Addison stood in front of her closet without a clue about what to wear. The restaurant Julia had chosen was The Capital Grille, typical D.C. see and be seen. But she was only going to see one person, and she wanted to look good for it.

She settled on a black cocktail dress with a daring, especially for the cold weather, neckline. When she arrived at the restaurant, the maître d' showed her to a private table in an alcove. Julia stood as she approached. In pants and a flowing blouse instead of the stiffly tailored suits she'd worn during the campaign, Julia looked relaxed and devastatingly beautiful.

Julia took her hand. "You look fantastic."

"So do you. The cameras don't do you justice."

"I think I lost about ten years when we won the election. Happens every time. I'm having scotch. Would you like a cocktail?"

"Scotch is great."

Julia nodded her approval and signaled to the waiter who hovered nearby.

While they waited for him to return, Julia said, "I like this place. It's quiet even when it's packed. Please tell me you're not a vegetarian."

"I love vegetables. With my steak."

"That's a relief."

Then the waiter appeared with another heavy crystal glass. Addison took a sip of the scotch. As the amber liquid glided across her palate, she tasted toffee, malt, spice, and a hint of smoke on the finish. Warm, smooth, expensive.

As if reading her mind, Julia said, "Johnny Walker Blue. I'm celebrating."

"Ah. And it is your celebration. Must be why you didn't ask me if I was a vegetarian before you invited me to a steakhouse."

Julia had the good sense to look sheepish, but Addison could tell she was used to having her way.

"Sorry about that. I guess I figured if you didn't like steak I couldn't date you, and I wasn't ready to find out over the phone."

"So, this is a date?"

"Frankly, I don't know what else to call it. I'm not a big dater, but I occasionally have dinner and other things, with a woman I'm attracted to."

Addison made a conscious decision to ignore the reference to "other things" and relish the fact that Julia found her attractive. She took another sip of her very expensive drink and decided to enjoy dinner and deal with anything else, if or when it came up.

They each ordered steaks and surrendered their menus to the waiter. A few beats of uncomfortable silence followed. Finally, Julia said, "I may not be fit for normal human interaction. I haven't had a meal in the last year that hasn't also been a strategy session. The last thing on earth I want to talk about is anything related to the campaign."

Addison laughed at Julia's refreshing honesty. "I'm well versed in human interaction, but it generally consists of dealing with faculty disputes, student grumbling, and an occasional interaction with a meddling board of regents."

"Well, we're a pair."

"I'm willing to give it a try, if you are. I'll start. Where are you from?"

"Look at you, starting with the softball questions. I'm from New York. My parents live in Rochester, but we're not close, so I don't get back there much. You?"

"I'm a Dallas girl. My father lives in Southlake, just north of Dallas. My mother died a few years ago. Cancer."

"I'm sorry."

Addison shook her head. After all this time, she still had trouble knowing how to respond to the socially expected niceties uttered by anyone who heard the news she'd lost a parent. But the kindness in Julia's eyes was deeper than the usual reaction she received. "Thank you. It's still hard. We were very close."

"Siblings?"

"A brother. He's deployed. Afghanistan. You?"

"Sister. She lives in Rochester with the folks. I think she always will."

Addison heard a twinge of bitterness and sensed it was time to steer the conversation away from family. "How long have you been a campaign guru?"

Julia shrugged and took a healthy drink of the wine they'd ordered to go with dinner. "For a while I guess."

"It seems like really interesting work. How did you get into it? I mean it's not like they teach a course in school called how to get a president elected, but you've done it twice now. You must be very good at what you do."

"I guess everyone has to be good at something. Sometimes you have to find out what you're really bad at before your true talents are revealed. Besides, considering where we were in the polls before Governor Briscoe imploded, some might say I'm not at all good at what I do."

The edgy bitterness was back, and Addison was relieved when the waiter appeared with their meal. She changed the subject, and they spent the next hour in a lively discussion of the best D.C. neighborhoods and their favorite restaurants.

Addison relaxed into the easy conversation, enjoying a night out, in public, with another woman. This was what she had wanted with Eva. Did she still want it with her or was she really ready to move on? Like Eva, Julia was accomplished, easy to talk to, and every bit as beautiful. As public a figure as she was, Julia didn't seem to give a rip about what anyone around them thought. Several times during dinner, Julia held out a fork for her to taste her food, grasped her hand to emphasize a point, and leaned in close to whisper a particularly politically incorrect story in her ear—all signs of intimacy other diners would have noticed.

By the time dessert was served, Addison decided it was safe to return to an earlier topic. She couldn't resist some discussion of the election. "I was so relieved Garrett was elected. If Briscoe were president, I'm sure we'd have another Burger or Rehnquist."

"There are plenty of safe, easily confirmable candidates he can choose."

"Really?" Addison tried not to telegraph how put out she was at the words "safe" and "easily confirmable," but she viewed both of those terms as buzzwords for conservative. "Like who?"

"Oh, I don't know. Gilbert or Montoya from the D.C. Circuit. They're both respected and balanced."

"Weir was a liberal powerhouse. You really think his legacy will be fulfilled by putting a justice on the bench who will go along to get along? Because that's what you'll get from either of those two."

"Hold on. I didn't say he would nominate either of those two. I'm only speculating, but if I were advising him on the heels of an election that could easily have gone the other way, I'd warn him away from a confirmation battle this early into his term."

"That's pretty chickenshit."

"That's politics. You have to make tough choices at this level."

Addison recognized the stubborn tone. She'd flashed it herself plenty of times, but she couldn't help but feel Julia had no right to push the point, and she didn't appreciate the condescending reference to tough choices. Of course, Julia thought about things in terms of how they could be spun, not how they really were. There was no arguing with someone whose ideas were swayed by the wind of public opinion. This evening had been enjoyable only because they hadn't talked about anything of substance. Favorite restaurants, best neighborhoods? Who cared if they liked the same food? She needed something more. She and Eva may argue, but she knew their debate came from strongly rooted beliefs, not poll results.

She pushed her plate of dessert aside. "I couldn't possibly eat another bite."

Julia looked contrite. "You're upset with me."

Addison laughed. "Do you really think I'm that vapid? That I would be upset with you for having a difference of opinion?"

"You're something."

She was something, but she wasn't sure if she wanted to say it out loud since it was likely to ruin the entire evening, and it had been going so well up to now. But hell, it wasn't like it was going anywhere anyway. Julia was packed and ready to leave the country. Her politics were the least of the issues standing between them.

"Dinner was great, but I should go. I have an early morning tomorrow." She reached for her purse, but Julia stilled her hand.

"My invitation. My treat." She held on. "I wish you wouldn't go."

"I think it's best."

"If you're not mad at me, then what's going on?"

She could tell the truth, but what was the point? Julia would get on a plane at the end of the week, and they'd probably never see each other again. She bit back her feelings and said it was nothing, that she was just tired, but as she walked away from Julia, her true feelings chanted a silent refrain. *Disappointed. I'm disappointed. And I so didn't want to be.*

CHAPTER SEVEN

For the first time in months, Julia slept until she woke up. Surprising, since she had a difficult time falling asleep after the awkward end to her date with Addison the night before. True, she hadn't been on a date in a very long time, but it bothered her that she couldn't seem to pinpoint exactly what she'd done wrong. She'd liked Addison from the start, had even envisioned seeing her again, but apparently, Addison didn't share her view.

When she finally decided to sit up in bed, she only barely remembered that she'd agreed to a meeting with President Garrett, and she already regretted the decision. She wanted to curl back up under the covers. Room service pancakes would've been nice too, but now that she was back in her own place, that wasn't an option. She didn't have to look to know her kitchen was bare. Hell, she didn't cook even when she was in town. She vowed to order pancakes from the Four Seasons in Bora Bora her first morning on the island. For now, she'd have to settle for going back to sleep.

The insistent ring of her cell phone killed that plan. She glanced at the display and recognized the White House line. "Hello?"

"Ms. Scott?" It was Sue Marks. "President Garrett asked me to call and remind you about your appointment today."

"Any chance he can serve pancakes for lunch?"

"Excuse me?"

"I was kidding. Never mind. Tell him I'll be there."

She rolled back into the covers, savoring the idea that the meeting with the president was the only thing she had to do today. After a year of a tightly packed schedule, it would take some adjusting to slow down her schedule, but a few weeks in an over-the-water bungalow in the islands should help. Her small D.C. office could handle things in her absence, especially since the time between now and the inauguration would be a period of recovery for everyone involved in campaign politics. The recent election would be dissected, but no one would be making hard and fast decisions about future elections until the new year. The meeting today at the White House was probably some kind of campaign wrap-up. The president's staff would be eager to get back to the business of running the country after a long haul trying to hold on to their jobs.

She was happy for the win, but she didn't feel the need to rehash it. Tangible proof of her good work was the money in her bank account, and she planned to spend a chunk of it traveling. But as a favor to the man who'd made her business what it was today, she'd show up for the meeting, nod, and smile at all the backslappers.

At eleven fifteen, she took a cab to the White House. After winding her way past a group of picketers hoisting placards with messages about abortion and gun rights, she made her way to the visitors' entrance. The Secret Service agent at the gate offered a rare smile and congratulations on the outcome of the election. He waved her through security, and within moments, she was in the building. As she walked through the halls, she couldn't help thinking of Addison Riley and the first time they'd met. Even with everything she'd had on her mind at the time, she'd been captivated by her. The way things had ended last night, she was certain Addison had no desire to see her again. The level of her disappointment surprised her, considering she barely knew Addison. Just as well, though. She didn't need to be dating at all, let alone a woman as strong-headed as Addison Riley. What she needed was a beach babe who cared about nothing more than helping her put sunscreen on those hard to reach spots. One more day.

When she reached the Oval Office, Garrett's secretary, Sue, stood and gave her a hug.

"Congratulations, Julia."

"Thanks, Sue. It's a good day."

"With many more to come."

There it was again. Everyone thinking about the future. They all expected Julia would join in, make plans for what happened next. After all, she'd directed every action, big and small, over the course of the last year and a half. She resisted the pull. "I'm sure the next four years have a lot in store. As for me, I'm headed to a faraway beach tomorrow."

Sue looked confused. "Beach? But I thought—"

"Julia!" Garrett stood in the doorway to his office. "Thanks for coming. Hope you're hungry." He didn't wait for her response, instead ducking back into his office. When she followed, he led her through the spacious room and out into a small corridor on the other side. Julia knew exactly where they were headed, and when they finally wound up in the president's private dining room, she nodded at the waiter arranging their lunch. Garrett motioned for Julia to have a seat at the table. While she dug into the delicious food, he steepled his fingers and appeared to be contemplating what to say.

Julia cut to the chase. "The food is great, but I'm pretty sure you didn't invite me here to feed me. As much as I enjoy your company, I have a trip to pack for. What's up?"

"I've been doing a lot of thinking. About how valuable you've been over the years. I'm not sure I ever would've been reelected to congress without you, and this election...well, it was nothing short of a miracle."

"I hesitate to say this since I haven't cashed my final check, but I think a lot of the credit for Tuesday's victory should go to Governor Briscoe. I don't think there's been an October surprise that incredible in my lifetime."

Garrett spoke. "We're still breaking down the numbers, but it's not that simple. Common wisdom says that when the conservative Right loses their candidate, they just skip that box on the ballot. But in our case, the numbers show Democratic voters were galvanized after the news break. I have to credit your judgment about how we handled the news for the bump in the polls. Because of that, the party won a ton of down ticket races that were too close to call as late as last week. We kept control of the Senate and no one predicted that would happen, even with Governor Briscoe's penis problem."

"Fine. If you're saying you want to give me a bonus, I'll take it."

Garrett took a deep breath. "I have a bonus for you, but it might not be the kind you're thinking of."

Julia had a sneaking suspicion she knew what he had in mind. "Out with it. I barely have time to hear what you have to say, let alone make you understand I'm not interested."

"You haven't even heard the offer yet."

"Mr. President, you've worked with me for years. You know what I will do and what I won't do. If you're about to ask me to take a job in your administration, then you could've saved yourself a lot of trouble, and you know that. I'm not cut out to work for anyone other than myself."

"At least hear me out."

"Fine, but dessert better be spectacular."

"With a team of pastry chefs at my disposal, I think I can guarantee that. Here's what we have in mind. Most of my staff, including Noah, are going to spend the next sixty days setting a second term agenda and preparing for a State of the Union no one thought I would be giving. But I have one other huge task that needs to be done as quickly as possible, and that's what I'd like you to help with. You'd be a senior advisor to the president, and you'd report directly to me. You'd have a team of your own choosing and any resources you need to get the job done. When it's over, you can get on the next plane to wherever your heart desires."

She sighed. "Okay, I'll bite. What's the job?"

"Help us vet the next chief justice and get him through the nomination process."

She laughed out loud at the irony. Last night, she'd told Addison she barely had any interest in the subject, and now she was being asked to head up the process. In response to the president's surprised look, she merely said, "Sorry, I was thinking of something else." She took another bite of her salad, and while she chewed she considered what he'd said. "Wait a minute, you said he? You already have someone in mind don't you?"

"Not necessarily, but while we were finishing up the campaign, Noah put together a list of names. There are some big issues pending before the court, and he thinks," he cleared his throat, "I mean I think it's a good idea to make the appointment a priority."

"Not to mention, you'd probably like to start your next term without all the protestors out front."

"True."

"Who's your guy?"

"Judge Landry, Fourth Circuit."

"Interesting choice."

"You think so?"

"Actually, I think he's probably the dullest choice you can make, which makes it a super safe selection. And he's been confirmed before, so it should be a breeze to get him through. Not sure what you need me for."

"I can't afford to start this term with any stumbles. I want this confirmation to go off without a hitch."

"Good plan. How do you see this playing out?"

"I'll provide you with a full team to help, and you can start vetting a group of candidates. You'll explore a wide range of possibilities, but settle on a short list where Landry shines."

Julia ignored his references to what she would be doing if she were to take the job. "By the time you name your choice, Landry will be the golden boy compared to the possible contenders."

"Exactly. His confirmation should sail through."

"Sounds like a piece of cake. You don't need me, and you, of all people, should know why I have no desire to get involved in Senate politics."

He reached across the table and grasped her hand. "I promise this is the last time I'll ask for your help. Noah thinks we can get this done on our own, and I know you don't believe in all that serve at the pleasure of the president crap, but I'd feel better, more confident, if we had you on our team. Just this one last time."

Julia avoided his eyes while she considered the offer, because she knew if she met his gaze, she'd see a reflection of the debt she owed and could never repay. She'd always been clear with him that she wouldn't take a job in the administration, but what he was asking was short-term, temporary. She ticked off all the other factors. Low government pay wasn't an issue. She made more money in one campaign than most people make in several years' worth of government work. These days, she was her own boss, in charge of her own destiny. She set her own hours and decided who she would work for. If she took this job, even for the short-term, she'd give up her freedom, not to mention her long-awaited vacation.

Clear blue ocean, strong cool drinks, and sandy white beaches beckoned. These were the things she craved, the reward for all her hard work. But even they wouldn't last. In a few weeks, she'd get the itch and she'd find another campaign to pique her interest. She knew he'd asked her to take on this task because it was a lot like a campaign. And a Supreme Court justice confirmation didn't come along very often. And her debt would be repaid.

"I'll do it. On one condition."

CHAPTER EIGHT

A week after her fateful date with Julia Scott, Addison Riley was completely immersed in end of the semester preparations. Her assistant, Roger Lloyd, sat in front of her desk, taking notes on his iPad.

"Please schedule a faculty meeting for the week before Thanksgiving. I'd like to make sure everyone has what they need for exams before they scatter for the holidays."

"Will do." Roger closed the cover of his tablet and stood. "It's almost lunchtime. Would you like me to order you something?"

"Actually, I got a call from Senator Armstrong just before you came in this morning. We're meeting for lunch. She made the reservations so I'm all set."

"Tell the senator I said hello." Roger had been with her for years, following her from the solicitor general's office, to private practice, to the law school. Addison thought him capable of so much more than running her professional life, but he'd insisted that working for her was as fulfilling a job as he could ever hope to have.

Addison spent another half hour reviewing the final details of the coming year's budget in preparation for the regents meeting that night, and then she grabbed her coat and took her car into the city. Senator Armstrong had chosen The Capital Grille, the scene of her disastrous date with Julia Scott. As she'd done many times since that night, Addison contemplated the conversation from that evening, as if she could cipher out a different ending. She couldn't make it work.

And why should she? Julia seemed committed to noncommittment. She'd just gotten a man elected to the most powerful office in the world, and her only concern was which white sandy beach would be best to place her towel. Her theory about the Supreme Court nomination likely had Weir rolling over in his grave. At the very least, it demonstrated how little Julia cared about the issues behind the politics that were her bread and butter. No matter how striking, no matter how magnetic, she needed to stop thinking about Julia. Definitely a case of flash over substance.

Senator Connie Armstrong was waiting just inside the restaurant and gave her a strong hug. They'd been friends since law school and had kept in touch despite their divergent career paths. The Texas senator came from a long line of lawyers who'd made their wealth in oil and gas. She'd worked at one of the state's largest, most prestigious firms that also happened to bear her family name. Her name recognition and money came in particularly handy when she'd run for statewide election. She'd chosen precisely the right time. Texas had turned blue again for the first time since Ann Richards had been elected governor, and she rode the wave of liberal enthusiasm to an easy victory. She'd served her state well, and many were predicting she'd be the presumptive presidential nominee in four years. But to Addison, she was simply Connie, the first person she met when she arrived at Yale Law School.

Once they were seated, Connie launched in. "We have a lot to talk about. Let's order big fat steaks and big glasses of bourbon."

Addison considered the rest of her day. No meetings scheduled, but tons of reports to review and the budget to finalize. "I'm in for the steak, but cut me off after a glass of wine. I've got a board of regents meeting tonight and a lot of explaining to do."

"Maybe you should serve wine at the meeting. A little red goes a long way."

"I suppose that's true, but I think I'd best be on the safe side this time."

"Always the good girl. I suppose I should expect no less."

They ordered and then Connie turned the conversation to the holidays. "Do you have plans for Thanksgiving?"

"Dad wants me to fly home. Jack's planning to be there, and I'd love to see him. Just a matter of timing and how much I can get done between now and then. Why in the world do we have exams planned to take place right around the holidays? It's a curse for students and staff. When you're leader of the free world, could you do something about that?"

"It's a rite of passage. We had to go through it. Why would you want to let everyone else off the hook? But you shouldn't let any of that get in the way. Go see your family. Family is important. Speaking of important people, anyone special in your life right now?"

Addison's mind flashed first to Eva and then to Julia. "No. I mean...no."

Connie laughed. "And your final answer is?"

"Don't make fun of me. I don't know what the deal is. I'm finally settled in a career that, despite being very challenging, doesn't require round-the-clock work, but the only women I meet are either intimidated by my position or they're turned off by it."

"Examples."

"The last two years, I've had a thing with one of the fellows, but according to her, our relationship has to be a secret because it just wouldn't be good for her reputation to be dating the dean."

"Don't shit where you eat. I get it."

Connie had always been crass, but Addison turned it back on her. "That's just the thing. She's perfectly willing to...you know, but it just has to be a secret."

"She scared for anyone to know she's a gal's gal?"

Addison shook her head. "She teaches Women in the Law. What do you think?"

Connie laughed her big, bold laugh. "Gotcha. Well, cross her off the list. She's not worth your time. Anyone else?"

Addison started to mention Julia, but stopped short, sticking instead with a vague reference. "No one who isn't where I was four years ago."

"Career first, love last."

"Exactly."

"You like this dean gig? Seems like it might be a little boring after what you're used to."

"I like it. Yes, it's different. I'm not on call twenty-four seven, which took some getting used to." As solicitor general, Addison had been charged with representing the federal government in cases pending in the Supreme Court. Even with a large staff, she'd had her hands full. As a former judicial clerk, she'd been well suited for the job, but as the youngest person to ever hold the position, she'd worked extra hard to make sure no one ever questioned she was the right choice.

"Just seems like you're wasting your talents."

"How so?"

"You spent years shaping the law. You really don't miss that kind of power?"

"I'm shaping young lawyers. That's pretty powerful stuff."

"True, true." Connie took a big swallow from her glass of bourbon. "Tell me about Justice Weir. What kind of person do you think he'd want to replace him?"

Addison wasn't surprised by the question considering Connie was the chair of the Senate Judiciary Committee and de facto gatekeeper to confirmation for whoever the president chose as Weir's successor. "I guess I'd have to say he'd want whoever took his seat to be honest, compassionate, and smart. Not necessarily in that order."

"I can't believe we lost him."

Addison nodded. "There will never be another like him. Whoever the president chooses will have big shoes to fill."

"Who would you pick?"

"That's a hard question. There are a lot of capable people who would do a decent job of protecting his legacy on the court, but I guess it's not really about that, is it?"

"What do you mean?"

"The tide goes in, the tide goes out. New president, new ideas about what's good for the times." She paused, considering whether to share what Julia had told her. "I heard a rumor that Garrett was going to nominate a moderate. As for who it might be, the list is endless. Seems if you want to get confirmed anymore, you can't make waves." Addison cocked her head. "Why all the questions?"

Connie's expression was unreadable. "Just curious. I have a feeling we'll be getting a list of possible nominees soon, and I just wonder what makes them tick."

"Your guess is as good as mine. When I was at the court, the justices were all unique in their approaches and ideals. Maybe that's the key—a good mix. Anyway, I'm glad I don't have your job. I can't imagine having to make the call on whoever the president nominates."

"If Garrett nominates the right person, we'll do the right thing."

Addison couldn't help but hear the ominous tone in Connie's voice. She raised her glass. "Here's to doing the right thing."

❖

Julia surveyed her office in the West Wing. She would've preferred using her own office on Capitol Hill for this assignment, but Garrett had insisted she remain as close as she had during the election.

She'd agreed to the concession, but only because he'd agreed to comply with her one, deal-breaking demand. Her phone buzzed and she rushed to answer, hoping this was the call she'd been waiting for. The secretary who'd been assigned to help her spoke softly into the intercom. "Ms. Scott, Gordon Hewitt is on the line."

"Excellent, thanks." Julia waited for the call to connect, and when she heard Gordon's voice, she practically shouted into the phone. "Gordon, where are you? I've got meetings set up for tomorrow and I need you here. And I've been trying to reach Barb, but she's not answering any of my texts or e-mails."

"Probably because she's on vacation, which is exactly what I was packing for when you left a dozen nine one one messages on my phone. I thought you'd be in Bora Bora by now. What's up?"

For a split second, Julia felt guilt. Gordon Hewitt and Barb Lowry were two very accomplished public relations consultants, and she hired them to assist every time she'd worked on a major campaign. They'd both worked hard on the Garrett campaign and, like her, had planned on taking some well-deserved time off. She'd wanted them both, but one would have to do.

"I'll explain when you get here, but it's important. Trust me—I wouldn't ask if I didn't really need you."

"Fine. Meet at your office?"

"Actually, no. West Wing. I'll have a pass waiting for you. See you tomorrow." She hung up before he could ask any more questions.

Explaining that she'd talked the president into letting her hire a PR consultant to serve on the Supreme Court appointment committee was a conversation better had in person. She just hoped she'd piqued his interest enough that he'd hear her out before realizing he'd have to postpone his vacation. Garrett had already given her a list of advisors who would be at her disposal, but she wanted someone she trusted on the team, not just the hotshots around here who thought they knew everything.

Now that Gordon was squared away, she buzzed the secretary and asked her to come into her office. Seconds later, the young blonde stood in her door. Her bearing said timid, which was surprising since she'd held her current position for several years. The advisor she'd been working for had gotten an offer from a big law firm in L.A. and had given notice as soon as the election was over, so she'd been assigned to Julia. Julia suspected she didn't have a clue about her future fate in the administration, and it was time to set the record straight.

"Susan, I think we need to have a talk."

"Cindy. Excuse me, ma'am."

"Sorry?"

"My name. It's Cindy. Cindy Tinsley." She shuffled in place, apparently uncomfortable about correcting her new boss.

"I'm sorry, Cindy. Have a seat."

As she sat in the one of the chairs across from Julia's desk, Julia stood and came around to sit in the other one. "Cindy, do you like working here?"

"Here in the White House?"

"Yes."

"Yes, ma'am, I do."

"Well, I don't. I'm only staying on as a favor and, if all goes well, I'm not going to be here long past the inauguration."

"I understand. I can have my things cleared out by the end of the day."

Cindy started to stand, but Julia motioned for her to keep her seat. "I'm not making myself clear. Over the next few months, I'm going to be dealing with a really delicate issue, and I'm going to need a strong right-hand person to be a gatekeeper."

Cindy nodded and Julia continued. "I can't promise you longevity, but I can promise that if you're up to the task, I'll give you an excellent recommendation, and I know a helluva lot of people."

"Yes, ma'am."

Julia cringed at the word ma'am, but plowed forward. "I have a few rules or special conditions, whatever you want to call them." She ticked off each item on her fingers. "If it has to do with furniture, office supplies, et cetera, you handle it. Don't even ask me. I'll deal with whatever you decide. I'm only picky about a few things, and I'll tell you what they are right now: pastrami not turkey, scotch not vodka, and when I say I don't want to be disturbed, that means no one comes through that door, not even the president.

"I'll be heading up the search team for the next Supreme Court justice. There will be several other people working with me, some I know well, some I don't, but I'm in charge and I make the calls on who is interviewed and when. No one will go around me, even if it's the president or his chief of staff."

By now, Cindy was scribbling notes onto her steno pad. Julia stopped and waited until she looked up again.

"And I have direct access to the president. You will face other gatekeepers, ones that have more experience, but you must not be deterred. My calls always get through. Do you understand?"

"Yes, ma'am."

"One more thing. Stop calling me ma'am. I'm Julia, Ms. Scott if someone important is in the room, but ma'am adds ten years to my age and I don't need any help. Deal?"

"Yes, ma—I mean, yes, Julia."

"Great." Julia handed her a list of names. "This is my team. The top name on the list can have full access to me. The rest will have to earn it. We'll start meetings tomorrow. Make sure we have a conference room on the main floor with as much visibility to visitors as possible."

Cindy wrote furiously. "Right. On it."

"Tell whoever you need to that we need the room available for the next three afternoons. Don't take no for an answer. That's all for now."

"Yes, thank you." Cindy stood and strode out of the room with purpose. She'd either work out or she wouldn't, but Julia liked the idea of sculpting a secretary out of a lump of clay. Whoever Cindy had worked for before had beaten her down with filing and insipid tasks. She wasn't in the business of underutilizing skills. Treating someone like they were capable was the first step in making them so.

A few minutes later, her phone buzzed and she heard new confidence in Cindy's voice when she announced that Noah was waiting to see her. Julia smothered a smile of amusement. Noah Davy wasn't used to being kept waiting. She told Cindy to send him in.

He entered the room with his signature swagger. "Nice office."

She assumed an air of nonchalance as she looked up and met his gaze. "Not as big as yours, but it'll work for my needs."

He didn't wait for an invitation before settling into a chair. "I would've bet you'd turn him down."

"The president's a persuasive man."

"I suppose that's true, and you do like to make history, don't you?"

Should she call him on his barely-veiled accusation of influencing the president to get this position, or should she ignore him like she always did? She'd never understand why Garrett had picked Noah to be his chief of staff, but it didn't look like he was leaving anytime soon. It was no secret he'd resented her influence during the election, and he'd probably counted the days until her job was done. That she was still here was likely a source of annoyance. She may not have to work with him, but she'd be working around him for a bit longer. May as well make the best of it.

"Guess we all have the chance to make a mark, although Judge Landry isn't likely to make a big splash in the history books," she said.

"You have a problem with the president's choice?"

His tone was aggressive, challenging. Telling. He was bucking for a fight, but he wasn't going to get one from her. "I commended him on it. Low profile, low risk. Good choice, considering."

His expression showed a trace of surprise that he quickly hid behind a fake smile. "Looks like we agree. That's good. What will be even better is if you realize you can place your trust in the people assigned to help you. Have a good day, Julia." He made long strides to the door and was gone in seconds.

None too soon. Once the door closed behind, him, Julia picked up the list the president had given her of people who would work with her to help select the next chief justice of the United States. She'd meet with them this afternoon to set the agenda for the next few weeks. She read the names and quickly realized Noah had selected the people who'd made the list. She'd met most of them during her work on the campaign. They were all capable, dedicated, but they were also all type A individuals who had something to prove.

That's okay. She and Gordon would be the real team. The rest were window dressing. She may not have wanted this job, but now that she'd taken it, she'd give it her all. She'd get President Garrett's choice vetted and confirmed. With no distractions, she'd get the job done in record time.

CHAPTER NINE

The next day, Gordon showed up thirty minutes before the first meeting. Cindy, following her instructions, let him into Julia's office without question.

"It's about time you got here."

Gordon gave her a big hug. "You do realize I don't actually work for you, right?" he said in a teasing tone. "I was packing for Paris. Whatever you need better be more important than a pain au chocolate and the Eiffel Tower."

"There's a bakery around the corner with decent pastry, and the guy who works the counter has a French accent. Quit your bitching and have a seat."

Gordon settled into a chair. "One day I'm going to ignore your call, but since I'm already here, tell me what you've got."

Julia glanced at her watch. "In a few minutes, we, along with a group of White House staffers, are meeting with several members of the Democratic Judiciary Committee to go over what we will tell them is the president's short list to fill Justice Weir's seat."

"Whoa." Gordon shook his head. "I figured when you said you needed me ASAP, there was some lurking scandal, but a Supreme Court nomination? Isn't that the kind of thing a bunch of lawyers sit around and cipher out? This place is full of them. Even if you needed my help, you won't need me until you're ready to spin the final choice for a smooth Senate confirmation. Plenty of time for me to cruise down the Seine and be back in time for the battle."

Julia waited, confident Gordon would figure it out. Didn't take long.

"Oh, wait a minute, you said 'what we will tell them is the president's short list.' In other words, he's already vetted someone."

Julia nodded. "Close. No vetting yet, but he does have a name in mind. You're the fourth person to know. It's Judge Landry, from the Fourth Circuit."

"Never heard of him. That's why you want me, right?" Gordon said.

"Bingo, but it's a tightrope. We'll want to raise his profile, but not so much that he's polarizing for either side."

"Deal. What do you want me to do first?"

Julia glanced at her watch. "I've got a meeting in fifteen minutes with the Democratic leadership. A bunch of White House staffers who think they're in charge will be there. You will be my wingman, a nice distraction for everyone involved. All I need you to do at this point is gauge reactions. The real work will start in a few days. Shall we head to the meeting?"

Gordon hesitated for a moment, but Julia knew he wouldn't be able to resist the exposure he would get from working on another high profile assignment so close on the heels of the presidential campaign.

When they arrived at the meeting, she greeted the staffers and introduced Gordon, but offered no explanation of his presence. While the rest of the group contemplated the new addition to the team, she sat at the head of the table and consulted the notes on her laptop while waiting for the Democratic leadership to arrive. The senators would be expecting to meet with Noah, with whom they had a solid working relationship. Well, they were in for a few surprises.

Senators Connie Armstrong, Lance Jones, and Maria Juarez entered the room, each with a staffer of their own. Thankfully, the room was big enough to accommodate them all. Julia made the introductions and accepted their congratulations on the hard-fought election.

Seconds later, Armstrong said, "Is Noah going to join us?"

"No."

A few beats of silence passed while Armstrong stared at Julia, apparently sizing her up.

"Interesting. Would have been nice to know who we were going to be dealing with."

"The president has asked me to be the point person and, as you can see, we have a full team assigned to make this process as expeditious as possible." She didn't bother trying to hide the cocky tone. The amount of ego in the room was off the charts, and the only way to stake her claim as the person in charge was to act like it was a given.

"Well, let's start over then. Julia, it's good to see you. We'll look forward to helping out with the process of selecting a new justice."

Nice pivot. Julia didn't bother to set her straight by pointing out the nominee would be the president's choice and no one else's. Armstrong knew she owed the president loyalty. Without his big win and the down-ticket victories that rode on his coattails, she would've lost her precious majority in the Senate. "We have a preliminary list for you to consider." She pushed a piece of paper toward the senators and waited.

Armstrong picked up the paper and held it at arm's length. She read the list and then passed it to her fellow senators. "Not a lot of imagination. President scared to go out on a limb?"

"These are all very qualified candidates that should garner full support."

"You mean easy confirmation. I get it. He doesn't want any waves."

Julia refused to be baited. No way would she concede that Garrett wasn't willing to do battle on this front. "I'm sure we can count on your support." She stood to indicate the meeting was over.

Connie Armstrong stayed seated. "Not so fast." She reached over to her assistant, took the sheet of paper handed to her, and pushed it across to Julia. "Don't you want to see our list?"

Julia glanced down at the table. As the head of the Judiciary Committee, Armstrong had a lot of pull. She might not get to select the candidate, but she could make the process arduous at best. Good strategy dictated that Julia should at least make a display of deference.

She picked up the paper and read the names out loud. There were three. "Clausen, really? Isn't he a Communist? And Taylor? I thought he was working for the ACLU. Let's see who else. Look. It's Gibbons. She's the poster girl for left wing nuts everywhere." Julia let go of the paper and let it float back to the table. "You're kidding, right?"

Connie smiled. "Never hurts to ask." She looked at her colleagues. "Every one of these candidates is as qualified, or more, than the names on the president's list. But I understand your guy being a little reluctant to go to bat for these folks." She paused, and Julia swore she did it for effect. "I do have another name for you. In fact, we'll put her at the top of our list."

"Whoever she is, she couldn't possibly be more controversial than these three. Who is it?"

"Addison Riley. She's a former solicitor general and she's dean of the law school at Jefferson, and…"

Armstrong kept talking, but Julia didn't hear her. She knew the high points of Addison's background, but just hearing her name in this setting sent her into a tailspin. Taking a deep breath, she struggled for control. Armstrong very likely expected her to point out that Addison was an out lesbian. If it were any other potential nominee for Supreme Court justice they were talking about, that would definitely be the first thing out of Julia's mouth. But she held back, lying to herself that it was because she didn't want Armstrong to see she was caught off guard.

"I know who she is."

"Then you must admit she's well-qualified for the job. Weir was her mentor. She was his favorite clerk. No better person to take his seat. Unless you have some other reason for not wanting to put her on the list."

Julia ignored the bait. "With all due respect, it's not Justice Weir's seat. It's just a seat. You know as well as I do that nominating a federal judge at any level is the president's purview and the choice will reflect his vision. Certainly you don't think if Justice Falco retired, President Garrett should nominate another conservative textualist, do you?"

Armstrong shook her head. "Of course not, but the president should be proud to nominate Dean Riley or any one of these other candidates, and I'd like to think he cares enough about the advice and consent function of the Senate to take our suggestions seriously."

This was a game of chess, and Armstrong had just called check. The senator had the power to either stall the process indefinitely or ram this nomination through. The path she took would set the tone for the entire first year of the president's second term. Julia could stand firm or she could acquiesce. The smart thing would be to go along and at least interview these potential candidates before finding a reason to take a pass.

Addison Riley. The memory of their brief interlude conjured up lots of images, but none of them involved black robes and legal rulings. Did Addison know Armstrong was throwing her name in the hat? Addison had brought up the subject of the vacancy on the court at their ill-fated date. Had she known then she might be on a list? Julia made a mental note to look into whether Addison had any connection to Armstrong, but in the meantime, she knew what she had to do to move things along. The extra steps would delay the process, but she'd speed it along as quickly as possible.

She pointed to the piece of paper on the table. "We'll set up preliminary interviews with these people. In the meantime, you'll review our list. Agreed?"

"And Addison Riley? You'll meet with her as well?"

"Yes. I'll meet with her myself. You have my word."

Armstrong smiled like she'd won a greater victory than she had, and Julia wondered what she was missing.

Ten minutes into the board of regents meeting, Addison wished she'd had that glass of whiskey at lunch.

At issue was the new moot court facility that she'd lobbied for continuously over the past year. Chadwick Barker, the board president, was completely behind her proposal, but a small contingent on the board, led by Mary Dempsey, had taken it upon themselves to question anything that wasn't classroom centric. They, of course, weren't lawyers, and couldn't seem to muster an appreciation of the importance of hands-on learning. Rather than defer to the members of the board who talked at length about how such a technologically advanced facility could give students practical real world experience, Mary and her pals had droned on about grade point averages and job placement.

She listened to Dempsey and watched her posse nod their agreement to her conservative approach to the budget. When she finally finished her big speech, Addison delivered what she hoped was a persuasive pitch. "Our placement as a top tier school isn't confined to GPAs and job placement. Clinical experience is a big chunk of the ratings, and if we don't take significant steps to give our students practical as well as academic success, they will be ill suited to the current marketplace. As the report in front of you details, the number of law school graduates this year is higher than ever before, and the number of jobs has significantly decreased. The best thing that we can do to ensure our graduates are ahead of the game is to equip them with real skills so they have added value in the marketplace. We've raised two-thirds of the money from private funds, but we believe the university will reap the most benefit from funding the rest of the project."

Addison paused to take a drink of water, hoping she had said enough to shut Mary up while Barker called for a vote. She breathed a sigh of relief when the proposal passed by a narrow margin. The slim victory reminded her of her days at the Supreme Court when decisions were almost always split five-four. When the meeting was over, she thanked Barker, and then ducked into her office to get a leg up on the next day's work. She was surprised to find Roger still at his desk.

"I know why I'm working late, but what are you still doing here?"

He looked up from his computer. "Same thing you are, probably. Maybe if we put in a few hours, we can get caught up."

"I don't feel like I'm ever going to get caught up, but I'll keep trying. You should go home."

"I think I have a bottle of ketchup and a six-pack in my fridge. I'd just as soon stay here, order takeout, and get caught up. How did the meeting go?"

"It went. The board approved the funding, but it was a battle. I don't understand why some of them can't see the value of practicality."

"Law school and practicality. Crazy talk."

Addison laughed. Roger had become well versed in the customs of academia, and both of them had heard tales from other staff members about deans beating their heads against the wall trying to change the age-old customs of traditional legal education. "You're right. But I haven't been doing this long enough to be discouraged yet."

"Don't let it get to you. You're on the right path. Trust your gut."

"Thanks. Why don't you order takeout? Put it on my credit card. I'm going to see if I can wade through the stack on my desk." She started to walk into her office, but stopped when he called her back, waving a piece of paper.

"I almost forgot. You got a call just as you were walking into the meeting. Someone named Cindy from Julia Scott's office."

Addison stopped short at the mention of Julia's name. Julia was supposed to be on a beach somewhere. Roger had said someone from her office called, not her. But why would she have someone from her office call? Funny, Addison hadn't really thought about Julia even having an office. She'd pictured her traveling around the country in planes and buses, at the whim of whatever candidate she happened to be pitching at the time. But of course, she had to have an office. And staff. She was a professional with a solid reputation, and she'd been doing this for a long time. She'd have all the trappings of success, which probably included plenty of women who wanted to date her. She might still be one of them. She took the paper from Roger's hand. "I'll return the call tomorrow."

"I told her you were in a meeting. She said to call back today, no matter how late."

She did, did she? Addison walked into her office and closed the door. Seated at her desk, she glanced back and forth between the stack of work and Roger's note. Curiosity won. She picked up the phone, dialed the number for an outside extension, and then punched in the numbers to Julia's office.

"White House operator, how may I direct your call?"

The White House? Addison stared at the number, certain she must have misdialed. "I'm sorry. I must have the wrong number."

"Who were you trying to reach?" The voice was friendly, helpful.

"Julia Scott."

"Hold please."

Well, that answered the wrong number question. Apparently, Julia was working at the White House. Maybe she'd called to tell her that. Ask her out again. Give their attraction another try.

"Ms. Scott's office. This is Cindy."

Cindy. The name on the message. "Cindy, this is Addison Riley. I'm returning your call. Is Julia there?"

"Um, hello, Ms. Riley. Ms. Scott would like to schedule an appointment with you tomorrow. Does three o'clock at the White House work for you? We'll leave a guest pass at the guard gate by the West Wing entrance."

A deeply ingrained sense of manners was the only thing that kept Addison from hanging up. Who did Julia think she was? They'd had one date and now she was having her secretary summon her to the White House? How about a call instead to say, "Hey, I'm back in town. Let's get together?"

Instead of saying all that, she asked, "What is this regarding?"

"I'm afraid I can't say, but Ms. Scott will fill you in at your meeting."

"I'm afraid I'm very busy tomorrow. Please tell Ms. Scott thanks for the invitation, but I won't be able to attend. If she'd like to discuss it further, she can call me here at my office during regular hours."

"But, Ms. Riley, I don't think—"

Addison had heard enough. "Thanks for the call. Have a good evening."

She hung up the phone, unable to believe Julia's gall. She'd actually harbored the delusional fantasy that maybe, when Julia returned from the islands, they might have a chance meeting, start over, and see if the spark from their first meeting would rekindle their attraction.

Fat chance. The only spark she felt right now was the flare of her temper. Julia Scott could find another woman to order around.

CHAPTER TEN

"What do you mean, she hung up on you?"
Cindy looked like she wanted to crawl under her desk.
"She was very polite about it, but she said she was very busy and if you wanted to discuss it further, you could call her yourself."

"Did you tell her you were calling from the White House, the West Wing?"

"I'm sure she knew, since the call came through the switchboard. I don't think she cared."

Julia had started scheduling meetings with the candidates on the Democrats' list, and every single one of them had jumped at the chance to attend a meeting at the White House. She'd considered calling Addison herself, but thought it best to maintain a sense of impartiality. Besides, what was she going to say? "Hey, I know our one and only date went badly, but I've got a job opportunity for you?"

No, that wouldn't do. Besides, it wasn't true, at least the last part anyway. Her one task was to get Landry confirmed. Addison was just one on a list of see them to please them candidates she had to wade through to get what the president wanted. An informal interview with her was going to be weird enough without having to reach out and broach the subject.

But she'd promised Armstrong she'd meet with Addison, and if the only way to get it done was to ask herself, she'd do just that. She turned to Cindy. "I'll need a car after my meeting with the minority leadership. Make sure it's waiting for me at the ellipse. If the meeting runs long, it's up to you to rescue me. Got it?"

Cindy nodded, her expression made it clear she was sufficiently upset with herself for blowing the other task. Julia didn't bother scolding her anymore. She made her way to the Roosevelt Room to meet with the Republican members of the Judiciary Committee.

The minority committee chair, Jeff Burrows, stood when she entered, shook her hand, and introduced her to the rest of the group. She'd only met him once before, and she'd been impressed by his courteous manners even if she hated his politics. He was young to have landed a leadership role on such a prestigious committee, but his pedigree as a former Supreme Court clerk and his rising star status in the party apparently gave him extra credit.

"Senator Burrows, good to see you."

"And you, Julia. How did you get roped into doing actual substantive work?"

She laughed and didn't answer directly. "It's amazing anyone could get me to do any work at all after the last year. What do you say we wrap this up and all go lie on a beach for the holidays?"

"We're ready to advise and consent." He leaned forward and placed a piece of paper on the table. "Here's a list of names I can guarantee we would support."

Julia picked up the paper and skimmed the names, careful to keep a neutral expression. As expected, it was the antithesis of the Democrats' list, each candidate an ultra-conservative sure to vote for the death penalty and against any law that impinged on the ability of states to curtail the rights of their own citizens.

She set the paper back on the conference table. "All men. All white. All as conservative as you can get. You do realize Governor Briscoe didn't get elected president, don't you?" She would make a show of considering his list, but she didn't have to act like a wimp doing it.

Burrows's smile was feral. "And you realize that if Briscoe had kept it in his pants, your guy would be looking at a long winter vacation instead of an inauguration?"

"Doesn't matter how the sausage is made as long as it tastes good." Julia was instantly sorry for the analogy, but she pressed on. "We'll take a look at these, um, gentlemen. We'll even interview a few. You should know we also have interviews set up with Judges

Gibbons and Taylor, and Addison Riley. You know Addison Riley, don't you, Senator? Didn't you two clerk together?"

He shifted in his seat. "I know her. She was Weir's girl. You think you're going to replace him with a justice made in his own image? Not too smart if you ask me. The court needs new blood, not a recycling of the same old ideas."

"Just working our way through the list." Julia kept her tone light, although his use of the term "girl" bothered her. There was a time to fight and a time to lay back and gather information. This was the latter. Something was up. Two powerful senators with very different opinions about a single candidate. She'd get to the bottom of why later, but she had a distinct feeling she was being played. She handed his list to Gordon and stood. "Thank you for your time. I promise we'll give these names careful attention, and we'll be back in touch as the vetting process continues."

Taking their cue, Burrows and his contingent stood and started toward the door. As he was leaving, Julia called out, "You know there is another name we're considering."

Burrows raised his eyebrows. "And who might that be?"

"Judge Landry, Fourth Circuit Court of Appeals."

Burrows's face was a mask. He nodded. "Interesting. I'll give it some thought."

Julia dismissed the rest of her group as soon as Burrows left the room, but she asked Gordon to stay behind.

"What do you make of that?" she asked.

"Hard to tell. Landry is a gift compared to the names on the Dems' list. He'll probably jump at the chance to confirm Landry when the time comes."

Gordon was right. She'd expected Burrows to play it cool when she mentioned Landry. He'd want her to review and reject her list before he finally gave in, as if he were the one offering her something in the negotiation. She pointed at the list in Gordon's hand. "Why don't you see what you can find out about that stodgy list of conservatives? I'm going to do a little research of my own. Meet you back here tomorrow?"

It was almost three. Julia stopped briefly at her desk, grabbed a folder of work, and then went to meet her car.

The law school at Jefferson University was a much larger school than the University of New Mexico law school she'd attended, but she could see a lot of the same trappings. A library full of students seated in groups, working on outlines for final exams. A food court with much of the same. It was definitely the time of the year where cramming was the norm. Did Addison find this environment as challenging as the other positions she'd held? Was she angling for something more? Time to find out.

❖

Addison was deep into budget reports when Roger knocked on her door. She looked up, surprised since she'd told him she needed to work undisturbed for at least an hour. "Come in."

He slipped in the door and shut it behind him. "There's someone here to see you. A Julia Scott. She looks really familiar, but I can't place her."

"She was President Garrett's campaign manager. You probably saw her on TV at some point during the last six months."

"I know you said not to interrupt, but she was very insistent. Said it was a matter of national security. I know that's probably horseshit, but I don't think anyone's ever used that one before. I have to give her credit."

Addison laughed. "Yeah, I'm pretty sure she's lying, but kudos for the try."

"You want me to send her packing?"

Addison took a moment to consider. Her first instinct was to say yes. She didn't have a clue why Julia had shown up, but after the strange call from her secretary the night before, she was more than a little curious. "No. I'll handle this one myself."

She arranged her desk into some semblance of order and then waited for Roger to knock again. When Julia appeared in her doorway, she took a deep breath. On TV, Julia was striking. In person, she was breathtaking. She knew better, but part of her wondered if candidates hired her in large part because of her captivating presence.

Well, she was no candidate, and she wasn't about to let Julia's good looks trump her own good sense. "Have a seat. I only have a few minutes. I told your secretary I wouldn't be able to make an appointment today, but perhaps you didn't get the message."

Julia slid into the chair in front of Addison's desk before the invitation was out. "Oh, I got the message all right, but what I heard was that you hung up on my secretary." She raised her hands in surrender. "My mistake. I should have called you myself, but I was trying to keep things on a professional level."

Professional. So, Julia wasn't here for anything personal. She should be relieved, but a tinge of disappointment traced her thoughts. Determined to focus, she asked, "What happened to Tahiti?"

"I'm pretty sure it's still there and I'll see it eventually. I got roped into a favor, and I'm hoping you can help me out."

"You have a funny way of getting people to do your bidding."

"Really, what's that?"

"You seem to expect them to act. You know, asking is customary. It's even nice."

Julia laughed. "I guess I'm not used to having time for niceties, but I'll give it a try. Addison Riley, I'd like to ask you a favor."

"Now you're patronizing me. What's your job at the White House?"

"How am I supposed to ask for a favor when you won't let me get any questions in?"

"You answer one and I'll answer one. Fair?"

"Fair. I'm working on a special committee for the president."

Addison shook her head. "Not very informative, but I suppose it's your turn."

"How do you know Senator Armstrong?"

That was out of left field. "Connie? She and I are old friends. We went to law school together."

"Have you kept in touch?"

"It's not your turn. Why did you have your secretary call me?"

"I wanted to see you. Back to Armstrong?"

"Sure, we keep in touch. We had lunch together just the other day."

"Did she ask you if you wanted to be on the Supreme Court?"

"It's not your turn—wait, what?" Addison was thrown and certain she hadn't heard Julia correctly.

"Connie Armstrong just threw your name in the ring to take Weir's seat on the Supreme Court. You mean to tell me you didn't know that?"

Addison leaned back in her chair and closed her eyes. She silently ran through her conversation with Connie. Sure, they'd talked politics, but nothing about their conversation would have signaled that she was being considered for the high court. She certainly hadn't brought up the subject.

"I didn't have a clue." She studied Julia's expression as it went from skeptical to accepting. "I don't understand. She actually asked the White House to consider me? Wait, that's the committee you're working on, right? You're on the search committee for the new Supreme Court justice?"

"Yes. You really didn't have a clue did you?" Julia visibly relaxed. "Well, in any event, I promised I would interview you."

Supreme Court. Addison let the words roll around in her head, savoring their promise. *Enjoy the moment. It's a pipe dream.* She'd already picked up on the pro forma tone of Julia's promise to interview her. "Garrett has already chosen someone hasn't he? You're just interviewing people to make the liberal camp happy, aren't you? I bet you'll be interviewing really conservative types too. Placate the extremes so you can meet in the middle. Am I right?"

"You're not entirely wrong. The president does have someone in mind, but he wants a thorough review process, and I'm in charge of that."

"Well, this is interesting. Bet you never thought we'd have a second date, let alone that it would be a job interview." Addison winced internally, wishing she hadn't referenced their attraction misfire, but Julia didn't shy away.

"I think that's the other way around. Pretty sure it was you that didn't like me very much after our first date."

"Not that simple. Besides, you were headed out of town. Dating seemed out of the question."

"So if I hadn't been headed to a remote island, you would have stuck around? Maybe even gone on another date?"

Addison studied Julia's expression, but couldn't quite tell if she was flirting or just curious. "Doesn't really matter now, does it?"

"I suppose not. Although there's no reason we can't conduct our interview over dinner."

Julia's tone left no mistake. This whole thing was nothing more than an exercise for appearances. She'd had a moment to enjoy the possibility of being chosen, but now that the moment had passed, she could at least enjoy something else. She let a hint of suggestion invade her tone as she asked, "Will the rest of your committee be joining us?"

"Do you want them to?"

"Let's start with just us and see how it goes."

"Exactly what I had in mind."

Addison was certain now that Julia was flirting.

And she liked it.

CHAPTER ELEVEN

Julia wanted to smack her head on the table. She'd been in this conference room for hours, and she was ready to climb the walls. Her committee of hotshots had spent the morning studying everything they could learn about the woman who sat in front of them and, in her opinion, she was worse in person than on paper.

The woman was Ninth Circuit Court Judge Sally Gibbons, aka Savior Sally. She'd been on the appeals court for ten years, enough time to author an enormous library of liberal opinions. She was pro-choice, pro-gay, pro-immigration. Sally had elevated liberalism to an art form, taking the most radical stance possible on every social issue that had been presented to the court. She was liberal even by Ninth Circuit standards, and that was saying something.

Julia had promised Armstrong she would interview Gibbons, but that would be as far as it got. The Senate would have a field day with Gibbons as a nominee. She'd authored numerous opinions, which meant her left-wing bias was written in stone for all the world to see. Gibbons would probably love the chance to testify before the Senate and tell them a thing or two about the laws they'd created that she thought impinged on the rights of citizens. If she were nominated, chaos would ensue.

Julia leaned back in her chair and let the rest of the team continue with their slate of questions, no longer caring about Gibbons's responses, none of which mattered since there was no way the president would put her name in contention.

It was four o'clock, just a few hours until time to meet Addison for dinner. Addison probably held a lot of the same opinions as Gibbons, but she had the advantage of not having authored judicial opinions that could be thrown back in her face. As solicitor general, she'd been charged with arguing the position of the administration whose opinions weren't necessarily her own. Any arguments she'd made in that role could easily be dismissed as those of her boss, not hers. As a dean, her role had been mostly administrative. Her biggest obstacle might be her lack of judicial experience.

Julia shook her head. Here she was acting as if Addison was a serious candidate. She wasn't. The only reason she was interviewing any of these individuals was to please the gatekeeper, Armstrong. She wasn't a fool. She could tell by the way Armstrong had handled their meeting that Addison was the one she really wanted. The others were just fluff. Or maybe all of these names were a scare tactic to get Garrett to agree to someone completely different.

Now she knew why Garrett had chosen her for the job. Gamesmanship. No one was better at it than her. She'd give them their money's worth. Starting now.

She waited for a lull in the conversation and then stood to indicate the meeting was over. Thrusting a hand at Gibbons, she said, "Judge Gibbons, it's been a pleasure. Your résumé is outstanding, and we will certainly pass along a glowing report to the president. I have a feeling he's going to want to talk to you soon."

Savior Sally fell all over herself as she left the room, and Julia doubted she would wait until she got home to leak to the press that she was being considered. Good, it would save her the trouble.

"You really think she has a chance at being confirmed?"

Julia looked at the aide who'd posed the question. Danny or Tommy, some name that ended in a "y." He worked in the counsel's office. Over his shoulder, Gordon made a face, and she struggled not to laugh. This young attorney could dissect every word of a potential nominee's jurisprudence, but probably didn't know jack about real world stuff like who played whom in the last World Series.

Grudgingly, she had to admit she couldn't really accomplish this task without these whiz kids. She knew the law as well as any regular lawyer, but these aides were constitutional scholars. She and Gordon would handle the politics, but maybe they could learn something along the way.

"You tell me."

"She's definitely left of center, but at the core, her message is one of social reform. Should dovetail with the Democratic platform."

"Platforms are for jumping off of," Julia replied. "They're ideas, meant for elections and speeches and flag waving. Once the election is over, we have to govern. After this confirmation process, the Dems in the Senate will have to go home and explain to their constituents why they voted the way they did. You think the voters in Mississippi and Arkansas are as liberal as the ones in California where Sally Gibbons sits in her ivory tower?

"We have a majority by the slimmest margin—one vote. For a person like Sally to get confirmed, she would have to get every single Democrat to vote for her because I can guarantee no Republican will cross the aisle for her."

"Well, that's probably the case with everyone on this list, so why are we even wasting our time?"

Julia sighed. "We're not wasting our time. It's strategy. We have to at least consider the Judiciary Committee's recommendations. It's part of the process." She was done giving political lessons for the day. She wasn't here as a mentor, but as a troubleshooter. When they got around to interviewing Landry, maybe they would get it, maybe they wouldn't. Not her problem.

Tommy reviewed the list. "I took constitutional law from Addison Riley at Jefferson. She was an amazing professor and she clerked for Weir. When is she coming in?"

"I'll handle that interview myself," Julia answered and then looked back down at her papers to signify the topic wasn't up for discussion.

Tommy didn't get it. "Really? I'd love the opportunity to talk to her."

Julia looked at him, trying to gauge whether he was questioning her strategy or if he really was dying to see his old law school professor. Her bullshit meter didn't detect anything. "If she gets a second interview, I promise you'll be in the room."

A few hours later, Julia handed her keys to the valet at the restaurant where she was meeting Addison. When she walked in the foyer and saw Addison waiting, her entire body thrummed with anticipation.

Addison was striking, classically beautiful. She had a strong, no-nonsense look about her. And she was tall. Julia met very few really tall women. She hadn't realized how excited she was to see her again. When she approached, Addison turned toward her, and her eyes lit up. Julia was entranced.

"Thanks for coming into the city. Again."

"I live in the city. Guess your vetting process hasn't gotten that far."

"Sorry, I just assumed you lived near the college."

Before Addison could respond, the maître d' interrupted. "Ms. Scott, we have your usual table ready."

He led them to a table near the bar, but out of the path of other guests. Once they were seated and alone, Addison leaned forward. "Do you have a special table at every restaurant in town?"

"Not every one."

"I guess you do a lot of entertaining."

Julia felt the blush creep up behind her ears. "Is that your way of asking if I get around?"

"Actually, I imagined you entertained for work, but judging by the fact your ears are red, I'm guessing you were thinking of something else. Bring a lot of dates here?"

Embarrassed further by her assumption, Julia laughed to clear the air. "Not here. There are a lot of places closer to my apartment."

"Is this a date or an interview?"

"Wow, you really like to cut to the chase, don't you?"

"I find directness to be refreshing. You don't?"

"I do. I just don't see it a lot in my line of work."

"Well, you can count on me to call it like I see it. Unlike some people, I'll actually answer a question that's asked of me."

"Ouch. Point taken. But my answer isn't that simple. Can't it be a date and an interview?"

"Not really. If the interview is serious, I doubt the date would be possible."

"Are you always this logical?"

"Mostly. Even more so when I'm liquored up."

"Then, by all means, let's order drinks." Julia signaled to the waiter hovering a few feet away. "Scotch again?" Addison nodded and Julia ordered the Blue again, telling herself she wasn't doing it to impress her date. Dinner companion. Whatever.

"How about we get the interview done and then we can decide what the rest of the evening should be?"

"Perfect. What's your first question?"

"You really like to dive in. Okay, what's your stance on *Roe v. Wade*?"

"Do you want me to tell you the law of *Roe v. Wade*? Because to the extent that it's still the law of the land, as a justice I would be bound by its precedents."

"I know the law. I'm asking would you vote to overturn it?"

"It wouldn't be prudent for me to offer specific commentary on issues that might come before the court."

"Then why did Sally Gibbons do that very thing this afternoon?"

"You're baiting me. Did you really talk to Sally about a spot on the Supreme Court?"

"We spoke with Judge Gibbons about her views, but we didn't talk specifically about the vacancy."

"Right. Well, I bet she's salivating at the chance to move up."

"I sense a bit of bitterness."

"Not at all. She's just a bit hard to take. Good luck getting her confirmed."

Julia considered what she was about to say, and decided there was no harm. "Between you and me, she doesn't have a chance of making the short list."

"Who's on your short list?"

"Are you fishing to see if your name is on it?"

"I'm perfectly happy not to know."

"Diplomatic response, but not really an answer."

"I don't really have an answer."

"Don't tell me you've never thought about it. Chief Justice Addison Riley."

"I'd be lying if I said I hadn't ever considered what it would be like. Could you imagine, the Riley Court? But it's like little kids imagining one day they will be president, long shot, little chance. All the hard work in the world and it all boils down to a piece of luck, a twist of fate. I'm not big on pipe dreams."

Julia took a sip of scotch. She liked Addison. More than liked her. She was drawn to her pragmatism. It was refreshing. Didn't change the fact she was as liberal as Sally Gibbons, but her views didn't define her in the same way. Sally would pick a fight for the sake of fighting. Addison was more likely to win people over to her side, which might work in most circles, but the Republicans on the Judiciary Committee would eat her alive.

"How well do you know Senator Burrows?"

"Jeff? We clerked for Weir together. You spend that many hours together and you're like family. We don't keep in touch as often as we should, but we keep up. I saw him at the funeral. Why?"

"Nothing. He seems a little pushy to me. Surprised Weir selected him."

Addison cocked her head. "I would've expected you to do more research about the justice whose seat you're seeking to replace. Every year, Weir picked one brilliant mind who was diametrically opposed to his general beliefs. He didn't want a crowd of yes-men as his clerks."

"Interesting."

"Are you considering Jeff?"

"What?"

"For Weir's seat? I mean you can't really be considering him, can you?"

"When pigs fly. No, we just have to deal with him on the process. Advice and consent and all."

Addison laughed. "You had me worried for a minute. I mean, we've always gotten along. He doesn't let his general beliefs affect his personal relationships, but on the court he'd be a nightmare for the Democratic party. You'd never overturn *Citizens United*, and *Roe v. Wade* would be a distant memory. Gay marriage? Forget about it."

"Just because we aren't interested in a big battle in the Senate doesn't mean we're suicidal."

"Yes, I imagine you have a nice moderate in mind. Let me guess. Is it Cocker? Southland? Landry?"

Julia tried to hide in her glass, but light sparked in Addison's eyes.

"It's Landry, isn't it?" She paused as if considering the news. "He's qualified."

"That's like saying your blind date has a nice personality."

"He's your date, not mine."

"What's your stance on gay marriage?"

"Wow, way to change the subject. We're back to me all of a sudden?"

"Dinner will be here shortly. I'd like to move this along so we can decide if this is a date or not."

"Fine. Gay marriage or as I like to call it, marriage, is a right that should be afforded to all citizens. The court took important steps by overturning part of DOMA, but leaving the rest to the states was delaying the inevitable."

"So, you think the court should overturn the rest of DOMA, force the states to recognize same-sex marriage?"

"I see no difference between this issue and the one in *Loving v. Virginia*. The Fourteenth Amendment applies to the states. Congress shall make no law that affects the equal rights of citizens. Whether it's the rights of a biracial couple or a same-sex couple makes no difference. If the states run afoul of the principles of equal rights, it's the court's duty to step in."

"And now I'm wondering why you answered that question, but not the abortion one."

"I suppose it's because I never plan to have an abortion. And I was speaking to you, not the Senate committee."

Julia munched a breadstick while she considered a response. Addison's little speech was loaded with passion, command of the law, and personal detail. Julia had never considered marriage except as a rite many people enter into and many discard, but Addison clearly regarded the institution as reverent and to be protected. Time to change the subject. She signaled to the waiter.

"I think I'd like to switch to a bottle of wine. Addison, do you have a preference?"

Addison raised her half empty glass of scotch in salute. "After this, I trust you to order the entire meal."

Julia gave the waiter her wine order and ordered some appetizers. "That'll get us started. How about we abandon all talk of law for the rest of the evening?"

"Interview over?"

"For now," she lied. The interview was over for good, but she was afraid telling Addison the truth would bring an abrupt end to their evening. Addison Riley wouldn't be a Supreme Court nominee, but she was definitely in the running for her attention.

Dinner lingered into dessert and coffee and Addison had no desire to see the evening end, but it was getting late and she had an early meeting the next morning.

"This is the most fun I've ever had at a faux job interview."

"I hear a but."

"But I have an early morning."

Julia looked at her watch. "Damn, it is late. I'll call my car and give you a ride home."

"Thanks, but I'm within walking distance. Dupont Circle."

"It's kind of cold."

"It's bitterly cold, but I'm used to it."

"I'll walk you home."

"That's sweet, but just because I enjoy a brisk walk, doesn't mean you have to endure it."

"If you can do it, so can I. Besides, I may not be done with the interview."

Again with the suggestive tone. They'd spent the rest of dinner talking about personal things, but mostly Addison's. The only additional details Addison knew about Julia were that she owned a townhouse on Capitol Hill and she didn't have any pets. Maybe she could find out more in the course of a few blocks. "All right, a walk it is."

Two blocks into the walk, Addison asked, "How did you get into campaign work?"

Julia shrugged. "Not a very interesting story."

"You managed President Garrett's campaign. Twice. Nothing boring about that. Didn't you work for Scholes & Thirsten? Is that how you managed to score a presidential campaign?"

"You've Googled me or you've had a very boring conversation with someone who knows my life history."

Seemed like Julia was dodging her questions. Funny, Julia didn't strike her as the kind of person who was shy about her work history. Addison let it pass. "Guess you caught me. Tell me you didn't Google me too."

"Guilty as charged, but you shouldn't believe everything you read online."

"If it makes you feel any better, I only read the entries on the first of two hundred pages."

Julia smiled, visibly relieved. "Then you know the basics. Single, no kids, workaholic. Sound familiar?"

"I can definitely relate. Where did you grow up?"

"Moved around a lot. You grew up in Dallas, right?"

Yes, Julia was definitely dodging personal questions. "The Dallas area. My dad still lives there, but I've only been back for visits since law school." Addison switched gears, determined to get at least one answer to her many questions. "Of all the places you've lived, what's your favorite?"

"You ask a lot of questions."

"So do you. The difference is that I actually answer yours."

"I guess I'm used to talking about whatever candidate I'm working for, not myself."

Addison nodded, pretending to accept the answer even though she sensed there was a lot more to Julia's reticence. Besides, they were in front of her apartment now and the evening was about to be officially over. "Okay, just one last question."

"Shoot."

"We met for dinner instead of at your office because I'm definitely not in the running, right?"

Julia looked strained, but she finally nodded.

"Don't worry. I'm not mad or disappointed. I just wanted to make sure where things stand."

"Good thing. Now that you know, I can do this."

Addison froze in place as Julia leaned in. She smelled like lavender and spice. Her lips were soft, and Addison let her eyes flutter shut as she forgot that she was a dean of a prominent law school, that Julia worked for the president, and that kissing women in public, especially on the first date just wasn't her style.

Good thing it was really the second date.

CHAPTER TWELVE

The next morning, Julia sat in her office in front of her computer. Her lack of productivity was epic. She blamed the kiss. The long, slow, delicious kiss. The kiss that made her forget the bitter cold, the people on the street, and her pledge to never get involved with women who talked about marriage as passionately as Addison Riley had.

It's not like she wants to marry you.

Good thing. The kiss had been the end of their evening together and the start of a long and sleepless night spent reviewing every moment of the time she'd spent with Addison. The only drawback of the night had been Addison's probing and personal questions, and the fact Addison had looked her up online.

She typed her name into her Google search bar. Addison was right. The first page was totally innocuous, mostly having to do with her work on the campaign. Some of the photos and quotes made her wince, but she supposed things always seemed more clever in the moment.

"I need a haircut."

"Excuse me?"

Julia looked up and saw Cindy standing in her doorway. Damn, she should've shut the door. "Nothing. Actually, would you see if I have some time on Friday to fit in a haircut? I can't remember the last time I actually had time to get more than a trim on the run."

"Sure. I know a good place too. Want me to make you an appointment?"

She started to say no, used to doing that kind of thing for herself whenever she had time, but reconsidered. "That would be great." She looked back at her computer screen before remembering Cindy must have wanted something, or else she was just a voyeur. "I'm sorry. Did you need something?"

"Actually, yes. Senator Armstrong is here meeting with the vice president. Her aide asked if she could have a few minutes with you while she's here."

Julia started to say no, but she knew she'd eventually have to deal with the senator. May as well get it over with. The clock on her computer screen read ten a.m. "Tell her I can be available at ten thirty. And would you mind shutting the door on your way out? I need to make a call. Thanks." She put her head back down to indicate they were finished. She appreciated Cindy's offer to get her a haircut, but she needed to make sure there were solid boundaries erected. She wasn't here to make friends.

Looking back at the computer screen full of results, she skipped from page one to page three, then six She clicked a few more times and finally hit the results she was looking for buried on page nine.

"Reliving your past?"

Startled, she looked up to see Gordon standing at her desk. She shut down the Web browser. "You could knock."

"Cindy said your door is always open for me. I would expect no less."

"What's up?"

"We spent the morning with the first name on Burrows's list. You really should have made the time. He's a real charmer."

"If he's still here, bring him by for a handshake. Don't want him to run crying to Burrows, although why he thought we would even talk to these guys is beyond me."

"You should've been there. It definitely would have been more productive than reliving all that." Gordon gestured at her computer.

"I don't know. Maybe being reminded of my frailty isn't necessarily a bad thing."

"Whatever. I say look to the future. Now that Garrett is back in office, you can officially write your own ticket. When are you going to realize you're an official D.C. badass?"

Before she could answer, Cindy buzzed through on the intercom. "Senator Armstrong is here to see you."

"Send her in."

Julia remained seated behind her desk. Armstrong may be powerful, but she wasn't about to be intimidated.

She came through the door like a tornado. "Julia, how nice to see you again. I understand Jeff Burrows has you chasing your tail with a bunch of right wing wackos."

"Hello, Senator, nice to see you too. You know Gordon Hewitt?"

Gordon stood and reached out a hand. Armstrong took a long moment to look him up and down before she finally returned the gesture. "Of course I know Gordon. You two moving on to work on your next campaign?"

The ray of hope was hard to ignore. Julia decided against enlightening her about Gordon's presence in her office. "Would you like to have a seat?"

Connie Armstrong sat on the couch instead of one of the chairs in front of Julia's desk, but Julia stubbornly refused to move. Gordon looked between them before taking one of the chairs. Armstrong couldn't quite hide her surprise that Julia hadn't asked him to leave for this conversation, but she launched into the reason for her visit. "Guess my list seemed like a dream come true after you've talked to some of Jeff's boys. They were all boys, right?"

Julia sighed and gave in. A little. "Yes, they were all men. All highly qualified."

"Really. I'm thinking Angus Sinclair is on that list. Do you really think his inability to believe that citizens are entitled to a right of privacy under the constitution makes him qualified? I guess Garrett is setting a low bar."

"I'm in charge of compiling the short list."

The instant the words left her lips, Julia wanted them back. She had no business letting the senator know how much or how little involvement the president had in the process. Even though it was well known that staffers generally did the preliminary work, it wouldn't do to actually say that to one of the most powerful women in Congress.

For whatever reason, Armstrong let her comment slide, instead changing the subject. "How about our list?"

"We've conducted initial meetings with everyone on your list."

"Cagey. Care to elaborate?"

"You really think you can get Sally Gibbons confirmed? She might actually burn her own bra on the Senate floor."

Armstrong laughed. "I'd give my government salary to have a first row seat to that. Seriously, you must know she's just a decoy for who I really want."

"So, it's about who *you* want?" Two could play this game. Armstrong had just let slip that she had a personal choice, and Julia knew exactly who it was. She braced for what was to come.

"Me, on behalf of the constituents of Texas. Not a small group, if you don't mind my saying."

"Let me guess. You and all your Texas friends want Addison Riley. May I ask why?"

"We want a judge who isn't afraid to tackle the big issues. Like Weir, God rest his soul."

"Polls say that people want a moderate."

"Stick a pole in the water and you get whatever fish you've baited. I know those polls and they're rigged. Those same people think the court was right to get involved in civil rights. The average person doesn't understand the difference. Don't pick Riley if you don't want to, but pick someone like her."

"Addison Riley is no different ideologically than Sally Gibbons. We pick anyone that liberal and we'll spend all our political capital in the first thirty days in office."

"No better time. You come out bruised and we still have plenty of time to recover before the midterms."

"Does anyone ever tell you no?"

"Not usually."

"How about George Landry?"

Senator Armstrong leaned back in her chair, her arms crossed. "You can't be serious."

"I am. He's qualified. More qualified than Riley—he has judicial experience. Not much in the way on controversy."

"That's because no one knows what he really thinks about anything. He rarely authors an opinion, and he almost never asks a question during oral argument. You'd have to hook him up to a machine to even know he has a pulse."

"Not true. He's just not a lightning rod. Put him on the court and you're virtually guaranteed a swing vote on the issues you care about."

"That's what you say. I'm not so sure."

"Would you like me to schedule a time for you to meet him so you can see what you think?"

"Probably not a bad idea. I'll have someone from my office call to set it up."

Of course Armstrong assumed it was a done deal. Julia made a mental note to have Cindy schedule a meeting with Garrett. He'd left this to her for now, but they'd never discussed when he'd release Landry's name as part of his short list or even as his final choice. She'd had the rest of her team vetting Landry and, except for receiving daily reports, she'd stayed out of the mix to avoid the press getting the information before they were ready to leak it. Garrett would have the final word on whether Landry would make himself available to meet with Armstrong at this stage, but she had every confidence he'd go along if she recommended it.

Armstrong stood to leave, and Julia followed suit to encourage her along. Armstrong stopped in the doorway. "You know, I find it hard to believe you met with Addison Riley and didn't walk away ready to dispense with a short list."

Julia shot a glance at Gordon, willing him to say something so she wouldn't have to lie. But what could he say?

Nothing. His personal politics were way left of center, but, like her, he put them aside when he was on the job. Addison would be a perfect justice. But Garrett had made it clear he didn't want to spend a ton of political capital on this fight, and Addison would take all they had. Her job, her allegiance, meant she would get her boss what he wanted. Personal politics and personal feelings couldn't be a factor.

She wasn't about to share her reasoning with Armstrong, so she opted to ignore her remark. "Thanks for stopping by, Senator. I'll be in touch."

❖

Addison sat in her office realizing she'd been staring at her computer for thirty minutes and hadn't accomplished a thing—except thinking about Julia's lips, her hair, her scent. When her phone rang, she grabbed the handset on her desk before she realized it was her cell phone ringing. She fumbled in her briefcase and finally located it in between some files. The display read private caller.

"Hello."

"Addison?"

"Yes, who is this?"

"It's Larry Weir. Is this a good time to talk?"

It wasn't, but Addison could hear the strain in his voice. It had been weeks since his father died, but it was obvious the grief was still a heavy burden. Addison looked at stacks of papers on her desk. She should probably welcome the opportunity to take a break from the tedious administrative tasks that took up eighty percent of her day. "It's perfect. What's on your mind?"

"Maybe it would be better if we met somewhere. I have some things to give you."

"I could meet you for a drink this evening. Does seven work for you? At the Old Ebbitt?"

"Perfect. I'll see you then."

She'd no sooner hung up then Eva popped her head in the door. "Want to grab dinner tonight?"

"Dinner?"

"You know, a meal that people eat in the evening. Sometimes even at a restaurant."

Eva, queen of the stay-in date, was suggesting they eat at a restaurant? Addison was almost too shocked to remember she'd just made plans. Almost. "Thanks, but I have plans. I'm meeting Larry Weir."

"Oh, my loss."

Eva looked truly disappointed, and for a second, Addison felt bad for turning her down, but the memory of her date with Julia, in a restaurant, and then the kiss, in front of God and tourists on her front steps took over. Could Eva see the warm blush she felt? She quickly changed the subject, just in case. "I don't think Larry's doing well."

"To be expected. I guess we all thought Weir was going to live forever."

"I suppose you're right. He and his dad were very close."

"I wonder who they'll get to replace him."

Addison was irritated that Eva was so quick to change the subject from a son's grief to the nomination process, but it was perfectly normal, expected even, for a well-respected law professor like Eva to be curious about the court. She was almost tempted to tell her that she'd met the woman in charge of the process, that her name had even been considered, even if only for a moment. Saying anything would raise too many questions, political ones she was probably expected to keep secret and personal ones she wasn't ready to reveal. She settled on a simple, "Hopefully, they can find someone to fill his shoes."

"Doubtful. I can't remember the last time we had an administration with any balls. They'll pick whoever they can get confirmed without a battle."

"I'm sure you're right." Addison thought for a moment, before venturing further into the topic. "What do you think about Judge Landry, Fourth Circuit?"

"You've got to be kidding. That would be a disaster. He swings whichever way the wind blows. Path of least resistance. We need a return to the Warren Court, but I doubt Garrett will make it happen."

Addison nodded. Eva was spot-on, but she didn't have to like it.

A few hours later, Addison drove to the restaurant and left her car with the valet. Larry was already waiting at the bar and she joined him.

"Thanks for meeting me. What would you like to drink?"

Addison flashed back to the memory of dinner with Julia. "Scotch, neat." She resisted ordering the forty-year-old stuff Julia had spoiled her with, but she'd welcome the memory the amber smoke provided. "Are you staying in town long?"

"I've been at Dad's house. It's going to take us a while to go through his things."

She'd been to the justice's house in Arlington on many occasions. He'd been fond of inviting his clerks for dinner with his family when his wife was alive. During those times, Mrs. Weir forbade them from talking business, so they'd had to make due by discussing current events without putting a legal spin on everything. For a group of people who lived the law, it was a challenge. After dinner, they would retire to the Justice's study where they could share all the law talk they wanted.

"I bet some museum is going to be very happy when you're done."

Larry smiled. "A line has formed already."

"Your father was very important to many people. His legacy will live on forever."

"I know you were his favorite. He thought of you like a daughter."

"He was the best mentor I could ever hope to have."

Larry raised his glass and they toasted Weir's memory. Then Larry pushed a small box toward her.

"What's this?"

"Two things. One a memento and the other I have a question about."

Addison set her drink down and opened the box. The first thing she pulled out was a Douai-Rheims Bible. She looked at Larry, waiting for an explanation.

"It's the bible that was used to swear him in."

Addison set it down in front of Larry. "You should keep this."

"The person who should keep it is the one it means the most to. I loved my father and I have no doubt that he loved me, very much. But the law meant more to him than anything else, and that was something you shared with him." He picked up the bible and placed it in her hands. "He would want you to have this."

She stared at the book, its edges showing little sign of wear. She flipped it open and read the words inside. *To Harrison Weir at his confirmation.* Weir hadn't been a religious man, but he did believe in a higher power. She doubted he'd ever set foot in a church after he'd been old enough to make his own decisions, but the book must've been special to him since he'd kept it and used it for his swearing in ceremony.

She looked up at Larry. "Thank you. I'll treasure this always."

"There's something else." He reached into the box and pulled out another book, this one showing lots of wear. "Dad kept journals. This is the one he was writing in when he died."

Addison didn't say anything, but waited for Larry to make his point.

"There are a few strange entries and I'm wondering if you have any insight." He handed her the book. "I've flagged them."

Addison took the book from him. She'd seen the justice writing in similar journals, soft leather-bound, slim like a brochure. She opened to the first flagged entry.

Pressure to retire. Aggravating. The young pretend to understand the minds of their elders, as if they can predict when we will lose our ability to make sense of the world around us. This one will be old himself when I choose to step down.

A month later, he wrote:

Today he comes back with a "friend," as if I don't know who my friends are. This isn't about friendship. It's about the legacy of this court. I'm healthy as a horse, and even if I weren't, I wouldn't be willing to leave the future of the court in the hands of a rogue like Briscoe.

Addison looked at the date of that entry. Six weeks before the recent presidential election. Made sense why he was referring to Briscoe who at that time was the indisputable frontrunner. She shuddered to think about Briscoe being in a position to select the next Supreme Court justice and gave a silent thanks for his flop on election day. Still, someone had been pressuring Weir to retire, and she wondered who it was.

The last flagged entry was the day before he died. Weir wrote about his plans to attend a concert at the Lincoln Center. And then he mentioned a phone call he'd received.

He called again, still at it. I suppose it was wrong to hang up on him, but as he said, life's too short. He wasn't content with platitudes when I chose him, but I suppose politics changes a person. Life may indeed be too short, but I'll spend mine doing whatever I want, and until they're willing to replace me with a courageous jurist, I'll die in my robe.

She looked up at Larry. "Sounds like someone was putting pressure on your dad to retire."

"It does, and I'm not a conspiracy theorist, but a couple of other things have been bothering me. The door to the garage at the house. The lock's been messed with. Not enough so you could easily tell, but it jammed, and it looks like someone took a screwdriver or some other tool to it."

Addison nodded, not sure how to respond. Larry was clearly looking for some sort of affirmation, but she wasn't entirely sure what he wanted her to agree with. "You said there was something else?"

"Yes. Dad used a digital recorder. You know, one of those handheld things. It was something he took up for work last year in deference to technology, even though he kept his paper journal for personal thoughts. He recorded notes so he could give it to his secretary to transcribe." He paused to take a drink. "It's missing."

Addison released a breath. She'd been braced for some ominous news, but Larry seemed a little paranoid. Weir never considered himself off work and probably had the digital recorder with him the night of the crash. In her most soothing tone, she said, "Is it possible it was lost in the accident?"

Larry flinched, and Addison remembered the TV coverage. Justice Weir's car had flipped end over end before bursting into flames. If any belongings stayed with the car it would have been a miracle, and even if they had, they would have been burned to a crisp. She shuddered, instantly sorry for bringing the graphic memory to Larry's attention. She reached over to hold his hand.

She was prepared for him to draw away or react in anger, but instead, his eyes were full of tears. "They wanted him gone and he wouldn't leave, so they killed him."

Addison reeled at the non sequitur. "What?"

"Don't you see? He was being pressured to retire, but he wouldn't do it. Then suddenly, he's dead. I don't think that's a coincidence."

Addison flicked a glance at his drink, wondering how many had preceded it. She knew Larry well enough. He'd been young when she'd clerked for the Justice, but he'd always seemed like a smart kid. Weir had kept her updated through the years. Whenever they'd met, he'd show pictures. Larry graduating from Harvard business school. Larry getting married. Larry becoming a partner at a Wall Street firm.

No, Larry wasn't drunk or crazy. He was just grieving, and grief makes people do strange things. Like conjure up murder plots where none exist. She thought of a dozen things to refute his assumption, but they all boiled down to one thing: why would someone want Justice Weir off the bench bad enough to kill him? Supreme Court justices were powerful, but so much of what they did was up to chance and the will of the eight other justices who served with them. Besides, no one could guarantee that whoever replaced him wouldn't be as liberal as he had been.

Well, that wasn't entirely true. She flashed back to her conversation with Eva. If Briscoe had been elected, he surely would have taken the opportunity to appoint a conservative hawk to the bench. And Garrett? Because of Julia, she happened to know he was going to take the safest route possible and nominate a man Weir would have called a coward. But still, it was a long way from political strategy to murder.

"Why are you telling me all this?"

"I'm not sure. Maybe I just needed to tell someone. Maybe I hoped you would have some ideas about what to do."

Forget about it. Let it rest until you've had time to give the whole thing some perspective, and you'll see that these things are all just coincidence. These were the things she wanted to say, but the desperate look in his eye kept her from offering honesty when he sought hope. She touched the envelope.

"Do you trust me with his journal?"

He nodded.

"I'd like to read it through. See if I have any ideas. I'll get it back to you soon. Would that be okay?"

"You don't think I'm crazy?"

"No." Crazy with grief maybe, but Larry wasn't mentally ill. She'd read the journal, give it a few days, and then tell him she didn't think there was a connection between his father's death and the pressure to retire. In a few days, Larry would feel better and more receptive to reason.

CHAPTER THIRTEEN

The next morning, Julia paced outside Garrett's office. She'd had two scheduled times to meet with him the day before, but they'd both been cancelled because of some emergency briefings. At least that's what Noah had told her. Today, she waited until she knew Noah was on the Hill to try to get in. Garrett's schedule was already two hours behind for the day, but Sue assured her she would have the next open slot. So much for the direct access she'd been promised. She was about to abandon the task, when the door opened and Brad signaled for her to enter.

Garrett waited for Brad to leave the room before he shut the door and invited Julia to have a seat on one of the couches in the office. He sat across from her, the table between them piled high with files.

"I'm sorry about the rescheduling. It's been hard to settle back into a regular routine since the campaign." He motioned to the scattered paperwork. "Seems like I'm spending all my time playing catch-up. Plus, I don't have you at the helm, guiding me through it all."

"Oh, I'm sure you'll get back in stride." She hoped he would anyway. The sooner she finished this job, the sooner she could enjoy having a life before the next campaign season started. And now that she might have someone to share the time with, she actually cared about a break from the usual grind. She shuffled through her notes. "You ready to talk short list?"

"Sure. Is your team working out?"

"They're great," she lied. Their constant jockeying to show who could cite more case law was annoying, but she'd learned to tune out everything except the high points. He didn't need to know that. People in power wanted results, not process. But there was one part of the process he should know about. "Not sure it was a good idea to have me here in the West Wing. Burrows and Armstrong have both been to see me."

"Really? In person? Any reason why they wouldn't just send the Judiciary Committee chief of staff?"

"They both came under the guise of being here for other business, but both of them brought lists of potential nominees." She handed over both lists.

Garrett glanced at the papers. "About what I'd expect. Have you tossed out Landry's name, yet?"

"Yes. Burrows seemed open about it."

"How did Connie take it?"

"Not well."

"That's surprising. She's a pragmatic woman. She has to know no one on her list will get the nod."

"Actually, she's got her sights set on someone completely different." Julia paused as she considered how to spin this. "Addison Riley."

"Really? Interesting choice. Solicitor general, dean of a prominent law school. What's her other experience?"

"Nothing judicial. She was a partner at Boyle and Downton."

"What practice area?"

"Litigation, primarily. She also taught at Jefferson while she was in practice. Constitutional law."

"Ambitious."

Julia considered the adjective. Certainly, Addison must be ambitious to have taken on so much in her life. Any one of her achievements—solicitor general, big firm partner, law professor, dean—were admirable, but the combination made her a bit of a superwoman. Accomplished was a better word and she said so.

"Have you met with her to discuss her interest?"

"We haven't really discussed her interest." Technically true since Julia had made it clear from the start, any consideration was only pro forma. She didn't offer Garrett any other details, and she wouldn't, not unless asked directly. If she'd ever thought Addison was a serious contender for the job, she wouldn't have kissed her. Missing out on that kiss would have been a shame. Addison was a powerfully good kisser, and the mere memory of her lips sent a rush of heat through her. She struggled to think of something else to keep from blushing. Damn, she'd turned into a giddy schoolgirl.

"Should I meet her?"

"Do you want a confirmation battle?" If he did, she would be on board, but it had to be his decision.

"I already said no."

Armstrong's parting words from the day before lingered. *I find it hard to believe you met with Addison Riley and didn't walk away ready to dispense with a short list.* He'd made it clear he didn't want a fight, and it was her job to get him what he wanted. "Then you don't need to meet her. There's no way she could be confirmed without bloodshed. She's Weir in a skirt. If you want Landry, you need to put all your weight behind him."

"No short list?"

"Only for show. We'll leak a few other names, but put the focus on Landry. Let's really pitch him as a centrist, a rational jurist who will use his position to interpret the law, not make history."

"I like it. Should I give Connie a call, get her behind the plan?"

"No. She'll just view it as strong-arming. She knows no one on her list, Riley included, can make it unscathed through confirmation. If you want a quick confirmation, we'll send Landry's name and be done with it. Burrows will fight you for show, but he won't be able to rally his people to fight this choice. The new Senate convenes January third. With any luck, you'll have a confirmation within a few weeks of inauguration."

"Okay. Give me the short list once you've picked out a couple of other names and get the FBI to start vetting them. I'll send the list to Armstrong and let her know we have much more efficient ways to spend our political capital. Right now, I have a meeting to discuss replacing some cabinet members."

Julia took the signal that she was dismissed and stood. It was hard going from the number one person on the campaign to being a one-task worker out of many. She watched the president start sifting through the files on the table, and she noticed one had Weir's name on it.

"Did someone from my team leave that here?"

"What?" Garrett followed her finger that was pointed at the folder. He snatched it up and shoved it into the middle of the stack. "No, no. Just some personal notes I made." He stuck out his hand. "Thanks for everything, Julia. I know this isn't your regular line of work, but I can't think of anyone better to get us through this process."

"Wait until you see my bill."

They both laughed, but Garrett's laugh seemed tinged with nerves.

Julia left the room and switched her cell phone back on. She scrolled through the half dozen missed calls, mentally noting which ones she would return now and which ones could wait. One number stood out, and she called it on her way back to the White House.

"Addison Riley's office."

"Is Addison in? It's Julia Scott."

While she waited for the call to connect, Julia reflected on her meeting with Garrett. She felt a tinge of guilt at tanking Addison's opportunity to be considered for the highest position a lawyer could ever imagine having. Maybe she should've let the president meet her at the very least.

No, he'd probably have been as charmed as she was. He wanted to nominate a moderate and avoid a politically taxing battle in the Senate. Her job was to make it so. As for politics, she'd rather have an Addison Riley than a George Landry any day of the week, but she knew that was about as likely as wishing for peace on earth. She'd been picked for this job because she knew how to get people what they wanted, and that's exactly what she was going to do. The only time she'd ever failed before was when she went off on her own, and that wasn't going to happen here.

Addison ate a deli sandwich while poring over the pages written in Weir's cramped handwriting. What she should be doing was reviewing the final budget that had just been delivered, but she'd made a promise, and the sooner she took care of it, the sooner she could do her job without distraction. With Connie's visit and Julia's talk of the nomination, she'd had more than enough distractions to last her a while.

After reviewing the entire journal, she was convinced that Larry was right. Weir had felt pressure from someone to retire. She imagined that many justices who'd been on the bench as long as he had, had felt such pressures, whether externally or internally. But the fact that he died in horrific circumstances soon after was likely an unfortunate coincidence.

She read the last entry several times. Something about it nagged at her. She read through the passage several times, but she couldn't pin down the source of her discontent. All too likely, she was reading it with an eye toward conspiracy after Larry's words. In a vacuum, the words didn't portend doom.

She placed the journal aside. She had plenty of other issues to deal with. She'd call Larry in a few days. Tell him that she'd thoroughly examined the journal, but didn't find anything that led her to believe his father's death had been anything except an accident. In fact, she'd do one better. She buzzed Roger.

"Roger, can you do me a favor?"

"Need more chips?"

"Not if you want me to be able to fit through this door."

He chuckled.

"No, but I do have another personal request. Nothing to do with my appetite. I'd like to see if I can get a copy of the accident report regarding Justice Weir."

"Is something wrong?"

"No, nothing. Like I said, it's a personal thing, for a friend. I was hoping that maybe if the request came from a lawyer, it might speed it along. Can you find out which agency did the report and request a copy?"

"Of course."

She hung up, satisfied she'd done everything she could for now. She just started reading the budget file on her desk when her extension buzzed.

"That was fast."

"Actually, you have a call. It's Julia Scott, on three."

Addison forced calm into her tone. "Great." She took a deep breath and punched the button to connect the call. "Julia, great to hear from you."

"Glad to hear that."

"What? Do some of the women you kiss not like to hear from you again?"

"Let's just say I was hoping you wouldn't be one of them."

"Your fears are unwarranted, although I would've expected you to call sooner. Kiss and run, is that who you are?"

"Sorry. It's been a little crazy around here. Plus, I probably shouldn't have kissed you in the first place."

Julia's tone was light, but her words sunk like rocks. Addison sat in silence for a few seconds before replying. "No, you probably shouldn't have."

"But I'm glad I did."

And just like that, Addison's spirit soared. "Me too."

"That's a relief. Are you free for dinner?"

Excitement immediately tempered by caution led her to ask, "And the reasons for why you shouldn't kiss me? All gone?"

"Well, since the president just sent his short list to the Judiciary Committee, those reasons officially no longer exist."

Addison rocked back in her chair as the weight of Julia's words sunk in. No matter what she'd told Julia or herself, finding out she was no longer even under consideration for the empty spot hit harder than she'd expected. She summoned a tough exterior. "Great. We'll celebrate. You pick the place and I'll meet you there."

"Why don't you come to my place and we'll have a glass of champagne before we head out?"

Apparently, this was going to be a real date, not a hybrid interview slash date. Despite her initial disappointment, Addison was excited at the prospect of an evening with no politics to come between them. She took down Julia's address and agreed to be there at seven.

The rest of the afternoon dragged on. Finally, at six, Addison told Roger she was headed out for the day. She ignored his questioning look as she left the office.

On the way to Julia's, she stopped at a high-end liquor store. Wouldn't do to show up empty-handed. Inside the store, she walked directly to the refrigerated bottles and scanned the shelves. She paused with her hand on the Dom, but decided that was too presumptuous. If she'd made the short list, that might have been a good idea. Of course, if she'd made the short list, she wouldn't be meeting Julia at her apartment, toasting with champagne, or any of the other things she'd daydreamed about doing with Julia all afternoon, none of which Supreme Court nominees did with their handlers. Shaking her head, she opened the glass door and let the cold whoosh of air curb her heat. She chose a bottle of Veuve Clicquot and touched it to her cheek. The chill felt good, but she'd need more than that to cool off.

Back on the road, she let her GPS lead the way while she let her mind wander to something other than the feel of Julia against her, like the nomination, or rather the not nomination. She hadn't thought she'd be disappointed, but she was. A little anyway. Not just for herself, but for the legacy of the court. Moderate judges were the only ones who could survive confirmation anymore, which meant the role of naming the next Supreme Court justice had essentially fallen to the Senate. The Democrats in the Senate may have held on to their majority, but with sticky procedural rules, they had to walk a fine line to get the big work done. Justice suffered because of it.

In addition to her concerns about the law, she wondered how long Julia planned to stick around. Her business was campaigning, which usually meant heavy travel. If the campaign was regional, it could even mean a temporary move to another part of the country. Now that a short list was on its way to the Senate, would Julia see the process through or would she move on to the next exciting project? Maybe she'd take her long awaited vacation to Tahiti?

For a brief moment, Addison pictured them both in lounge chairs on the beach, under a big umbrella. No papers to grade, no budgets to write. No emergency calls to handle campaign issues, no press conferences. Just white sand, stiff drinks, and—

"Your destination is on the right."

Addison shook away the fantasy and turned off the GPS. She punched in the code to the gate, parked, and made her way to the front door. Julia answered on the first knock.

Addison held out the wrapped bottle of champagne. "My contribution to the celebration."

Julia took the bottle and smiled. "Very thoughtful of you. Do you mind if I put this in the fridge? I already have a bottle open and ready for us."

"Not at all."

Julia led her through the foyer into a living area. "Have a seat. I'll be right back."

Shelves lined the room from floor to ceiling, full of hardcover books. The rest of the room was a bit like a museum, and Addison wondered how many of the curios were the real thing. A beautiful antique champagne stand was situated near a bar in the corner of the room, and Addison wandered over. Waves of icy condensation floated off the bottle of Dom Perignon. Julia had apparently decided this little celebration was worthy of the best.

As if on cue, she appeared in the entry. "Let me pour you a glass."

"Thanks. This is a beautiful room." Addison meant it, but what she didn't say was that it didn't fit with her image of Julia at all. She pictured Julia as kind of a nomad and figured her apartment would be sparsely furnished.

"I have a good interior decorator. I told her, make it look like someone substantial lives here. She went a bit crazy."

Addison rubbed her hand on the ice bucket stand. "She did a great job. This piece looks like it should be in the Smithsonian."

"I like nice things."

Addison looked up, but instead of looking at the bucket, Julia was staring directly at her. She met her stare and replied, "Me too."

After a few beats of silence, Julia blinked first. She poured them each a glass of champagne and raised her glass in a toast. "To nice things. And to nice people."

Addison made a silent vow not to let her residual disappointment ruin what could be a perfect evening. She touched Julia's glass with her own. "I'll drink to that."

Julia drank down half a glass in an attempt to calm her nerves. This was the first time she'd had a woman over, and now she cursed her decision to book a table at the hottest place in town when all she wanted to do was finish this bottle of champagne with Addison and see where it led.

They talked about the various art pieces in the room while she finished the glass. She started to pour another for both of them, but

Addison stopped her. "I shouldn't. Not until I've had something to eat. I won't be responsible for my actions, otherwise."

Julia stopped with the bottle in mid-air and stared into Addison's smoldering eyes. Unlike her trysts on the road, Addison had substance. She didn't want their first time together to be the result of too much to drink. She placed the bottle back in the bucket and took Addison's hand. "It'll keep."

On the drive to the restaurant, they covered a half dozen subjects ranging from foreign affairs to Capitol Hill gossip. Addison held her own no matter what the topic. No, she was nothing like the women she'd bedded on the road.

The restaurant was chaotically busy, but Julia's recent success secured them a secluded table. Once they'd ordered, Addison turned the subject to personal things. "What are you doing for the holidays?"

"Holidays?"

"You know, Thanksgiving, Christmas or Hanukkah, whatever you celebrate."

"Oh, you mean the high holy times of shopping? I haven't given it much thought. If I'm not working, I usually get out of town to avoid all the tourists who want to see lights in the capital. This year, I'll probably just hole up in my townhouse and order Chinese."

"Sounds very Currier and Ives."

"You're funny. How about you? Do you have big plans?"

"My father wants me to come home for Thanksgiving. My brother, Jack, is scheduled in for a visit."

"He's on his second tour, right?"

Addison cocked her head. "So, you really did do some research on me."

"Just the basics. I know you graduated from high school at sixteen. You had an undergraduate degree in poli-sci from Berkeley by the age of nineteen, and you are one of the youngest to ever matriculate from Yale Law School at the ripe old age of twenty-two."

"Wow, I'm impressed. And you, what's your growing up story?"

Julia dodged the question. "I'm still growing up. Do you think your brother will get his leave?"

"Your guess is as good as mine. The military is a fickle master."

"I sense a bit of bitterness."

"I fully support the military. I'm just not sure how long we can keep supporting this war when it's no longer a real war, to the extent it ever was."

"Garrett ran on a campaign to bring our troops home."

"I hope he keeps his promises."

Julia didn't want to talk about Garrett or politics of any kind. She raised her glass and offered a toast. "To all this evening promises."

"You're pretty good at this toasting thing."

"I might be good at other things too."

"Is that so?"

"I'll let you be the judge."

She cringed at her choice of words, but Addison laughed and said, "Do you think they'll bring our dinner soon?"

"Giving up so soon?"

"We could have them wrap it up and we could go back to your place. Finish that bottle of champagne and…"

Julia grinned. "That's a perfect idea." She looked around. "Hold that thought." She placed her napkin on the table, leaned over and kissed Addison on the cheek, and went in search of their waiter.

A few minutes later, having found the waiter and given instructions for their meal to be wrapped to-go, she walked back to the table, not even trying to hide her swagger. When she got close, she froze in her tracks.

Connie Armstrong was in her chair, chatting with Addison.

Julia watched for a minute. Their conversation seemed lively, but friendly. No sign of trouble. She'd sent Garrett's short list over to the Judiciary Committee's chief of staff just this afternoon. She supposed there was a chance that Armstrong hadn't seen it yet. She took a deep breath and strode over to the table.

"Senator Armstrong, how good to see you."

Armstrong stood, turned slowly toward her, and fixed her with steely eyes. She knew and she was pissed. But seriously, what had she expected? Neither Sally Gibbons nor Addison Riley was moderate enough to survive confirmation. Armstrong overestimated the extent of her influence.

"Julia. I was just talking to Addison about the holidays. I had no idea who her dinner companion was, but now that I do, I must say I'm very surprised."

"Okay." Julia wanted to duel, but she wasn't going to do it in front of Addison. The names on the list were good names. Respected jurists who could win, would win, approval from the Senate without creating a battle the newly re-elected president didn't need.

"You care to explain what you're doing?"

"Having dinner with a friend."

"A friend? That's rich."

Before Julia could reply, Addison piped in. "What's up with you two? I thought you were both on the same side."

Julia looked down at Addison, who was genuinely perplexed. "We are." She offered a half-hearted smile. "Senator Armstrong, I hope you have a nice evening." She sat down and prayed this would be the end of it.

But the powerful senator refused to be so easily dismissed. "So, she's good enough to share a meal with, but not worthy of consideration?"

"I'm right here. If you're talking about me, please have the courtesy to recognize I'm in the room." Addison looked between them. "One of you care to tell me what's going on?"

Julia considered her options. Addison already knew she hadn't made the short list. She'd known Armstrong would be pissed off, not just because Addison's name was missing, but because there wasn't a single woman on the list, but it wasn't her job to affect the judicial makeup of the court. It was her job to get what her guy wanted. She wasn't a policy maker. She was a play maker. The play the president wanted was Landry, and she'd been hired to make that happen. Addison's name on the list would have been a distraction, and that's why she'd advised the president not to even meet with her.

"I guess Julia didn't mention I put your name in to replace Weir on the court."

"Matter of fact, she did. Connie. I appreciate you going to bat for me, but you and I both know I'm not Supreme Court material."

"What's that supposed to mean? You're smart enough. You're savvy enough. And hell knows you're so young, you'd outlast all those right-wing assholes who threaten to take away our rights at every turn."

Julia watched their conversation for a minute before jumping in. "You're right, but you don't have the votes to get someone like Addison confirmed."

"Too bad, we'll never even get a chance to test your theory." Armstrong turned to Addison. "Did she tell you that she advised the president not to even bother meeting you? That it would be a waste of time?"

Julia felt each word punch her gut, and it took every ounce of strength she had to face Addison. When she did, she was met with a calm stare that seemed to last forever but was really only a couple of seconds. Then Addison turned to Armstrong.

"Connie, I appreciate your concern, but Julia tells me everything she thinks I need to know. Speaking of which, we were just discussing a private matter and I'd like to get back to it. Can I give you a call next week?"

Julia sighed with relief as she watched Armstrong give Addison a quick hug and make her way out of the restaurant. Addison stared after the senator, and Julia followed her lead by remaining silent. When Armstrong was out of sight, she looked at Addison. "Sorry about that."

"I want to leave."

"What?"

"I want to get the check, pay the bill, and I want you to drive me back to your house so I can get my car and go home."

"You had me at drive you back to my house, but the rest of it? Come on, Addison. Are you really angry at me?"

"Angry? No, that doesn't describe how I feel."

"I told you about the short list."

"What exactly did you tell Garrett about me?"

"The president wants a moderate."

Addison stood. "I'll find the waiter."

Julia grabbed her hand. "Don't. Please sit. Let me explain."

Addison looked around and resumed her seat. Julia cleared her throat. "He wants Landry, and it's my job to make that happen. If he interviewed you, it would distract from the goal. His entire short list needs to be controversy free."

She paused to see if that was enough, but she could tell it wasn't. She didn't know what Addison wanted, but she plunged on, giving every detail, hoping one would satisfy and they could resume their date. "He knows you're qualified. He asked why you weren't on the short list and I told him what I just told you. He asked if he should meet with you and I said no. I may have said it would be a waste of time, but only because he wants to get this wrapped up quickly, before the holidays, so the Senate can vote on it right after the break."

"Okay."

"Okay?"

"Okay. I'm ready to go now."

"But…" Julia didn't know what else to say. She wasn't accustomed to begging, and that's exactly what she felt like she was doing. "I don't know what I did wrong here. Why are you mad at me?"

"I suppose you might have told me the advice you gave the president instead of letting me find out from a friend, but I'm not mad at you."

"You're something."

"You're right. I'm disappointed."

Julia was used to being not available, too busy, even infuriating at times, but disappointing? That's one she tried to avoid at all costs.

❖

The short drive home took forever. When Addison finally reached her building, she sat in the car, not ready to face the loneliness of her apartment.

She didn't have to be lonely. She could call Eva and fall back into their relationship limbo.

No, Eva would just be another reminder of someone who was more concerned about appearances than substance. Eva wanted her, but only if it didn't affect how the world saw her. Julia would always view things in terms of what whoever had hired her wanted. As much as she wanted someone to love and to love her, she cared more about not giving up who she was to be with someone.

She poured a glass of whiskey and curled up on the couch, noticing the difference between her place and Julia's. Instead of expensive artwork, her walls were decorated with family photos.

She'd kicked off her shoes and left them in the foyer and she might not pick them up for a day or two. She thought about Julia, in her perfect home with its fake personal touches. Was she so desperate for affection that she was attracted to the illusion that Julia projected?

Julia. She probably still didn't get why Addison had abandoned their date. If she'd just been honest and told her that she'd advised Garrett not to consider her.

What? Would you have said, "That's cool. I didn't really want it anyway"? Right. So much for being honest.

She had wanted it, and why not? A federal judgeship was the pinnacle of a law career, and a place on the Supreme Court would be the achievement of a lifetime. But even if it wasn't for her, she was mad they weren't even considering someone with any backbone for the job.

She was mad at Julia for that. Julia should push for someone who would retain the integrity of the court, not let it backslide. If she cared...

But that wasn't fair. It wasn't Julia's job to push an agenda. It was the president's. He's the one who didn't have a backbone. At any point, he could've told Julia he would put his force behind a real contender, not a spineless jurist like George Landry. But Landry was his pick, and Julia had been hired to make it so. Addison knew it was irrational for her to be angry with Julia for doing her job, but the disappointment lingered.

They were both better off. She'd probably just been a fling to Julia until the next project came around. A substitute for the beaches of Tahiti while she was stuck doing winter in the capital.

Addison reached for her phone, carefully considering the call she was about to make. Finally deciding what she needed, she pulled up a number and hit dial, hoping it wasn't too late to call.

"Addison?"

"It's me, Dad. Set an extra plate, I'm coming home for Thanksgiving."

CHAPTER FOURTEEN

A re we going to be here much longer?"
Julia looked up from the stack of papers in front of her.
The members of her committee were gathered around the conference
table, and they all looked like they had one leg out the door.

"What's the problem?" The edge in her tone was designed to
dare them to respond.

"Nothing."

"They have plans for Thanksgiving," Gordon said.

"Thanksgiving?"

"It's tomorrow. You know, turkey, dressing, family?"

"I know what Thanksgiving is." She contemplated what to do.
They'd worked hard over the past two weeks, but the Senate would
start informal interviews with the potential nominees next week, and
they still had a lot to do to get them prepared. Of course, the nominees
would probably want to enjoy the holiday too, so they could probably
knock off for a day without sending the entire schedule onto the skids.

She glanced at the clock on the wall. It was after five. She'd keep
working, but they could go. She told them as much and then gathered
up her work. She may as well work in her office if she was going to
be by herself.

She stood and found Gordon and Cindy still standing in the
room. "What's up? Don't you both have somewhere to rush off to?"

Gordon spoke first. "I do, and you should too. You could take a
day off every now and then."

"Would you believe me if I told you I had nothing better to do?"

"Yes." He gave her a hug. "Have a nice day working your brains out. See you Friday."

Julia turned to Cindy. "And you, don't you have somewhere else to be?"

"I don't go home until you do."

"Well, that's probably a bad rule since I'm not going anywhere for a while."

"Don't you have plans?"

"Plans? Oh, you mean for tomorrow? No."

"There are a few of us who get together. Holiday orphans. Nothing fancy, but it's fun. You're welcome to join us if you want."

Julia was taken off guard. "Uh, thanks, I appreciate the offer, but…"

Cindy pressed a piece of paper into her hand. "No pressure. Here's the address. It's fun. You could use some fun. And it's only for a day. Think about it. Now, let's get these files back to your office. I assume that's where you're headed."

Julia stood still for a moment, watching as Cindy gathered the files and led the way. She appreciated the kindness and was sorry she'd fumbled at the offering, but she wasn't going to change her ways. Tomorrow would be a day just like any other. At most, she'd have a turkey sandwich. When they reached her office, she sent Cindy home.

Contemplating the files on her desk, she wondered what Addison was doing for the holiday. She'd mentioned her family, that her brother might be on leave. She searched her mind to remember everything she'd learned about Addison's personal life. Addison's mother was dead. Her father lived in Dallas. One phone call to the DOD and she could find out if Jack had returned home. She had that kind of access, but why should she be concerned about a woman who wasn't concerned about her?

Because Addison's assessment of her had stung. Disappointing. She could deal with anger, frustration, just about anything other than disappointment. Especially since Addison's disappointment meant they were done. They'd parted after Julia drove her back to her house with barely any good-bye, definitely not a see you later.

"Are you trying to show everyone up by working through the holiday?"

Julia looked up at Noah who was standing in her doorway, his broad frame filling the space. The bonus of working here on the second floor was not having to deal with him very often. She'd never get what Garrett saw in the guy, but they'd been friends since childhood and in the eyes of many, Noah had earned the coveted spot at the right hand of the most powerful man in the world.

"I could say the same to you. Don't you have a family?"

"Mona took the kids to her parents in the country. I may fly out for the day tomorrow. Haven't decided yet. I'm sure I can find something to do here in the city." He winked as he delivered the words, and she was reminded of the rumors she'd heard about his penchant for getting some on the side. Of course, in D.C. a philandering nature wasn't a bar to power, and as chief of staff, Noah was practically guaranteed the second most powerful spot for the next four years.

All she had was the project on her desk. When that was done, she was technically unemployed. Sure, she'd had dozens of inquiries after the election. Everyone with a seat up for election in the midterms was already vying for her services, and they'd all be willing to pay top dollar.

She didn't need the money, and after successfully helping Garrett get elected, she wasn't in the mood to take on a House or Senate race despite the fact that picking the right candidate might put her in line to run another presidential campaign four years from now. Two years, four years, six. She'd spent her entire adult life measured in these increments, the project in front of her the only deviation. For the first time, she realized she was tired.

"I heard you royally pissed off Connie Armstrong."

She looked at Noah, having completely forgotten he was still there. "I suppose I did. Nothing personal."

"Everything's personal. She's always had a rocky relationship with Wes. You should check with me for pointers next time you have to deal with her."

Never going to happen. But Julia wasn't in the mood for a fight. She only wanted to finish her work, go home, and be alone with a glass of whiskey. She smiled sweetly and lied. "I'll do that. Thanks. I thought the president went to Camp David. Why are you still roaming the building?"

"I have a few meetings set up for this evening."

"About the nomination?"

He shifted. "Uh, no. No. Just some housekeeping details about the inauguration."

He was lying and Julia wondered why. The inauguration committee wouldn't be working late on the night before Thanksgiving. She was curious, but not enough to keep him here any longer. The sooner he left, the sooner she could finish and leave too. "Well, don't let me keep you. Have a good Thanksgiving."

When he was finally gone, she tried to focus on the files in front of her, but the words swam on the page. She was tired and frustrated and she didn't need to be here to feel this way. She packed her briefcase and called for a car. She could be tired and frustrated at home.

Addison was already reaching for her phone when the plane screamed to a stop on the runway. She sent a quick text to her father to let him know she was on the ground and she'd be at the house soon. He'd wanted to pick her up, but since the only flight she could get was on Thursday morning, she'd insisted on using a car service. He was likely in the middle of trying to prepare all their holiday favorites, insisting that just because their mother was gone, they didn't need to change the way they celebrated the holidays.

Truth was she hadn't been home since the year after her mother died, three years ago. Offering excuses about work, she'd managed to avoid the emptiness that no amount of turkey and dressing could fill. She and her father had never been particularly close. An ambitious man, he expected the same of his children. Jack's career as a Delta Force officer, now commander, had him bursting with pride, but she could never quite get it right. When she'd left her partnership at a prominent law firm to teach, he'd been astounded.

"You've got to be kidding me. With your experience, you could be anything, but you're going to throw it all away on a gig at a liberal law school? Your mother and I had higher hopes."

Her mother was alive when he'd made the pronouncement, but only barely. Addison wasn't sure what infuriated her more, the fact that he'd written her off or that he presumed to speak for her mother. Mom would have been proud of her if she'd been a ditch digger, as long as she was happy. She knew her mother had loved her father very much, but she'd never understand how she'd been able to see past his conservative view of the world. Making money is good. Making a difference is okay as long as you're making money doing it. Money equals success.

She loved him because he was her father, but she'd never understand him, and she wasn't coming home for him. She was coming home because for the first time since her mother died, Jack would be there, and even though she barely saw her brother anymore, his company was the closest thing to home she had anymore. And right now she needed to be grounded.

Addison walked off the plane and headed to the ground transportation area, bypassing baggage claim. She was only here for two days and had packed lightly. Once at the doors, she looked around for the various drivers gathered there, holding signs with the names of their fares. A tap on her shoulder surprised her, and she whirled around to face an even bigger surprise.

"Jack!"

"Addy!"

Before she could remind him no one called her that anymore, he had her in his arms, swinging her through the air.

"Put me down." She whispered the words into his ear in a fierce, but loving tone.

He shook her in the air one last time and then set her down gently. "It's great to see you."

She hugged him hard. "It's great to see you too." She leaned back to give him the once-over. He was slimmer than she remembered, but still ruggedly handsome. "You're thin. They feeding you over there?"

"They feed us plenty, but heat and hard work make it go fast. Quit worrying."

"Somebody has to now that—" She stopped, letting the word drop. Jack squeezed her arm.

"I know. I miss her too."

They both stood silent for a moment before Jack said, "Speaking of parents, Dad's going to be so happy you made it."

"Uh-huh." Addison wasn't at all sure how she and her father would get along now that her mother wasn't there to referee, but she opted not to push the point.

"Did you check a bag?"

"No." She glanced around. "I ordered a car, but it doesn't appear to be here yet."

He reached down to his bag and picked up a small white board with her name on it that was resting on top. "I high-jacked him. He's over there." He pointed to a suited driver with a cap. Mind if I tag along?"

"Pretty sure you planned it that way."

Once they were seated in the car and headed to Southlake, the suburb where she'd grown up, she reconsidered her remark. "I thought you were getting in yesterday."

"Me too, but you know how it is."

"Right. You could tell me, but then you'd have to kill me?"

"Exactly."

Seriously, is everything okay?"

"It's as okay as it can be."

Addison heard the words for what they were. Jack took his career seriously, and he would never divulge information about the dangerous missions he and his team faced in the ongoing war, but she could tell something was up. She wouldn't pry. "I think about you all the time. I can't wait until you can come home."

"Me too."

The admission was huge, but Addison didn't make a big deal about it to keep him from clamming up. "How's Dad?"

"Do you think it's strange that I know more about how he's doing than you do and I'm seven thousand miles away?"

"Not in the least."

He gave her a knowing look. "He's good. He's functioning really well, but holidays are hardest. It means a lot to him that you're here."

"I'm sorry I'm not more available. I know my job doesn't seem like a big deal to him, but it's more challenging than working at the firm ever was. More challenging than even the solicitor general's office."

"You still love it?"

She hesitated. She did love it, or at least the thought of it, but she'd had more fun when she was teaching than she did now pushing paper, crunching numbers, and resolving disputes. "I wish I had more time to teach, but yes, I still love it."

"That's all that really matters. Anyone special in your life?"

Same question Jeff had asked when she'd seen him at the funeral. She cringed for the second time. "How about you?"

"Nice dodge. No, it's hard to find that special someone when you spend all your time surrounded by a bunch of burly guys who don't bother shaving most of the time."

"No G.I. Janes yet?"

"Not yet. Someday though. Things are changing."

"No more don't ask, don't tell."

"I'm glad folks can start living their lives out in the open, but the guys in our unit are still pretty uptight about it. I'm not sure anyone could take the hazing that would come with an outing."

Addison nodded, sure that was true. All the more reason civil rights were important. Judges like Landry would let the court backslide, she was sure of it.

"I was sorry to hear about Justice Weir. I know you were close."

"Thanks. He was a giant and he'll be missed." She started to tell him about Julia, but what was the point? She wasn't going to see Julia again, and she definitely would have no part in the appointment process. Garrett would appoint Landry, the nomination would sail through, and life would go on. What was important to her and the lessons she taught generally escaped the notice of the everyday person. People didn't usually care about rights changing until it affected them personally, and by then it was too late. Connie had called her before she left for Dallas, but she hadn't returned the call.

She decided to focus on the issues in front of her. "So, Dad's really cooking dinner? Should I have eaten something on the plane?"

"Oh, like you're one to talk."

True. Her mother had been amazing in the kitchen, but she'd never been interested in anything even slightly domestic, preferring instead to keep her head buried in history books. Her father had been her biggest champion, saying she didn't need to learn those things—when she was president, she could get someone to do them for her.

What neither one of them counted on was Addison having no desire to run for political office, and even if she did, it wouldn't have been for the party her father preferred.

In her teen years, she'd become increasingly liberal, which put her at odds with her father on just about every issue discussed at the dinner table. Her mother had served as de facto referee until Addison left for college at sixteen. Future discussions of ambition were confined to Jack's career, and Addison was content to let him have the spotlight since it relieved her of the pressure to live up to her father's standards.

As they pulled up to the house, she said a little prayer for peace. After the tumult of the last week, she just wanted to relax, enjoy time with her brother, and avoid conflict.

John Riley stood in the doorway with a spatula in one hand and flour in his hair. "Boy, am I glad to see you two. I'll get your luggage. Please just go in the kitchen and see what can be salvaged."

Addison looked at Jack. "This seems like a job for Special Forces. Don't you people make whole meals out of things you find in the forest?"

"Very funny, sis. I'm happy to let you help Dad do the heavy lifting while I check the oven." He shot her a grin as he headed off to the kitchen, and she quickly realized she'd just lost her buffer.

Her dad had one bag and she grabbed the other. "Where do you want us?"

"Any reason your old rooms won't do?"

"Not a one."

She followed him up the stairs to the second story. The wall along the stairway was lined with a lifetime of memories. Birthday parties, graduations, Jack in dress uniform. And her mother, present for every celebration, the backbone of the family. Gone forever, gone too soon.

"I miss her every day."

Addison looked up and met her father's eyes. As much as she missed her mother, he'd had the greater loss. She'd never understood how they'd come together, but their relationship had worked. With Mom gone, he'd lost not only his soul mate, but the glue that held them all together. He'd spent the morning trying to take her place, and it made her sad. "I miss her too."

"I know. I'm trying."

She sniffed the air and smiled. "You might be trying a little too hard. I'm not sure even Emeril could salvage what you've got roasting downstairs." She hefted the bag in her hand. "Why don't we get these put away and go out to eat. My treat?"

"I really wanted to make today like every other Thanksgiving."

"Things have changed. We'll change with them. Besides, this way we don't have to fight about who's going to do the dishes. Deal?"

"Deal." He took the suitcase from her hand and jogged up the last few stairs.

Two hours later, they were seated at Copeland's, tearing into Cajun-fried turkey and a half dozen side dishes.

"Dad," Jack said between bites, "I have no idea what you were trying to cook, but this is the best meal I've had in a very long time."

"Thank Addison. She's paying."

"Someone had to save you two from food poisoning, and I didn't make a quick trip just to spend it all in the kitchen."

"How long can you stay?"

"I need to get back on Saturday. Lots of work to do before the end of the semester." She considered telling them about all the things that had distracted her from her work over the past two weeks. Meeting Julia Scott, the visit from Connie Armstrong, the narrow shot at a Supreme Court nomination. Great stories, but telling them would come at her expense since she didn't have anything to show for her recent experiences. No relationship, no judgeship. Military types like Jack and her dad measured life in terms of success—mission accomplished. The only thing she'd accomplished in the past two weeks was to be distracted. And she was distracted now.

While she ate turkey and sweet potatoes and way too much pecan pie, was Julia sitting in her immaculate townhouse eating Chinese takeout? While she listened to Jack and her father debate the strategies of war, was Julia sitting at the desk in her museum-like study, making notes for the Senate confirmation hearings? While she wondered what Julia was doing, was her own life passing her by?

CHAPTER FIFTEEN

Julia sighed. It had been a week since Thanksgiving, and this was the fifth meeting with Judge George Landry. Multiple meetings were to be expected, but they were nowhere near where they needed to be to get him through the process. Garrett might think Landry was a perfect candidate not to ruffle any feathers, but he sure got under her skin.

She turned to Tommy, who, after a couple of lessons from Gordon, had proved very effective at role-play. "Okay, this time you be Senator Burrows and I'll be Armstrong. I'm telling you, he's going to get hit from both sides and you can't be this easy on him."

"Excuse me, but I'm sitting right here."

Julia glanced at the tall, imposing man seated to her right. What Landry didn't have in intelligence, he made up in size. "Pardon me, Judge. I'd like to run through this one more time before we head out to our meetings. We'd just like you to be prepared for each of the different methods of questioning you're likely to face." It took every ounce of resistance she had to keep her tone even and respectful. If he'd been a candidate for political office, she'd have been much rougher, and they probably would've made more progress by now. At this rate, they'd be lucky to have him ready for confirmation when the term opened after the New Year. Whether he would be prepared for the first round of interviews with several key senators this afternoon was in major doubt. "Tommy, I mean, Senator Burrows, you have the floor."

Tommy puffed out his chest and did an uncanny imitation of Jeff Burrows's brusque style. "The Supreme Court has made it clear that corporations are people with First Amendment protections when it comes to political campaigns. Do you accept this precedent even though it's only a few years old, or do you have some baseline you would apply when the court's decisions are firmly rooted?"

Julia nodded at Tommy, and then waited for Landry to answer. He twisted in his seat, silent.

"Your Honor?" Tommy prodded him.

Landry broke role and turned to Julia. "Surely you know that several cases are winding their way up from the circuits to challenge the decision in *Citizens United*. I can't be expected to comment on the issue since it's very likely to come up when I'm on the court."

Julia gritted her teeth. She wanted to tell him his likelihood of joining the Supreme Court was waning by the second. Instead, she said, "This prep will only work if you stay in character." She pointed at Tommy. "He's Senator Burrows. Tell him what you just told me. With conviction." *Not like the whiny ass you've been all morning.*

An hour later, he finally got the hang of answering without actually providing any insight. It wasn't smooth, but it would have to do for now. Julia stopped the role-play. "Thank you, Your Honor. Let's take a lunch break. We're due in the lobby of the Hart Building at two." She stood and walked him to the door. When he was out of earshot, she turned back to Tommy and Gordon. "I want you both to go with us this afternoon. In fact, I want you to meet him at his hotel and bring him directly to Armstrong's office. I don't want him left alone for a minute in that den of vipers."

"I wouldn't worry so much," Tommy replied. "He might not be the brightest bulb, but that probably means he's not going to piss anyone off."

Gordon snorted. "Really? You think being part stupid and part pompous isn't irritating? He may not rub the leadership the wrong way on the issues, but it's important that he not make them think Garrett is filling Weir's seat with a dolt. Trust me. I know Armstrong and Burrows. Either one of them senses any attitude, and they're going to jump all over him."

Tommy shrugged like it was out of his hands, but promised to do his best.

Julia walked back to her office, stopping at Cindy's desk on the way. "Have you finalized the afternoon schedule? Can we fit everything in this afternoon, or are we going to have to block out the morning as well? I'm not sure I can take another day with Landry, and I'd love to put him on a plane home. Tonight, if possible."

"Don't worry. I spoke with Senator Armstrong's aide. No votes scheduled today, so there's no reason you can't fit the major players in this afternoon."

"Great. Will you—"

"Send the schedule to Judge Landry? Already done."

"Thanks. I'm going to find some lunch."

"There's a pastrami sandwich on your desk and coffee. Don't thank me again. You don't have time. Go get ready for your afternoon. It's going to be insane."

Julia dutifully complied. Cindy was right. She had a whirlwind schedule of interviews set up with all the key members of the Judiciary Committee and only a couple of hours to finish organizing her files before she escorted Landry through the gauntlet.

The pastrami sandwich was heaven. The layers were paper thin, just the way she liked. The coffee was in a French press. She didn't know if Cindy had any leads on a more permanent position, but as she savored her lunch, she vowed to try to steal her away at the first opportunity. She'd lost her last assistant a month before the election. Not unusual, she went through them like pages in a trashy novel. She could do without the extra help, but Cindy was spoiling her from trying.

As she ate, she glanced through her files, matching notes for specific interviews with the time slots each senator had been assigned. She thumbed through the pages, but couldn't find her copy of the questionnaire Landry had completed. The document was thick and should be easy to locate. After combing through every file on her desk, she buzzed Cindy on the intercom.

"I can't find the questionnaire."

"Bottom right drawer. Second hanging file folder from the left."

Julia found the file exactly where Cindy had described, further solidifying her resolve to poach her from this office. She pulled out the entire hanging folder and thumbed through it until she found the questionnaire. Once she had it, she started to replace the hanging folder, but a document near the front stopped her. The lists Armstrong and Burrows had given her. She traced the names with her finger, practicing responses to refute them all in favor of Garrett' choice. The process was easy until she remembered one name that wasn't on this list.

Had Addison gone home for the holiday? Had she sat around a table with family and friends, telling stories about D.C., eating home-cooked food? Had they decorated the house for Christmas? Gone shopping? Had Addison talked about her or even thought about her?

Of course she hadn't. And whatever else she'd chosen to do on her own time, in a world far removed from the brief time they'd shared, was none of her business. She placed the list back in her drawer, but she couldn't help but wish she was taking Addison instead of Landry for the round of meetings this afternoon.

"Did you have a good trip?"

Addison looked up at Eva who was standing in her doorway, looking sexy as always.

"Matter of fact, I did. You?"

Eva strode across the room and took a seat. In a fitted sweater and wool skirt that barely skimmed the top of her tall leather boots, she looked more like a fashion model than a law school professor. Seated, she crossed her legs, and Addison couldn't help but be a bit distracted at the hint of skin the subtle action revealed.

"I stayed in town. Had dinner with friends. We're all orphans—family too far away or not interested in spending time with us. Lots of wine and too much food." She smiled her dazzling smile. "I had a great time."

"Good." Addison considered expanding her story. Telling Eva she'd always felt like a bit of an orphan herself, having left for college at sixteen and never able to please her demanding father, but that wouldn't be fair to the memory of her mother or the very real presence of her brother even though she didn't see him nearly enough. Besides, she wasn't in the habit of sharing such personal details. She settled instead on a few small facts. "My brother was home from Afghanistan and, since it was just the three of us, we went out to eat. Turkey, but no dishes. It was a quick trip."

"Are you like me and ready for something other than turkey?"

"Absolutely." The minute she said the one word, Addison saw the sure expression on Eva's face and saw that her question hadn't been a casual one.

"Great. I'll pick you up after work. Sushi?"

This was the second time Eva had asked her out since they'd broken up. Time to nip this in the bud. "I meant what I said before."

"It's dinner, not a lifetime commitment. I'm trying here."

Suddenly, it struck Addison that if she went out with Eva tonight, this would be the first time they'd gone on an actual date, in public, in the evening. And it was the second time Eva had asked. Maybe these invitations were Eva's way of telling her she was ready to try for something more.

Addison's thoughts turned to Julia, and she felt a rush of guilt as if by dating Eva she was betraying her true feelings.

Nonsense. Julia had been a passing fancy. Julia wasn't interested in anything more than a fling. If she had been, she wouldn't have manipulated her. The last thing she should do was let lingering desires obstruct the road to something real. Eva, beautiful and accomplished, was standing in front of her right now. Offering something more. She'd be crazy to turn her down for a pipe dream that had already proven it wasn't and wouldn't ever be real.

"Sushi sounds great. I'll be ready at seven."

CHAPTER SIXTEEN

So far, the interview with Burrows was going well, and Julia took a moment to check the news sites on her iPad. With Gordon in the wings to orchestrate, the president had made his announcement about his nomination the afternoon before in a press briefing in the East Room. He used well-planted buzzwords like "respected jurist" and "constitutional scholar" and spoke about how Landry's addition would lend dignity to the court. Blah, blah, blah. Buzz in the press room was that Landry wasn't a very daring choice, but he was qualified and would likely be confirmed quickly. Garrett was generally lauded for his wisdom in avoiding a confirmation battle after such a contentious election.

All good, and based on Burrows's reaction to Landry, the news accounts were spot-on. So far, they'd covered everything from gay marriage to whether corporations should be treated like people for purposes of political campaigns. Landry had deferred to precedent, dodging direct answers to the senator's probing inquiries. Finally, Burrows asked his final question.

"What about the right to life? Can you commit to enforcing laws that protect the life of an unborn child?"

Burrows had saved this one, letting Landry get comfortable before delivering the big punch worded in the most incendiary way possible. Julia silently answered the question the way they'd practiced, willing Landry not to buy into the premise.

"The court's precedent is clear, and many decisions have already been written which address the balance of rights and protection of life. I cannot comment on how I would rule on a particular case, but I can promise that I have always been guided by well-established precedents and principles in my decisions on the bench."

Burrows stared a hole in Landry, but the judge didn't balk. Finally, Burrows stood and shook the judge's hand. "That's all I've got. Thank you, Your Honor, for your time and your thoughtful consideration of the issues."

Julia breathed a sigh of relief as she ushered Landry out of the room. She wasn't completely at ease. They still had the interview with Connie Armstrong, but she'd purposely saved it for last to give Landry time to warm up to the questioning. This whole process would be very different from what he'd encounter at the actual confirmation hearings, but it was a testing ground nevertheless. Once the camera crews were in evidence, all the senators would begin posturing for a place in history with questions masked as slick speeches intended for their constituents.

"I think that went rather well."

She glanced at the judge as they walked through the hallway. "It went okay. He doesn't like you, but you're better than some of the other names the Dems floated around. This next interview is crucial, and I hope you've got a tough skin. Connie Armstrong wanted the president to pick someone else, and she's going to be gunning for you. If she's nice, it only means she's saving it for the cameras. If she's mean, she's trying to get in your head. It's up to you to keep things on an even keel. I'll do my best to redirect if things get out of hand, but this interview will be the true test of your mettle." She stopped in front of the massive oak doors. "You ready?"

He nodded and pushed through the doors with Julia and Tommy close on his heels. Julia took charge and spoke to the interns at the front desk. "Please tell Senator Armstrong that Judge Landry is here to see her."

The oldest looking one rose and wandered back into the suite of offices while the one who looked all of twelve asked if they wanted something to drink. Julia and Tommy declined, but Landry said he'd love a cup of coffee.

The youngster returned with a mug of steaming coffee and Senator Armstrong in her wake. Julia made the introductions and waited for

Armstrong to escort them back into her office, but Armstrong seemed content to carry on inane conversation in the reception area. Julia glanced at her watch, thankful she'd scheduled this meeting last.

Finally, Armstrong looked Landry square in the eye. "Well, Your Honor, shall we get started?"

Landry offered the ingratiating smile Julia had seen way too much of that day and raised his mug as if in a toast. Maybe they shouldn't have told him to be extra nice to Armstrong. Anyone would be able to see through his act, especially the astute senator. Oh well, nothing to be done about it now. Julia signaled to Tommy, and they started to follow Landry and Armstrong back toward her office. They'd only taken a couple of steps before Armstrong turned, stopping them in their tracks.

"Excuse me?" Armstrong raised her eyebrows. She was an iron wall.

"Your office?" Julia responded.

"I think that Judge Landry can handle a little discussion on our own." Armstrong touched the judge on the arm and stared up into his eyes. "Right, Your Honor?"

Landry looked around like a scared rabbit, but he really had no choice. Be eaten alive with or without an audience. If he chose the former, he was done for, but if he survived the ordeal on his own, he might just win Armstrong and all the votes that came with her for a smooth confirmation. He cleared his throat. "Certainly, Senator. It would be my pleasure to visit in private."

Julia stood, frozen in place, and watched as the cunning Connie Armstrong escorted the unwitting judge into her office. She'd done all she could do, but she feared it wouldn't be enough.

A vivid image burst into her mind as she imagined Addison Riley in the same situation. Would she want Julia's help? No, she'd likely resist being managed, but then again, she would bet money that Addison could handle the likes of Connie Armstrong or anyone else who challenged her knowledge or ability. Not for the first time today, Julia regretted how things had turned out between them.

❖

"How is it I haven't been here before?" Addison took another bite of the Fire Dragon roll and enjoyed the slow burn of the spicy food. "Amazing."

"It's a hidden gem. I found it when a friend stayed here over Thanksgiving," Eva said, referring to the hotel. "I don't usually think about eating at hotel restaurants, but this one's sublime."

Addison considered asking about the "friend," but decided she didn't really want to know. She did have another question itching to be asked. She set down her chopsticks. "I don't mean to start an argument when we're having such a good time, but you do realize this is our first meal in public. What gives?"

Eva met her eyes, her gaze sultry. "I've been listening to you. I asked you out before Thanksgiving, but you had plans with Larry Weir. How is he, by the way?"

Addison considered whether she should let Eva change the subject or whether she should press for more information about her change in attitude about public dating. A tiny voice inside told her to let it go, enjoy the night. She followed the advice and reminded herself she needed to follow-up with Larry to tell him she'd read through the journal. She'd left a message for him on Monday, but then missed his return call. "Larry's okay, but he's still grieving for his father. It's hard to let go."

"I imagine. I know Justice Weir was old, but I don't think anyone ever dreamed there'd be a time without him. The Weir court made such huge advances in our generation, but there was still so much to be done."

Addison took a drink of sake and murmured her agreement. As with her father, she was sorely tempted to mention her near miss at the nomination, but what was the point? It was a nonissue, and because she hadn't made the short list, she wouldn't even be a footnote in history. She decided to steer the subject in an entirely different direction.

"I'm thinking about taking a step back from administration. Focus more on teaching. Maybe even take over as clinic director next year."

Eva's eyes widened. "Really?"

"Really. Is that such a crazy idea?"

"It's a little crazy. Do you think the board will go for it?"

"I don't know, but if they don't, I have lots of options. I know it's been a while since I've had a full load, but my skills are still in demand."

"I didn't mean to imply anything about your skills." Eva placed extra emphasis on the word. "I guess I've always known you as the dean and you're quite good at it. I've taught at several schools, and I've never seen one run as smoothly as this one. Jefferson would suffer a great loss if you were to step down."

"That's sweet of you to say. I'm not sure how much of it is true. We have a good faculty, and I couldn't get the job done without them, but what I do, it isn't fulfilling anymore. Budgets, paperwork, logistics. Do you know what I mean?"

"When did this all come about?"

Addison dodged the truth. "I guess it's been brewing for a while. But end of the semester is when it hits the hardest. I decided it was time to make it official. I'll finish out the year, but then I'm not sure what the future holds."

Eva raised her glass. "A toast to uncertain futures and the excitement of the unknown."

Addison met her smile and raised her own glass. She felt more agitated than excited, but she hoped the anxiety would pass. From the moment her last date with Julia ended badly, she'd been on edge, like she was looking for something she'd lost. She didn't know what it was, but she did know she wasn't going to find it looking in the same old places.

Eva's hand on her arm tugged her out of her thoughts.

"Isn't that Judge Landry?"

Addison sucked in a breath and slowly turned in the direction Eva had motioned. George Landry sat in a booth, chopsticks in one hand and a glass of wine in the other. He laughed a big round laugh that carried across the room, and then he plucked a piece of a roll and shoved it in his mouth. The woman seated across from him made a face, and Addison recognized the expression. Julia had made the same face when Addison had talked about marriage.

She put down her glass of sake, suddenly no longer hungry, no longer interested in enjoying this new place with an old flame who only served to remind her that her mantra about not looking in the same old places should apply to both her personal life and her professional one. "Figures."

"What?"

Addison looked up and saw that Eva was staring at her with a puzzled expression on her face. "Nothing. I'm sorry."

"So, that's our next chief justice. Hard to believe."

"Indeed."

"Isn't that Julia Scott with him?"

"Yes, it is. Pretty sure it's her job to ram Landry down the throats of the Senate."

Eva laughed. "Tell me how you really feel. So, you know her? She seems quite captivating."

"We've met." Addison decided a tiny lie of omission was in order. "She does have a certain charm."

Eva cocked her head. "Sounds like there might be a story there."

"Not an interesting one. Would you like another glass of sake?"

Eva was not going to be deterred. "She's on her way over here."

Addison cursed her bad luck. She should've excused herself from the table the minute she spotted Julia. Feigned illness, a fire at her apartment, anything to avoid this meeting. Bad enough to run into Julia, but with Landry at her side, it was salt in the wound.

Well, there was no escaping it now. She'd face Julia, share a few meaningless niceties, and resume her date with Eva. Tomorrow, she'd continue to work on her plan, and soon she'd find the peace she sought in a career change that was long overdue. All she had to do was get through the next five minutes and she'd be fine.

"Addison?"

That voice. Husky, but soft. Sweet, but spicy. She looked up to meet Julia's eyes, and her resolve crumbled.

Julia had suggested the restaurant in the hotel for her debrief with the judge. She'd instructed Cindy to put Landry up in a nice place, but not one of the D.C. mainstays like Hay Adams or Watergate. The Donovan House near Thomas Circle was close to the White House, but far enough away to make it unlikely they would run into anyone they might be trying to avoid.

She would've preferred a nice steak rather than the sushi this restaurant was famous for, but maybe because they didn't have to cook the food, she could get out of here faster. Gordon had bailed, citing his kid's school play and she'd had enough of Tommy's incessant law talk for the day, so it was just her and Landry. As they followed the waiter to the booth, she ticked off a list of questions she had about the afternoon, but once they were seated, it was clear she wasn't going to get quick answers. Landry made quite a fuss over the menu as he dallied over which delicacies to order. Julia wondered if he put as much thought into his rulings and decided probably not. When he finally finished ordering for both of them, she started her interrogation.

"Tell me everything she said and don't hold back."

"She was very charming, in an Annie Oakley sort of way. I suspect her constituents love her and feel like she represents them well."

Julia gritted her teeth and resisted pointing out that she hadn't asked for a personality profile of Connie Armstrong. She could write the book on that. Instead, she tried to ease into the subject. "What topics did she cover with you?"

"Oh, we discussed a lot of interesting subjects. Did you know she's very interested in several charitable causes in Somalia?"

Enough. "No, I didn't. I also don't know what I need to know to get you confirmed. And what I need to know is this: what did you and Senator Armstrong spend the better part of two hours discussing?"

"She certainly didn't grill me like you are now."

"Respectfully, Your Honor, the grilling I'm giving is nothing compared to the showboating you're going to experience when the cameras are on. Connie Armstrong may have had on her kid gloves today, but she won't when the world is watching. I can't prepare you for what's to come unless I know more about what's happened before."

"I understand, but I'm telling you, we didn't really discuss any major issues. She did ask me a few questions about specific issues, but she seemed to accept my standard answer—that I couldn't, wouldn't comment on issues that are or could be pending in front of the court. The whole conversation was really quite polite."

Julia shook her head. Polite, meaning exactly the opposite of the way she'd been acting toward him. She knew most federal judges expected a certain amount of deference, but it wasn't her job to sugarcoat this process. If he wanted to be the next Chief Justice, he had a lot to learn, and he could either learn it from her the easy way or take a licking on nationally televised hearings. If it didn't mean potential embarrassment for Garrett, she'd be tempted to let him take a beating.

But it was her job to grease the wheels, and she would do just that. She made a mental note to have Gordon contact some of his friends in the Senate to see what he could find out about Armstrong's meeting with Landry. Armstrong may have held the meeting behind closed doors, but nothing stayed locked up tight on the hill. Information was currency.

"So, what's the next step?" Landry asked the question between big bites of raw tuna.

"The Senate will adjourn for the holidays soon, so not much between now and the end of the year. The FBI will continue to vet you and will provide a report to us and the Judiciary Committee by the first of the year. When the Senate reconvenes, they'll begin formal committee hearings. If all goes well, the hearings will last a few days and then your nomination will go to the floor for a full vote. The president would like you sworn in within days of his inauguration."

"Very prudent not to let the seat remain vacant. There are some big issues pending before the court."

Julia looked at him, trying to read his tone. This was the first time he'd referred to matters pending at the court, although the reference was vague. She'd spent quite a bit of time with the solicitor general's office, learning enough to ask probing questions about important court cases. Several controversial cases were working their way quickly through the system. Attempts to expand gay marriage and the first real shot at repealing the decision in *Citizens United*. Neither one of these petitioners had a shot once Landry was on the court, and she knew that reality factored large in Connie Armstrong's strategy. Armstrong hadn't grilled Landry on those subjects, and that probably meant she was planning to roast him in public. That, or else she had resigned herself to the fact she couldn't put her side through a nasty battle so soon after a bloody election.

"Do you think those ladies are with the press?" Landry interrupted her thoughts and pointed a chopstick at a table across the room. Julia followed his gaze. She didn't recognize the woman facing her, but she noted she was gorgeous and staring intently at them. She was with another woman, and although Julia couldn't see her face, she felt a chill of recognition as she stared at her back. Before she could tear her gaze away, the woman turned and the chills intensified. Addison Riley.

Julia jerked her eyes away and focused on Landry who'd apparently forgotten the women he'd pointed out and had moved on to some other topic that Julia couldn't possibly focus on. He droned on and on, but all Julia could think about was Addison, seated mere feet away.

On a date. With a beautiful woman. It should be her seated at the table with Addison. She'd gladly eat raw fish for the chance. She lost the ability to focus on anything Landry was saying, and she no longer cared. She stood and placed her napkin on the table. "Excuse me for just a moment."

The hundred feet between her table and Addison's weren't enough time to prepare, but her feet propelled her forward even though her mind was screaming for her to run in the opposite direction. When she finally reached their booth, she planted her feet and stared down the other woman's curious gaze.

"Addison?"

She looked up, and Julia caught her breath. She looked incredible, at ease, beautiful, carefree. The table was free of books, papers, any other work paraphernalia, and Julia had no doubt Addison was here on a date. Damn.

"Julia. Good to see you."

Didn't sound like it, but Julia ignored the tone. "Good to see you too. Although I wouldn't have figured you for a sushi fan."

"Really? I guess your research didn't turn up everything after all."

Dark and mysterious cleared her throat, and both Julia and Addison turned toward her as if surprised to find her seated at the table.

"I'm sorry," Addison said. "Julia Scott, meet Eva Monroe, she's—"

"I'm a professor at Jefferson law school. Is that Judge Landry at your table?"

Julia smothered a grin at the fangirl expression on Eva's face. So, she and Addison had already noticed them. Probably even discussed them. But the most interesting piece of information Eva had revealed was that they weren't here on a date. At least not as far as Eva was concerned. She'd wouldn't have abruptly interrupted Addison's introduction otherwise.

"Yes, that's Judge Landry. Would you like to meet him?" She waved to the judge and pointed at Eva with a questioning look. He waved back and signaled for her to come on over. She warned Eva as she slid out of the booth. "He's a talker. We'll see you again someday."

When Eva was settled at the judge's table, Julia slid into the booth across from Addison.

"Stealing my date?"

"She didn't seem to think she was your date."

Addison crossed her fingers. "That's been a bit of a problem. I thought we were past it."

"She's pretty, but you shouldn't settle."

"She's gorgeous, but I'm not about to take advice from the biggest settler I know."

Julia looked across the room at the judge, actively engaged in conversation with Eva. He was probably telling her the same story she'd just heard. No point denying Addison's observation. The judge was boring, a follower, and most likely to never upset precedent. He was the perfect candidate for a confirmation battle and precisely the wrong nominee to affect social change.

"Touché."

"Wow, no argument? That's a change."

"After a day with posturing senators, I'm all out of argument. Your date does seem to like him though."

"Stop calling her that."

"Sorry."

"No, I'm sorry. I know you're just doing your job."

"Sometimes, my job sucks."

"Why do it?"

"Do you enjoy everything about your job?"

"Yes." Addison shook her head. "I mean no. How did you get so good about turning everything around?"

"Seeing all sides of an issue is my specialty. You're a lawyer. Don't you view the world the same way?"

"Just because I can see all sides, doesn't mean I think they're all right or even worthy of consideration."

"I guess that's what makes us different. I'm not much into absolutes. I get paid to seize opportunities."

"Hmmm."

Julia was out of things to say. The big thing that stood between them seemed destined to block any intimacy they might have shared. She glanced at Eva and the judge. "I suppose I should get back over there."

"I suppose you should."

"It was good to see you."

"It was good to see you too."

There didn't seem to be anything else to say. Julia stood, but when she started to walk away, a nagging feeling held her back. Two steps later, she put her finger on it and turned back to the table. "Addison?"

"Yes?"

"If this whole nomination thing hadn't gotten in the way, do you think...Do you think we could have..."

"Gone on another date?"

"Yes."

"Does it even matter?"

Julia shook her head, frustrated that she'd even asked the question. Of course it didn't matter. Why had she placed so much importance on what Addison thought of her? She wasn't in the habit of caring what the women she dated thought of her. Not in years.

And now she remembered why. The pain of falling short wasn't worth the risk. Not then, not now.

She spoke her last words to Addison Riley while on the move. "I hope you find what you're looking for."

CHAPTER SEVENTEEN

Two days later, Julia looked up to find Noah standing in her doorway. Cindy must have gone for coffee, because no way would he have gotten past her. She finished her call with Senator Burrows and hung up.

"Noah, what can I do for you?"

"I'm headed to the oval. Come with me."

The order was annoying, but she stood and followed him, wondering what was up. By all accounts, Landry's nomination was on track. Burrows had just called to say that he could promise there would be no Republican filibuster and he could deliver enough votes to guard against the unlikely event of Democratic defectors.

She knew Noah well enough to know pumping him for information was useless. If they were headed to the Oval Office, Garrett would be the one to speak. When she arrived, she was surprised to see Connie Armstrong with the president. They were already engaged in heated conversation when she entered the room, but suddenly got quiet when she entered.

"Don't stop talking on my account. What's going on?"

Garrett gestured to the couch nearest him. "Have a seat, Julia." He waited until she was settled before resuming the conversation. "Senator Armstrong has some strong concerns about Judge Landry, and we thought it would be wise for us to hear them all at once."

Connie set a folder down on the table between them. "This is what happens when you put someone in charge of the nomination who doesn't have a keen legal mind." She pointed at the folder. "Go ahead. Read it."

Julia pulled the folder toward her and opened it. Inside she found a small stack of paper filled with single spaced lines of type. She glanced through a few pages and noted it was a law review case note. She glanced at the date and the name of the journal. It was from Landry's law school during the time he'd served on the editorial board, but there wasn't anything on the paper to indicate who the author was. The title was *Privacy: Constitutional Overreach.*

She skimmed the first page and then looked up at the rest of the group. "Someone want to help me out?"

"It's Landry's," Armstrong said, "He wrote it and you either failed to find it, or worse, you didn't think it was important."

"Are you sure it's his?"

"His pals on the law review say it is."

"This is almost thirty years old. And how do you know he wasn't just taking a position for the purpose of argument? Keen legal minds do that on occasion." Julia couldn't resist the dig.

"You can try all you want to cover your ass, but the truth is you've wasted our time with this cardboard cutout of a judge who doesn't even believe in the right to privacy. I wonder what else you've overlooked."

Julia shot a look at Garrett, who shrugged. Great. Apparently, he was willing to throw her under the bus over his own choice. Well, that wasn't going to happen. "I'm certain President Garrett's handpicked candidate believes in the right to privacy. In fact, he's on his way over. Why don't we ask him ourselves?"

"Oh, I already wasted more time on this guy at my office than I planned to. That one won't shut up. If you thought for one minute you'd get him through the hearings without this coming out, you were sorely mistaken. He'll crater in the first hour.

"No, he's your problem now, but I can guarantee you won't get a majority for confirmation. We may not be able to stand strong on everything, but the caucus will band together when our fundamental rights are threatened. And shame on you, Mr. President. Winning by the skin of your teeth doesn't give you license to pull the wool over our eyes." Armstrong stood, excused herself, and left the room.

Julia waited until she was sure she wasn't coming back, and then said, "What was that all about?"

President Garrett spread his arms. "I thought I could talk her down, but she wasn't having any of it. How did we miss this article?"

Julia stared at him, unable to believe he wasn't willing to take the blame himself. He'd insisted on advancing Landry, even before he'd been fully vetted. It was just her bad luck that her team hadn't found the law review article, but if Landry had such fundamental differences with their party, then why had Garrett nominated him in the first place?

The advantage to being a paid consultant instead of an employed lackey was the ability to walk at anytime. And this was the perfect time. Feeling a sense of relief that her job was almost done, Julia said, "Landry's due here any minute. What do you want me to tell him?"

"Find out if he wrote the article. I want him to say it. If he did, we're going to cut him loose. I want to see the list Connie gave you, and I want a meeting with each of those candidates no later than tomorrow."

Julia started to remind him that Sally Gibbons was on that list and there was no way in hell she'd get confirmed. She started to tell him that Burrows was totally on board with Landry and he might be able to get enough Democrats to cross the aisle and join him. She started to say a lot of things, but then decided she was done. She'd talk to Landry, set up the other interviews, and then she'd tell him she quit. She could almost feel the sun on her skin and the sand between her toes. Hell, she'd even give him Addison Riley's name. She was done. She'd messed this up, but as far as she was concerned, her debt was paid.

"Yes, sir."

"You have several messages, but only one of them that you need to return right away."

Addison took the slip of paper from Roger's outstretched hand. "Since when are you handwriting messages?" He usually sent her an e-mail summarizing all the phone calls she'd received.

"Two reasons. One, I thought you might think it was spam, and two, I didn't want to create an electronic trail."

Addison was tempted to laugh at his serious expression, but instead she just reached out a hand. "Am I supposed to eat this after I read it?"

"Just read it."

His anxious tone piqued her curiosity, and she skimmed the note. Then read it slowly twice more, anxiety fighting with excitement as she digested the implications.

Roger's voice cut through her haze. "Did you know about this?"

She looked up from the paper. "I didn't have a clue."

"What do you think it's about?"

She closed her eyes. "I need a minute."

"You're going, right?"

"I don't know."

"What? It's the White House."

Addison raised the note and read the words again. She didn't need to—she'd memorized them.

President Garrett would like to meet with Dean Riley. Today at three p.m. Please advise if she would like us to provide transportation. Please contact the president's chief of staff for details.

She looked up at Roger who said, "I've already contacted them and made the arrangements."

Great. At least she didn't have to make that decision. But of course she was going. She replayed the last week's worth of news in her head searching for a clue as to why she was being summoned. The president had made an appearance in the press room with his nominee of choice, Judge Landry, and George was being squired around to meet with senators in preparation for a smooth confirmation.

Maybe she was being tapped to take Landry's seat on the court of appeals. But those kind of appointments, while important, rarely merited an in person visit to the White House. No, usually a prearranged phone call from the president was the closest connection between the nominee and her benefactor. One of the federal district judges she'd clerked for while in law school had taped his call and played it for visitors to his chambers, but he'd never actually had a face-to-face with the president who'd appointed him.

Would she see Julia there? Doubtful, but the very idea spurred a sense of nervous anticipation. *Get over yourself. You should be more nervous about the scheduled meeting, not a chance run-in with a woman you lusted over.* The heat of a warm blush spread across her face, and she looked up to see Roger waiting for instructions.

"Tell them I'll be there, but cancel the car. I'll drive."

"I think it's easier on them if they send the car. Security and all."

"I'm perfectly capable of finding my way to the White House. This meeting is a little last-minute, which means I'm having to cancel my entire afternoon, so I'm not overly concerned about what's easier for them."

"Okaaay." Roger gave her an I think you're a little bit crazy look and then spun on his heel and left the room. After he shut the door, Addison paced the room. The suit she had on wasn't the one she would've chosen for a meeting with the president, but red would have to do since she didn't have time to run by her apartment to change.

The next two hours sped by as she made a vain attempt to focus on work. Finally, she shoved her draft lesson plans into her briefcase and told Roger she was leaving for the day after she swore him to silence on her afternoon activities.

When she left the building, she shivered. The temperature had dropped significantly since she'd entered the office early this morning, and the gray skies promised snow. When she got in the car, she tuned to the local news to check the weather report. She'd been right about the snow, but thankfully, there was no ice in the forecast. But for now it was dry, and she made the drive into the city in record time. She valeted her car at The Hay-Adams and walked the block over to Pennsylvania and Fourteenth. She gave her name to the Secret Service agent at the gate, and he checked his list and passed her through. Anticipation rising, she walked the short distance to the second checkpoint and passed through the metal detectors, finally giving her name to the last gatekeeper before entering the area of the White House open to the general public. He motioned for her to wait in the lobby while he made a call.

She took a seat on a bench and gazed at the wall of portraits depicting past presidents and first families, seeking out her favorite—former first lady Grace Coolidge hugging her pet raccoon. She'd just about memorized every picture on the wall, when a young woman approached her with her hand outstretched.

"Mrs. Riley, I'm so sorry to have kept you waiting. I expected you at the West Wing entrance."

She stood. "No one specified, so I came here. And it's Ms. Riley. I'm not married."

The youngster look flustered, which hadn't been her intention. She smiled to soften the formality between them. "What's your name?"

"I'm sorry. I'm Ella. Mr. Davy asked me to come and get you. Follow me?"

Addison stood and followed the young woman through the corridors of the historic building, trying not to look like a tourist. It was hard. She'd been here a number of times on business during her tenure as solicitor general, but there was never any time to look around and absorb the history of the place. When they reached the West Wing, the hallways were bustling with staff, managing the world, but nothing about the frantic pace negated the historical significance of the building. Finally, they arrived at the suite surrounding the Oval Office, and Ella handed her off to an elderly woman seated behind a large desk.

"Good afternoon, Dean Riley. May I get you something to drink while you wait?"

Addison envisioned coffee spilling down the front of her shirt and politely declined. The woman picked up her phone and notified someone that she was waiting. Addison settled back in her chair and took calming breaths as she contemplated what would happen next.

She recognized the man who came out to greet her. She'd seen him on the news. He was President Garrett's chief of staff.

"Dean Riley, I'm Noah Davy. A pleasure to meet you." He shook her hand in a barely touching kind of way and turned to the woman behind the desk. "We're going to head to the Mural Room for a few minutes, but we'll be right back."

He led the way, and Addison followed until they were both ensconced in the dark confines of the Mural Room. She resisted the urge to look at the paintings on the wall, instead focusing on reading Noah's expression. His face was steel, which made it hard. Finally, giving up on her observational skills, she asked, "Any chance you could fill me in on why I've been summoned?"

"I'm sure you know."

"I haven't a clue."

He stared at her, but she didn't waiver. Finally, he looked away. "You know we're vetting potential Supreme Court nominees."

"Of course, but I was also under the impression you'd settled on your pick."

"Things change."

"That's cryptic."

"In a couple of hours, Judge Landry will officially withdraw his name from consideration for personal reasons."

Addison started to ask how Julia felt about that, but held her tongue. For all she knew Julia had no idea she was even here. She'd glanced around as she'd been escorted through the building, but hadn't seen any evidence of her presence. "That doesn't really answer my question about why I'm here."

"President Garrett would like to meet you. He's in the Oval now. I'm supposed to take you there."

Addison recalled the public announcement about Landry's nomination. Garrett had held a press conference with Landry at his side. He made a brief speech touting Landry's accomplishments and told the Senate via the reporters gathered, that he hoped for a swift confirmation process to enable the important work of the court to continue unabated. She remembered scoffing at the television screen as she watched the beginning of a huge setback to progressives everywhere.

Apparently, things had changed. Landry was out, and she was about to meet with the man who'd chosen Landry to fill shoes twelve sizes too big for him. The only thing she knew for sure was that Noah wasn't happy about her being here and she said as much.

He was quick to reply. "No, I'm not and I think the only reason you're here is your friendship with Senator Armstrong."

"I like when people say what they think, but I have to ask, do you know anything about me other than the fact I know Connie Armstrong?"

"I know enough. You're the dean of a liberal school. You're a member of the ACLU. You clerked for the most liberal judges this country has ever seen, and you're big on expanding the constitution to suit a liberal agenda. The only thing in your favor is that you haven't had the opportunity to author any opinions as a judge, so you're only a judicial activist in waiting."

"Wow, you forgot lesbian."

He waved her off. "It's not like you're sporting a chick on your arm or babies in tow. In fact, it looks like you barely date enough to register on the sexual activity meter. For all the world knows, you're just one very focused woman, the career-minded spinster. Yes, your sexual orientation is a concern, but it's not the biggie."

Surprised as she was that he'd obviously marshaled resources to monitor her sex life, she could tell he wasn't quite done, and she focused on what he had to say next.

He paused long enough to create a sense of drama. "I have two words for you. Anita Harwood."

Addison winced. She, like the rest of the world, had followed the confirmation hearings for Garrett's first court of appeals nomination, one year into his first term. He'd taken a huge risk. Judge Harwood was one of the most liberal judges ever to serve on the federal bench. A senior federal judge in the Northern District of California, she'd authored dozens of opinions on everything from gay marriage to immigration to a woman's right to choose. She had been a Weir in the making, and as a young and vibrant judge, she had a lifetime full of pushing the envelope ahead of her.

She'd been crushed. The right had dug up every aspect of her life and held it under a microscope for the world to see. It wasn't unusual for federal judges to receive death threats, but public displays of vitriol against Judge Harwood bordered on the insane. From burning crosses in her front yard to boxes of hate mail, she underwent a constant public hazing while all the major news outlets streamed coverage of only slightly more civilized hazing in the Senate. After a brutal series of hearings and numerous histrionic speeches from the Senate floor, Garrett, facing the prospect that he'd never get any of his judicial appointments confirmed, had withdrawn Harwood's nomination and settled on a safe moderate choice that everyone could agree on.

Addison remembered the day of the announcement well. She and her peers had moaned the shifting center of the court over beer and bourbon at the Old Ebbitt. The news about Landry's nomination echoed the same bland refrain from the post-Harwood days, and she had to admit she was happy to hear Landry was withdrawing from consideration, while hoping his family emergency wasn't serious.

"Why am I here?"

"Do you seriously not know?"

"I have a feeling, but I need to hear you say it."

"Well, that's not going to happen." He stood and motioned for her to follow, stopping back in the reception area. "Someone else wants to tell you what he has in mind." He nodded to the secretary and she picked up her phone and whispered a few quiet words into the handset before looking up.

"He's ready. Go on in," she said.

CHAPTER EIGHTEEN

Some of the furnishings had changed, but the Oval Office still contained the same swirl of power Addison remembered. The seal on the floor, the Resolute desk, the museum show pieces on the walls. All the elements combined to overwhelm and intimidate visitors. She took a moment to ground herself before reaching to meet the president's outstretched hand.

"Dean Riley, thank you for coming on such short notice."

"My pleasure, Mr. President." It would be more of a pleasure if she knew why she was here.

"Have a seat." The president motioned to one of the two couches in the room and she settled on the one closer.

"Noah, thanks for taking care of Dean Riley. I'll take it from here."

Addison watched Noah's expression. He was obviously torn and had no desire to leave them alone, but the president's tone had made it clear he was being dismissed.

"Thank you, sir. Let me know if you need anything else."

President Garrett waited until Noah had cleared the door and it clicked shut to begin speaking. "Would you like something to drink?"

Three o'clock was too early to think about having a whiskey, wasn't it? "No, sir. Thank you."

"Do you know why you're here?"

"I only know what Noah told me and that wasn't much."

"What did he say?"

"That Judge Landry has pulled his name from consideration. For family reasons."

"It wasn't for family reasons."

Addison leaned back against the couch. She was growing tired of cagey politicians. "I don't suppose you're going to tell me what the real reasons were, but I imagine it had something to do with anticipated trouble for the confirmation hearings. Frankly, I'm surprised. Judge Landry is no Anita Harwood."

With every word, she anticipated a prompt dismissal. What she got instead was a big laugh, and she couldn't help but join in. After a few seconds of laughter, the president settled back and said, "You're right, of course. Judge Landry is a good man, but he'll never cause a ruckus like Judge Harwood did. In fact, I thought his confirmation would be quick and easy."

"Exactly what you need right now." She hadn't meant to speak the words aloud, but when he raised his eyebrows, she finished her thought. "The election was brutal. More divisiveness would not be in your best interest or the interest of the country."

"You are much more politically minded than Judge Landry."

"I'm a lot of things Judge Landry isn't."

"Let's talk about some of those."

"First, I need to know why I'm here. If we're just chatting or if you'd like my input about a potential nominee, then I'm happy to share my opinions with you, but…" She didn't want to presume. Thankfully, he saved her the trouble.

"You're on the list of potential Supreme Court nominees."

"A decoy?"

"Good guess under other circumstances, but that's not the case." He leaned forward. "Dean Riley, you're near the top of the list. I don't take the time to meet with decoys. I have my staff do that."

"If you were to appoint me, you're going to have a battle like you did with Judge Harwood. Ideologically, she and I are very much alike, not to mention the stakes are higher now."

"I misjudged the timing when I put her name forward. I was too new, too green. I made a lot of mistakes then that I've since learned from."

"Yet, you nominated Judge Landry."

"I have my reasons for making the change. I won't share them, but I will tell you I'm committed to selecting a more vocal candidate."

"I have no judicial experience."

"Only clerkships with some of the top judges in the country, including the man whose shoes you would be filling. What better legacy for Weir's court than to have his protégé take his place?"

"Do you really believe that? We've barely even met and already you think I'd be the perfect fit?"

"I didn't say that. I guess I'm just trying to gauge your interest. If you have no interest, then there's no point in starting the interrogation."

He smiled to soften the point, but he'd made it. And that was the key. Since Julia had first broached the idea, she had been so busy thinking about what would be good for the court and good for the country, that she hadn't taken the time to decide how she would answer the call to service, if asked.

She'd walked the halls of the Supreme Court building, sat in the chief justice's chambers, and written large portions of opinions that helped change the course of history. When the gallery of the courtroom for the highest court in the land filled with spectators, she'd had a special seat near the front, and she'd witnessed more historic events in one year than most people see in a lifetime.

But she'd always been one step removed. She didn't wear the robe. She didn't get to attend the Friday conferences where the justices entered their initial vote and determined who would author the majority opinion that would become the law of the land. Her name wasn't on the opinions, wouldn't be in the history books.

Maybe working one step away from power was her destiny. As solicitor general, she'd championed the arguments of the president, not her own. Her job in big law was more of the same, except the clients were corporations, wealthy enough to pay the huge fees she commanded. Even now, she was on the periphery, dealing with administrative issues, so others could teach and write. Was she ready to step out of the shadows, run the country's highest court, direct the future of legal precedent?

It wouldn't be easy. Just getting confirmed was likely to be a battle, no matter who was in her corner. Anita Harwood was still a household name—everyone remembered the scathing examination of her life and the persecution she suffered for not being bland, comfortable, centrist. She wondered if Anita would do it all again. She thought she knew, and all at once, she knew her own answer.

"Yes, Mr. President, I'm interested."

"Great. Then I'd like to continue this conversation, but include the chair of the search committee."

Addison nodded and he pressed a button on the phone nearest him and told his secretary to "send her in." She was still so swept up in her decision to go forward she didn't think about who would be joining them until Julia walked through the door, looking every bit as delicious as she had the very first time they'd met. Here, at the White House.

President Garrett stood when Julia entered and waved a hand between them. "I don't know if you two remember, but you met at Judge Weir's funeral."

Addison's head spun as the memory of that day came crashing back. After the solemn scene at the Supreme Court building and the emotional service at Saint Matthew's, the reception at the White House had been the first moment in days she'd been able to take a breath, enjoy the company of old friends, and share tales of the giant man who'd loved her like a father. And then, like a faded romance cliché, she'd spotted Julia across a crowded room. Her energy had been intoxicating and her obvious nonchalance about the power she commanded had made her even more irresistible.

Remember? Hell, she'd never be able to forget.

"Yes, sir," Julia said. "I remember." She extended her hand to Addison, embarrassed about the formal gesture, but too uncertain about the reaction she might face from a friendlier move. "Nice to see you again, Dean Riley."

Addison winced at the title, and Julia bit her lower lip. She knew where this meeting was headed. Noah had already paid her a visit, ripping her a new one for adding Addison's name to the short list. She took the scolding in stride, knowing it was easier for him to take his anger out on her than the real target of his temper, Senator Armstrong who, encouraged by the stable Senate majority, was throwing her weight around on a number of issues. Noah had made it clear that her job was to keep the president focused on his moderate choices. Sally Gibbons and Addison Riley were window dressing—added to the list to keep the left happy, but in no way to be seriously considered.

She'd assured him she agreed and would do everything she could to make sure the president stayed focused. She'd start now. First things first, take the temperature of the room. It was already friendlier than she liked considering Addison had been here for forty-five minutes and the president was just now starting to ask her about issues that were likely to come before the court.

"Let's talk about reproductive rights," Garrett said. "Certainly we can expect—"

"You mean the right to privacy," Addison interrupted. "What you really want to talk about is the right to privacy and whether it's even addressed in the constitution, let alone should it apply to laws enacted by the states."

"I'm not interested in discussing a global right of privacy, but I would like to discuss the specific issues for which the court has interpreted certain rights."

"And most of them boil down to this one thing. If you take away the right to privacy, many of your specific issues will tumble down like a house of cards."

Garrett leaned forward. "I can't tell if you're trying to avoid the question, or if you're just being clever."

"Those things aren't mutually exclusive. A woman's right to choose, birth control, illegal searches and seizures—all of these things are bound up in a constitutional right to privacy. You know that. You must also know that Justice Ronald believes that because it isn't specifically enumerated in the Constitution, no such right exists. If the center of the court continues to broaden, many scholars believe the group that votes with Justice Ronald will continue to grow, thereby endangering the cases predicated on the right to privacy."

"That sounds vaguely like a threat."

"It's a reality. I'm only telling you what is bound to happen."

Julia couldn't help but interject. "Unless we put an activist on the court."

Addison shook her head and then turned her way. "No, Ms. Scott. Activists have no place on the court. An activist is someone who is set on advancing his or her own agenda. The court is no place for that, and if Justice Weir were alive, he would tell you that himself."

"Call it whatever you want," Julia said. "Judges who support abortion rights believe in a woman's right to choose—there's no doubting that."

"Why is it when a judge is progressive, we call him or her an activist, but when a judge is conservative, we don't do the same? Are you saying the circuit court judges who decided *Citizens United* didn't actually believe corporations should have the same right to free speech as individuals, but only came to that conclusion after a clear reading of precedent? Because that's clearly not the case.

"A judge isn't an activist if he decides an issue based on the law that happens to coincide with his personal beliefs. As long as judges are actual people and not automatons, we will be forced to believe in coincidence or the system must fail.

"And don't you want judges that support things like a woman's right to choose? Isn't that the beauty of this intersection of politics and lifetime appointments? That you get to select a justice to put on the bench to create a legacy that outlives your time in office?"

Julia answered for the president. "If only it were that easy." She stared at Addison, watching while she pondered her response. For this entire back and forth, it'd felt like they were the only two in the room, sparring about the issues. She couldn't help but be as attracted to Addison's mind as she was to her body. When Addison finally spoke, the attraction flew off the charts.

"If you want easy, there are lots of other jobs." Addison steepled her fingers and stared directly at her and said, "I'm not campaigning for this job, but as a legal scholar, I beg of you to choose someone who can walk in Weir's footsteps, if not fill them. If you do that, you'll have a legacy you can be proud of."

Julia waited until Addison finally looked away before she turned to Garrett. His curious expression let her know he noticed Addison had directed remarks at her that were surely meant for him. Or had she? Was she talking about Julia's legacy? If she was, it only exhibited that she didn't know her very well. The only legacy she cared about was success on Election Day for each of her clients. Once this little side venture was over, she'd find another client and build the next brick in the only legacy she would ever have. That all her accomplishments belonged to other people didn't bother her in the least.

Or did it?

She didn't have time to ponder the question. Garrett stood, and she and Addison followed suit. He shook Addison's hand and told her they'd be in touch. Addison took her hand as well, and she lingered with the touch. Warm, firm. She didn't want to let go.

When Addison was gone, Garrett asked her to stay for a moment. "I like her."

"She's very likable, sir, but likability in a person doesn't always translate to widespread appeal."

"She doesn't have to appeal to everyone. Connie Armstrong says she can get her confirmed."

"Senator Armstrong has a tendency to overestimate her strengths. We managed to hold a majority in the Senate only because of your strength at the top of the ticket. If you hadn't won, those down ticket races would have gone very differently."

"And you don't have to remind me that my win was pure luck."

"Well, that doesn't say much about my abilities. Yes, we had a lucky stroke at the end, but the point is no one has a mandate, and that includes the Senate. Unless Armstrong and her pals are willing to exercise the nuclear option, Addison Riley's name may never come to a vote. That empty seat could sit idle for God knows how long. What kind of legacy would that be?"

The minute she asked the question she was sorry she had. The word legacy had triggered his curiosity about the conversation she'd just had with Addison, and she braced for the question on his lips.

"You two seem to be acquainted. How long have you known her?"

She scanned his face, trying to determine if his was an innocent question or whether he already knew the answer and was trying to catch her in a lie. Her instincts told her he knew nothing about her personal relationship with Addison, such that it was. If ever she was going to say anything, now was the time to do it. Later, it would seem, well, unseemly.

But what would she say? I'm crazy attracted to her, but we disagree about practically everything? She's got an incredible brain, if only she would be more practical, we might have a chance?

Nothing she came up with sounded plausible, so she went with a vague response. "We've had coffee, dinner. I've met with her several times to discuss the possibility of an appointment. She has a lot of interesting things to say about the court."

"Most of which you do not agree with?"

"Most of which are not politically expedient. Sir, you knew when you asked me to do this job, what you could expect. I'm here to get you what you want with as few casualties as possible. If you choose to nominate Addison Riley and Senator Armstrong doesn't deliver, then you will have used up any residual goodwill you might have had before you even take the oath again. If that happens, you can take your legislative agenda and throw it in the trash. And if the Republicans are successful in blocking Riley, it'll be blood in the water as far as the rest of your judicial appointments. Mid-terms will be hell."

"For the rest of your clients, you mean."

She shook her head. "It's your party you'll be tanking. Meet with the rest of the list. Your instincts about Landry were right. He just wasn't the right guy. There are other names on the list that should sail through committee. Armstrong will come around when she realizes Burrows and his clan aren't going to confirm someone like Riley without a fight."

"Do you like her?"

"What?" The question threw her off.

"Riley. Do you like her?"

"I don't see why that matters."

"It's a simple question. Either you like her or you don't. I'm just curious. Indulge me."

But it wasn't simple. Yes, she liked her. She more than liked her—she wanted to get to know her better. Reel back the heated topics from their dating attempts and start over with something innocuous, something that had nothing to do with politics. But since politics were her life, that wasn't likely. Especially now that the president seemed intent on putting Addison's name on the short list of potential Supreme Court candidates. No, there was nothing simple about her relationship with Addison, but judging by the set of his jaw, he wasn't going to let her go without an answer.

She cleared her throat and answered his not so simple question. "Yes. I like her. I like her a lot."

CHAPTER NINETEEN

Addison looked up at the knock on her office door and called out, "Come in." When Roger appeared in the doorway with a cup of coffee, she smiled. "Thanks. Guess I've been in here a while."

"You could say that. Working on secret plans to take over the world?"

"Maybe." She pointed at a chair. "Have a seat."

He set the coffee on her desk, shut the office door, slid into the chair beside her desk, and waited while she contemplated what she was about to ask. Since yesterday's meeting with the president, she hadn't been able to focus on anything but being short-listed for the high court.

Except Julia. Truth was her sleepless night had been split between thoughts of a judgeship and the possibility of a relationship. Stupid really, since if one happened, the other wouldn't. Couldn't. If the president nominated her, she'd probably be spending a lot of time with Julia, but none of it would be about them and, judging by their interaction yesterday, most of it would be spent arguing.

She shifted in her seat at the memory of their heated exchanges. She seriously needed to focus.

"I need some help, but it's not university related and I hate to ask."

"I'm yours. Whatever it is."

"First, don't laugh if I tell you it's top secret."

Roger drew a finger across his lips. "Agreed, but I should tell you that I know about the lesson plans."

"What?"

"The lesson plans you've been working on. I ran across them when I was sorting your files and mail the other day. Are you thinking about stepping down from administration?"

"I was considering it. I planned to take on a couple more classes and see how it went. I miss the classroom." She waved at the stacks of paper on her desk. "I miss doing something besides all this."

"Nothing wrong with that, but did I catch the past tense there? Is there some reason you're not thinking about that anymore?" His eyes lit up. "Did it have something to do with your last-minute trip to the White House the other day? Let me guess, Garrett wants to replace his solicitor general, and since you have experience in the job, he's looking at you?"

"Good guess, but that particular job never came up in conversation."

"But he did want to talk to you about an appointment?"

"Yes." She paused. She had to trust someone with the news. "Apparently, Judge Landry is about to ask the president to take his name out of the running, and there's a very slim possibility that I'm about to be vetted for chief justice." She waited for his reaction and she wasn't disappointed by his astonished look.

"Justice Weir's seat? Holy shit, really? You'd be the first female chief justice. Wow, that's amazing!"

"Before you get too excited, you should know it's still very much up in the air. I'm sure there are many more qualified candidates, and I'm only window dressing, but I have been given these questionnaires to answer."

She slid a folder across the desk. The large envelope had arrived at her condo the evening before, and she'd spent the evening parsing together the information requested before the White House would even begin the vetting process. Roger picked up the folder and started skimming through the contents.

"I could use your help compiling all this information. They need names and contact info for references, plus a ton of detail about work history, but it'd have to be outside of normal business hours. And totally secret. I'll pay you for your time."

"You'll do no such thing. I'm happy to help. Who knows? I might be helping make history. When will you know more about whether you've made the short list?"

"I don't have a clue. These things have a life of their own. I assume Julia, I mean, Ms. Scott, the search committee chair, will let me know about the next step."

Roger stood. "Well, we better be ready. I'll go through this tonight and fill in the details." He started for the door. "I know you want to keep this a secret for now, but what do we do when the FBI starts showing up to do their background check? People are going to notice."

"I doubt it will ever get to that, but if it does, I assume we'll have plenty of notice."

Not even five minutes later, Roger was back at her door. Addison looked up from the lesson plans she was now only half-heartedly interested in. "What's up?"

"Turn on your TV. Any of the news channels."

She swiveled in her chair, switched on the cable, and flipped through the channels, landing on Fox News first. When she saw the image on the screen, she stopped. George Landry looked pale and lost.

"It is with much regret that I must withdraw my name from consideration for chief justice of the United States. Family issues prevent me from giving this position my full attention, and I have told the president that, while I appreciate his confidence, I will remain on the Fourth Circuit Court of Appeals where I can still accomplish the great work envisioned by our forefathers."

"So, he's not quitting the bench, just not accepting a promotion? That's odd. It's not like he'd be in for more work on the Supreme Court, just more prestige."

Addison considered Roger's words. Landry's reasoning was vague, but it wasn't her place to question such a personal decision. The chief justice was not only the head judge of the Supreme Court, but of all the federal courts. He ran the court's conferences, the hearings, and the entire Supreme Court docket. He was the public face of the court. And the he had never been a she. Would she be the first woman to hold the position?

Before she could think about it further, the phone rang. Roger reached for the receiver. "I'll get that."

Addison shook her head. "That's okay." She punched the line and picked up the handset, almost positive she knew who was on the other line.

She'd barely said hello when Julia asked, "Did you see the announcement?"

"I did." Julia sounded out of breath, but Addison couldn't tell if she was excited or exerted. She wanted to ask, to enjoy a moment of plain old political gossip with this woman who so intrigued her, but Roger was sitting mere feet away. "I guess things will start to move quickly now."

"Understatement. The president has asked me to let you know that you're officially being vetted for the position of chief justice. He's in a meeting with the French ambassador right now, but you'll receive a call from him personally later today.

"We'll need your completed questionnaire by tomorrow, and you should expect people close to you to start getting contacted by the FBI for your deep background check. You should go ahead and clear your schedule for the rest of the week. We'll be scheduling a press conference with the president and prep time here followed by your interviews in the Senate. We'll get back to you with specific details, but right now, do you have any questions?"

Addison barely heard what Julia said, instead trying not to read too much into the formal, straightforward tone. Of course, Julia was focused. Finding the next Supreme Court justice and getting that person confirmed was a daunting task. Julia would have a lot on her plate, and the last thing she would want was to be distracted by the undeniable attraction between them. Time for her to focus as well. She'd confine her questions to the process. "Who else?"

"What?"

"Who else is on the list?"

Julia laughed. "Well, it's a pretty short list. You're the only one on it."

Addison tried to hide her gasp, but she was pretty sure Julia heard her surprise. In an attempt to hide her shock, she kept silent.

"Addison?"

It was the first time in a while Julia had called her by her first name. Her voice felt silky nice, making her name sound like an endearment. She barely managed to snap out of her reverie long enough to say, "Yes?"

"You're the president's choice, and it's my job to get you confirmed. I'll do everything I can to make that happen. And that means…"

Addison wasn't sure if Julia's voice had actually trailed off, or if she'd been no longer able to hear any words beyond "president's choice," "of the United States," and "short list—you're the only one on it." Before she could fully process her thoughts, Julia's words penetrated, picking up where she had dropped out of the conversation.

"…okay, just so that's clear. I'll talk to you tomorrow and we'll set the schedule for next week. Good-bye, Dean Riley."

Addison held the phone for a few minutes after Julia disconnected the line. Dean Riley.

Leave it to Julia to make even that dry title sound sexy.

Julia set the phone down and let out a deep breath. That had gone as well as could be expected, but it had been a struggle to maintain her composure. Part of her wanted to congratulate Addison, ask her out for drinks to celebrate her good news, but a bigger part dreaded the fight to come and what it might do to her and to any chance they might get to know each other better.

"Julia?"

She looked up to see Noah standing in her doorway. "Yes?"

"I'd like to go over the president's schedule. He wants to make the announcement by the end of the week. Rose Garden if it's sunny, which it's supposed to be. I have a number of things for you to get done by then."

Annoyed at his commanding tone, and that Cindy never seemed to be at her desk when he came by, she didn't try to mask the imposition from her voice. "Am I always to expect a personal visit from you when you want to tell me how to do my job?"

Ignoring her tone, he sank into a chair and took over a corner of her desk with his stack of files. "Maybe I like seeing you."

"Maybe you should get a new hobby."

He laughed. "You're refreshing. No one here talks to me this way."

"That's because they're all scared of you. You have the power to send them packing."

"And you're immune?"

"Let's just say I don't care if you fire me or not. I'm doing this as a favor for the president, not because I need the work. In a month, I'll be moving on to a long list of clients who want me to perform the same miracle for them that I did for your guy. Translation, cash. Lots of it. Like I said, I don't need this gig."

"Why don't you step down then? Take that trip you planned? I'll talk to him, pave the way. I know several qualified candidates who could take your place."

Julia started to say "if only," but then she realized he was serious. The steely expression lurking behind his veneer of nonchalance started her wheels spinning. *He wants me to quit. Badly.*

It was one thing to know she had the power to quit whenever she wanted, but she wasn't about to be pushed out, especially when she suspected Noah had an ulterior motive behind his idle suggestion. No, she'd gotten Addison Riley into this by passing along her name, and she was committed to seeing it through. She had no clue what Noah was up to, but she made a silent vow to see the process to conclusion.

The words she spoke next were ones she'd never expected to say. "I serve at the pleasure of the president. If he would like someone else to handle the confirmation process, then he can tell me so himself."

Noah laughed and stood. "Take it easy, Julia. It was just a suggestion. Hey, you're the one who said you were doing this as a favor. I was just trying to give you an out. No harm done."

She studied his face. His features were firmly fixed in a broad smile and his tone was casual and confident. Maybe she'd imagined the ulterior motive. After all, she was used to looking for the hidden twists in any situation, and sometimes things were just exactly as they appeared to be. She reached for his hand, a truce of sorts. He looked startled at the gesture, but stopped gathering his files to reach out and meet her halfway. As he did, the stack of folders fell to the floor.

"Damn, I'm sorry," Julia said as she released his hand and bent to help pick up the scattered papers. Noah practically dove to the floor and began scooping up the files, hugging them to his chest, but not before Julia got a good look at one of them and its contents. It was familiar. She'd seen the same folder only days before, on the president's desk. She hadn't asked then, but she had to now. "Noah, is there a reason the president was looking at the police report about Justice Weir's accident? It was an accident, right?"

His reaction was swift. Eyes downcast, he shook his head. "Yes, it was. A horrible accident. The president wanted me to see if there was anything about the roadway that night that could've contributed to the accident so I could speak to Mayor Dandridge about it. But it appears it was just a matter of human error. Sad and such a great loss."

His words offered a plausible excuse, but his downcast eyes and the slight hesitation in his voice told her he was shading the truth, if not covering it up entirely. But why? He had every right to request and read a police report involving the death of a highly placed official. No reason to lie about it.

She kept her reaction to herself, and chose to respond by echoing his sentiment. "Yes, a very great loss." Then, quickly changing the subject, she said, "the Rose Garden will be a great spot for the announcement. Let me know when the schedule is finalized and I'll follow-up with Dean Riley."

A few minutes later, after he was long gone, Julia stood and walked to her door. "Cindy, may I see you for a moment?"

When Cindy was in her office, Julia motioned for her to take a seat and then she shut the door.

"I'd like you to get a copy of the police report for Justice Weir's accident. Can you do that?"

Cindy cocked her head and Julia could've sworn she looked insulted by the question. "I can do anything you want me to."

"Can you also keep it quiet? I don't want anyone to know why you're asking for it or who asked you to get it."

Cindy nodded. "Not a problem."

"Aren't you going to ask me why?"

"If you wanted me to know you'd tell me."

Good, a woman who appreciated a need for discretion. A thought struck Julia. "Cindy, who did you work for before me?"

Cindy shifted, obviously uncomfortable with the question. "I've worked for a number of people in the administration. Some wouldn't mind if I told you, some might."

"Do you work for anyone else now?"

"Just you. Mr. Davy said you needed someone and asked me to fill in. I was happy to do so." She frowned. "Are you unhappy with my work?"

"Not in the least. And thanks for keeping this matter just between us. It's just my idle curiosity, and I'd rather not have anyone thinking it was anything else."

Cindy stood. "Is that all?"

"Actually, no. I'm sure the press office is going to handle the details of the announcement, but you should know the president is going to announce Addison Riley as his nominee for the Supreme Court. I'll contact her myself to talk about the schedule for her Senate interviews, but I need you to find us a space to meet to prepare and I'll also need you to coordinate with the Judiciary Committee's chief of staff."

"No problem. I'll get right on it." She walked toward the door, but paused before she crossed the threshold. "Interesting choice, by the way."

Julia looked up from the papers on her desk. Something about Cindy's tone made her think she disapproved. "Really? How so?"

"Nothing. It's just she's very different from the president's first choice."

Julia continued to stare, trying to read the meaning behind the words. "Yes, she is. Addison Riley is a rare breed."

CHAPTER TWENTY

Addison kicked off her shoes the minute she crossed the threshold of her condo. What a day. President Garrett had called within an hour of her conversation with Julia, and Roger had nearly fallen out of his chair with excitement before he burst into her office to tell her who was on the line. After the brief discussion in which the president asked and she agreed to be the nominee, she'd spent the next hour clearing her schedule and warning Roger to keep things under wraps until the White House made the official announcement.

She'd managed to pour a glass of wine before her phone rang again. She didn't recognize the number, but answered anyway. It had been a day for strange calls, and she didn't expect that was going to end anytime soon.

"This is Addison."

"Addison, hi, it's Jeff." The man on the other end of the line paused and then cleared his throat. "Jeff Burrows."

Addison relaxed into a chair. "Oh, hi, Jeff. Good to hear from you."

"Sorry to call you at the last minute, but I was wondering if we could meet for a drink. It's important."

Addison glanced at the glass of wine in her hand and the shoes she'd abandoned in the foyer. She really didn't want to go back out, but he sounded like whatever he wanted to talk about was urgent. For a brief moment, she considered inviting him over, but decided against it. If she met him somewhere, she'd be able to leave when she was ready. Whatever Jeff wanted, she was going to get a good night's sleep. She'd need it to make it through the rest of the week.

"Sure, how about Old Ebbitt? Say half an hour?"

"Perfect. See you there."

She hung up the phone, placed her wine glass on the kitchen counter, and wandered off to find a warm coat and a pair of boots for the walk to the restaurant.

The Old Ebbitt was the oldest restaurant in D.C. and a popular power circle venue. She knew Jeff, the consummate Washington insider, would know the place, but she'd chosen it mostly because she was starving and a plate of their famous grilled oysters sounded wonderful right now.

The walk took only twenty minutes, but by the time she pushed through the brass and wood revolving glass door, she was eager to enjoy the heat and hospitality inside.

Jeff was waiting at the bar and she made her way over. When she got closer, he looked up and stood.

"Don't stand on my account," Addison said as she hugged her old friend.

Jeff leaned back from the embrace. "You're freezing. Did you walk?"

"My place isn't far."

"You're a braver soul than me. I don't know what I'd do without my driver."

"Law school deans don't exactly merit those kind of perks."

"I suppose not. Well, unless you'd like a drink now, we have a table waiting."

She looked around. There was plenty of seating at the bar. "We can just sit here if you want."

Jeff looked around, and Addison followed his gaze to the man seated two places down, head buried in the *Washington Post*. "If you don't mind, I'd rather we sat somewhere more private."

Addison shrugged. "We can sit in the basement if you want, as long as I can get some food."

A few minutes later, they were tucked away at a booth in a secluded corner of the restaurant. Addison recalled the first time she'd come here for lunch. Soon after, she'd started as solicitor general. As legal counsel for the United States, she'd been notable on her own, but she'd quickly realized how notable didn't mean much in a city full of powerful political celebrities. She'd barely been noticed in the sea of important men and women who ate like everyone else. One mouthful at a time.

Tonight was no different. Long removed from political life, she was barely noticed except as a woman joining the powerful Senator Burrows for dinner. In just a couple of days, that would change. Her face would be plastered on every front page, every news outlet. Her entire life would be examined, from her opinions on trending legal issues to her favorite foods. Was she prepared for that kind of notoriety?

"Addison?"

She looked up into Jeff's inquiring eyes. He'd obviously just asked her something and she'd zoned out. "Sorry, what?"

"What would you like to drink?"

She started to say a glass of wine, but reconsidered. A stiffer drink was in order after the week she'd had and what was still to come. "McCallan. Neat."

Jeff turned to the waiter. "I'll have the same. Make it the eighteen-year."

As the waiter started to leave, Addison called him back. "And an order of grilled oysters."

For the next few minutes, they made small talk. Jeff relayed stories about his family and asked about her brother who had resumed his tour in Afghanistan. When the waiter returned with their drinks and appetizer, Jeff motioned for her to take the first oyster. As Addison placed it in her mouth and reveled in the salty brine, he dropped the bomb.

"I'm amazed you can eat after all the excitement."

Now she knew the real reason for the meeting. It wasn't to catch up on their personal lives. Jeff was here in his role as senator. She'd almost forgotten he'd recently been elevated to minority chair of the Judiciary Committee. After all, before this week, she'd had no personal reason to remember that fact. She'd been told not to reveal her upcoming nomination, but of course, he'd know who was on the president's short list. No harm in discussing it with him now.

"It is pretty exciting."

"I'm sure Justice Weir would be proud."

His statement was flat, signaling he might not agree with the deceased justice's assessment of her abilities. His support would go a long way toward an eventless nomination process, something she was sure the president needed right now. No sense waiting to find out if the waters were going to be choppy. She plunged in. "And you? What do you think?"

Jeff picked up the heavy tumbler full of scotch and twirled it around in the glass before taking a deep drink. "I like this one. No burn. Smooth from start to finish. Well worth the price."

Addison set her fork down and faced him. "I wasn't talking about the scotch, but I think you know that. We both know you didn't invite me here for small talk, Jeff, or should I call you Senator Burrows?"

"You can call me whatever you like. I'm here as a friend, and I'd like to offer a little friendly advice. I think you'll find that being dean at a prestigious law school is a much more satisfactory occupation than any other you should care to seek."

"No need to dance around the subject. You're saying I should withdraw, aren't you? I can guess why you'd like to see me withdraw from consideration, but you must realize that if it's not me, it will be someone like me."

"Not necessarily. When the president realizes he's not going to get another Weir, he'll turn to more moderate names."

"Like Landry?"

"Yes. The president caved to threats from his own party on that one, but when he learns that we, along with our majority in the House, will block all of his legislative initiatives, he'll cave. It's not like he's got a lot of political capital to waste on wars like this one."

Addison held back a wince at the word "war" and pointed out, "He was reelected you know."

"A fluke. Never should've happened. Everyone knows it."

"And you do realize your job is only to advise and consent? And you're not in the majority?"

"Don't pretend you don't understand politics, Addison. We both know you're not that naive. There are many things we can do to prevent a nomination we don't like. I'm just trying to save you from the trouble of going down with the ship."

"How gracious of you." Addison stared at the unfinished platter of oysters. She'd completely lost her appetite. "Tell me, did you harbor ill will toward Justice Weir while we were clerking for him, or did you only develop your animus after the fact?"

He looked surprised. "I don't have any ill-will toward Weir or you, for that matter. I actually like you. You're smart and well reasoned, but I don't want a mini-Weir on the bench. He was dangerous, and the court is better off without his leadership."

"You're wrong. The court issued some of the most important decisions ever under his guidance."

"Fighting corporations' right to free speech? Curbing citizens' rights to bear arms? Setting the stage for gay marriage to be accepted in violation of states' rights? I don't think so. Of course, that last one may be of particular importance to you, I suppose. Would you recuse yourself from a discussion on the issue or will you let your own bias inform your decisions?"

His ire was palpable. Addison stared at the man she'd considered a friend. His fury came from some place deep, and she wasn't about to engage. "We'll have to agree to disagree."

"Actually, no. We need to agree that you will pull your name from contention."

It was clear he expected her to say "Sure, whatever you say, Jeff. I'll bow out." Had life as a senator so insulated him that he thought his power was boundless? She took a long drink of her scotch, not for fortitude, but to give him time to back down. When she placed her empty glass back on the table, it was apparent nothing had changed, but she decided to give him one last chance to clear the air.

"Jeff, I don't know what's going on here, but I assumed you wanted to meet to catch up, talk about old times. It never occurred to me that you asked me here in your capacity as a senator, as minority leader of the Judiciary Committee. Frankly, I feel sandbagged, but I'll tell you this. On Friday, the president is going to announce my name as his choice for chief justice. You and I both know I'm qualified for the position, and I hope I will have your support."

Jeff stood up and threw a few twenties on the table. "I've lost my appetite, but feel free to enjoy your meal." He leaned down and in a low voice said, "You have until noon tomorrow to let the president know you're not interested in the position."

"Or what?"

He shrugged. "I can only advise you as to what I believe will be the miserable experience of having your entire life placed under a microscope. These hearings can be pretty rough. I offer this advice as a friend. I hope you'll take it to heart."

Addison raised her empty glass and toasted the air. "Sure, Senator Burrows. Thanks for the advice." She waited until he was completely out of sight before letting the glass thud back to the table. She grasped the edge of the table with both hands, willing the shaking to stop.

Friend. Why had she ever thought he was a friend? They'd spent a year at the court arguing points and had barely spoken since. News reports, professional announcements, and Christmas cards were the only reason she knew anything about his life, his family, or he hers.

When her nerves calmed, she paid the check with her own money, left Jeff's cash on the table for the waiter, and headed home. The cold air cleared her head, and as she crossed the threshold of her apartment, she decided she'd blown things out of proportion. Jeff was a politician. They talked tough, but it was mostly bluster. Of course, he didn't want a liberal on the court, but he was probably resigned to the probability it would happen. After all, he knew the stakes as well as anyone: when you win an election and your party has control of the Senate, you get your pick. Two months ago, when Garrett was so far down in the polls he was expected to crash his entire party's ticket, Jeff probably thought a conservative justice was a lock, but now? Now, he'd have to live with the president's decision.

And so will I. Addison considered calling Julia to tell her about the encounter. She even picked up the phone, but stopped before she could dial the numbers. She didn't need Julia to fight her battles for her, and she knew that wasn't the real reason for the call anyway. She wanted compassion, comfort. She set the phone down. Julia would be many things to her in the coming weeks—her handler, her champion, her advocate—but she was paid to do all of these and nothing more. As long as she was going forward with the nomination, Julia was off-limits for anything personal.

She sighed as she felt the first pang of regret since she'd told the president yes.

CHAPTER TWENTY-ONE

Y ou really couldn't get him back here?" Julia stood in the middle of the East Room and looked up from the list on her iPad to bore holes in the deputy press secretary. She was already exasperated because the weather wasn't cooperating with her first choice of the Rose Garden. Cold was one thing, but snow had been coming down for the last twenty-four hours and wasn't expected to stop anytime soon. "Did you tell them it was important?"

The guy didn't back down. "He's not exactly a regular enlisted man. He's Special Ops. We can't just pull these guys out of the field at a whim. Or at least that's what I was told."

Julia shook her head. She knew he was right, but she'd really wanted the visual of Addison flanked by her veteran father and her soldier brother while the president touted her accomplishments. Oh well, she'd settle for Dad. "Okay, well, let's move Larry Weir up to the front row, closer to the podium. He's brother-like and a good image for all the Weir fans who'll be watching." She ignored the deputy's disapproving look. It wasn't her job to be politically correct. All she had to do was get the candidate elected. Or in this case, smoothly through Senate confirmation.

A young woman poked her head in the doorway. "She's here. Do you want me to send her in?"

"No, take her to my office. I'll be there in a minute." She took a deep breath and gave the room a final look. All the preparations were in order. Guests would start arriving in the next hour and, after being screened by Secret Service agents, they would be ushered in by interns. All that was left on her list was to go over the protocol with Addison and make sure she was ready for the onslaught that was about to begin.

So why was she the one who was nervous?

She took a few moments to ensure the room would be arranged exactly as she wanted, and then headed back to the West Wing. And Addison.

When she approached her office, Cindy was sitting at her desk, all smiles.

"What? Do I have something on my suit?"

Cindy shook her head. "No, you look great. And so does she. I can't believe we're going to have a woman chief justice."

Julia held a finger to her lips. "Shhh, you're going to curse it."

"Seriously, you're superstitious?"

"Hell, yes. If you'd lived through as many crazy elections as I have, you'd be superstitious too. For all we know, Governor Briscoe wasn't wearing his lucky tie the night his affairs became front-page news. There's absolutely no reason to tempt fate." She started toward the office door. "Any messages?"

"I e-mailed you a couple. Nothing urgent. But…" Cindy reached into a drawer on her desk. "I was able to get the report you wanted."

Julia reached out her hand to take the folder Cindy handed to her and glanced at the cover. "Ah, thanks." It was the accident report from the D.C. Police Department.

"Don't be too thankful. There's not a lot there."

Julia frowned. "What do you mean?"

Cindy started to reply, but then her expression changed and her eyes became fixed on something over Julia's shoulder. Julia turned and suddenly she was standing very, very close to Addison. Heat swept through her.

"Sorry," Addison said, "I didn't mean to interrupt, but I was wondering if I could get some water?"

Julia cleared her throat. "Of course. Cindy?"

Cindy nodded and dashed off. Julia escorted Addison back into her office. Once they were seated, she took a moment to observe the woman she'd been hired to elevate to the most powerful court in the land. Addison wore a perfectly tailored charcoal gray suit. The light blue shirt highlighted her eyes, although Julia avoided lingering on them too long for fear she would lose her bearings. Black pumps with heels, not too tall, not too short. Long, toned legs. Serious expression, but with a hint of a smile in her eyes. If she'd had to cast the part, she couldn't have done better than Addison. Why had she resisted the nomination?

Because despite the attractive package, Addison came with plenty of baggage. Liberal, lesbian, untried. The Senate Republicans would say her lack of experience was doubly problematic because they couldn't evaluate a nonexistent record. They'd be forced to extrapolate who she was into opinions that would take the court to the left. And if she answered questions the way every candidate since Robert Bork had—by not offering any specifics as to how she would apply her judgment to controversial issues, she wouldn't be giving them any reason to assume differently.

"Are you comparing me to Justice Weir?"

"Excuse me?"

Addison pointed at the folder on her desk. "I didn't mean to spy, but I saw his name on your folder. I made an assumption."

Julia placed the folder in her desk drawer and sidestepped the question. "You don't strike me as the type to make assumptions."

"It's not my usual mode of operation. I guess I noticed because Justice Weir's been on my mind a lot recently. I had an unusual visit from his son recently."

"Unusual how? He's going to be here today, supporting your nomination. If there's any bad blood between you, I need to know about it before the press gets wind of it."

"You are a one-track mind, aren't you? No, no bad blood. It's just…" She glanced at her watch and then shook her head as if she decided not to get into it. "Let's just say he had some questions about his father's accident."

Julia fixed her expression into careful nonchalance, but her hand instinctively reached for the folder. Was it a coincidence that Justice Weir's son was concerned about an accident the White House seemed to have taken a special interest in? An investigation that was closed? As much as she wanted to look into the folder now, there wasn't time.

Instead, she murmured, "It was a terrible tragedy. Are you ready to head to the East Room?"

If she was disturbed by the abrupt change in subject, Addison didn't show it. "Of course."

"Great. When we get there, you'll stand to the side of the president while he tells everyone how great you are and then he'll welcome you forward to the podium. Your comments are on the teleprompter. Have you used one before?"

"Cindy walked me through it yesterday. Besides, I can wing it if there's a problem."

"Wing it? This is your first chance at a first impression. You're being nominated as the first woman ever to head the court, and you'll wing it? I don't think so."

Addison laughed and, despite herself, Julia was charmed by the sound of it. "Relax. My comments are brief, and I have them memorized. Years of practice doing oral arguments before the court have honed my ability to memorize and speak on my feet. I'll be fine." Her expression became serious. "I assure you that I get how important this moment is, and not just for me."

Julia sighed. "Thanks for shaving a few years off my life. Hopefully, the Senate finds your sense of humor a credit."

Addison leaned close, and Julia could feel her breath on her neck as she whispered in her ear. "I'd be fine if only you did."

Before she could respond, Addison was already out the door, standing at Cindy's desk, waiting to be escorted to the event that would change all their lives. Julia lingered for a moment, savoring the impact not of what was about to happen, but of the memory of Addison, standing close, talking only to her, and conveying the utmost intimacy in the simplest of acts.

Addison barely had time to figure out the configuration of the room before President Garrett shook her hand, congratulated her, and said, "You'll do great." Within moments, he was standing at the podium, extolling her accomplishments, and she waited out the time by studying the audience. Some man she didn't know was seated in the place that had been reserved for Larry Weir, and she did her best not to let his absence affect her mood. In anticipation of seeing him today, she'd called him again yesterday, but like every other time she'd tried to reach him in the past few weeks, she'd had to leave a message. Was it possible he was angry with her? True, she thought his theory about his father's death was farfetched, but she had at least tried to get a copy of the accident report. Roger's efforts in that regard had been stonewalled with excuses about family privacy issues. She should suggest that Larry request a copy of the report himself to allay his suspicions.

She vowed that when the dust settled from her nomination, she would find him and do whatever she could to settle his mind about his father's death.

Her own father was seated in the front row, next to the stranger who'd taken Larry's place. Dad looked proud. A relief. Of course, it wasn't every day your daughter was poised to become the next Supreme Court justice, even if you didn't agree with her politics.

Within moments, the president stepped aside and she took center stage. The teleprompter was a blur, so she relied on her instincts and recited her speech from memory. Thanking the president, her family, her school, and her mentor, Justice Weir, she kept her comments brief.

When she finished, the crowd erupted in applause, followed by the shouted questions of reporters. After she'd answered a few questions from the major news outlets, the president escorted her out of the room, while the White House press secretary took the podium to field additional questions. As they left, she heard someone ask if she had children. The sensation of having that many people curious about her life, personal and private, was a bit disturbing.

As if he could read her mind, the president said, "You'll get used to it."

"I doubt that."

"At least once you're on the court, you'll never have to go through this again. Imagine having to run for reelection every few years."

"I guess you'll never have to worry about it again either, sir."

He laughed. "I've got the next four years for them to poke and prod at me before I can stop worrying about my privacy."

"With all due respect, you could have selected someone less of a lightning rod. Someone more like Landry. Might've made the ride a little easier."

"True. There are lots of people who say that I don't have a mandate, that I shouldn't overstep my bounds. I almost believed them and, no disrespect to Landry, that's why he made the cut in the first place. But you're going to be the next chief justice, and I couldn't be more proud to be the guy who appointed the first woman to the spot."

A man Addison assumed was a Secret Service agent touched the president on the arm and whispered in his ear. He shook her hand and walked off. She watched him leave, wondering about his change of heart from Landry to her.

"That went well."

Addison turned to see Julia standing directly behind her. "I didn't faint or slur my words. How was the press conference?"

"Diane has them all under control. She's probably showing them pictures from your first birthday party right now."

"Lovely."

"Seriously, the press will be writing about you constantly during this process. First, you're a woman. Second, you were like a daughter to Weir. Those things combined would be enough to gin a dozen human interest stories, but then add in that your brother is Special Forces and your dad's a vet. You're like a goldmine."

"And to think you didn't want me."

Julia raised her eyebrows, and Addison could feel the blush rise up her cheeks. "You know what I mean. Didn't want me to be the president's choice."

"It's my job to take what I'm given and win with it."

"I get it. It's all business. So, what's a win in this situation?"

"A smooth confirmation. No surprises. Step one is the reception. Several senators from the Judiciary Committee will be on hand. Shall we go schmooze? Surely, as dean you've had to do your share of schmoozing."

"I can schmooze with the best." As Addison spoke the words, she remembered the abrupt ending to her drinks with Jeff Burrows. Would he be here for the reception? Doubtful, but should she mention their meeting to Julia just in case? She hesitated for a moment and then decided on full disclosure. "I should mention that I had drinks with Senator Burrows night before last."

"Really?"

Julia at once assumed a defensive posture, and Addison responded in kind. "He's not big on me being nominated, but I assume you expected that."

"Actually, I'd hoped that because you are friends, we might have expected a gentlemanly agreement not to protest too much."

"You may have overestimated our friendship. We're acquainted, but we haven't kept in close touch since we clerked for Justice Weir."

"You seemed very friendly at the funeral and the reception."

"I suppose absence makes the heart grow fonder. Trust me, he's completely over it." Addison wished she'd never broached the subject and that wish led her to keep quiet about the threatening tone of her conversation with Jeff. She'd enjoy the celebration of this day before she had to face her detractors in the harsh environment of a Senate hearing room. "I'm sure you'll win him over. Isn't that part of your job?"

A flash of something, disappointment maybe, crossed Julia's face before she replied. "You bet. Now, let's go. I'm sure your dad's wondering where we've spirited you away to."

The reception was a blur. Addison had attended plenty of White House events, and they were always a production, but she'd never been the center of attention. Everyone, even steadfast conservatives angled to get close to her as if their proximity would make them part of history. Julia, apparently deciding she could handle herself, left her side and started working the rest of the room. At one point, Addison spotted her father, likely one of the staunchest conservatives in the room, bending the ear of President Garrett. She considered saving the leader of the free world, but that might mean she'd be the one stuck hearing her father's latest theories on the war or the economy. No, the most powerful man in the world could take care of himself.

"You handled the press like a pro."

Addison turned at the sound of the familiar voice. Connie Armstrong stood behind her with a whiskey and an entourage. "Thank you, Senator, but I think Diane did all the heavy lifting. I'm saving myself for your committee."

"You'll be fine. We'll have you over for interviews before we start the hearings, but I expect a quick yay vote."

"I think you're going to get a lot of pushback from Senator Burrows."

Connie shook her head. "Don't you worry about Burrows. He likes to throw his weight around, but he's only been the minority chair for a few months. He'll learn his place." She took a healthy drink and added, "Don't you worry about a thing. You'll be on the court quick as you please. I'll take care of that. After all, we need you. We have a lot of important cases coming up."

Addison glanced around and then gave a silent thanks that no one else was in earshot. "Senator, you know I won't comment on pending cases on which I might be expected to eventually give a ruling."

Connie leaned in. "Save it for the hearing, Addison. You don't need to play the part for me. I get it. Would you like another drink?"

The abrupt change in subject made Addison's head spin, but she recovered enough to shake her head before Connie waltzed off to the nearest bartender, leaving Addison alone for the first time since the reception had started. She stared at Connie, trying to process her words. Did she really think she was buying a vote on the court with her support?

Connie seemed oblivious to her observation. She got her drink and then moved on to monopolize the conversation happening between a couple other senators. Addison looked around the room and found her father, who was now talking to one of the president's aides. She should save the poor aide. She started walking toward them, but stopped when she felt a tug on her arm.

"You look a little bewildered. Everything okay?" Julia asked.

Peeved that she'd let her agitation show, she smiled. "No, not at all. Anyone else I should talk to?"

"I think you've worked the room sufficiently. You should get some rest. We'll start up in the morning with prep for the interviews next week. Senator Armstrong has assured me she's going to fast-track the hearings, but everyone's going to want a chance to talk to you one-on-one before they get started."

Back to business again. "Understood. What time should I be here?"

"Let's start at ten. I'm not much of a morning person."

"Thank goodness." She glanced around. "I guess I should find my father."

"I think he's taken over the West Wing. Going to clean out the place."

"He's a bit much, I know."

"He's fine. Gives you broad appeal to have a soldier brother and a conservative dad."

"Glad I could use my family for something."

"Too bad your mother couldn't be here or you'd have the perfect pedigree."

Addison looked away to hide the tears she could feel forming.

"I'm sorry. That was a jerk thing to say. I only meant…"

"It's okay. I know what you meant. She was a great woman and she would've loved this."

"I'm sure she would've been beyond proud, but I'm sure your father is proud too."

"In his way."

"Hey, would you like to have dinner? I mean, we could talk about the senators on the committee, get an early start on prep…"

Julia's voice trailed off, and Addison sensed she was sorry she'd asked the question. Well, she'd give her an easy out. "Thanks, but Dad's staying the night and I promised him the thickest steak east of Dallas."

"Of course. Of course. Enjoy your evening. See you in the morning."

Julia started to leave, but Addison touched her shoulder. "Wait." Looking into Julia's expectant eyes, Addison lost her words. She'd stopped her from leaving without any plan as to what she would say if she stayed. A few beats of silence passed before she recovered and said, "Why don't you join me? Us. For dinner. Dad would love it."

Julia's grin was infectious. "Well, if Dad would love it, I can hardly say no. I'll pick you up at seven."

She turned and was gone before Addison could reply. She watched Julia cross the room and strike up a conversation with a young woman she didn't recognize. They stood close and engaged in whispered conversation, heads together, like conspirators. Or something more.

A moment later, the woman Julia had been speaking to crossed the room and said, "Ms. Scott asked me to help you and your father find your way out whenever you are ready to go. I'm Violet, an intern."

Her jealousy had been wasted. Feeling silly, Addison nodded to Violet, even as she scanned the room. Julia was gone and she couldn't wait to see her again.

She turned back to Violet. "I think we're ready to go now." No sense pretending there was anyone else she wanted to see as much as the woman who'd just left the room.

CHAPTER TWENTY-TWO

Julia pushed her plate away and leaned back in her seat. "I can't eat another bite."

"Me neither." Addison turned to her father. "Dad, how about you? The desserts here are amazing."

As if on cue, the waiter appeared, dessert and after-drink menus in hand.

John Riley tossed his napkin on the table. "Not me. I'm stuffed and too damn tired to shove another bite of food in my mouth." He turned to Julia. "Can I trust you to make sure my daughter gets home? I think I'm going to call it an early night."

Julia shot a look at Addison. Would she leave with her father or stay behind? She knew what she wanted her to do, but Addison's furrowed brow said she was undecided. In an effort to tip the scales, she said, "I do have a few more items to go over with her, and I promise I'll take good care of her. Let me get my driver to give you a lift."

John stood. "Not a chance. I need to stretch my legs." He shook her hand and then leaned over and kissed Addison on the cheek. "Enjoy the rest of your evening." Seconds later, he was out of sight.

"Well, I guess no one wanted to know how I felt about being left behind," Addison said.

"Did you want to go with him?"

"And spend another few hours listening to him talk about politics? I've had all I can take for a while." Addison shook her head and then looked at Julia, her eyes wide. "Wait, please tell me you don't plan to spend the rest of the evening discussing the confirmation process. Do you?"

Julia drummed her fingers on the table and drew out her words to keep Addison in suspense. "I guess we could find something else to talk about. After all, we're going to spend the next few weeks talking about nothing but the hearings. Did you have something particular in mind?"

"How about I buy you a glass of that scotch you like to celebrate with, and we take it from there?"

Julia raised an imaginary glass to toast the proposition, but before she could say anything else, she was interrupted by a voice over her shoulder.

"Dean Riley, Emily Pierson, from the *Post*. I waited until I saw you were done with dinner, but I wondered if I might have five minutes to ask you a couple of questions."

Addison opened her mouth to answer, but Julia beat her to it. "Dean Riley is not giving any interviews this evening. You should have your paper's White House correspondent contact the press office if you'd like an interview. They will be happy to make the arrangements." At the last word, she turned her back on the reporter, willing her to vanish.

She hovered a moment longer, but then slunk away in defeat. When she was gone, Addison leaned over and whispered, "Think you might have been a little hard on her?"

Julia smiled at her naiveté. "You have no idea how many alleged reporters are going to crawl out of the woodwork in the next month. They will all want a piece of you or to tear you into pieces. The gay rags will want you to be their poster girl, and the conservative pundits will serve you as the main course for the mid-term elections. That kid is a blogger. She doesn't have White House credentials, and she never will because all she ever does is write subjective pieces with little to no fact-checking. The White House correspondent for the *Post* probably doesn't even know her name. Trust me, by the time this is over, you will wish I'd been harder on these leeches."

"I got some press attention when I was appointed solicitor general. I think I handled myself pretty well."

"From Beltway insiders, right? And mostly because you were a novelty since you were so young. Most Americans don't know what a solicitor general is or even that there is such a thing. This is a whole new game. You're bright, you're beautiful, and you're up for a lifetime appointment to the highest seat in the highest court in the land. You're going to attract a ton of attention, and part of my job is to keep things on track until you're confirmed. Talking to two-bit reporters on the fly is out of the question." She finished her speech and took a drink of water. Addison was staring at her with an unreadable expression on her face. "What?"

"Beautiful, huh?"

Julia grinned. "Absolutely." For a moment, she wanted to believe she was here with Addison for no reason other than to enjoy the evening. Enjoy each other. They'd order after-dinner drinks and linger over them while talking about whatever people who went on dates talked about. She'd have to work on that part, but she was willing. More than willing—she wanted to.

But they weren't on a date, and their every move was likely being watched by D.C. gossips and local reporters. She glanced around. For all she knew the waiter had accepted a bribe to relay the details of their conversation to the highest bidder. She should say good night to Addison and they should go their separate ways. Tomorrow, they could start fresh, as colleagues working toward a single goal.

And then she had a better idea. "What do you say we share that celebratory drink somewhere more private?"

Addison's grin lit the room. "Great idea."

Before she could change her mind, Julia flagged down the waiter.

"Did you change your mind about dessert?" he asked.

Forcing back a smile at the double entendre, she asked for the check.

The waiter shook his head. "The gentleman who was with you paid the bill."

Julia looked at Addison who shrugged. "He's old-fashioned like that."

"Then I guess I better take good care of you, like I promised. Wouldn't want him to be waiting at the door with a shotgun when I finally bring you home."

With the subtlest of motions, Addison slid a hand onto her knee. "I'm a big girl. I can stay out as late as I want. Shall we go?"

Warmth flooded Julia. Could Addison see the blush rise in her cheeks? Did she care?

She should. She was about to take Addison back to her house, pour her drinks, and see where that led. Warning bells clanged loudly in her head. She's a candidate, a client, a…

No matter where her thoughts led, she kept coming back to one thing. Addison was a beautiful woman who sent sexual signals only an idiot couldn't read. Julia knew what should happen. They should say good night. Go their separate ways. Let hours of sleep and space get between them so they could focus on the job ahead.

Knowing what she should do did nothing to stop the cascade of anticipation that came with what she wanted to do. If she didn't take Addison home, see where things led, she wouldn't sleep. And hours of separation would only make her want her more. Willing her internal voices to shut up, Julia stood and accepted Addison's invitation. "Let's go."

Julia's home looked exactly the same as it had the last time she'd been here. Not a thing out of place, not a speck of dust, no shoes by the front door, no coats hanging over the back of chairs. Addison followed Julia to the kitchen, noting that it too looked pristine. "Do you actually live here?"

Julia, head in the fridge, looked over her shoulder with a puzzled expression. "What?"

Addison wiped a finger along the counter. "You're either a huge neat freak, which scares me a little, or this is really a model home that you bring…" She let the words trail away, not ready to name the reason she was here, in Julia's house, so late in the evening.

Julia emerged from the fridge with a bottle in her hand and a grin on her face. "I'm not a neat freak, but my housekeeper is. I'm a little scared of her to tell the truth." She pointed at the bottle. "I have one last bottle of Dom. Are you game?"

Addison reached for the bottle, eager to do something with her hands. As she worked the champagne cork, Julia leaned against the counter, appearing to ponder something.

"The idea of having a place just to bring women home to, isn't a bad one though," Julia said. "I'm just not sure I have the energy to keep up those kind of appearances. When I'm in town for long periods of time, you're likely to find socks on the floor and dirty dishes in the sink. I'm kind of a slob."

"I doubt that." Addison handed her a glass. "So, do you have much need for such a place?"

"Place?"

"You know, to bring women home to?"

"Are you asking me if I bring women home with me on a regular basis?" Julia scrunched her brow as if she were giving the matter some thought, while a slight smile played around the edges of her lips. "Well, if you must know—"

At that very moment, the cork shot across the kitchen with a loud pop. Addison set the foaming bottle on the countertop and threw her hands in the air. "Damn, that was loud. I'm sorry. I'm usually not such a klutz, and I promise this is not the first bottle of champagne I've opened." Julia stepped to her side, so close she could almost feel her. The idea that she could lean just slightly to the left and be in her space sent a flush through her. She rambled to stave the heat. "Guess it's a good thing sommelier is not one of the skills required for the Supreme Court. Tell me where I can find a towel and I'll—"

Her long speech was halted by the hard press of Julia's lips against hers. Julia's soft, yet firm touch was exactly as she remembered from their first, their only, kiss. She parted her lips and enjoyed the rush of heat that flooded her body at the expectation Julia would move deeper, but when she did, her knees buckled from the intensity as their tongues touched. When Julia pulled back, Addison was certain her life had changed.

"Do you need to sit down?" Julia asked.

"I have lots of needs right now, but that's not on the list." She leaned against the counter. "You are an amazing kisser."

Julia poured them each a glass of the now settled champagne and raised her glass in a toast. "To amazing kissers."

She bowed and Addison felt the warm glow of a blush. Or maybe it was just the heat from being so close to this amazingly attractive and charismatic woman.

"Oh, and I was saying before you decided to spray bubbly all over my kitchen, I've never brought another woman here."

"Here?" Addison was certain her ability to hear was impaired by the fact all of her senses were focused on the thrum of arousal beating just below her skin. All she could think about was Julia's lips and her hands, touching, taking.

"Here in my house." Julia paused and then said, "You're the first woman I've ever asked here."

Addison shook away the haze, conscious that Julia had just made a big admission, one that deserved more than a hazy nod. She pulled Julia closer and raised her glass. "Then let's toast to first times."

They clinked glasses and then set them on the counter. An awkward moment of silence followed, as if neither of them was able to decide on the next move. Addison spoke first. "Are you glad you asked me here?"

"Of course."

"What would your boss say?"

"I work for myself."

"You know what I mean."

"I have no doubt he would approve in my choice of a date." Julia took a long swallow of her champagne. "In the abstract, anyway."

"No sleeping with the candidates?" Julia's face darkened, and Addison regretted her words. "Sorry, I suppose your professionalism is not really my concern. You don't work for me, and I have to tell you that right now I'm so attracted to you, I'm not sure I would care if you were a Republican." She smiled to add some levity, hoping Julia's lighthearted mood would return.

Julia shook her head. "No, I'm the one who's sorry. It's nothing you said. Well, it is, but it's not your fault. I have a bit of a reputation that I've spent a long time running from. What you said about sleeping with candidates hit a little close to home."

Addison motioned to the kitchen table. "This sounds like a conversation to be had while sitting."

Julia's expression was pained. "I'm not certain I want to have this conversation with you at all."

She'd thrown up a barrier, and Addison had two choices. Break it down or walk away, because she knew that after months with Eva and her self-imposed boundaries, she couldn't be with a woman who put obstacles in their path. She stared at Julia, who, for the first time since they'd met seemed vulnerable, hesitant. As much as she was attracted to the super confident, headstrong version, she found herself strangely drawn to this side of Julia, and she wasn't about to let anything get in the way.

"Well, let's see," she said. "If you don't already, I imagine in the next few weeks you will know absolutely everything about me from my favorite food to the details of my first short and silly relationship in college. And not only will you know, but your staff, the president, the president's chief of staff, and at least a handful of senators will have a full file of my exploits, good and bad, at their disposal."

"I sincerely doubt you've ever done anything that you're ashamed of."

Addison heard the fear in Julia's voice, the trepidation, and she reached out a hand and waited until she had her full attention before saying, "Everyone makes mistakes."

"My job doesn't allow for them."

"No, what you mean is that because everything you do is in the public eye, your mistakes are magnified. That doesn't mean they are really bigger, just means they feel bigger."

"Are you always this rational?"

"Yes." In response to Julia's widened eyes, Addison grinned. "Okay, no, not always. But here's the deal. You've already admitted you have a bit of a reputation, which means whatever's keeping you on guard, is already available for public consumption. Telling me isn't going to make it more real. In fact, owning it, right here, right now, might remove some of the sting. Now that you've gotten me curious, don't you think I could find out anyway?"

"Spoken like a true lawyer."

"Takes one to know one."

Julia put her hands in the air. "Touché, counselor."

"Ah, now we've moved to pet names. Don't think you're going to charm me off the subject." Addison squeezed Julia's hand, hoping she felt the strength she was sending her way. Whatever it was Julia had to share, she needed to get it off her chest. And once she had, maybe they could explore whatever was happening between them.

❖

Dredging up the past had not been on Julia's list of planned activities for the evening. Then again, none of this had been planned. From Addison's impromptu invitation for her to join her and her father for dinner, to John Riley leaving them alone at the restaurant, to inviting Addison back to her house.

No, if she were going to plan an evening with Addison, she would have put a lot more thought into it, which was a deep departure from her usual ways, but it would definitely not have included sharing her biggest personal and professional failure.

"It wasn't a candidate." She blurted out the words and waited to see if they met a soft landing. Addison nodded and took a drink of her champagne. The neutral reaction spurred her on. "And the sleeping with part, well, that was just one, albeit humiliating, piece of the puzzle."

Addison sat forward on her chair, their knees now almost touching. Attentive, close, but not smothering. Julia kept talking. "I always wanted to work in politics. Dreamed about it from my very first debate in junior high. I was a congressional page in high school, and I interned every summer of college and law school with various representatives. When I graduated, I started working in legislative affairs, reporting directly to the Speaker of the House. I never wanted to be a politician, but I loved being at the heart of lawmaking, and I was really, really good at what I did."

"I'm sure you were."

Addison's words were delivered in an even tone. Easy, light, encouraging. Julia pressed on. "Didn't take long before I was brokering big deals between parties and with the White House. I had all the power players on speed dial, and they always took my calls. That kind of influence makes you feel like you're on top of the world."

Antsy now, she stood and walked across the room. "Do you want some water? I'm thirsty. Are you?"

Addison stayed seated and called out. "Water would be great."

The whoosh of cold air cooled Julia's flushed skin. The anticipation of relaying this embarrassing tale was taking its toll. She should rush the telling instead of dragging it out, but measuring

Addison's reactions at each point of the story seemed more important than her own comfort. She pulled two bottles of water out of the fridge and returned to her seat, ready to unveil the first big piece. "You know Kate Bramwell?"

"I know who she is. Everyone knows who she is. A Republican, really?"

Despite Addison's teasing tone, Julia felt the warmth of a blush crawl up her neck. The powerful former deputy chief of staff for the late President Erickson was a familiar name to anyone inside the Beltway. She had run the Republican president's legislative agenda with an iron hand, and now she hosted a pundit talk show on Fox News.

"I know. I can't really explain it other than to say there's something to that whole opposites attract theory. I was sleeping with her when I worked for the Speaker. Wait, that makes it sound like it was just sex. To me, it was more. We weren't living together, but we spent every bit of what little free time we had together. Mostly at her place, mostly naked, but it felt like we had a connection. One that would last beyond who we were in the eyes of everyone else."

"It must've been hard to have a relationship in a fishbowl, especially being on different sides of every major issue."

"We tried to be discreet, but people knew. We were determined not to let it get in the way of our work or vice versa."

"But it did."

"Yes, and it was my fault." Julia found something interesting to stare at in the bottom of her champagne flute while she told the rest of the story. "The Speaker was pushing an expansive gun control initiative. It was going to be the crowning jewel of his career, and for once, it seemed like we had the votes to carry it through both in the House and the Senate. It was going to be tight, and I was working with the Whip to make sure we hung on to every pledged yea vote on our side. Late night meetings, phone calls, whatever it took to keep the majority in line, especially our members in the Deep South, where the NRA lobby is strongest, and they had the most to lose by staying strong.

"I could barely spare a moment away from the office, and when I did, I was constantly on the computer or on the phone, helping whip the vote. The day before the measure was to go to the full floor, Kate called to pick a fight with me about how I'd let work interfere with what little time we had together. It took me by surprise."

"I imagine she worked long hours too."

"More than me, most of the time. But I had neglected her. I couldn't not work the night before the big vote, but she offered to make me dinner if I would agree to work from her place." Julia looked up from her glass, willing Addison to read her mind for the next part so she wouldn't have to say the words out loud.

"I remember that bill. The entire Southern Democratic delegation defected. It died on the floor, and the Senate never took it up."

"Yes. The White House made sure of it. Every one of those reps was either threatened with a challenger in the primary or bribed with some pork barrel initiative. I guess you know how they discovered which weaknesses to exploit."

"Julia, surely you don't blame yourself? If those House members had vulnerabilities, they weren't secret."

Addison reached out to touch her, but she drew back. "She made the calls herself. She waited until I fell asleep, went through my computer, read my notes, and then one-by-one, with threats and bribes, she took apart the coalition I'd built. I know where she got her information because the punishments and rewards were tailor-made.

"I was fired the next week. No one would hire me after that. Took a few years for me to get any solid work, and I had to open my own business to make that happen."

"Wow. Really?"

"I had a job and I failed. My work's a zero-sum game. You either win or you're out. Kate advanced her career by exploiting our relationship, and I got all the blame for letting what I had with her get in the way of my job. I should've known that whatever we had was second to who we were."

This time when Addison reached out, she didn't have the energy to resist. Her arms were strong and held her tight. She murmured comfort. "What you do for a living isn't who you are. You are so much more than that."

"You don't know me well enough to know that."

Addison leaned back and titled Julia's chin up so they were eye to eye. Her smile was indulgent. "It's a universal truth, but if you're going to be stubborn, then let me get to know you." She ran a finger along Julia's cheek, her touch soft, inviting. "I promise I'm right. You want to know how I know?"

Julia stared deep into Addison's eyes, knowing that right now she was too entranced not to believe anything she had to say. She nodded.

"Because I may be a Supreme Court nominee, but right now, all I can think about is how attracted I am to you—mind and body. I'm not entirely sure you couldn't talk me out of the job if I had to choose between it and the chance of getting to know you better."

"Yeah, right." Julia couldn't let herself believe Addison might be distracted from what would be the pinnacle achievement of any lawyer's career, let alone that she was the possible other choice.

"Trust me, it would be a hard choice."

Julia wasn't sure what to do with Addison's revelation. She knew what she wanted to do and she knew what she should do, but Addison stood in front of her, smart, beautiful, funny, and sexy. A tangible reminder of the type of relationship she'd given up to guard her success. Since Kate, she'd assumed that personal and professional choices were mutually exclusive. Did they have to be? Did she want them to be?

Deep in her heart, she knew the answer. She took a deep breath and made the choice to risk everything.

"What if you didn't have to choose?"

CHAPTER TWENTY-THREE

Addison answered with her lips, but no words. The earlier kiss had been eager, insistent, but this time, she relaxed and enjoyed the taste of Julia, knowing there would be plenty of time to savor her soft lips, her playful tongue, and the surges of arousal pulsing through her every time they touched.

Only the need to breathe broke their connection. Gasping, Addison used the moment to ask, "Bed?"

"Upstairs."

Julia grabbed her hand and led her out of the kitchen, down a short hall, to a staircase. They paused at the landing and kissed again. Fused at the lips, Addison began unbuttoning Julia's shirt, eager to touch her skin, dying to know if the heat burning inside her was reflected in Julia's body. The buttons were tiny, stubborn gatekeepers, and Julia reached down to help, tearing through them with one hand while her other hand reached under Addison's sweater, circling her waist.

Addison groaned in anticipation as Julia tugged her sweater over her head and tossed it onto the floor. Next thing she knew, Julia dipped her head as she arched into Julia's embrace. She ran her hands through Julia's thick, soft hair. "You feel incredible. I want you. All of you."

Julia raised her head, and her grin was hazy with lust. "That's the plan. Think you can make it the rest of the way up the stairs?"

Addison nodded and followed her lead, almost running into Julia when she stopped short in the doorway of a room at the top of the stairs. Julia turned to face her, a strange look on her face.

"What is it? Change your mind?"

"Um, no. It's just I wasn't expecting guests."

Addison leaned around her, peering into the room. "Ah ha. The true Julia Scott, finally revealed. Is that a sweater hanging over the back of that chair? And, no, it can't be possible, but I think your bed might be unmade."

Julia shuffled in place. Addison could tell she was embarrassed, but she looked adorable and sweet, nothing like the vixen who'd nearly taken her on the staircase. Hoping to coax her sexy mood back, she pulled Julia close and whispered in her ear, "I'm so hot for you right now, I wouldn't care if all you had was a mattress on the floor and empty pizza boxes lining every surface. An unmade bed only saves us time." She traced her tongue along the edge of Julia's ear. "Do you want me?"

"Badly." The word was drawn out with a slow, jagged breath.

"Then take me. Please." Her words weren't a plea, they were a command, and they set Julia into action. She undressed, slowly, ducking out of range, every time Addison reached to touch her. When she was completely naked, Addison sagged at the knees. Flat stomach, full hips, and long, long legs. She was breathtaking.

Julia stepped closer and left a trail of kisses along Addison's neck as she removed her clothes. As each piece fell away, Addison teased back, desperate to taste and touch every inch of this beautiful woman. When Julia was finally naked, Addison pulled her closer, sparks flying as their skin touched. "How about that bed?"

Julia tugged her toward it, leaning back when she reached the edge, pulling Addison along with her. Addison nestled a thigh between Julia's legs and bent to caress her full, beautiful breasts. Heady with lust, she licked and nipped as Julia rose off the bed to meet her hungry lips and tongue. She could have stayed locked against her chest forever, but the heat and wet against her leg signaled Julia's growing arousal, and she didn't want to miss a moment of the impending climax. She flicked her tongue along Julia's abdomen, kissing her way to the tangle of red curls, glistening with anticipation.

She swirled her tongue around Julia's folds, savoring how she bucked with need at each pass. Raising her head, she asked, "Tell me what you want."

Julia groaned, writhing. "Lick me, fuck me. Whatever you want. Anything you want. Any way you want. Please touch me. Don't stop."

Addison smiled at the string of comments each punctuated with a heavy breath. This was nothing like the sameness of sex with Eva. After one wild night, they'd settled into a couple of favorite positions that always worked. There was a lot to be said for a guaranteed orgasm, but excitement fast became a forgotten feature of their time together. In this moment, she couldn't remember ever being so aroused, ever being so excited about devouring every inch of another woman. No limits, no boundaries.

"I have no intention of stopping." She stroked Julia's inner thigh, delighting at the shiver that met her touch. "I just hope you can handle everything I have to give."

Julia barely heard the words before Addison's tongue flattened against her clit and removed her ability to speak, think, reason. She grabbed the pillow above her head and held on tight as she arched into Addison's mouth, the tender heat of her lips and tongue lifting her up onto waves of pleasure. As each wave receded, she barely had time to catch her breath before the cascade began again. And then pressure, glorious pressure, as Addison entered her, fingers pulsing as her tongue stroked her into stiff pleasure.

"Oh, God, I'm coming. Don't stop."

Addison's answer came in powerful thrusts and teasing kisses, and the waves grew higher and higher until Julia began bucking out of control. Addison stayed with her, her tongue and fingers drawing out every ounce of the most powerful orgasm Julia had ever experienced in her life.

Spent, Julia finally let go of the pillow and reached down to touch Addison, who lay still between her legs. "Hey, you."

Addison lifted her head and gently kissed Julia's still quivering clit. Julia twitched.

"Seems like you might not be done."

Julia managed, somehow, to lift herself on one arm. "Done? No, I'm not done, but if you touch me again right now I think I might burst into flames. That was...you are amazing."

"Good orgasm?"

"Fantastic orgasm." Julia closed her eyes. "Best ever." She sighed, and when she looked again, she saw a grinning Addison. "You look pretty proud of yourself."

Addison pointed at her chest. "Who me?"

Julia tossed a pillow at Addison's head. "Yes, you."

"Okay, maybe a little bit. Nice to know I'm qualified for other things besides being a judge."

"Don't even think about showing any senators your special skills." Julia reached down and tugged at Addison's hand. "Come up here with me. Please."

Addison slid along her body until she lay in the crook of her arm. "Mmmm. I was perfectly prepared, and happy about it, to spend the rest of my days between your legs, but…" She nuzzled into Julia's neck. "This is nice too."

Julia turned and caught her lips in a kiss. A moment ago, she thought she was completely spent, couldn't imagine how she would ever move again, but the musky scent of Addison's arousal sent adrenaline through her veins. She rolled over onto her side and took one of Addison's small, firm breasts into her mouth, trailing the pebbled edges of her nipple with her lips and grazing it to a stiff point with her teeth.

Addison's breath quickened, and Julia reached for her other breast, teasing it to a hard point with her fingers. Addison's eager response made her quicken her pace. She drew closer and traded tongue for hand on each breast until Addison rocked beneath her. She didn't have to reach down to know Addison was dripping wet, but she had to feel it, had to revel in it. She slid down between Addison's legs, enjoying the slick trail of arousal she left behind, and slowly licked inside one thigh and then the other, enjoying the sharp thrusts against her touch.

She'd always cared about making her lovers happy, even though for years, she'd barely known anything about them except how they looked naked and willing. But this was different. Addison was different. Brilliant, engaging, kind. She wanted to know Addison, please her in ways she may have only dreamed about. Addison was the kind of woman people aspired to be. The kind of woman people pledged forever to.

The idea stopped Julia cold. She wasn't a forever kind of person. Nothing was forever. Things were always changing, and that was a good thing. Change meant variety. Change made life interesting. Just like candidates who moved in and out of public office. You worked at something, you enjoyed something until it wasn't right anymore, wasn't working out. Every lover since Kate had been a temporary indulgence, someone to enjoy until the pleasure faded, and Julia had accepted, embraced even, the inevitability of change.

"Julia? Is everything okay?"

Addison's voice was edged with concern, but also raspy with want. For now, anyway. But everything would change, and she wouldn't always want her. Addison would get her seat on the bench and she would be one of the most powerful women in the country, busy with the law, busy with a new crowd of D.C. elite. Julia would choose from one of the many candidates who were begging for her help, and she'd be back on the road, working her magic. Everything would change, but right now...right now, in this moment, she would leave her mark. When this temporary indulgence was over, they'd both have amazing memories of this night, no matter where life led them.

She pulled Addison against her mouth and murmured. "Everything's okay. More than okay." She stroked and thrust the rest of her response with her tongue and her fingers. First gently, then with increasing pressure as Addison answered with bucking hips and loud moans of pleasure. As Addison thundered into orgasm, Julia did something she hadn't done in years. She cradled her lover in her arms, kissed her hair, and promised more. At least for tonight, she could deliver on the promise.

CHAPTER TWENTY-FOUR

Julia woke the next morning to sunlight streaming across her face. She reached across the bed, hopeful, but she felt nothing but sheet and pillows. And then she remembered.

Addison had left in the middle of the night to return to her apartment. Her stated reason was that her father was there and she'd promised him a ride to the airport to catch his early morning flight back to Dallas. They both knew that as much as they didn't want to leave the heat of the bed and each other, Addison couldn't be seen leaving her place the next morning, wearing the same clothes she'd had on the night before.

After a prolonged good-bye that involved lots of hands-on and an impromptu orgasm in the kitchen, Julia had called for her driver and arranged for him to take Addison home. She'd made him promise to wind around the city and make sure they weren't followed. She shouldn't have even trusted him, but in a city where gossip could make or break a career, you could either worry everyone was going to sell their story or you could just use your best instincts. Hers were well-honed.

She looked at the clock on her nightstand. Nine a.m. Was Addison on her way back from the airport? Maybe she'd be interested in brunch? Lord knows she'd worked off last night's dinner hours ago.

Julia reached for her phone, but stopped mid-air. Last night had been fun, perfect even, but it was time to get back to work. The Senate would be taking their holiday break soon, and the White House wanted a firm commitment to confirmation by the first of the year. She should check in with the FBI agent heading up the vetting process and making a list of questions to prepare Addison for next week's grilling with the Judiciary Committee. If she spent any time with Addison this weekend, it should be at the office, prepping for the week ahead.

But they'd have to eat, wouldn't they? They could work over brunch. Go to a restaurant where they could spread out their papers on a table and enjoy a nice meal. In public. Where there was little chance of a repeat performance of last night's activity. What had she called it? A temporary indulgence.

Ignoring the nagging internal voice that suggested her characterization might be off, she plucked her phone from the nightstand. She started to pull up Addison's number, but the list of missed calls and voice messages on the screen stopped her cold. Someone from the White House had been trying to reach her since seven that morning. She checked the ringer and then remembered turning it off sometime between the first kiss they'd shared in the kitchen and getting naked in her room. Damn.

She checked the first message and got Noah's caustic voice, telling her to call back right away. By the third message, he didn't try to hide his anger, barking the command for a return call. She scrolled through her contacts and dialed a number that was answered on the first ring.

"Cindy?"

"Yes." She whispered the word.

"You at the office?"

"Um, yeah."

"Is Noah right there?"

"Absolutely."

"Okay. I'm on my way."

She wasn't ready to spoil last night's memory by tangling with an angry Noah, especially not over the phone. She'd show up in person and see what he wanted. Let him know he couldn't push her around. Brunch was out, but there were other meals. Maybe once she got things squared away, she'd call Addison and see where things stood.

When she arrived at the West Wing, she was met in the lobby by a Secret Service agent from the president's detail. She'd planned to go directly to her office upstairs, but he insisted she accompany him. He led her back to Noah's office at a fast clip, the sense of urgency almost palpable. When they arrived, Noah was huddled in his office with Jed Reeves, the deputy director of the FBI, and they both looked up when she entered the room.

"Have a seat," he told her. "Diane will be here in a minute, but we have a situation."

Julia remained standing. "Are you sure you want me here? I'm not big on situations."

"It involves you and your little project."

Julia ignored the edge in his voice. He wasn't going to get over the president giving her another chance and putting her in charge of the confirmation, and she wasn't going to figure out why he cared. It wasn't like if she were out of the picture, he'd be doing it. Hell, he wasn't even a lawyer. All she cared about right now was why she'd been summoned. "What's going on?"

"Larry Weir took a bottle of pills and chased it with a fifth of whiskey. He's dead."

"Holy shit." Julia sank into a chair. "When? Where?"

"His apartment. Not sure when yet, but it's probably been a couple of days."

She ran through a quick timeline in her head. Cindy had talked to him Thursday morning, and he confirmed he would be at the White House for the official announcement about Addison's nomination. According to Cindy, he'd gushed about the president's choice and said he'd be honored to support it. Had Addison heard the news? How would she hold up? She'd described Justice Weir as a father figure. Had Larry been like a brother to her? If so, she'd likely be devastated to learn he'd died so close on the heels of Justice Weir's death.

"That explains why he didn't show up on Friday." She heard Noah's door open and she looked behind her to see Diane Rollins, the White House press secretary enter the room. She didn't wait for Noah to speak and called out, "Diane, have you heard about—"

Noah cut her off with an annoyed expression. "She doesn't know yet." He took a minute to fill Diane in.

She sat on the edge of her chair. "It's going to break soon. I got a question about why he wasn't here for the announcement, but I brushed it off. It was Josh Gander from the *Times*, and if he thinks there's an angle, he's not going to let it go."

"Give me a break," Julia said. "Addison was like family to the Weirs. Would anyone believe Larry didn't show up because he didn't approve of the president's choice? Doesn't his death explain his absence?"

Noah shot her a withering glance, but Jed was the one to answer. "Actually, ma'am, one might reach another conclusion."

"Jed, don't call me ma'am, and I promise I won't call you a jackass, okay?" Julia waited for his reluctant nod before continuing. "What's the other conclusion?"

"Well, it's possible he was unhappy about the president's choice."

"Is that so? Then how come he told my assistant we couldn't have picked a better person for the job?"

"Well, maybe he changed his mind. We have reason to believe he harbored reservations."

"That's pretty vague. Care to elaborate?"

Jed flicked his eyes at Noah before answering. "Not at this time."

Julia waved a hand at Diane. "Help me out here. Can you explain to them that if there's an issue that could cause a shit storm for Addison Riley's nomination, we need to know what it is, and we need to know right now if we're going to have any chance at containing it?"

"She's right. If Larry Weir was against the nomination, we need to get out in front of that, and we need to start right now."

Noah shook his head. "You're going to have to find a way to put Gander off for now. But Larry Weir's suicide is not the only thing that's going to make the news today."

"Big news day for a Saturday."

"That's for sure. How much do you know about Addison's girlfriend?"

Noah's question landed like spikes to her brain. "Girlfriend?"

"Don't act so surprised. Surely your little committee knew about this one." He tossed a picture on the table between them. "She's a looker, that's for sure."

Julia looked down. She knew about this woman, had met her even, but she didn't remember her name. What had she called her? Dark and mysterious. This beauty had been Addison's date the night she'd run into them in the restaurant at Judge Landry's hotel. She vaguely remembered some mention of her in the preliminary background check. A professor at Jefferson, and, except for the night she'd seen them together, she'd never been seen socially with Addison. What had Addison said about her? She implied they weren't serious. She forced calm into her voice. "Do you really think it's a problem that Addison may have dated a professor at her law school?"

"They are colleagues, aren't they?" Noah said. "Grown people can date whoever they want, and if you insist on putting a lesbian forward, there's a better than even chance she's going to be dating a woman. No, that's not the problem. Here's a copy of a report about your pretty little future Supreme Court justice's lady friend that's going to run on Drudge this afternoon. They'd like our comment."

Julia picked up the paper and started reading. As the words blurred on the page, she flashed back to another time when she'd let her personal feelings get in the way of her judgment. How could this be happening again?

Despite his insistence that he would take a cab, Addison drove her father to the airport. It was the least she could do after staying out half the night. He hadn't mentioned anything about it, but she knew years of military training meant he always woke up at the slightest noise.

There wasn't a sound in the car for the first few miles to the airport, neither one of them prepared to say anything about the night before or willing to discuss the many ways that Addison's life was about to change. As they drew within sight of the airport, her father finally spoke. "Guess you'll be too busy to come home for Christmas."

"To tell you the truth, I hadn't even thought about it." She should have. Jack wouldn't be able to come home again so soon, and she didn't have a clue if she could schedule a trip away with the confirmation hearings drawing near. She reached a hand across the console and squeezed his arm. "Maybe you could come back here. They're predicting lots of snow. Come back and have a white Christmas with me."

He smiled and his eyes were full of mischief. "I have a feeling you won't be spending much time at home."

"What's that supposed to mean?"

"I think you know. I'm surprised you can keep your eyes open after getting in at three this morning."

She detected no judgment, only teasing in his voice. "I'm sorry. We had a lot to talk about."

"Addison Riley, you're no teenager and you don't live in my house. You can do what you want with your life, and if you'd rather spend the night with a pretty lady than get a good night's sleep, that's not only a respectable choice, it's none of my business." He paused and his voice cracked a bit when he spoke again. "I only want you to be happy."

Knocked off kilter, Addison wasn't sure how to respond. Before now, these were the kind of talks she would've had with her mom, never her dad. She'd always known he cared about her, but she couldn't remember the last time he'd said so. "I want you to be happy too."

"I'll get there. It's hard, but knowing you two kids are living a life that would do your mother and I proud helps."

"Thanks, Dad. I'll make time over the holidays. The Senate will be shut down." Now at the airport, she pulled over to the skycap and turned to face him. "I'm sure I can escape for a couple of days."

He shrugged. "I'll be fine. I was thinking of visiting your aunt Donna and uncle Charlie. I'm sure they'd love to see you, but if you can't get away, I'll be well taken care of."

Her dad's sister, Donna, and her husband, Charlie, lived in Montana. A nonstop to Dallas might be possible, but traveling to a remote area of Montana for a two-day hop was probably out of the question. "You should definitely go see them. We'll catch up later. No matter what happens, when this is all over, I'll come back out to Dallas and buy you a real Texas-sized steak. Deal?"

"Deal." He reached over, gave her a hug, and said with a gruff voice, "Love you, kid." He grabbed his bag out of the backseat and took off toward the airport doors.

Addison drove off and considered her next move. It was only seven thirty a.m. She really wanted to call Julia, hear her voice and the flood of memories it was sure to bring back, but she couldn't bear the thought of waking her so early.

Her office beckoned. She had a ton of paperwork to clear out before end of the semester, especially since she might not be back for the spring term. Who was she kidding? She knew she wouldn't be back. Even if she didn't get confirmed, she'd go forward with her plan to resign as dean. She'd help out until they found someone to take her place, but she was going back into the classroom, where she could use the talents she had spent a lifetime cultivating, instead of raising money and pushing paper.

When she pulled into the law school parking lot, she was surprised to see several cars already there. Apparently, she wasn't the only one trying to get a jump on semester's end. She parked in her reserved spot and started to head into the building, but stopped when her cell phone rang. Hoping it was Julia, she answered on the first ring without taking time to look at the number on the screen. "Hello?"

"Addison, it's Roger. I saw your car pull up. Are you in the building yet?"

"No." She glanced around. Roger's whispered voice made it seem like something clandestine was about to go down. "What's the matter?"

"A couple of reporters have been by. One was Josh Gander from the *Times*. I just got here a few minutes ago, and they were wandering around. I told them you weren't here, but their cars are still in the lot and they're probably still on campus. I'll meet you at the door and walk you back." He hung up and she stared at the phone, puzzled about too many things. What was Roger doing here on a Saturday morning? And Josh Gander, White House reporter from the *Times*? Saturdays were generally slow news days, and there'd been a ton of articles about her nomination that ran the day before. Why would a big shot reporter like Gander be trolling around, looking for her at her office, early on a Saturday?

She didn't have time to consider it further before Roger cracked open the door and waved her in. When she walked through, he locked it behind her.

"I should've had it locked to begin with, but I never imagined anyone would show up so early."

"Why are you here bright and early on a Saturday?"

"I figure we have a lot of work to do, now that you're headed off to Number One First Street."

Addison laughed at his reference to the famous address of the Supreme Court building. "Don't. You'll jinx it. What did the reporters say?"

"He was vague." Roger held up finger quotes. "Big story, wanted to get your side of it." He shook his head. "I mean, I expected you would get inundated with requests for interviews after yesterday's announcement, but it's Saturday and it's kind of early."

Addison nodded, a nagging feeling beginning to take hold. What exactly did "get her side of it" mean? "I'm going to head back to my office and see if I can plow through at least one pile. Don't bother answering the phone if anyone calls. And let me know when you're ready to take off. I'd appreciate it if we could leave together."

"You got it."

When Addison entered her office, she shut the door, picked up the phone, and dialed. Five rings later, she reached Julia's voice mail. Of course, she was probably still asleep. Addison listened to the sound of Julia's smooth and confident professional voice, but hesitated when the time came to leave a message. She knew Julia would want to know she was being stalked by reporters, but she didn't want the first words she spoke after the intimacy they'd shared the night before to be all about business. She settled on a vague, "Good morning. I can't wait to see you again. And I have something I need to talk to you about. Could you call me as soon as you get this? Thanks."

She hung up, wishing she hadn't sounded like a sixth grader with a new crush. Nothing to be done about it now. Determined to make the most of the time spent waiting to hear back, she dug into her work. When Roger knocked on her door, she looked at the clock, surprised to see it was almost noon. She glanced at her phone, surprised she hadn't heard from Julia yet.

"Come in."

Roger poked his head in, but kept the door pulled to.

She cocked her head. "You ready to head out?" Feeling a little silly for thinking she needed an escort, she made a snap decision to stay now that she was swept up in her work.

"Uh, no, but Professor Monroe is here to see you." He lowered his voice to a whisper. "She doesn't look happy."

Eva. The events of the past few days had been such a whirlwind, she hadn't discussed any of it with Eva, and, after last night, she wasn't at all sure what she would say. *Hey, in case you hadn't heard, the president nominated me to be the chief justice of the United States.*

That woman who came over and talked to us while we were out on the one date in public we've ever had? Well, she's going to walk me through the confirmation. Oh, and we're sleeping together.

Right. Eva would certainly already know about the nomination by now, and Addison wasn't about to say any of the rest. Sometime in the last week, she'd known that she and Eva were over, but she owed her the courtesy of making it official. "It's okay, Roger. Send her in."

Eva swept into the room, arms waving. She didn't wait for the door to close before launching into an interrogation. "What the hell were you thinking? You give my name to a reporter? You tell her we're in a romantic relationship? I've barely seen you in the last week. You think if I were your lover, you would've at least told me that you'd been nominated to the fucking Supreme Court."

Addison had been prepared for angry, but Eva's words didn't make sense. She hadn't talked to a reporter, and she never would've given Eva's name or characterized their relationship as romantic, even if they were still sleeping together. She reached out and touched Eva's arm to try to stop the spiral of emotions. "Hey, let's talk about this." She jerked her head toward the door. "Quietly, okay?"

She motioned to a chair and waited until Eva took a seat. "First of all, I didn't give your name to a reporter. I haven't talked to the press at all besides a few comments at the press conference yesterday, and I can promise you that your name did not come up. And I'm sorry I didn't tell you what was going on. It was all very hush-hush until the official announcement, but you're right. I should've given you a call."

"I sort of understand the not telling me part. I know things have been rocky between us for a while. But the reporter told me she spoke to you last night. She was very specific."

"What was her name?"

Eva pulled a business card from her pocket and handed it over. Addison scanned the card. Emily Pierson, *Washington Post*. She recognized the name, but it took her a moment to place it. The reporter from the restaurant last night. She looked up at Eva. "I saw this woman last night, but I assure you I didn't talk to her. Julia, the woman who is working on my confirmation, sent her packing." Addison justified the half-truth about Julia's role in her life with the very same right to privacy Eva apparently wanted for herself.

Eva sighed. "I'm sorry. I should've known you wouldn't talk to a reporter about me. Besides, her questions were more about me than you. I'm just so upset, I needed to lash out."

"Is the prospect of being linked with me really that upsetting?"

Addison smiled to show she was teasing, but Eva shook her head and said, "You don't understand. A long time ago, when I was young, I experimented with different things. One of them was men. I was in college, drunk, at a party. We had sex. It was fun, but it wasn't for me. Figures that the one and only time I have sex with a man, I got pregnant."

Addison braced for Eva's next words, already sure what she was about to say.

"I had an abortion."

"Which you're legally entitled to do."

"Legally entitled to doesn't grant you immunity from societal judgment. Even those who say it's a woman's right to choose, usually only mean it in the abstract. You know, for rape victims or those poor people who don't have good access to birth control. But I was a trust fund kid, attending an Ivy League school. My parents wouldn't have cared if I'd shown up at spring break, baby on the way. They would've loved it. But I didn't want a baby to interfere with my own dreams."

Addison walked over to Eva's chair and took her in her arms. She wasn't in love with Eva, but she did care about her, as a former lover. As a friend. "I'm so sorry. It's my fault. I should've told you about the nomination. Maybe you would've been more on guard when the reporter showed up. I would never have put you through reliving these memories."

Eva shook her head. "Don't you see? It's not just me. The Right is going to go after you with everything they've got. Your baby-killing girlfriend is just the beginning. You need to contact the White House because they are going to need some serious spin if you're going to get confirmed."

Addison looked at her desk. Julia hadn't returned her call from this morning. Was she really still asleep or was she regretting last night? Either way, it was time to tell her everything about her encounter with Jeff Burrows the night before the president's announcement.

CHAPTER TWENTY-FIVE

The West Wing was buzzing with activity as Addison walked with her escort through the hallways to the chief of staff's office. Her call to Julia hadn't been answered, but Noah Davy had made it very clear Julia would be here today for the meeting for which she'd been summoned.

As they reached the door, her escort slowed. Addison looked her way, but couldn't quite decipher the look on her face. She struggled to remember her name. *Cindy*. Right. "Cindy, is everything okay? There seems to be a lot going on around here for a Saturday."

She looked around before answering, "It's a busy place." Then she ducked her head and said, in a quiet whisper, "Whatever happens in there, know that you are the best possible person they could have picked for the job."

Cindy knocked on the door as she delivered the final words, and once the person inside shouted "be right there," she disappeared down the hall.

The few seconds Addison waited for the door to open were the longest in her life. Why had she been summoned here on a Saturday? Had someone tipped the White House off about the story on Eva? But hadn't Julia said that Emily Pierson was a blogger, not a real reporter? Although nowadays, it didn't appear that the general public drew a distinction between the two. Didn't matter. If the White House was scared of what a blogger might say about the fact a woman she'd once dated had exercised her right to choose, she was prepared to argue the point. She'd practiced her arguments on the way over. You can't support the right only in the abstract. If you want the court to preserve

Roe v. Wade, then you have to stand firm and stop letting states chip away at the law with arbitrary restrictions. Besides, it wasn't like she'd had an abortion herself or even known Eva when she'd had hers.

Engaged in thought, she was startled when Julia opened the door. She looked like she hadn't slept at all the night before, but her eyes didn't have the sleepy haze of the sated, but instead were laced with restless anxiety. She'd wanted to cause the one, but definitely not the other.

"Are you okay?"

Julia shook her head. "It's been a long morning."

"This isn't how I wanted to see you...after..." Addison let the words fall. She read nothing encouraging in Julia's expression, and this was no place for a personal conversation. Maybe they could talk later. Alone. She'd invite her over and they could forget politics for an evening, try to recapture the heady passion of last night.

"Noah's waiting, and there are a few other people here." She shook her head, opened her mouth like she wanted to say more, but then shook her head again.

Addison placed a hand on her arm. "It's okay. We'll talk later."

She followed Julia into the crowded room. *Later.* They'd talk about last night, but it would have to be later. Right now, she was prepared to deal with whatever they were ready to throw her way.

Noah was at his desk. Gordon and Diane were seated in chairs across from him with another man she didn't recognize. Julia stood off to the left, slightly out of her line of sight. Noah stood and the rest followed suit. He motioned for her to take a seat, and once she sat down the others did as well.

"Dean Riley, thank you for responding so quickly. We have a few items we need to discuss with you, and we wanted to do this in person."

He picked up a piece of paper and started to say something else, but Addison raised a hand to stop him. "Excuse me, Mr. Davy, but I haven't been introduced to one of your guests."

Noah looked around the room, his eyes finally settling on the stranger in the room. "Oh, yes. Jed Reeves, Deputy Director FBI."

"I know that being nominated to fill a Supreme Court seat is a big deal, but do you really assign the deputy director to perform my background check?"

Gordon and Diane shifted in their seats, and the room became thick with tension. Noah's eyes narrowed. "Well, now that you mention it, Deputy Director Reeves isn't here about that." He set down the paper in his hand and crossed his fingers. "How well did you know Larry Weir?"

Addison's gut response—that they were like siblings—caught in her throat. "How well did I know him? Why? What's happened to him?" She searched their faces for an answer, saving Julia for last. Surely, if something had happened to Larry, she wouldn't have kept it from her? She could rely on her to clear up this misunderstanding. Couldn't she?

"He's dead. He committed suicide."

Julia's voice was quiet and edged with pain, but Addison took no comfort from that. Larry was dead. He'd come to her, grief-stricken, angry with hurt, and she'd brushed off his concerns. She should have recognized the cry for help. Done more than try to reach him by phone to assuage his worries. She should've known something was wrong yesterday when he didn't show up for the press conference. Yet, instead of worrying about his well-being, she'd been at Julia's house, indulging in pleasures he would never again feel.

"When?"

"They're not sure yet, probably a couple of days."

The knowledge that she couldn't have done anything about it if she'd skipped her celebration wasn't a relief. She still should have reached out to him. Should've done more to fill the void he must have felt after his father's tragic and inexplicable death. Waves of nausea flooded through her, tangible guilt and sorrow. She had to get away, be alone with her grief. "I need a few minutes."

"Dean Riley, I'm sorry about this news, but we have several urgent, important things to cover."

Noah's words sounds light years away, but it didn't matter. Julia crossed the room in long strides and motioned for him to shut up. Addison watched the scene play out as if she were up in the air, above it all. Seconds later, Julia took her by the arm and led her from the room.

❖

"Hey, you're going to be okay. You're going to be okay." Julia hated repeating the useless phrase, but she didn't think Addison was in any shape to process more. Seeing her so visibly shaken was disconcerting, and her own anger and disappointment faded in the face of Addison's distress. At Weir's funeral, she'd been strong, calmly delivering her mentor's eulogy, but now she was broken, and Julia didn't know how to fix it.

She led her into a nearby room and shut the door behind them. Addison slumped into a seat, but Julia paced the room. "I'm sorry you had to find out like that."

"How long?"

Addison's voice was a whisper. "What?"

"How long have you known about Larry? Last night? Did you know last night?"

Julia flashed to the evening before. All she'd known then was how much she craved contact with the now grief-stricken woman seated before her. All she'd known then was that she was likely making a huge professional mistake, but she'd cared more about how good it felt than the consequences. "No, I didn't know last night. I found out this morning."

"And you didn't think I should know? Didn't think you should call me?"

It had been her gut instinct to call Addison the minute she'd learned the news, but she'd ignored it, certain she was letting personal feelings get in the way of doing what was necessary to contain the story. And then there'd been the news about Eva. She'd let her anger get in the way. Or hurt. She hadn't had time to decide which. "There wasn't time. Besides, I found out about Larry around the same time I found out that your girlfriend is about to be outed in the national news as a pro-choice poster girl. Think you might've told me about that?"

The words weren't fair and she knew it, but once she started hurtling down this path, she couldn't seem to stop herself. Besides, she'd be just as tough on any other candidate. Last night had seemed so good, so right, but it had been a huge mistake if it was going to get in the way of doing her job.

Addison stood and walked over to where she was standing, her jaw set and her eyes steely. Sad, grieving Addison was gone.

"Eva Monroe is not my girlfriend. If she had an abortion, a legal abortion, that's her business and no one else's. You might want to check with your boss, but I think the right to privacy is one of the key issues the Senate is going to ask about at the confirmation hearings, and this is exactly the kind of situation that right to privacy is supposed to protect.

"As for Larry, I don't even know where to begin. I told you yesterday that he and I have been in touch, that he was concerned about his father's death. I feel horrible that he took his own life and I didn't catch the signs of his depression in time to stop him. You should have known I would want to know as soon as you did and that I wouldn't want to find out in front of a room full of strangers."

Julia opened her mouth to respond, not at all sure what she would say, but Addison wasn't finished.

"What we shared last night was special to me, but I see now I was wrong to think that intimacy was any part of it. Winning is so important to you that you forget what you're trying to achieve. Well, I'm perfectly clear now on what to expect from you, from this process. Let's go back in there and do whatever needs to be done to make sure you get your win. The sooner I'm on the bench, the sooner you'll be free to move on to the next job."

Addison strode to the door and was through it in a flash. Julia remained rooted to her spot completely confused. She couldn't have asked for a better out. What had she told herself last night? She'd enjoy the temporary indulgence before it was time for them both to move on. Fun without strings attached. It was her way, it was familiar, and it was what she wanted.

Wasn't it?

"Show me what you have about Eva Monroe." Addison injected a hint of challenge in her voice. She wanted everyone in the room to know she wasn't about to take any of this lying down. She'd committed to this path and she was going all the way. If her career went down in flames, she wouldn't be the first person not to survive the confirmation process. Hell, she could probably command top dollar on the speaking circuit as a cautionary tale.

Noah nodded at Gordon and he opened a folder and slid a photo her way. The resolution wasn't great, but it was clear enough to show her and Eva in a restaurant booth. She squinted and then realized she didn't have to work hard to figure out the location since she and Eva had only had one public dinner in D.C. during the whole of their relationship. It was from the night they'd gone to sushi, a couple of weeks ago. But why would someone have been photographing them when she hadn't even been in serious consideration for the court at that time?

"Is this it?"

"There's this one too." Gordon handed over another photograph. Same booth, her and Eva, but this time Julia was in the photo, standing close. That explained the photographer. Julia had been at the restaurant with Judge Landry. The reporter had likely been following Julia and Landry and had snapped these photos out of curiosity. Damn. Eva's privacy would probably still be intact if they hadn't shared that one dinner out.

As she studied the photographs, she heard the door open. Out of the corner of her eye, she saw Julia take a seat. She sighed and handed the photos back to Gordon. "Eva and I are colleagues. Who's to say this isn't a business dinner?"

"Does Professor Monroe wear plunging necklines every time you meet for dinner?"

Diane's question was delivered in a dry tone, but Addison got the point. "I won't deny we were involved, but we aren't anymore, and what Eva did when she was a young college student should have no bearing on my confirmation."

Noah started to speak, but Gordon raised a hand to stop him. "Let me give this a try." He gave her a steely look. "Dean Riley, you'd be more likely to support abortion because your girlfriend had one, isn't that right?" He shook his head. "Now, which part are you going to deny first?"

"I don't have to deny anything. Professor Monroe and all women have a right to privacy. Court precedent is clear on a woman's right to choose, and I have no intention of breaking new ground in this area of the law. As far as specifics, I happen to know there are a number of state cases making their way through the appellate process now and, out of deference to the court's work, I will not comment on pending cases." She leaned back in her chair and waited for the inevitable criticism.

"We're going to have to work on that," Noah said.

"Oh, I don't know," Diane said. "I thought she nailed it. If a woman's right to choose hinges on a constitutional right of privacy, then shouldn't that right of privacy extend to allow her to keep her choice private?"

Gordon chimed in. "Diane's got a point. We can finesse the wording, but the point's the same. She's effectively tossed the question back to them. If you don't like the law, change it, but until then, I'll apply the law that's on the books. If she can handle every question they throw at her in the same manner, she'll do just fine."

Addison watched the exchange, wondering if it was even necessary that she be in the room. Unable to help herself, she glanced over at Julia who seemed to be engrossed in a spot on the wall. Julia would probably rather the president had nominated Sally Gibbons than her at this point. She wasn't sure she didn't agree.

"We need to get back to the subject of Larry Weir. Dean Riley, you think you can handle some tough talk on this subject now?"

Addison faced Noah and nodded.

"It appears Larry may not have supported your nomination. Any idea why?"

She'd been prepared for talk of a memorial service, even gruesome details about his death, but she hadn't been prepared for this. "I don't know what you're talking about. Care to elaborate?"

Noah shot a look at Jed, but Addison couldn't read their expressions. She waited until finally Jed took over the line of questioning. "Larry made a phone call to Josh Gander before he died. He told him he was mailing him a copy of his father's journal and he alluded to a confrontation Justice Weir had with one of his former law clerks before he died. Larry was evasive in the call, but he told Gander he'd have plenty for a story once he read the journal."

Addison's mind wandered to the original of the journal still in her desk at home, but she kept a poker face. "Did Gander get the journal?"

"No, not yet. And our agents haven't found it at either Larry's or Justice Weir's residences."

"And you have some reason to think the former law clerk is me?" Out of the corner of her eye, Addison saw Julia's head snap up, the spot on the wall no longer commanding her attention.

"Is it?" Noah asked.

"No, it isn't, but apparently, before he died, Justice Weir was getting pressure from several people to step down."

"And you know this how?"

"Because I have the journal." Addison braced for their reaction. She didn't have to wait long.

"You realize you could be charged with obstruction of justice?" Jed said.

Addison stood up. "I thought the FBI had better training in the law. I can't be charged with intent to do anything that I did not intend. I have the journal, yes, but I don't have anything to hide. If you want to hear what I have to say, then you'll take your tone down a notch."

Reeves bristled at her reprimand, but Noah made it clear who was in charge. "If you want a seat on the most powerful court in the land, you'll sit down and answer our questions."

She'd had enough. All she wanted to do was leave this office, this place. Go home and grieve. Too many losses. First Justice Weir, then Larry, now this opportunity.

And Julia. If they'd met under any other circumstances, they might have had a chance, but now it was Julia's job to either build her up or take her down, depending on the winds of politics. Too flimsy a foundation for any kind of relationship, and she'd been a fool to think otherwise.

She started to the door, but stopped when she felt Julia's hand on her arm. She looked into her eyes and saw the silent plea. "I'm not the one you're looking for."

"The president chose you."

And it all boiled down to that. Julia stopped her from leaving because it was her job. Not what she wanted, but what she'd been hired to do. Addison may not like it, but she was right. President Garrett had chosen her for the job, and she was qualified. She could walk away, but she'd never shied from a fight, and this opportunity was worth fighting for even if it meant she would lose something she wanted more.

CHAPTER TWENTY-SIX

Julia walked Addison back in the room and waited until they were all back in their seats before taking charge. She addressed her remarks directly to Noah.

"Here's the deal. You may be on the government dole, but I'm the one the president asked to run this process, and unless he says otherwise, I'm taking the lead from here on out." She waited a few seconds to judge his reaction. Silence. "Great. Let's talk about Larry Weir. Addison, tell them what you know."

Addison spoke, looking directly at her and no one else. Her rich brown eyes were sincere and her mouth twitched with sadness. "Larry contacted me after his father's death. He believed it wasn't an accident. That the car wreck was intentional."

Julia listened while Addison relayed the conversation she'd had with Larry when he handed over the journal, but her mind kept wandering to the accident report of Justice Weir's death. She'd had a copy of it in her desk, but she hadn't taken the time to look at it. With a silent apology to Addison for her rudeness, she pulled out her phone and sent a text to Cindy, asking her to bring the file. When Addison finished talking, she said, "Did you find anything in the journal?"

"Nothing nefarious. As I said before, it seemed Justice Weir was getting pressure to consider retiring in the week before his death. He did mention a former law clerk, but it wasn't that specific. Like it could've been just a clerk who worked at the court, not necessarily one of his."

Julia glanced around the room, ready to pounce if anyone challenged Addison. "Do you have any ideas about who it might be?"

"I don't. To be honest, I thought Larry's grief had clouded his judgment. He did say it appeared as though the garage door at Justice Weir's home had been tampered with, but I gather he told the police and they didn't think it meant anything. I even went as far as trying to get a copy of the accident report, but my office was told it wasn't being released out of deference to the family. I planned to tell Larry he should request it himself when I talked to him again, but..."

As Addison's voice cracked, Julia wished everyone would vanish so she could take Addison in her arms, comfort her, tell her everything would be okay. The best she could do under the circumstances, was get some answers. At that moment, she was saved by a knock at the door. Cindy. She took the folder and glanced inside at the D.C. Police Department accident report, remembering Cindy's words when she delivered it to her originally. Yep. It had been heavily redacted, more wide black lines than legible type. She handed the folder to Noah.

"Well, I've got a copy of the accident report, but it's so marked up, it's not remotely helpful. How about you show me your copy and we can get to the bottom of this."

Noah shot a nervous glance around the room. "I don't know what you're talking about."

"Yes, you do. I saw a folder with the report on the president's desk and you had the same folder when you were in my office last week. I'm thinking your copy wasn't full of holes, like mine. Care to tell us why you were interested in the report?"

"I told you."

"You told me some bullshit about road safety. Given what we've been told about Larry's suspicions, I don't believe that was your primary interest."

Noah jerked his chin at Addison and shook his head. "Not everyone in this room has clearance to know what I know."

"Really?" She walked over to his desk and picked up the phone. "Should we call the president? Ask him what was in the report? Because I'm pretty sure if he trusts Addison Riley to head the Supreme Court, he will trust her with this little piece of information." She stood, holding the phone, waiting for him to call her bluff, but she was surprised at who spoke up.

"Julia, I should leave the room. Let you all talk about this. If you do go through with my appointment this could be a source of conflict someday. Separation of powers and all."

"No, please stay. You deserve to know what happened to Justice Weir, and I'm certain the president would agree. What do you say, Noah?"

He held up his hands in defeat. "Fine. I'll tell you, but if anyone outside these doors breathes a word of this, I'll hold every one of you responsible." He turned to Jed. "Tell them what you told me."

"Basically, Justice Weir's vehicle was rigged to explode. It was a very sophisticated mechanism, designed to go off in short bursts which caused him to wreck and his vehicle to roll before the series of blasts ended and the vehicle caught on fire."

Addison sank in her chair, her hand over her face. Julia resisted the urge to go to her. She needed to find out the rest. "How long have you known?"

"It's taken a while to analyze all the evidence from the wreckage."

"Not an answer."

Jed looked at Noah, who tapped his foot and then nodded. "We knew something was up from the witness accounts following the accident. You wouldn't know it unless you examined them all together in close detail, but there were definitely reports of sounds that mimicked an explosion right before Justice Weir lost control of the vehicle. We would have examined the evidence from the scene carefully no matter what, but coupled with the reports, we knew we were looking at something criminal from the get-go."

"Why would someone want to kill him?"

Julia looked over at Addison, who looked as if the one question were all she could manage. She looked back at Jed who looked at Noah before turning back to face her. "We don't know. But this information about the journal could be helpful. Maybe someone really did want him to retire badly enough to arrange for his death. If we knew who was pressuring Weir to retire, that could lead us to the suspect or suspects."

"But I don't understand. Who would benefit from his death so close to a hotly contested presidential election?" Addison asked, seemingly recovered enough from the shock of the news to start weeding through its implications. "If they wanted him to be replaced with a younger version of himself, there's no way the process could've been completed before the election, and we all know the election could have gone the other way."

Julia saw Agent Reeves shake his head at Noah, and she waited for the inevitable.

"Dean Riley, I'm going to need you to leave. Julia and Gordon, you too."

Julia had expected he wouldn't allow this conversation to go much further in front of Addison, but she hadn't anticipated she would be dismissed as well. She started to argue the point, tell him she had a right to know anything that could affect her ability to get Addison confirmed, but she decided it would be pointless. She would find out what was going on, but she wasn't going to beg Noah for the right to information. To encourage Addison not to press the point, she stood and motioned to her and Gordon. Addison followed her to the door, but stopped and turned back to Noah before she exited the room.

"Mr. Davy, I have every confidence if there was foul play, you will make sure whoever was responsible will be brought to justice. In the light of day."

After a few beats of silence, he nodded curtly, and Addison followed her out of the room. Julia walked beside her, noting Addison was tall and proud. Like she belonged in important places. Like she was in charge. She'd read the ballsy subtext of Addison's message to Noah: if he tried to cover up whatever happened to Justice Weir, she would go public with the conversation she'd just witnessed. Julia knew she meant it and she couldn't respect her more.

Respect was a safe enough emotion.

When they reached Julia's office, Addison leaned against the door, but she didn't follow Gordon and Julia inside. She desperately wanted to escape this place, where controversy and conflict were the norm. As she watched Julia settle in at her desk, looking like she was raring for a fight, she wondered how she'd ever thought they could start a relationship in the midst of a political battle during which no one could be trusted and everyone put up a front to get what they wanted. Where did her wants, her desires figure in?

"Addison, please come in and shut the door."

Julia's invitation was gentle, but she stayed put. "I'm going to head home. It's been a long day already." She considered her next words and then edited them due to Gordon's presence. "And to top it all off, I didn't really get any sleep last night."

"Excited about the nomination?" This from Gordon.

"Something like that." She avoided Julia's gaze. "But today, lack of sleep and the news of Larry's death, has taken its toll. I need a little time to rest and reflect."

"Gordon, could we have a moment?"

Julia's question was more a command, and Addison acted swiftly to avoid the awkward moment. Unsure of what she might say or what she might do, she couldn't, wouldn't be alone with Julia right now. She edged away from the door. "I really have to go." She looked over at the desk outside Julia's door. Cindy was deeply engaged in untangling a pile of paperclips. "Cindy, would you walk me out?"

With a furtive look at her boss's office, Cindy nodded.

They walked in silence down the corridors of the West Wing. Unlike her offices back at the law school, the halls here were bustling with activity despite the fact it was a weekend. Politics never took a day off. No, that wasn't fair. The people here were working for policies, not just politics. Without a doubt, the majority of them were passionate about making the world a better place. Unfortunately, most of their efforts would be compromised, if not thwarted, by the power of opposing forces and the rush of time until their party was inevitably voted out of office.

If she was confirmed, she'd be a Supreme Court justice for the rest of her life, and there would be no ticking clock on her ability to make a difference. No matter what she might say in public about the duty of a judge not being able to affect change, she knew the reality. The person who sat in that seat made a difference. Look at Weir. Without his take no prisoners style of liberalism, the body of law styled by his term as chief justice would not have made the inroads it had on civil rights issues.

She was ready to take up his mantle. She only wished she didn't have this gauntlet to traverse before she could carry on his tradition.

Thankful she lived in a fairly secure building, she parked her car in the garage underneath and made it into her apartment free from encounters with reporters. The crowd of protestors on Pennsylvania Avenue had been disconcerting enough. She kicked off her shoes and turned on her TV, determined to find something silly and distracting to take her mind off the events of the last two days.

No sooner had she settled on an episode of *Southpark*, when her phone pinged to signal an incoming text message. Tempted to ignore it, she was drawn to the device, hopeful even. It wasn't Julia. It was Jack.

Hey, sis. Skype?

Gladly trading her solitude for the rare chance to see Jack's face, she typed *yes*, and then reached for her laptop and signed on, impatiently waiting for the line to connect. When he finally appeared on the screen, she breathed a sigh of relief to see her brother, whole and smiling.

"You have no idea how much I needed to talk to you right now."

"Guess you've had a big week, Madam Justice. Don't even try to tell me this wasn't in the works when I saw you at Thanksgiving."

"It sort of was and it sort of wasn't. It's a long story, and I promise I'll tell you everything when we can talk in person."

"This is probably as in person as it gets for a while, and I can see by the look on your face, everything"—he formed air quotes to emphasize the word—"isn't fine."

He knew her too well. She couldn't exactly tell him everything that had gone on in her meeting at the White House over an unsecured line, but she desperately wanted to. She settled on a vague summary of her current circumstances. "Yesterday was fantastic. Today sucked. And I have no idea what tomorrow holds."

"Dad says you have a girlfriend."

Vowing to beat her father next time she saw him, she shook her head. "Not hardly."

"He said she's pretty."

Pretty wasn't the word she would have used. Pretty was ribbons and bows, flowers and sunshine. Julia was none of those things.

She was sleek and feisty, stunning and sexy. Addison ached at the memory of Julia naked and vulnerable, hers for the taking. Boiling her attraction down to a G-rated phrase, she said, "She's like no one I've ever met."

"What's her name?"

"It doesn't matter. It's over."

He made a show of counting on his fingers. "It hasn't been that many days since I saw you. Not a lot of time to get into and out of a relationship."

Relationship. Ha. What she'd shared with Julia had been a flash in the pan. Satisfying while it lasted, but leaving both of them hungry and wanting. She'd known Julia felt the same way when she'd seen her earlier that day. She was pained too, but neither one of them was willing or able to do what it took to overcome the obstacles. The barriers were too high, the risk too fierce. She'd been a fool to think, even for a moment, that they could make it work. Last night had been a drug, but she was sober now and she could recognize the experience for what it was. Fleeting.

"Jack, I promise when I meet the one, you'll be among the first to know. In the meantime, tell me about you. I worry."

"You shouldn't. I'm doing well. I'm sorry I couldn't be there for your big day, but the longer this tour, the more likely it is I get to come home for good."

God, she hoped so. He was on his fourth tour. He'd done his part. Maybe Garrett would make good on his word and bring Jack and all his buddies home soon. Pretending it was a foregone conclusion, she said, "What will you do when you come back?"

"I don't know. I don't think I'm cut out for a nine to five, but if I don't stay in, maybe I can get a job in security."

"In Dallas?"

"Maybe. Dad could probably use the company."

"Right. You'll meet some pretty girl and be married off and having children within a month."

"I don't think so, sis."

"Really?"

"This life…it changes you. I've seen things no person should ever have to see in his lifetime. The pretty girl, well, that might work out at first, but there will come a time when she hits a wall with me because there are parts of me I will never share. Wouldn't be right to put another person through that."

Even with a world between them and a fuzzy connection, Addison saw the pain in his eyes, and her heart ached for the life he'd chosen and what it had robbed from him. "Everything changes us, but that doesn't mean we have to accept less because of it. Don't give up on a full life for yourself before you've even given it a chance. Promise me?"

His nod was slight, but she hung on to the small sign as hope for his future. It wouldn't be right for him to have given so much for others only to be left with nothing for himself at the end of it all.

When the call was over, she was out of sorts. She didn't want to watch TV, she didn't want to review materials for her Senate interviews, she didn't want to be in her own skin. Her own words played over and over in her mind. "Don't give up on a full life for yourself." She was on the edge of becoming the next chief justice of the United States, but if it really happened, she had no one to share the success with, no one to toast her success. Had she given up on a full life, or was she only capable of professional success? She wasn't sure she wanted to know the answer.

CHAPTER TWENTY-SEVEN

Julia stood outside the Oval Office, bargaining with Sue. "I swear I'll only be a minute."

Sue shook her head. "I can get you in first thing tomorrow. You know, before his schedule hits the rails. He's supposed to be getting ready for dinner with the Brazilian ambassador and his wife. The first lady will have my hide if he's late."

Julia was only slightly afraid of Veronica Garrett. They hadn't seen each other since the night Garrett had won the election, and she was pretty sure Veronica was just as glad about that as she was. "There'll be press at that dinner, right?"

"There's a photo op before, maybe a couple of questions."

"I have to brief him before he goes to that dinner. I'll handle Mrs. Garrett."

"Good luck with that," a booming voice sounded from behind.

Noah. Julia turned to face him, calculating strategy in lightning fashion. She'd hoped he was still in his office down the hall with Reeves, plotting their response to the press explosion that was about to occur when word broke about Eva's abortion and/or the details of Larry Weir's death. Ostensibly, she had every right to go over his head to talk to the president, but she didn't want to share her real reason for the urgent meeting, not with Noah. Not now. "I thought you were still busy with Reeves. What's the plan?"

"I don't know. What is the plan? Looks like you might be hatching one on your own."

Julia shot a look at the closed door, willing it to open. Magically, it did. President Garrett rushed out with his arms loaded with folders.

"Sue, please cull through these and send whatever can't wait up to the residence." He looked up, seemingly surprised to find Julia and Noah standing at the edge of Sue's desk. "Everything all right?"

"No."

"Yes."

Julia looked at Noah and didn't try to control her expression of surprise. "Seriously? Do you lie to him all the time?"

Garrett looked between them and then at Sue who pretended not to be listening. "How about we take this into my office?"

"Mr. President." Sue pointed at her watch. "You only have ten minutes before your guests arrive."

"I'll be done in five." He walked into the Oval, and Noah and Julia followed him in. None of them sat down.

"It's Saturday night. Veronica and I are hosting the ambassador from Brazil and his wife for a private dinner so I can smooth over some of this NSA mess. What have you two cooked up that's going to ruin our plans?"

Julia so didn't want to do this in front of Noah, but she didn't have a choice. "Who killed Justice Weir?"

"I don't know what you're talking about." Garrett's face showed only a slight flush, but otherwise was firmly fixed in denial.

"She knows," Noah said.

"The whole world's going to know unless you tell me what's going on so I can put a lid on it."

"I don't understand." The president looked genuinely puzzled.

Julia plowed ahead. "I have a feeling someone from the *Times* is going to be at your little photo op. Josh Gander talked to Larry Weir before he died. Larry suspected foul play, and now Gander's sniffing around. Problem is he thinks a former law clerk may have been involved in Weir's death." She paused to let the words sink in. "Do you see how it might have been important to keep me in the loop now?"

Garrett sank into a chair. "Shit." He rubbed his temples for a moment. "You really think Gander might consider Addison Riley a suspect in Weir's death?"

"It's ridiculous, I know, but he's got a lead and he's going to keep digging. I may trust him to keep quiet, but this could all blow up fast if some third-rate blogger gets wind of his investigation and they decide to get a quick and easy story out of it, truth be damned."

"Do you have a suggestion?"

"Get Gander in here now and promise him an exclusive on the investigation if he holds off for now."

"He won't do it," Noah said.

Julia shook her head. "He will if he hears it straight from the president. But it has to be right now."

"Damn it," said the president. "Veronica is going to kill me."

"It won't take long. He's in the building."

"Fine. Tell Diane to bring him back and I'll talk to him. And, you two, schedule a meeting with Sue for us to talk more about this tomorrow. I want to know who killed Weir, and I want to know yesterday."

"Mr. President, there's one more thing."

Julia waited as Noah delivered the news.

"Apparently, a former girlfriend of Dean Riley, a professor at her university, had an abortion."

"What? Like just now?"

"No, about fifteen years ago."

"Oh my God. So what? Deal with it. Now out. Both of you."

Julia followed Noah back to his office where Reeves was waiting. She waited until they were both inside with the door shut before asking, "What's your plan?"

"It's not your concern."

"The hell it's not. Anything that could affect this nomination is my concern."

Noah wasn't budging. "Prepare your nominee and we'll take care of the rest."

Julia stared at both men, but their faces made it clear they were shutting her out. The Senate interviews would start on Monday, which meant they only had one day to prepare. Based on Addison's mood when she'd stormed off, working with her was going to take most of her energy. She should leave the matter of Weir's death to the professionals and focus on getting Addison ready for the senators and doing damage control with the press. "Fine, see that you do your part, and I expect you to keep me informed."

Reeves stopped her as she reached the door, "One more thing. We need to get that journal from Ms. Riley."

Julia started to tell him Addison had left for the night, but she didn't want him going to her house, startling her even more than they had already. "I'll get it and bring it to you." She made sure her tone told him any other solution was off-limits.

When she returned to her office, Gordon and Cindy were waiting, ready to get to work. She was ready to work too, but without Addison, there wasn't much point. It was almost six. She'd thought this day would have gone so differently. Brunch with Addison, maybe a leisurely afternoon in bed. Delivery for dinner. More champagne. More kissing, more touching, more of many things she wasn't likely to experience with her again. If things had gone the way she'd planned, she wouldn't be working. So why should she work now, especially since Addison had made it clear she was done for the day?

Mind made up, she started barking out instructions. "Cindy, get me everything you can find out about Eva Monroe. Gordon, we need a statement about her abortion, not directly addressing it, but talking about how the administration is not going to comment on this woman's private life, assuming there are no skeletons we haven't already found out about. I don't trust the agent assigned to the vetting, so we're going to need to follow up on everything. Get with Diane on the language since the statement will come from the press office.

"Also, tell everyone, especially Tommy, to be here at eight sharp in the morning. He makes a great Burrows, and he's going to be Addison's first interview on Monday. She's going to think she has this one down because she knows the guy, so tell Tommy to prepare to be a total hard-ass during prep. Connie Armstrong may think she's got this confirmation in the bag, but it's going to be a brawl, and everyone needs to get ready for a fight. Understood?"

She grabbed her coat and started for the door.

"Where are you going?" Gordon asked.

"I've been deputized. I'll be back, but it may be late. Call me if you need me."

She left the White House with only a hazy plan in mind. It started with showing up on Addison's doorstep and ended with delivering Justice Weir's journal to Reeves. The in-between part was fuzzy, but full of possibilities and pitfalls.

Half her thoughts were occupied with seeing Addison, but the other half were full of fear that once again she was treading on fragile and familiar ground. At any moment, her inability to separate her personal and professional life would be her downfall. The confirmation process would explode into a fierce battle with stalemate the only logical outcome. The president would be forced to withdraw Addison's name and then be forced to nominate someone weaker than even Judge Landry. She should be concerned about how such an outcome would affect her business, but she was only worried about what Addison would think. Surely she already thought she had no standards, no absolute barometer, but to have Addison think she was weak and ineffective would be even worse.

She would get the journal, but she had no idea what would happen beyond that. She wouldn't allow herself to either hope or dread.

Tired of her own company, Addison decided to walk down to Shake Shack to get some food. A little grease and fat was exactly what she needed to soothe her soul. Dressed in jeans, boots, a long coat, and a knit cap, she didn't look anything like a Supreme Court nominee, and she slipped out a side door of the building, completely unnoticed. The few blocks walk in the cool night air calmed her, and she felt almost like a normal person when she placed her order. If the place hadn't been packed, she might have even stuck around, hung out and pretended to be like anyone else, enjoying a casual Saturday night outing.

When her food was ready, she started the walk home. She should be preparing for the Senate interviews, but she couldn't bear the thought of spending another minute at the White House, pretending politics weren't the only force at play, pretending Julia was just someone she worked with.

But that's clearly all it was. Last night seemed light years away, their connection broken. Julia was distant, and she didn't have a clue why. Whatever it was, she didn't think it could be fixed. Didn't know if she wanted it to be. Why did everything have to be such a struggle? Everything worth having, anyway.

Was Julia worth fighting for? Was anyone? Shouldn't falling in love be easier than this?

The last question pulled her up short. *Falling in love.* Was that what was happening? Surely not. They barely knew each other. Well, not entirely true. Julia knew loads about her, probably more than she remembered herself. And what did she know about Julia?

Enough. Enough to know she was passionate about her work, she'd been hurt before and was leery about taking personal risks. But she'd taken a big one last night. What would the president think if he knew they had slept together? Julia could've lost everything she'd worked for. Maybe that was the reason for the cold shoulder today. Julia regretted what they'd shared. The only thing Addison regretted was that it wasn't likely to happen again.

About a hundred feet from where she would make the turn onto her street, she saw Julia cross the street, walking toward her. She stood still, frozen to the ground, as Julia approached. "Well, this is a surprise. Lose your way?"

Julia's smile was tentative. "I hope there's something in that bag for me. I'm starving."

"I only bought enough for one. I'm not sure how I would've known to buy more."

"Addison, about last night—"

Addison spoke quickly to cut her off. "Worst way to start a sentence. Ever. I'm not interested in rehashing it. It was beautiful, it was lovely, it was an experience I'll always remember, but I don't want to hear any excuses about how it can never happen again. Why don't you walk on and we'll pretend it never happened?" At that moment, her cell phone rang. She started to reach into her pocket to answer, but Julia's hand on her arm stopped her.

"I don't want to pretend it never happened, but it's true, it can't ever happen again." Julia's eyes were sad as she delivered the death knell to whatever might have been. She waited until Addison's phone stopped ringing, and then said, "Today, when I got word the paper was about to print a story about your 'girlfriend,' I went ballistic. I have no business letting my personal feelings get in the way of this process. It's too important. You're too important. I can't do my job if I'm distracted. It'll cause us both to get ambushed."

She was right, but Addison desperately wanted her not to be. The only solution would be for her to withdraw her name, and it was too late for that. She'd made a commitment to the president, to herself. This opportunity was bigger than both of them, bigger than any potential relationship. How ironic that the thing that had brought them together was also the thing that had torn them apart.

"You're right. Whatever this was, it's over, but I need a little space. I promise I'll show up tomorrow, ready to be grilled by you and your staff. When you see me again, it will be like nothing ever happened." Maybe by tomorrow, she'd believe the lie. The only thing she cared about now, was getting back to her apartment, away from the temptation of Julia's presence. She started walking, but Julia reached out to pull her back.

"Wait. Look, I know you're ready to be out of my sight for a while, but I need to get something from you."

"What?"

"Justice Weir's journal. Reeves wants it. I told him I would get it from you."

So that's why Julia was here. Was the whole talk about relationships a secondary concern? Didn't matter at this point. Addison tucked her disappointment behind a smile. "Come up with me and I'll get it for you."

"I can wait downstairs if you'd rather."

"Don't be silly. We're both adults. I promise not to jump you if you promise to leave as soon as you get the journal."

"You really don't want to share those fries, do you?"

Julia's grin was infectious and Addison couldn't help but laugh. "You're impossible. And no, no fries for you." She turned the corner onto her block and pulled up short. Two D.C. PD squad cars were parked in front of her building. She knew they could be there for any number of reasons, but her gut clenched and she pushed through the lobby doors and went straight to the concierge. "What's going on?"

He looked up and then moved around the desk, leading her away from the center of the action. "Ms. Riley, my apologies, but it appears there's been a situation. I called you as soon as I heard."

Must've been the call she'd ignored. "Situation?"

"Yes, one of your neighbors found your door wide-open and they called the police. I tried to reach you, but there was no answer when I called."

"The police? Do you know who called?"

"I don't. A Detective Conland arrived with a uniformed officer. I wouldn't have let them up, but they knew your apartment number, and you have been getting quite a bit of attention lately. I wanted to make sure we take appropriate precautions."

His expression was nervous, and Addison was quick to put him at ease. "You did the right thing. Where are the police now?"

"They are upstairs. Would you like me to accompany you?"

"I'll go with her."

She'd almost forgotten Julia was right behind her. "Thank you."

The elevator ride was interminably long. When they finally reached Addison's floor, Julia stopped her just outside the doors. "Are you okay?"

"Yes," she lied. She didn't give a lot of thought to her personal safety. She lived in a secure building, worked on a friendly campus. She rode the Metro, walked at night, and never considered the possibility she'd be the target of crime. As she walked down the hall, she braced for the worst.

A man in uniform was standing outside her door. She held out a hand. "Good evening. I'm Addison Riley. I understand there's been a break-in."

"Good evening, ma'am. It's a bit hard to tell at this point. Nothing seems to have been disturbed, but your door was open, and, well, because of the recent, you know…"

"You mean because she's a future Supreme Court justice you thought you'd better give it special handling?" Julia stepped forward. "I'm Julia Scott with the White House. Thanks for being thorough. Can Ms. Riley have a look around inside? See if anything is missing?"

The officer responded quickly. "Detective Conland is already inside. He told me not to let anyone in, potential crime scene and all, but I'm sure he'll want to talk to you." He opened the door and signaled for them to wait while he went inside, but Julia pushed in behind him, leading Addison by the hand.

A moment later, a tall thin man in a suit came out of Addison's bedroom. Addison shuddered at the second violation to her privacy. First burglars, now the police. She wanted to be alone, only not here. Anywhere but here.

The detective seemed to share the sentiment. He barked at the officer. "You thought it was a good idea to let them in here?"

"She owns the place."

"And it could be a crime scene, not that you'd know one if it bit you on the ass."

The officer shot a look their way as if to apologize for his superior's behavior. Addison started to tell him it was okay, anything to get them out of here faster, but Julia spoke first.

"Excuse me, Detective Conland. Do you know who this is?" She pointed at Addison. "Ms. Riley is the next chief justice of the United States. If there's been a break-in, it could be a matter of national security."

"Oh, is that right? Guess they should've called the feds then. But they called me. Looks like she might not have shut her front door real tight. Best I can tell nothing's been disturbed. I'll file a report and you can get a copy from records."

He started toward the door, but Julia stopped him. "Shouldn't she look around? Make sure nothing's been taken?"

Conland shook his head like it was the worst idea he'd ever heard. D.C. Police already had a bad reputation, and after meeting this guy, Addison had no doubt why. "I'll only be a minute." Under his watchful gaze, she wandered through her apartment, opening cabinets and doors. As she started toward the bedroom, Julia's phone rang.

"Sorry, I have to take this." Julia ducked outside.

Addison couldn't explain why, but she felt a chill at being left alone with the detective. Resolved to make the ordeal as short as possible, she walked to her bedroom. When she entered, she could feel Conland on her heels. She shot him a back-off look and walked around the room, her eyes focused on the empty space on her nightstand. As she looked back toward the door, she noticed he was watching her every move, but his expression wasn't the curious look of an officer investigating a crime. It was prurient. It was predatory. She took another few seconds to confirm her initial suspicion and then hurried to get him out of her private space.

"Well?" he asked as she swept past him.

"Looks fine. May I have your card? If I notice anything later, I'll get in touch."

He reached for his pocket and stopped midway. "Sorry, I remember now I don't have any on me. Guess I was expecting the evening off." He turned and motioned for the other officer to follow. "Call us if you need anything. Have a good evening, Ms. Riley."

When he cleared the door, she couldn't shut it fast enough. She flipped the deadbolt into place and sank into the nearest chair where she focused on processing what had just happened. Moments later, a banging at the door disrupted her thoughts. She looked through the viewer.

Julia. Damn. She'd left to take a call. Addison pulled the door open and tugged her in and then checked the hall before she shut the door. "Sorry. I guess I was distracted."

"No problem. That was Noah. I told him I'd fill him in when I returned with the journal."

"Well, that might be a problem." Addison motioned for her to sit. "The journal's gone."

"What?"

"It was on my nightstand. It's not there now."

"Are you sure you haven't moved it? Maybe you took it to your office?"

"Not a chance. I saw it there this morning."

"What did Detective Conland say when you told him?"

Addison looked down at her lap. She didn't anticipate Julia, or anyone else would understand how she'd handled the situation. "I didn't tell him."

"Seriously?"

"I don't know how to explain this, but the guy gave me the creeps. Something's off about this whole break-in. My door was wide open so a neighbor called the cops? Well, have you looked at my door? There's no sign of forced entry and I damn sure didn't leave it open. My neighbors would likely have called the concierge and let him decide about calling the cops. And why would a detective have come at the first call? Seems like they would've sent patrol cops and they would've called in a detective. And why didn't they talk to this neighbor to find out if they saw someone leaving my place?"

"Whoa, there. Lots of questions. I'm sure there's a reasonable answer for all of them." Julia tapped her finger on her phone. "I think I should start by letting Reeves know that the journal is gone, and then we'll figure out the rest."

"Fine." Addison watched while Julia made the call. Julia probably thought she was nuts, but her gut told her something was off. Very off. Par for the course.

While they waited for Reeves, Julia resisted the urge to ask Addison one more time if she was sure she hadn't left the journal at her office or anywhere else. She might not know Addison well, but she knew enough to know she wouldn't jump to wild conclusions without cause.

After a few moments of silence, Addison excused herself to the bedroom, leaving Julia on her own in the living room to process what was happening. Addison was obviously upset. She would be too if her home had been violated. She wanted to go to her, to comfort her, but she sensed it wouldn't be a good idea. Lately, she didn't have any good ideas when it came to dealing with Addison, personally or professionally.

When she heard the knock on the door, Julia rushed to answer it, relieved to have something to do. After confirming it was Reeves, she opened the door and looked around. "You came by yourself?"

"Pretty sure I'm capable of handling this on my own."

"Someone needs to talk to the concierge. And the neighbors."

He glanced around the room and whispered. "We need to keep this as quiet as possible for now. You don't want to start a shit storm for your special little friend over there, do you? Word gets out that her apartment was broken into, the media will go crazy. And if they find out Justice Weir's journal was the thing they were after, Josh Gander is going to have a front page spread, and he's not going to wait for the president's okay."

Julia heard all the words, but only certain ones stuck. "Special little friend." Not just the words, but his tone implied he knew there was more to their relationship than the professional connection. Well, he could just file any details he and his FBI friends had gathered away with the dossier of all of Addison's other past relationships. All she cared about right now, all she could care about right now, was Addison's safety.

She pressed a finger to Reeve's chest. "You keep it quiet, but you better be thorough. I don't care how you do it, by yourself or with a team of suits, but we need some answers and we need them now. And if you don't think I'm serious, you should know I have a direct line to the president. How many hoops do you have to go through to get direct access?"

"I'm sure he'll do his job."

Julia looked up to see a very tired Addison holding a small suitcase. "I'm sorry." She directed the words at Addison to make sure she knew the apology was meant for her. "Where are you going?"

"I imagine Agent Reeves will want to get some information from me, but then I'm headed to a hotel. Just for a night or two. Until the locks are changed." She handed Reeves a sheet of paper. "I made some notes. My neighbors' names and phone numbers. The name of the concierge on duty, everyone else I could think of who might have seen or heard something, and I'll answer all your questions, of course."

Julia looked at Reeves, willing him to vanish in a puff of smoke. All she wanted right now was to have a conversation alone with Addison. Soothe her fears, pull her into her arms, and tell her everything would be okay. But she couldn't do any of the things she wanted. Not in front of him. Instead she said, "Why don't you go ahead and talk to her? I have to make a phone call, but I'll do it outside."

Once outside the door, she called Gordon. He barely got a hello out before she said, "I need you to find out from Gander who else he's talked to about the Larry Weir story. Do it quickly and quietly and call me back. Okay?"

"Everything okay?"

"Better if you don't know. Don't want him to read anything from your end. If he asks why you want to know, tell him it's just for background, so when the president gives him an exclusive, he'll be prepared for the interview. Be nonchalant, like it doesn't really matter. You're just filling in the details."

"Okay, but, Julia, it does matter, doesn't it?"

She sighed. "Yes. It matters a lot." She said good-bye and hung up before he could read anything else into her request. Noah would be pissed if he knew she'd sent Gordon to mine information, but she wasn't confident Noah would press hard enough to get answers, so she'd get them on her own. Next, she dialed his number.

"What's going on?"

"Do you always answer the phone like that?"

"I do when the president's freelance help is mucking up our work."

"Your work? If you had your way, we'd have a gutless wonder heading the Supreme Court."

"Not like you to care either way, as long as you win. A successful confirmation should be your only concern."

Julia bit back a retort. Fighting with Noah wasn't a good use of her time right now. She focused on the reason she'd called him in the first place. "Addison's leaving here to check into a hotel. I need you to get a detail assigned to her."

"A detail of what? Apparently, she doesn't trust the D.C. cops enough to tell them she's been robbed. The Secret Service isn't authorized to guard judicial candidates, and she doesn't get security from the Supreme Court cops unless she's confirmed."

"FBI then. I don't care, but I don't want anything happening to her between now and the time your pal Reeves figures out who stole the journal from her apartment."

"And if word gets out we have her under guard? That news will eclipse any play you'll get from the interviews next week. No one's going to confirm a nominee who's got security problems."

"Noah, you need to put aside your single-minded political hat for once or I'll go directly to the president. I don't care if I have to camp outside the residence to get his attention. I want a detail outside her door or I'll go to the press myself." She hung up before he could reply.

When she walked back into Addison's apartment, Reeves was standing, apparently finished with his interview. He offered to have an agent escort Addison to her hotel, but Julia interrupted. "Could I have a word with Ms. Riley in private?"

He looked between them and then stepped outside. *File that away with the rest of your personal information, Agent Busybody.* Once they were alone, she asked Addison to sit down. "They'll provide you with a detail. They'll be discreet."

"Thanks."

"You could come home with me." As the words fell out of her mouth, Julia searched for a spot on the wall, the ceiling, anywhere but Addison's face, where she would surely see rejection.

Seconds later, she felt Addison's hand on hers. "That was dumb. Forget I said it."

"I won't forget. It was sweet, but you know I can't. If we're over, we're over. I'm not strong enough to share your house and not want more."

Julia nodded. None of the words she wanted to say mattered. It was too late. She couldn't believe they were over when they'd barely begun.

Chapter Twenty-eight

Addison stifled a yawn and looked around the room. Tommy, Gordon, and the others all looked hatefully energetic despite the fact they'd been at this all day. Only she and Julia showed signs of wear. She knew the reasons for her exhaustion: apprehension, an unfamiliar bed, longing for something, someone she couldn't have. What was Julia's excuse?

"Is that the only thing you have to say, Dean Riley?"

She tuned back in and faced Tommy, who she was beginning to wish would fall into a hole in the floor. His Jeff Burrows's imitation was spot-on. "I'm sorry. I think I need a short break."

Tommy looked puzzled, like he wasn't sure if he was supposed to respond as the senator or himself.

Gordon took over. "Not a problem. We've been at this for hours. I'm sure we could all use a break." He stood and hustled everyone out of the room, leaving Addison alone with Julia. Not exactly the relaxing break she'd had in mind.

"Are you okay?" Julia's voice was gentle, her question tentative.

"I'll be fine. I'm staying at The Hay-Adams, but it's not home." Addison instantly felt stupid. Julia likely already knew where she was staying, probably knew her every move since they'd parted ways last night. She'd read in this morning's paper a short bit about how she'd moved into the hotel because of a plumbing issue at her apartment. One of the building managers was even quoted as saying they were sorry for the future justice's inconvenience, but they were doing everything they could to get things back in working order. No doubt,

Julia had worked into the night to seed the story, but as focused as Julia was on her business, she hadn't called to check on her, hadn't shown up to make sure she was okay. They'd had no contact until they met here at the White House this morning, in the company of a half dozen others.

The distance was what she wanted, wasn't it? She should be grateful Julia was backing off since the alternative was painful proximity that could lead nowhere. All she had to do was get through the next month or so. Interviews, holiday break, confirmation hearings, swearing in. One day at a time until she was wearing a black robe and Julia was on a flight to the islands. Excellent outcomes for both of them. So why did she feel so empty at the prospect of an end to whatever was left of their relationship?

"I'll do everything I can to get you back home as soon as possible. I promise."

Addison met her gaze. She saw caring, comfort, but she knew it was all business, or at least it had to be. She answered with a simple, "Thank you." She rotated her neck to work out some of the stress. "You know I really think I can handle myself with Jeff. Maybe we could move on to some of the other members of the committee."

Julia smiled. "You about ready to punch Tommy in the face?"

"I might be a little beyond that." Addison laughed and enjoyed the ease at which they could slip back into playful banter. They could be friends, couldn't they? Maybe keep in touch after this was all over. Go out for drinks, share a movie.

No, she'd always want more. Before she had a chance to process the difference between what she wanted and what she could have, Gordon stuck his head in the door.

"Julia, Noah needs to see you. Said it's urgent."

Addison looked between them, hoping for a clue. Had they found out more about the case? Would Julia tell her if they did?

Julia told Gordon she'd be right there and he ducked back out of the room. She turned to Addison. "I'll be right back. I promise I'll let you know whatever I find out. Just wait here for me, okay?"

Addison nodded and watched as Julia walked away. She wanted to say she'd wait even longer. She'd wait until after the confirmation. After the inauguration. She'd wait until whenever Julia was free from feeling like she had to balance work and play, but the words seemed hopeless and she stayed silent. Better to keep the memory of the intimacy they'd shared. The reality of Julia's political life loomed large. There would always be conflicts, from off limit topics to hectic cross-country campaigns. She hadn't wanted to settle for the lukewarm commitments Eva was willing to make. She'd be crazy to let the leftovers of a life with Julia be enough, no matter how much she wanted her.

She boxed up her feelings and prepared for the next round of inquisition, but one thought stuck with her. The one night with Julia soared over anything she'd shared with anyone else. Ever.

❖

"You're telling me that Senator Burrows might be involved in Justice Weir's death?"

Julia watched as Reeves and Noah tried to figure out how to respond. Noah finally nodded at Reeves who started talking. "What we know at this point is limited, but there is no record of a call to D.C. Police Department about a possible break-in at Ms. Riley's apartment. We've spoken to her neighbors, and none of them observed or reported any suspicious activity. And Detective Conland has close ties to Senator Burrows. In fact, he recently transferred to the D.C. Police Department from the Capitol Police. We pulled Conland's phone records, and he placed a call to Senator Burrows yesterday, shortly after he left Riley's apartment building."

Julia didn't bother asking what kind of strings they had to pull to get phone records so quickly. "Holy shit. What are you going to do next?"

"If it was anyone besides a U.S. senator," Reeves said, "I'd show up and start asking questions, but we have to be very careful, or ranks will close and we won't get any information. We're pursuing a few other leads, but in the meantime, we should keep a tight lid on this so he doesn't suspect anything."

"And the journal?" She asked. "What if Conland already took it to him and he's destroyed it?"

"If that's already happened, it's too bad, but you can bet if we push him into a corner, he'll definitely destroy it. And we have to consider the possibility that Burrows didn't have anything to do with Weir's death. What if he got the journal just so he could use it against Ms. Riley? Make it look as if she had something to do with Weir's death."

"Bullshit."

"Julia, settle down," Noah said. "Of course, it's bullshit, but we have to account for everything."

She sank into a chair. They were right, of course. Gordon had come to her first thing this morning and told her that Gander, the reporter from the *Times*, had talked to Burrows as part of his investigation. If Burrows knew about the journal entry, no doubt he would try to pin the law clerk connection on Addison, especially since he would do just about anything to keep her from the bench. But what if he was involved in Weir's death? She focused on the timeline. When Weir died, everyone was certain, her included, Garrett wouldn't be reelected. It would have been nearly impossible for him to get a nominee confirmed, which would have left the decision about Weir's successor to Briscoe. And if Briscoe had won in a landslide, the Democrats probably wouldn't have held on to their majority, which meant Jeff Burrows would start the next term as the majority chair of the Judiciary Committee, perfectly positioned to ensure a conservative nominee made it to the bench.

If Burrows was behind Weir's death, Addison could be in danger. The very idea sent waves of horror through Julia. Here she was spending the day preparing to send Addison to meet with the man who at best wanted to ruin her and at worst wanted to see her dead. "Addison's supposed to meet with Burrow's first thing tomorrow."

"What time?" Reeves asked.

"Does it matter? No way is she going, not if you think he's in any way involved with all of this."

"She has to go or you'll tip him off," Reeves said. "And you can't tell her about any of this. He gets wind that he's under investigation, there's no telling what he'll do."

"There's no telling what he'll do either way. At least if we cancel the meeting, you can be sure of her safety."

"She'll be safe. She's going to be in his office, not in a back alley. What's he going to do? Stab her with a letter opener?"

Julia shook her head. "I'm not sending her in there unless she knows what she's going into." She owed Addison that much.

"Bad idea," Noah said. "You tell her about Burrows and she'll do something to tip him off. She won't be able to help it. Then she either gets hurt or she winds up being a witness against him. Talk about a conflict. Your nominee will be tied up in Senate hearings, but they'll be about Burrows and his crimes. Her confirmation will be permanently derailed. Is that what you want?"

Failure. No, that wasn't what she wanted. Not for her, not for the president, and especially not for Addison. But above all else, she wanted Addison to be safe. If Addison knew what she was headed into the next morning, she would likely feel compelled to draw Burrows out, expose him for any part he might have played in killing her mentor. Office setting or no, a man backed in a corner would come out swinging. She stared at Noah and willed him to feel her resolve. "Fine. But nothing better happen to her, and you both better make sure of it."

On the walk back to her office, she decided they would call it a day. She could pretend the decision was because she knew how tired Addison was, but the truth was she didn't think she could be in the same room with her and keep this information to herself.

Besides, she should start getting used to not spending time with her. If all went well, Addison would be confirmed just after the New Year, and their paths would split. Addison would spend her time in the company of legal scholars and she would hit the road. With luck, she'd get hired for a campaign far enough away that she wouldn't run into Addison and politically bloody enough that she wouldn't have time to think about her.

The odds were against her.

CHAPTER TWENTY-NINE

The entire day had gone terribly and it was only eleven a.m. Addison glanced around the expansive waiting area outside of Jeff Burrows's office and considered making a break for it. Surely there was a food cart somewhere, or maybe she could just catch the Metro, ride back to The Hay-Adams, and order room service. Anything would be better than sitting here, waiting to be grilled, and trying to ignore Julia who was obviously trying to ignore her.

From the moment they'd met that morning, she'd known something was off. Julia had barely spoken to her, leaving all the explanation about how the morning would go to Gordon and Tommy who had both accompanied Landry on a similar journey just weeks ago. Now the four of them had been kept waiting in a hostile senator's office while he had pressing business at the Capitol building. His secretary kept insisting he would be right back, but now their schedule was completely off the rails. She didn't care, but Julia had become increasingly agitated at the prospect of waiting.

Addison wanted to go to her, find out what was really wrong, but she couldn't. They couldn't have a personal conversation in front of the rest of the group, but mostly she held back because she didn't trust that her concern would be well received. Instead she just watched as Julia paced the carpet and texted messages into her phone with ferocious finger punching. Finally, the outer door opened and a young woman ushered them into Senator Burrows's inner sanctum.

Jeff stood but didn't invite any of them to sit. "How nice of all of you to come, but Dean Riley and I have known each other for many years. I think we can have a little conversation in private."

After her last meeting with Burrows, Addison had looked forward to being insulated by the group for this session, but no way was she going to project weakness. "Fine with me, although perhaps you could find a more comfortable place for the group to wait. We've been relegated to the benches out front for a while now."

Julia shot her a grin at the admonition and she smiled back. It was the closest thing to a connection they'd experienced since she'd discovered her apartment had been burglarized.

Once inside Jeff's office, she didn't wait for an invitation to take a seat and she settled onto a couch to the side of his massive desk. Jeff sat in a chair across from her and glanced at his watch.

"How long should we stay in here? Will half an hour be long enough to convince everyone I'm well acquainted with your positions? Or is fifteen minutes sufficient?"

Addison settled back against the cushions, more comfortable now that he wasn't trying to project a veneer of friendly banter. She'd already glimpsed this version of him, and she was prepared for the worst he could deliver. "Why even bother meeting with me? You obviously don't want to even debate the issues. I may not agree with you on most subjects, but I've always thought you had the power of conviction behind your principles. Was I wrong about that?"

"I'm very principled, certainly more so than the cardboard cutout of a president who saw fit to nominate you, but principles don't get you elected. It's all about appearances. Meeting with you, smiling while we agree to disagree, that's how I come to be viewed as a statesman instead of a crackpot."

"I guess you've gotten pretty good at fooling people."

He laughed. "You have no idea, but aren't you supposed to be sucking up to me?"

"You know that's never going to happen. I've always respected you, but I'm beginning to think my regard was misplaced."

"Looks like we're even." He looked at the closed office door, and then back at her. "Shall I be perfectly honest?"

"What? Up to now you've been sugarcoating your feelings?"

"I have no doubt your baby-killing girlfriend is just the tip of the iceberg. You have other skeletons, and I will find them. You have no idea what you've unleashed. When it gets really bad, when you wish you could crawl in a hole somewhere, remember I warned you."

He'd demonstrated his power by digging up Eva's past. Maybe she should be afraid, but the only feeling she could muster was anger. Anger that he thought he had the power to subvert the process, anger that he'd harm an innocent bystander to get his way, anger that she'd ever considered him a friend.

She stood and made a show of looking at her own watch. "I think fifteen minutes is plenty of time, don't you?"

He made a mock bow. "Fine by me. Enjoy the rest of your pointless afternoon of interviews. I hope you haven't already resigned from your job at the law school."

She smiled a big Cheshire cat grin and left without another word. *Asshat.* Forcing a slow pace, she strolled up to the secretary's desk and asked where she could find Julia and the rest of the group.

"Conference room. Over there." The mousy woman pointed toward another door.

"Please let them know I'm waiting for them outside." She walked out into the hall and began to pace. Seconds later, Julia appeared at her shoulder, her voice soft, but urgent.

"Are you okay?"

Addison looked into her eyes, trying to read the source of her concern. "I'm fine. Where to next?"

"You were only in there ten minutes, fifteen tops," Tommy said.

Julia turned to him and made a slashing motion across her throat, but Addison placed a hand on her arm. "We're old friends. Jeff, I mean Senator Burrows, already knows all he needs to about me and he wanted to respect the limited time we have."

Julia's eyes narrowed, and Addison could tell she wasn't fooled. She wasn't even sure why she didn't tell them the truth, but somehow Jeff's continued animosity toward her nomination was almost embarrassing. She didn't have time to sort things out, but she could avoid an interrogation from Julia. Spying a sign for the restroom, she said, "I need just a second to freshen up. I'll meet you by the elevators."

She took off walking before anyone could respond. Down the hall, around the corner, until finally she was alone. In the restroom, she leaned against the counter and took a few deep breaths. Her reflection surprised her. She looked confident, poised, not at all flustered by the confrontation with Jeff. She could pull this off. If this interview was the worst, and it had to be, then she was in for an easy few days.

Composed inside and out, she stepped out of the restroom and started back down the hall. As she turned the corner, she nearly ran into a man coming from the opposite direction. She opened her mouth to apologize, but recognition stopped her cold.

"Detective Conland?"

"Excuse me?" He glanced around nervously.

Her gut told her to walk away. She knew he was the detective who'd been at her apartment Saturday night, but why was he acting like they'd never met? And what was he doing here? He couldn't be looking for her, could he? If so, he wasn't a very good detective because even in a suit, she didn't look much different than she had when they'd first met. For a brief second, she considered needling him about the investigation, but the strong sense that he'd had something to do with Weir's journal disappearing from her apartment held her back. She flashed back to the predatory look he'd worn while watching her in her bedroom and she abandoned interaction. "Nothing," she said as she kept walking.

By the time she reached the elevator, a churning sense of dread rumbled through her. Julia, Gordon, Tommy, and some other people she didn't know were laughing about something as she walked up. Standing several feet away, she remembered her calm reflection in the restroom mirror. She briefly closed her eyes, willing composure to return, but when she opened her eyes, Julia was staring right at her, no longer laughing, her eyes piercing their way to her heart. She edged her way toward Addison and pulled her aside.

"Something happened. What did Burrows say to you?"

"Nothing I haven't heard before. I promise, he was only honest. Don't expect his support."

"There's something you're not telling me."

Addison shook her head. She wanted to tell Julia about the encounter with Conland, but she didn't want that to become the focus of the afternoon. "It's nothing. I just saw that detective from Saturday. Conland. He acted like he didn't remember who I was."

Julia pulled her closer and waived Gordon over. As he walked over, she whispered, "Where? Where did you see him?"

Addison pointed down the hall. "Around the corner. We ran into each other literally, he was—"

Julia cut her off as Gordon appeared at her side. "Gordon, take Addison to her next meeting. I have to make a phone call. Don't let her out of your sight." And a second later, she was gone.

Addison stared at the space where Julia had been, confounded by her sudden disappearance. One more disappointment in an already very disappointing day.

Julia waited until she rounded the corner to pick up her pace. So far no sign of Conland in the hall, but she figured she knew exactly where he was headed, and she was on her way there. She was just a few feet from Burrows's office when she heard a voice call out to her. She turned and saw Connie Armstrong headed her way. Julia glanced back at the doors to Burrows's office. She couldn't ignore Armstrong, but she had to know if Conland was in there. She settled for assuming a position to the left of the doors and waiting for Armstrong to come to her.

"Where are you headed in such a hurry?" Armstrong asked. "Is Dean Riley meeting with Burrows?"

"No. She just met with him. She's on her way to her next interview. Senator Jimenez."

"Any particular reason you're not with her?"

"You do realize she's quite capable of talking to these people without someone holding her hand?"

"It's your job to make this process as smooth as possible. The president assured me he would do everything possible to get Addison confirmed. Pretty sure he expects you to shepherd her through the process."

Julia looked at Burrows's door and then back at Armstrong. As much as she hated to admit it, Armstrong was right, but the interviews were the easy part of the process. For all she knew, Conland was in there, handing over Weir's journal to Burrows who would probably destroy it. But would he stop there or would he take more drastic action to make sure Addison didn't take Weir's spot? If he was capable of conspiring to kill a sitting Supreme Court justice, it wasn't much of a stretch to believe he would and could eliminate a potential successor, especially one he vigorously opposed. Armstrong was right. She should be with Addison, but wasn't protecting her more important than promoting her?

Instinct fueled a blurted out question. "Who do you know and trust with the Capitol Police?"

The senator's brow furrowed. "What?"

"Please, it's important." She willed Armstrong to get the urgency of her request without further explanation.

"Lieutenant Burke heads my detail. I trust him implicitly."

Of course. Julia had forgotten that Armstrong, as president pro tem of the Senate would have her own security detail. "Can you ask him to come here right now? It has to do with Addison, and I promise I'll explain."

Connie Armstrong apparently got it, because she didn't ask any more questions. Instead, she pulled out her phone and sent a text. Seconds later, her phone buzzed with a response. "He'll be right here. Now, I need to know what's going on."

"I promise I'll tell you, but I have to make a quick call. Do you mind waiting here for Burke?" She started to walk away to make a call, but then added, "And interrupt me if anyone tries to leave that office." Ignoring Armstrong's annoyed look, she walked a few feet away and dialed Reeves. When he answered, she launched in.

"You need to get that search warrant right now. Detective Conland is here at the Capitol, probably in Burrows's office with Weir's journal. I've got someone from the Capitol Police headed here to make sure he doesn't leave, but for all I know they're in Burrows's office having a bonfire right now."

"I don't have enough to get a warrant yet. No federal judge is going to give us permission to search a senator's office with what we've got. We need something more concrete." A few seconds of silence preceded an apparent revelation. "Wait, did you see Conland take the journal into Burrow's office?"

"No, but why else would he be here?"

"Not good enough. Did you say you have someone from the Capitol Police there?"

"Lieutenant Burke. He's assigned to Senator Armstrong." Julia looked over at Armstrong and saw she'd been joined by a man in a suit. "Hang on." She walked over and stuck out her hand at the man. "Julia Scott. And you are?"

"Lieutenant Doyle Burke. Senator Armstrong said that you asked to speak to me."

Julia looked at her phone and then handed it over to him. "Tell the man on the other end who you are and then do whatever he says."

She watched while Burke exchanged a few short phrases with Reeves and then he handed the phone back to her. She put it up to her ear. "Yes?"

"You and Senator Armstrong make yourselves scarce. He's going to detain Conland when he leaves and question him about why he's in the building. I'll be joining him, and if he has any information to implicate Burrows, rest assured, we'll get it out of him. When he talks, we'll get our warrant."

"But what about the journal? If Burrows has it, he could be destroying it as we speak. Maybe I should go back in there."

"You think he's going to let you in if that's what he's doing? There's nothing we can do about that without tipping him off, and if we tip him off now, we'll never get a confession out of him or Conland. Trust me. This is our best chance. If Conland confesses, we won't need the actual journal to implicate Burrows."

He was right. She had no choice but to trust him, but with Addison's safety in the balance, she didn't want to trust anyone. "Fine, but I want additional security on Dean Riley until this is resolved. And I want to be kept informed about what's going on. The minute you have Conland, let me know." She had no right to make these demands. She was a contractor, not a regular employee of the White House, and her duties did not include directing the government's law enforcement resources or even merit receiving reports about the results of an investigation. She prepared for pushback, but Reeves was either beat down or he was willing to delay engaging with her.

"I'll call you as soon as we know something. And we'll arrange for additional security. Thanks for letting us know about Conland."

After the call ended, Julia stared at the phone. She wanted to call Gordon and tell him to get Addison out of the building, back to her hotel where she could sit under guard until this ordeal was over. But Burrows might get wind of the change to her schedule and take action. The best thing they could do was to act as if nothing was going on. She glanced over at Senator Armstrong, still standing a few feet away. She owed her the truth. She'd tell her what was going on and then rejoin her group. If she couldn't whisk Addison away to safety, she would at least stick with her for the rest of the day, vigilant about any potential threat.

Chapter Thirty

W hat are you still doing here?"
Addison looked up at Roger who was standing in her office doorway. She thought he'd left hours ago. It was Christmas Eve and the building was deserted. Perfect time for her to get some work done. "I don't think I'm ever going to catch up. Last week put me so behind."

"Does it really matter? If things go the way they should, this"— he gestured at the piles of paper on her desk—"will become someone else's problem."

"Key word 'if.'" She was cautiously optimistic. With the exception of the meeting with Jeff Burrows, her interviews on the Hill had gone surprisingly well. Even the staunch conservatives seemed to warm up to her once they got to talking, proving it was always easier to hate an abstract. The thing that really had her off-balance was the distance between her and Julia. She understood, even if she didn't like, the arm's length handling of their personal relationship, but Julia had put a healthy dose of professional distance between them as well. Julia had accompanied her on interviews, but had avoided small talk in between, often disappearing for an hour at a time, leaving Gordon to escort her through the gauntlet of meetings. She hadn't spoken to Julia this week at all, although she'd seen her across the room at the small memorial service given for Larry Weir. Julia had slipped out of the church before she could find her, and she had spent the afternoon wondering what she'd done to earn the cold shoulder. If she could figure out a way to shake the discreet security detail that followed her everywhere, she'd show up on Julia's doorstep and demand an explanation.

Silly thought since Julia didn't owe her anything. Even during the night they'd shared, naked and intimate, Julia had never promised anything beyond the moment. She was doing her job, and she'd never pretended to offer Addison anything more. She'd do well to focus on her own work and stop letting her thoughts wander to a judgeship she may not get and a woman whose every action made it clear she was off-limits for the long term.

She turned back to Roger. "You should go home, enjoy the holiday. I promise I won't stay long, and the suits out front will run interference in case any stray reporters don't have anything better to do than hound me the day before the holiday."

She'd finally moved back into her apartment building a few days ago and, with new locks and a security detail, she felt practically anonymous. The Drudge report about Eva's abortion still had protestors picketing the White House, but the D.C. police had been vigilant about keeping the protestors away from her block. Eva had left town immediately at the end of the semester to wait out the storm. Addison hoped this was all worth it, for her and everyone else involved.

Which brought her back to Julia. Did she have plans for the holiday or was she working? Addison cast back to what Julia had told her about how she'd spent Thanksgiving. Ordering in Chinese food. Didn't sound like much fun, but that's what she'd probably be doing herself this holiday since her father was in Montana and Jack was in Afghanistan. In the meantime, she'd focus on her work.

Roger reluctantly agreed to leave, but as he started through the threshold of her office, Addison's phone rang. She glanced at her desk phone and then realized it was her cell. Roger waited in the doorway while she answered.

"Hello?"

"It's Gordon. Are you near a television?"

Addison motioned to Roger to turn on the TV. "What channel?" she asked into the phone.

"Take your pick. The FBI is executing a search warrant on Senator Burrow's office."

"What?" Addison sank into her chair as she struggled to digest the news. "Why?"

"I, um, well I don't know the whole story, and it's probably better if we don't get into it over the phone anyway. Julia just wanted me to let you know so you wouldn't be blindsided by any reporters that may get past your detail."

Julia was thinking about her, but she hadn't called. The obvious snub stung, but Addison refocused on the content of what Gordon had to say. "Are you sure about this? And hasn't he already left town?"

"Surprisingly, no. He flew his family in to spend Christmas in the capital. I don't think it would've mattered if he was here or not. The FBI was in a big hurry to do the search. I get the impression they've been working on this investigation for a while."

Addison shook her head. None of this made sense, and the vague bit of information was more frustrating than helpful. She wanted to reach through the phone and make Gordon cough up more details. No, what she really wanted was for Julia to be on the other end of the phone, taking a personal interest in her as she'd done from the start. But apparently, Julia had better things to do.

"Okay. Is there anything I should be doing?"

"There's the likelihood you'll get some questions about this, since Senator Burrows is an old friend of yours. No comment is the best answer you can give for now. We'll put together a statement for you in case it gets to that point."

Gordon was only doing his job, but she seethed at the handling. She didn't need a lesson in discretion, especially not from someone who couldn't or wouldn't give her all the details in the first place. Suppressing a blowup, she simply said, "Got it. Thanks."

"Okay. Well, call me if you need anything. Have a good holiday and I'll see you after the first."

He hung up and Addison stared at her phone. Have a good holiday. Really? She was alone and lonely, in complete limbo about her professional future, and the woman she craved, the woman she might be falling in love with, couldn't be bothered to pick up the phone and tell her about a momentous event.

She looked up at Roger who was still waiting in her doorway. "Let's get out of here."

❖

"It's done. Only a matter of time now."

Julia listened to Noah's words and heaved a sigh of relief. She'd been on pins and needles all week waiting to hear the status of the FBI investigation into Weir's death.

All she'd known up until this morning was that Detective Conland had been fairly quick to jump ship rather than protect his former benefactor, Senator Burrows. He finally admitted he'd taken the journal from Addison's apartment after faking the call about a possible burglary, but he hadn't delivered Weir's journal to Burrows when Addison had seen him at the Senate office building. Instead, he'd gone to see Burrows to negotiate for a bigger payout. Before his visit, he'd done a little investigating and learned the FBI had taken over the investigation of Weir's death. That, coupled with Burrows's intense interest in the journal, told him he had a gold mine on his hands, and he planned to stake his claim. Burrows had promised him more, but said he'd need a few days to make the arrangements. They'd made the exchange this morning and, threatened with the prospect of many years in jail, Conland had worn a wire and goaded Burrows into several incriminating statements.

After the meet, agents tailed Burrows back to his office, where he no doubt thought he'd be alone on Christmas Eve to read the journal and dispose of it however he wished. He'd barely shut the door when Reeves showed up with a contingent of Capitol Police, warrant in hand. Burrows wasn't under arrest, yet, but it was only a matter of time. Neither he nor Conland had admitted having anything to do with Justice Weir's death, but Noah had assured Julia the FBI had already developed some credible evidence. He also promised her both men would be under constant surveillance until the attorney general obtained an indictment.

"And you'll keep the security detail in place on Dean Riley?" The formal name sounded flat, but she'd spent all week keeping up the appearance of formality with Addison. No sense stopping now.

"Yes. Until after the confirmation and then the Supreme Court cops can take over."

His tone had changed, and it was clear he'd gone from assuming the nomination was a disaster to realizing Addison's confirmation was a foregone conclusion. The optimism was contagious, and given how things were going, she should be ecstatic. It was still too early to predict exactly how the confirmation process would play out, but the FBI investigation was sure to render Burrows impotent. The Senate minority leader had already made a vague statement to the press implying that he wouldn't let anything get in the way of the work of the country. When the news broke that Burrows might have had something to do with Weir's death, the path would be clear for Addison's nomination to sail through. It was all a matter of timing now.

"What are you doing for Christmas?"

"What?" Julia tuned back into the conversation. "You know I hadn't really thought about it. I suppose I'll work. My office is a wreck, and since it looks like this little gig is about to be over, I should get things in order before I finally get my well-deserved vacation."

"Vacation. I don't even know what that means."

Neither did she. She couldn't remember the last time she'd taken off, really off. Shut the phones down, no Internet, fun in the sun kind of off. She'd looked so forward to the prospect, but now that it was almost time, apprehension hit. What if a big fish called? If her office couldn't get in touch with her, would the candidate wait or find someone else to hire? Would she be able to cope with several weeks of indulgent lassitude?

Breathing deep, she got a grip. She'd be fine. Normal people went on vacations all the time without repercussions.

But did they go alone? She couldn't deny it—the solitude she'd craved after spending the past year surrounded by campaign workers, press, and clamoring crowds of voters sounded like a drag now that she'd met Addison. For a brief second, she considered showing up on her doorstep with plane tickets. *Hey, I know you're about to have the job of your dreams, but I was thinking you might throw it all away for a few weeks in the islands with me.*

No, that window had closed, if it was ever open in the first place. And it was entirely her fault. She'd pushed Addison away, citing crap like ethics and professionalism. Crap that might keep her employed, but had long since stopped fulfilling her dreams. Undeniably, her dreams were peppered with memories of Addison naked, willing, and ready for anything, even if anything meant risking what she'd worked for. She had no idea if she was willing to make a similar sacrifice, but she supposed her indecision told her everything she needed to know. That night had been a single, solitary exception, and the further from it she got, the easier it would be to accept that it wouldn't happen again.

No plane tickets, no phone calls, no contact. That was her safest route. She'd have to talk to Addison again just before the confirmation hearings, but for right now she would shove her feelings aside and pretend there was nothing between them. After all, she made a living convincing people to believe what she wanted them to.

CHAPTER THIRTY-ONE

Addison clicked the remote quickly through the channels. She was at once drawn and repulsed by the coverage of her upcoming confirmation hearings, although she had to admit that hearing Rachel Maddow wax poetic about the potential of her as a chief justice was a mind-blowing experience.

Pathetic. It was Friday night, New Year's Eve, and she was home alone, scouring the television for something to watch besides conversations about her qualifications or hordes of drunks waiting for a ball to drop out of the sky. This week had been the busiest and loneliest time of her life. She'd spent much of it at work, making sure her office was ready for whoever took her position in the new semester because, no matter what happened with the confirmation process, she wasn't going back. She'd given notice, and if her confirmation failed, she'd take the semester off and come up with a new plan for her future. Maybe she'd take a trip. Go somewhere exotic.

She laughed at her own transparency. Like she'd have a chance of running into Julia in the islands. And what would she say if she did? Come here often? Want to share a hut?

Not a chance, especially since she hadn't heard from Julia once during the past week. Every day, as the press broadcast and blogged twenty-four seven about the FBI investigation into Jeff Burrows and the upcoming confirmation hearings, she kept expecting something, anything. A phone call, an e-mail, a text, but she got nothing. Not a word. She'd started to pick up the phone several times to break the silence between them, but stopped when she realized Julia's silence was a clear message. She'd hear from her when there was work to be done. She'd pushed the point herself, the night her apartment had been invaded, basically telling Julia not to tempt her if they were over. She didn't want anything if she couldn't have everything. Well, now she knew where things stood, and she had no one else to blame for her current lonely situation.

She finally settled on a mindless movie she could pretend to watch when her phone rang.

"Hello, Ms. Riley, it's Agent Liland, downstairs. There's a Ms. Julia Scott here to see you and we don't have her on the list for this evening."

Addison hadn't put anyone on the list of people security could let through this evening, but she would have expected Julia could push her way past any number of apartment security guards and a contingent of FBI agents. Apparently, this particular agent didn't have a clue who he was keeping waiting.

"Tall, red hair, green eyes?"

"Yes, ma'am. Her ID checks out."

Addison stifled a laugh. They'd been extra careful since the incident with Detective Conland, and she appreciated their caution. "Please send her up. Thanks, Agent."

While she waited for Julia, she walked to the master bath and looked in the mirror. Her hair was down and a bit wild. She barely had on any makeup, and she was dressed in a pair of faded jeans and her favorite bulky sweater. The contents of her closet, with rows of suits, well-shined shoes, and a few fancy dresses mocked her, but there wasn't time to change. As she walked back through the apartment, she took in every detail. It wouldn't be up to Julia's housekeeper's standards, but it was neat enough.

Neat enough for what? She could hardly believe that after a week of no contact, Julia would just show up at her door. Whatever she had to say must be important. Maybe the president was pulling her nomination. Although she was generally an optimist, she refused to believe the in person visit could signal anything except bad news.

When the knock finally came, she assumed a steely veneer and swung open the door. Julia stood in the doorway, flanked by agents. The agents looked to her for confirmation, but all she could do was nod. As they slipped back into the recesses of the hallway, Julia stepped into the room, shut the door behind her, and produced a champagne bottle from inside her coat. After a few painful seconds of silence, Julia handed her the bottle. "I know it's probably bad form to regift a bottle of bubbly."

Addison reached for the bottle, her motion completely rote. "What?"

Julia shot her a puzzled look. "I didn't have any other bottles in the house and figured this would be a bad night to be out looking for good champagne. I hope you don't mind."

The ground started to settle, and Addison slowly nodded as random thoughts fell into place. People used champagne to celebrate. Julia brought a bottle all the way across town. She wouldn't do that to deliver bad news. She squinted at the label and smiled when she recognized the bottle of Veuve de Clique she had brought to Julia's house the night she found out Julia had tried to convince the president not to nominate her for the Supreme Court. Were things coming full circle, or was this a sign?

"We have two things to celebrate. Well, one really, but the one makes the other." Julia cleared her throat. "I'm sorry. I'm making a mess of this. What I'm trying to say is Jeff Burrows is resigning from the Senate. He'll officially announce on Monday, but the president got a call from the minority leader this morning."

Addison took a moment to digest the words. Burrows was resigning. Confirmation hearings started on Monday, and her nemesis wouldn't be there to grill her either in public or private. She could handle his brand of bullying, but she hadn't been looking forward to it. She glanced down at the bottle in her hand. Now that Burrows was out of the picture, she felt a profound sense of relief, but relief alone didn't merit a celebration, did it? She looked up at Julia who wore a huge smile.

"You can ask anyone who knows me. I'm superstitious as hell. Never count a win until all the votes are in, but the minority leader implied that in the wake of the Burrows scandal, he isn't interested in waging a war over a quote 'unquestionably worthy nominee.'" She pointed at the bottle still in Addison's hand. "I suggest you have a glass. Lord knows you deserve it."

They both stood in place, several feet apart. Addison looked into Julia's eyes, searching for a sign. Something, anything to tell her what to do next. Appropriate phrases floated through her head. *Take off your coat. Sit down. Have a drink. Make love to me. Stay.*

No matter where her mind wandered, all thoughts led to the same conclusion. She wanted Julia to stay. Here. Tonight. Forever. Did Julia want those same things? Did she have the courage to ask, or would it be braver not to? She was on the verge of a lifetime appointment, her future set in stone. Until she retired, she'd never live anywhere else, never wonder what opportunities lay in store. Julia, on the other hand, lived her life on the fly with both her work and her residence determined by whatever exciting new campaign captured her attention. Could they make a relationship work?

She only knew one thing. She had to try. Without breaking eye contact, she set the bottle on the counter and stepped closer. Inches from Julia, she drank in the scent of her—citrus and wood, fresh and warm. Julia's breath hitched, and she leaned in closer, running her fingers along the soft skin of her strong neck. Tall and proud, mesmerizing and sensual. She longed for the feel of her lips, the press of her body. The ache between her legs spread through her soul, and she could hold back no longer. When she finally closed the distance and captured the kiss she'd been burning for, warmth flooded through every cell of her being. Without a doubt, she was in love.

Julia arched in anticipation. The ache of the intensely slow lead in to the kiss left her melting into Addison's embrace. When Addison's lips finally touched hers, she nearly exploded with want, with need. When they finally broke for breath, her lips were bruised and swollen and her mind was consumed with taking Addison to bed.

Funny, since she'd refused to consider the possibility when she'd left her house, bottle of champagne in hand. She'd told herself this trip was about congratulations and the prelude to good-bye. The past day had been full of news. Although Burrows's resignation wouldn't be officially announced until Monday, the rumor mill was rampant, and people were already jockeying for a spot in the inevitable special election to fill his seat. She'd gotten a call just this afternoon from the congresswoman from Montana who wanted to talk about the possibility of running for Burrows's soon to be vacant seat. They'd set a meeting for Monday evening and, if all went well, once the confirmation hearings were over, she would head out West to begin another battle.

Addison's incredibly arousing kiss threatened to steer her off course. If arousal was all she read from it, then it would be easy, but there was more. Much more and they both knew it. What she needed was a few seconds without Addison's body pressed against hers. Distance was the only way she could navigate this terrain. She walked over to the table where the icy bottle of champagne dripped condensation onto finely polished wood. "Shall we toast?"

"Depends on what we're toasting." Addison's voice was silky smooth, her tone filled with portent.

A cold drink wasn't going to be enough to give her perspective. What she should do was forget the toast, lead Addison back to her bedroom, and spend the night pretending their lives weren't headed in completely separate directions. The impending divergence was a good thing. She couldn't deny she cared about Addison, but to let her heart wander beyond that would be dangerous. If candidates thought she was dating Addison, they'd believe she had influence. They'd never accept that the girlfriend of the chief justice didn't have the inside track to all kinds of information about pending cases.

Girlfriend. Not a word she used in reference to anyone. Relationships, especially ones born of professional contact, were bad news. No strings, only flings had been her philosophy since Kate, and her life was less complicated because of it. If she'd never kissed Addison, she'd be better off because she wouldn't be standing here having an internal debate about what to do with the attraction between them.

She watched while Addison poured two glasses of champagne, unable to tell her no, but knowing she should. She compromised. One drink and then good-bye. *It's only right to toast success. She deserves this. Don't ruin it.*

She took the glass and raised it high. "To you. You deserve every good thing that comes your way."

Addison tilted her glass to hers and the soft clink was the only sound in the room. After a few beats of silence, she spoke. "I was just thinking about all the good things that have come into my life. Like you."

Her gaze was a magnet, and Julia couldn't look away even though she was certain she wouldn't survive the pull. She watched Addison's lips moving, knew she was still talking and whatever she was saying was important, but the words floated in the air between them, none of them landing save the last three.

"I love you."

The words were like rocks crashing against her resolve. She expected something—talk about promises, incremental and ordinary, but not this. I love you meant commitment. I love you went beyond a promise and said we're a done deal. For a brief moment, she met Addison's gaze. She saw raw, naked vulnerability coupled with complete confidence. Addison was so sure, but surely she hadn't thought it through, hadn't considered all the complications. Outside the bubble they'd been working in, they couldn't work, not as a couple, not for forever.

"This is where you're supposed to say something."

Addison's eyes still held hope, but it was waning. Julia knew it was her turn to meet Addison's words with a declaration of her own. Show Addison she was worthy of what she was offering, that she could dive into the naiveté of romance and, against the odds, let love conquer all.

But she couldn't fit her world into the reflection she saw. Love couldn't conquer all, and there was no point in considering whether she loved Addison, let alone any purpose in making promises she knew she wouldn't keep. She had only one choice. Two steps to the door and two words to cut through the intoxicating trance that was Addison Riley.

"I can't."

CHAPTER THIRTY-TWO

January 19, the day before the Inauguration

Addison approached the entrance to the West Wing, and a Marine guard held the door open for her. As she stepped across the threshold, the Marine said, "Good morning, Madam Chief Justice." He pointed to a middle-aged woman standing to his left. "This is Margaret, Mr. Davy's secretary. She'll take you back to his office."

Madam Chief Justice. She wasn't sure she'd ever get used to the mouthful of a title or the deference it afforded to her. She followed Noah's secretary through the familiar halls, every footfall a reminder of the last time she'd been here, nearly a month ago.

Noah stood to greet her and ushered her into his office as if they were old friends.

"Congratulations, Madam Chief—"

She held up a hand. "Please. This conversation is going to last forever if you have to use all those words every time you want to say something to me, and I know you must be insanely busy with other things today. How about just inside these four walls, you call me Addison, or Justice Riley if formality is necessary?"

He smiled. "Justice Riley it is. Thanks for coming in."

She took a seat. "I should thank you for the run-through. It'd be nice to have my first judicial act go off without a hitch." Tomorrow, she would stand in front of an audience of millions and swear Wesley Garrett in for his final term in office. Considering she herself had been sworn in only yesterday in a quiet gathering at the Supreme Court building, the prospect of presiding over the presidential inauguration was daunting. Thankfully, Noah had volunteered to walk her through what to expect during the ceremony.

"I'm surprised you had time for this," she said. "You certainly could have had someone on your staff give me the details."

"Actually, most of them are busier than I am. When you have a big staff, you get to delegate most of the work. And since I've given notice, most of what I'm doing now is preparing this office for whoever the president can talk into taking my place."

"You're leaving?"

"I only ever promised him I would serve one term."

"Any ideas who he's going to get to replace you?"

"I gave him a list of names, but I don't think he's made a decision yet. I told him I'd stick around for the next month to make sure there's a smooth transition. It's all for the best. He needs a different kind of consigliere for his second term. Someone who's more of a statesman than a hard-hitting politician will give him a better chance at addressing big-picture issues."

His words reminded her of Julia, always working the angle, moving from one political gig to the next with no anchor, nothing permanent to ground her. Or tie her down.

She hadn't talked to Julia since the confirmation hearings ended almost a week ago. During the hearings, Julia had always been close, ever ready to offer advice and deal with scheduling, but in every way that mattered, she'd been distant, acting as if Addison had never spoken about love, never asked for more. But she had asked for more, and her request had sent Julia running. The message couldn't be any clearer. She needed to stop wishing they'd met under other circumstances, stop wishing Julia was someone she wasn't, and focus on the next phase of her career. Anyone else would have been ecstatic to achieve what she had.

Yesterday, she'd placed her hand on the same bible Justice Weir had used when he was sworn in, and taken the oath of the Supreme Court judiciary in front of a small group of invited guests. Her father and Jack sat on the front row of the courtroom, but the only person in the room she noticed was Julia who stood in the back, by the door, looking like she was ready to bolt at any moment. And she had. Addison had looked for her during the small reception, but she was nowhere to be found. And why not? Julia had accomplished her mission, and now it was time for her to take a vacation, take a new job, anything but take a chance on her.

She listened while Noah went over the details of tomorrow's ceremony. In a little over twenty-four hours, she would stand on the steps of the Capitol building and swear the president in to his second term in office. Just a few months ago, her biggest concerns had been placating faculty, courting alumni, and a girlfriend who wouldn't commit. Her life had changed drastically, but one thing remained the same—she had no one to share it with.

"You have a bad habit of asking me for favors when I'm headed out of town." Julia sat on one of the couches in the Oval Office. "Let me guess. You want me to look over your speech."

The president laughed. "No offense, Julia, but when it comes to sound bites, you're the expert. Lofty speeches, not so much."

"Fine, then tell me what you want and I'll get out of your hair. I have places to be."

"The islands calling to you?"

Julia shook her head. She'd stopped pretending taking a long, leisurely vacation was her style. Bora Bora was a paradise, at least it appeared to be online, but paradise was for lovers. She'd given up the opportunity to be with Addison because of work, so she should put her everything into it. "No, I'm headed to Montana. Congresswoman Shelley is announcing for Burrows's seat in two weeks."

"Well, she definitely would be hiring the best if you take the job."

She heard the if, but ignored it. "Already done."

"The congresswoman and I are friends," he said.

She recognized the tone and preempted what he was about to say. "Sir, I hate to say it, but I think my debt has been paid."

"This isn't about debt. It's about opportunity. You go work for Shelley, you'll be done in six months and on to the next big thing. You stay here and work for me, you can do big things every day."

"What, as one of a dozen senior advisors? I'll be sitting at a desk, pushing paper, writing reports no one will see. No, thank you."

"You'll have a desk for sure, but it would be in the second biggest office in the building. Noah's retiring, and I want you to take his place."

"Noah is retiring?" She held back saying she would've thought they'd have to pry him from the building at the end of Garrett's second term. Davy was the consummate politician's right hand, always thinking a dozen moves ahead, always plotting for power. While she was an expert when it came to campaign strategy, she had to concede he was a formidable ally for the president on the operation of the executive office, and she was shocked to be considered for his job. "And you want me as your chief of staff? You're kidding, right?"

"I'm not kidding, and trust me when I say there's no one else I'm considering to take his place. I have big plans for my second term. Just think of all the good things we can do."

"You're a little quick on the 'we.' I already have big plans."

"You have plans, but they're not big. I'm talking about carte blanche to run my agenda. No one gets to me without going through you. You'd really rather settle for short-term campaigns on lower ticket races? Come on, Julia, in the space of the last eighteen months, you've managed to get me elected president even though my approval ratings were in the low thirties, and you got the first woman ever confirmed as chief justice of the United States. A special election Senate race in Montana, of all places, is a huge step down, and you deserve better than that."

Chief of staff. Once upon a time, when she was a young intern working her way up, she'd dreamed of such a powerful position. Before Kate, before she'd lost all credibility in the legislature. Could she really be this close to achieving the pinnacle success of her career? Did she really deserve it? She'd done everything in her power to get the president elected to his second term, but she had to admit that Governor Briscoe's missteps were the real reason behind Garrett's win. As for Addison, she'd started out believing her nomination was doomed to failure, so how much credit could she legitimately take for her ultimate confirmation?

She pictured Addison, standing in the well of the Supreme Court Chamber, taking her oath. Her father and brother sat on the front row, brimming with pride, while she'd lurked in the back of the room too ashamed to claim any of the glory of Addison's special day. Unlike her, Addison deserved her success. At every step along the path, she'd remained steadfast in her beliefs, true to her convictions. Julia wondered how that felt. She'd spent years pushing the beliefs of the people that hired her until she wasn't sure where their principles stopped and hers began. She'd come around to champion Addison, had grown to truly believe in her, but Addison deserved to love someone who matched her strength of conviction, not a chameleon who sold her soul to the highest bidder.

If she accepted the president's offer, she would naturally see Addison more. They'd both be in town, showing up at some of the same events. Addison deserved to move on without tripping over her, and she didn't think she could handle seeing Addison moving on without her. Montana was a long way away and, after six months, someone else would need her services. She could spend her future on the run under the guise of doing her job. Her mind was made up.

"Thank you, Mr. President, but I've already made a commitment. Gordon flew out yesterday, and the congresswoman is waiting for me to prepare her announcement. I leave tomorrow."

Garrett sighed. "I guess I was overconfident. You were the only one on my short list. Are you sure you can't at least stay for the inauguration tomorrow?"

She resisted the last tugs of temptation. "Flight leaves at one. I figure the lines at the airport will be short since everyone in town will be at the National Mall watching you getting sworn in." As the words left her lips, she thought of Addison, standing on the steps of the Capitol administering the oath of office to the president. No way could she witness that in person and maintain her resolve. "I should go. I still have to pack."

Moments later, she was making her way down the hall to the lobby, when she heard pounding footsteps running up from behind. As she turned toward the sound, she heard a young man's voice call out, "Madam Chief Justice!" and her eyes locked with Addison's. They both froze in place with twenty feet between them. Addison had just rounded a corner, and hot on her heels was one of Noah Davy's interns waving an envelope. Neither she nor Addison broke their gaze as the young man explained to Addison that Mr. Davy wanted her to have tickets to the Commander-in-Chief's inaugural ball. He rambled about how there were three tickets in the envelope, one for her, her father, and her brother, and that Mr. Davy hoped they would attend. Addison took the envelope and tucked it under her arm and the young man disappeared around the corner. Julia wished she could disappear too, but since she couldn't, she said the most innocuous thing she could think of.

"Congratulations."

Addison closed the distance between them. She was breathtaking, she was beautiful, and Julia had to struggle to hear her words over the din of arousal flooding her consciousness.

"I saw you at the swearing-in. I wanted to thank you for everything, but I couldn't find you afterward."

"I had to be somewhere." Anywhere but in the same room with you, pretending I didn't want to take you in my arms and say whatever you wanted to hear so I could be with you one more time.

"I understand. Will I see you at the inauguration tomorrow?"

"Actually, I'm headed out of town." She started to say more, tell her about the Shelley campaign and dish about the many candidates who were lining up to take Burrows's spot in the Senate. The game was on, and political strategy was her language, but it was also the language that posed a barrier between them, so she let it go.

"Too bad. I'd hoped to see more of you."

Addison's eyes probed deep, and Julia had to look away to keep from falling under her spell. How could Addison want to see more of her after she'd been such a shit, running away like a scared chicken? Could Addison be holding out hope that she'd come to her senses, or was she just being polite?

"I'm sorry." The words fell short, vague and lifeless. What she really felt was regret she didn't have it in her to give Addison what she deserved. Regret she didn't deserve Addison. "I miss you."

The words tumbled out before she could stop them, but she rushed to recover. "I mean, we were spending so much time together, it feels strange to go days without seeing you. I guess it's that way every time I work on a campaign. Twenty-four seven with the candidate and then after it's over, well, it's over." The words skidded to a stop, and Julia wished she could melt into the ground. She finally mustered the courage to look at Addison's face, and she was met with kind, but questioning eyes.

"I hope I wasn't like every other candidate you've worked for."

They were close now, inches apart. Julia couldn't ever remember this corridor being so quiet. The solitude was dangerous, and her body ached to pull Addison into her arms, forget about their futures, and dwell only on the intimate moments they'd shared. She practically panted her response. "You were like no one else. Ever."

Addison smiled, radiant and hopeful, and in the few seconds after, Julia shared the glimmer of hope. Maybe they could find a way to make a relationship work. She'd spent her life fighting other people's battles. Maybe it was time to fight for what she wanted.

She sought the words that would reopen the door between them, but as she cast about for the best pitch, a group rounded the corner and headed toward them carrying on a heated discussion about the next day's inauguration address. She looked at Addison, but the moment was gone. Her silent thoughts had forged a chasm. Instead of hopeful, Addison looked resigned. Julia knew she should feel relieved, but all she felt was bottomed out and alone. It was time to say good-bye.

Chapter Thirty-three

Inauguration Day

"Are you sure you don't want to use my ticket for a date?"

Addison punched her brother in the shoulder. "The tickets to the ball are for us." She pointed. "You, me, and Dad." They were sitting around the table, enjoying an early breakfast before the car service came to take them to the Capitol for the inauguration. The last thing she wanted to do this evening was attend a ball, but she wouldn't deny her dad and Jack the once in a lifetime opportunity, especially since the gala was in honor of military servicemen.

Her father pointed his butter knife at Jack. "Your sister was dating a very pretty lady, a redhead named Julia Scott, but I imagine she can get her own ticket. She's important around here."

"She's important in a lot of places, and she won't be at the ball," Addison said. "Julia's on her way out of town."

"When will she be back?" Jack asked. "I was thinking of sticking around for a few days."

Frustrated at the turn the conversation had taken, Addison rushed to get back on track. "Guys, if you don't hurry, we're going to be late."

"Someone doesn't want to talk about her new girlfriend."

Jack's singsong voice was teasing, but his eyes asked a ton of questions. Addison wished she had the answers. Yesterday, for the few brief moments she and Julia shared, she'd dared to hope that maybe, possibly, Julia would meet her halfway, but here she was on her way to the Capitol, and Julia was probably well on her way to

Tahiti. She wasn't ready to talk about it with Jack or anyone else, but it was time to move on.

An hour later, Addison left her dad and Jack with one of the ushers and walked toward the rotunda, flanked by a couple of Supreme Court Police, to wait for the president. Just before they reached the entrance, one of them tapped her on the shoulder. "Madam Chief Justice." When she turned, he pointed to Jack who stood a couple of feet away.

"Give us a moment," she said to her security detail. She waved Jack over. "What's up? You don't like your seats?"

"Seats are great. It's you I'm worried about."

"I'm fine."

"Fine. My married buddies tell me that's what women say when things really aren't great, but they don't feel like talking about it. Is that what's going on here?"

She looked around. The Capitol steps were packed with dignitaries being ushered to their seats. In less than an hour, the attention of the entire world would be focused on this stage. "Jack, this isn't really the time to have this discussion."

"I get that, but I can tell something's wrong, and I just don't want you to let it ruin one of the biggest days of your life." He pulled her into a hug and whispered in her ear. "I'm here if you need me. No teasing, only listening. Okay?"

She held him tight. She wanted to tell him everything, spill her guts so she could move on and enjoy every moment of this day, but there wasn't time, and this definitely wasn't the place. "Please don't worry about me. I'm going to be all right."

He studied her face for a few seconds before finally saying, "Okay."

"I love you."

"I know. I love you too." He gave her one last squeeze before heading back to his seat.

Addison watched him walk away, thankful he was here to share in her success. Today was bigger than any one person. She would put aside her own feelings of loss and focus on what she had, not on what she couldn't have.

❖

So much for shorter lines. Julia tapped her foot and drummed her fingers on the railing in front of her. Increased security measures because of the inauguration meant every person and every piece of carry-on luggage was being hand-searched. She understood Homeland Security's need to make sure no one brought a bomb onboard a plane that might fly over the Capitol when most of the nation's leaders were gathered in one place, but it didn't make the waiting any easier.

Ever since she'd left the White House yesterday morning, she couldn't wait to get out of town. Seeing Addison and the surge of feelings she evoked made it clear that physical distance was the only way she could move on. She'd even gone so far as to try to secure an earlier flight, but the airlines were booked. So here she was, moving at a snail's pace toward a future she was no longer sure she really wanted.

When she finally made it through the line, she found a seat near the gate, opened her laptop, and started reading through the e-mails Gordon had sent to get her up to speed on the burgeoning campaign she was about to lead. She'd barely made it through the first e-mail when she was interrupted.

"I can't believe you skipped your own party."

She hadn't heard that voice outside of her TV set for years, but she'd recognize it anywhere. Julia looked up from her laptop into the sky blue eyes of her former lover, Kate Bramwell. She was almost as pretty as she was on TV, but without her on set makeup, a few wrinkles showed up here and there in the airport lighting. Guess life as a political strategist for Fox News wasn't as stress-free as she made it seem when the cameras were on.

"Hello, Kate."

"Why aren't you at the inauguration?"

Just like her to be so abrupt. "Why do you care? You doing a story about it?"

Kate sank into the chair next to her. "Hardly. I'm headed out of town. New job possibilities await."

Julia glanced at the ticket in Kate's hand and realized they were booked on the same flight. Holy shit. She knew exactly where Kate was headed and why. "I thought you only talked about politics for a living. You're really thinking of getting back into the game?"

"Walter Hayes is going to be the next senator from Montana, and I'm going to make it happen. Word is you're heading up Shelley's campaign. Pity you don't have a chance. Shelley's election to Congress was a fluke. No way will she take the Senate seat. It's been held by a Republican for longer than you or I have been alive. You're wasting your time. You should stay in town and go to a few inaugural balls. At least here you have something to celebrate."

Walter Hayes was the former mayor of Billings and a wealthy Republican entrepreneur. Julia had expected his name to come up as possible opposition to Shelley, but the news that Kate would be his campaign manager was a complete surprise. "And how many years has it been since you've run a campaign?"

"Like riding a bike."

Julia stared at her laptop, unable to focus on the work in front of her. Her escape had just turned into a nightmare. Seconds later, things got worse.

"Look, you should watch this. I promise it will be the last time we see a Democrat taking the presidential oath of office for a very long time."

Julia, unable to help it, followed Kate's pointing finger and focused on the television hanging from the ceiling. At that moment, someone cranked the volume and the entire waiting area was transfixed as Addison Riley asked the president to repeat after her. The phrases were short and quick, and Julia barely had time to register the moment when she saw Addison reach out her hand and say, "Congratulations, Mr. President."

The wind whipped Addison's hair, and her face was pink from the cold, but she'd never looked more beautiful. Julia ached at the sight of her, so close, yet worlds away.

"I don't know how you got her confirmed, but you should definitely go buy a lottery ticket. That kind of luck doesn't come around often."

"It wasn't luck." Julia kept her eyes on Addison who was stepping away from the podium so the president could address the nation. "She's brilliant, charming, and she has more integrity in her little finger than you or I have in our entire beings. She's the best thing to happen to the Supreme Court, since, well, ever."

When it became clear the cameras weren't going to show Addison anymore, Julia turned to face Kate who was staring at her like she'd grown a second head. "What?"

Kate shook her head. "Nothing. I mean, I don't remember ever hearing you sound so passionate about something before."

"We haven't seen each other in a long time."

"I watch the news. I've followed your career. You've represented dozens of candidates over the years, and I'm sure you believed in some of them, but..."

Julia tuned out Kate's words as she focused on a revelation of her own. She *was* passionate about Addison, but as a lover, not a nominee. A lover that she wanted, no, craved. A lover she'd given up for no good reason she could think of. Past hurt? Looking at Kate now, she couldn't recollect ever feeling for her what she felt for Addison. How had she ever weighed the prospect of a bright future with Addison against the betrayal-laden past she'd shared with Kate?

The gate attendant called for first class boarding, and the crowd around them started to stir. If she got on that plane, in a few hours, she'd be far from Addison, fighting another political battle. She could win every one of these battles, but in the end lose the war they waged on her personal life. Was she really ready to throw away the chance of a future with Addison for a string of short-term victories won for other people?

She shut her laptop, grabbed her coat, and stood.

"You boarding?" Kate asked.

"Not my group." She edged away. "Not my group anymore. Have fun in Montana." She fumbled in her bag for her phone as she walked away from the gate. She hit speed-dial and kept walking as the rings sounded in her ear. She was at the airport exit when the call connected.

"Hello?"

"Cindy, where are you?" Julia had gotten Cindy a job working a temporary position in the White House counsel's office when her tenure ended. Thank God she'd kept her number plugged into her cell.

"I'm headed into the office. They gave us the morning off since it was going to be a madhouse with the inauguration. I guess they figured we wouldn't get much done anyway.

"I need a miracle. Pull it off and I promise you a huge promotion. Can you help me?"

She'd need more than a miracle if she was going to convince Addison to give her another chance, but she'd won uphill battles for plenty of other people before. Now it was time to win her own.

CHAPTER THIRTY-FOUR

Julia stepped out of the car and looked around. Cindy had promised to meet her at the entrance to the National Building Museum at exactly seven o'clock when the doors were scheduled to open. The party didn't officially start until eight thirty, but no way was she going to risk missing either of the guests she was here to see.

"Julia, over here."

Cindy was standing about twenty feet away, waving wildly, and Julia rushed over, trying not to trip over her dress. "Did you get it?"

"I had to make some pretty big promises, but"—Cindy brandished an official ticket to the Commander-in-Chief ball—"here you go."

"And?"

"And the president is scheduled to be here at eight thirty on the dot. He'll dance with the first lady and then do a video chat with some troops in Kandahar who're joining the party via live feed."

"Any word on the chief justice?" Julia did her best to sound nonchalant, but she couldn't hide the hitch in her voice that came from asking the only question that mattered.

"She's scheduled to be here with her brother and her father. I couldn't find out any information about what time." Cindy delivered the news as if she'd failed miserably.

"Thanks, that part was a long shot. Her detail shouldn't be leaking the timing of her movements anyway. I'm surprised you got as much information as you did."

"I believe you said something about a promotion."

Julia laughed. "Indeed I did, and I'll take care of that tonight. Expect to hear from me tomorrow. I can't thank you enough."

Once Cindy was gone, Julia faced the entrance of the building and took a deep breath. She had the ticket to get into the party; now she had to make the most of it.

The gargantuan columns of the Great Hall were lit up in red, white, and blue, just like they had been for the last inaugural ball four years ago. Julia had shown up for that party, done a quick run around the room, and left. Celebrating had never been her strong suit, but she hoped that would change tonight. She looked around for the best vantage point to see all the arriving guests. She settled on the balcony and, after grabbing a glass of champagne from a passing waiter, took the elevator up to the second floor.

She spent the next hour wishing she'd worn a disguise. All she wanted to do was sip her drink while peering out over the crowd, but guest after guest approached and offered their congratulations on the president's reelection. Just when she thought she'd fended off the last of them, Senator Armstrong walked up and stood between her and the balcony rail.

"Well, hello, Julia. I didn't expect to see you here."

"It's the ultimate victory party. How could I miss it?"

"I heard Lisa Shelley is expecting you in Montana."

"I talked to the congresswoman this afternoon. Told her I've had a change of plans."

"Is that so? I'm not aware of any other big campaigns going on right now. You thinking of switching to the other side of the aisle?"

"Not a chance." Julia edged over slightly so she could see around the senator. Armstrong turned as if to see what she was looking at and spotted Addison first.

"Look down there, Chief Justice Riley has arrived. Chief Justice Riley. Doesn't that have a nice ring to it?"

Julia ignored the question, laser focused on Addison who was sleek and gorgeous in a dark blue gown. Julia wished she could fly straight down to the ballroom floor and take Addison in her arms. She couldn't fly, but determined to get downstairs as fast as she could, she turned to Connie Armstrong and said, "Excuse me, Senator, but I see someone else I simply have to talk to." She didn't wait for a response, but took off at breakneck speed to the nearest elevator. After punching the down button in vain for several minutes, she gave up and headed for the door marked exit, hoping she wouldn't pitch headlong down the stairs.

When she finally reached the ground floor, she pushed through the door and encountered a sea of people. She struggled to make her way across the room, ciphering where she'd last seen Addison and her family. She reached the edge of the dance floor when the band started playing and the familiar strains of "Hail to the Chief" flooded the hall.

Everyone froze in place as President Garrett and the First Lady entered the room. After greeting several dignitaries, they took to the center of the floor and danced the obligatory first dance of the night. While the guests oohed and ahhed, Julia did her best to wind through the crowd, looking everywhere for a sign of Addison. She didn't see her anywhere.

"Julia, what are you doing here?"

She turned and saw the president waving her over. Intent on her search, she hadn't noticed when the music stopped. She wanted to keep looking, but she couldn't ignore him. Besides, she had something very important to ask him.

"Good evening, Mr. President. Madam First Lady, you look wonderful, as usual."

Veronica Garrett smiled and turned to her husband. "Wes, Julia wants to talk business with you. I recognize the look."

She took the arm of the naval commander next to her and asked him to escort her around, while Garrett told his Secret Service detail to give them a moment. He and Julia stepped to the side of the dance floor. "What's up? I thought you were headed to Montana."

Julia continued to pan the room while she spoke. "I told the congresswoman I couldn't make it. Is your offer still open?"

"To be my chief of staff? Of course. It's not like I had time today to ask anyone else to fill the spot."

"I want it. I can start whenever you want."

"You seriously already quit Shelley's campaign? Did you just assume I wouldn't be able to find anyone else so quickly?"

She barely registered his last few words when she spotted Addison, dancing with her brother, no more than a dozen feet away. "I took a risk, sir. I hope it's a good night for taking risks."

She didn't wait for his reply. Instead she squared her shoulders and strode onto the dance floor, hoping it was indeed a good night for taking risks.

❖

Addison walked into the Great Hall of the National Building Museum, flanked by Jack and her father, who both looked dashing in their dress uniforms. Thank God she'd let the saleswoman at Neiman's talk her into the midnight blue Armani gown or she'd feel decidedly underdressed.

The room was packed despite the fact they were a few minutes early for the official start of the festivities. Moments after they made it through security, she heard the band begin to play "Hail to the Chief." She and Jack, and even her staunchly conservative father, applauded as the president and first lady took to the floor for their first dance of the evening. They were a striking couple.

When their dance was over, Jack took her hand and nodded toward the dance floor.

"Oh, no. I don't feel much like dancing."

"You're seriously going to deny a soldier a dance?"

"You're impossible. Okay, one dance."

They fell into an easy rhythm. As he turned her around the floor, she took in the sea of uniforms and experienced a sense of pride to be in the company of so many service personnel. Once more around the floor and she saw the president talking to a woman whose back was to her. She had gorgeous red hair, and for a second, Addison wondered, hoped, that maybe it was…Before she could finish the thought, the woman turned and Addison ducked her head.

Julia. Julia was here.

"Addy, are you okay?"

She looked at Jack and then back at the spot where she'd just seen the president and Julia, but both of them were gone. Could she have imagined she'd seen her? Did her feelings run so deep they'd caused her to hallucinate? She had to get a grip. "I'm okay, but I might need to find a drink soon."

"No problem."

Jack guided them to the edge of the dance floor, but just as they were about to disengage, Addison looked up to see Julia standing directly behind him, and their eyes locked. Jack, following her gaze, looked over his shoulder, and Julia, without breaking eye contact, asked, "May I cut in?"

Jack looked back and forth between them, and Addison finally nodded. He leaned in close to her before he stepped to the side and whispered, "Dad was right. She's a very pretty lady."

The band started playing the next song, and seconds later, she was in Julia's arms and they were gliding around the floor. Addison had a million questions, but she couldn't prioritize, so she simply said, "You're an excellent dancer."

"Lots of parties, lots of practice. One of the hazards of my former occupation."

There was a clue there, but, distracted by Julia's bare porcelain shoulders and the way her sea green gown caused her emerald eyes to flash, she couldn't dissect it. She started with the facts she knew. "I thought you were leaving town."

"I decided that would be a terrible idea."

"Oh, you did, did you? And when did you make this decision?"

"Earlier today, while I was at the airport, but I should have made it long before."

Addison heard the closing notes of the song. They didn't have much time before the dance ended, and she had no idea what would happen after. Julia held her close, and the touch of her body was intoxicating. She longed to forget whatever had kept them apart, agree to whatever terms Julia needed to make this moment last as long as possible, but she couldn't suppress her need to know exactly why Julia had chosen to be here tonight. The band played its final phrase, and couples began to file off the dance floor. She stood perfectly still, tucked in Julia's arms, and simply said, "Tell me."

Julia's voice shook, but her gaze was steady. "I should have made the decision to stay on New Year's Eve, the night you told me you loved me. I was scared to commit. Afraid I didn't deserve you, that we couldn't make a relationship work in the context of our careers. But I can't imagine my life without you. You're all I think about. So I guess what I did tonight was kind of stupid, but I told the president I would take Noah's job, which I know will make things between us even more complicated, but it'll mean I'll be here, in town, and by sticking around, maybe I can find a way to make it work and I guess if we—"

Addison placed a finger over her lips to stop the ramble. She didn't understand half of what Julia had said, but she got the gist. Julia was staying in town and she wanted more. It was a lot. The music was starting up again, but they both remained still. She should dance the next dance and then take Julia home, make love to her, and wake up tomorrow ready to start figuring out what more meant to them.

No, she already knew what more meant to her. It meant rings and vows and forever. It meant I'll be with you to the very end, when careers and ambitions had faded into hobbies and the status quo. She could keep dancing and wondering what the future held or she could be sure. She looked deep into Julia's eyes, willing her to understand the importance of this moment, willing her to know what hung in the balance. "Tell me."

Julia cleared her throat, and this time when she spoke there was no tremor. "I love you. I've loved you since that first moment when you cut short our first date because you didn't like my politics. I'll always love you, even when we disagree, even when our work divides us, because you are the smartest, kindest, sexiest woman I know, and I want to be with you for the rest of my life."

It was the first time Madam Chief Justice kissed a woman in public, but it wouldn't be the last. Addison pulled Julia closer, and as their lips met in a searing kiss, everything else—the crowd, the band, the politics—fell away and they started their future with a celebration of their own.

THE END

About the Author

Carsen Taite's goal as an author is to spin tales with plot lines as interesting as the cases she encountered in her career as a criminal defense lawyer. She is the author of ten previously released novels, *truelesbianlove.com*, *It Should be a Crime* (a Lambda Literary Award finalist), *Do Not Disturb*, *Nothing but the Truth*, *The Best Defense*, *Slingshot*, *Beyond Innocence*, *Battle Axe, Rush*, and *Switchblade*. She is currently working on her twelfth novel, *Lay Down the Law*, another tale of romantic intrigue. Learn more at www.carsentaite.com.

Books Available from Bold Strokes Books

Courtship by Carsen Taite. Love and justice—a lethal mix or a perfect match? (978-1-62639-210-6)

Against Doctor's Orders by Radclyffe. Corporate financier Presley Worth wants to shut down Argyle Community Hospital, but Dr. Harper Rivers will fight her every step of the way, if she can also fight their growing attraction. (978-1-62639-211-3)

A Spark of Heavenly Fire by Kathleen Knowles. Kerry and Beth are building their life together, but unexpected circumstances could destroy their happiness. (978-1-62639-212-0)

Never Too Late by Julie Blair. When Dr. Jamie Hammond is forced to hire a new office manager, she's shocked to come face to face with Carla Grant and memories from her past. (978-1-62639-213-7)

Widow by Martha Miller. Judge Bertha Brannon must solve the murder of her lover, a policewoman she thought she'd grow old with. As more bodies pile up, the murderer starts coming for her. (978-1-62639-214-4)

Twisted Echoes by Sheri Lewis Wohl. What's a woman to do when she realizes the voices in her head are real? (978-1-62639-215-1)

Criminal Gold by Ann Aptaker. Through a dangerous night in New York in 1949, Cantor Gold, dapper dyke-about-town, smuggler of fine art, is forced by a crime lord to be his instrument of vengeance. (978-1-62639-216-8)

The Melody of Light by M.L. Rice. After surviving abuse and loss, will Riley Gordon be able to navigate her first year of college and accept true love and family? (978-1-62639-219-9)

Because of You by Julie Cannon. What would you do for the woman you were forced to leave behind? (978-1-62639-199-4)

The Job by Jove Belle. Sera always dreamed that she would one day reunite with Tor. She just didn't think it would involve terrorists, firearms, and hostages. (978-1-62639-200-7)

Making Time by C.J. Harte. Two women going in different directions meet after fifteen years and struggle to reconnect in spite of the past that separated them. (978-1-62639-201-4)

Once The Clouds Have Gone by KE Payne. Overwhelmed by the dark clouds of her past, Tag Grainger is lost until the intriguing and spirited Freddie Metcalfe unexpectedly forces her to reevaluate her life. (978-1-62639-202-1)

The Acquittal by Anne Laughlin. Chicago private investigator Josie Harper searches for the real killer of a woman whose lover has been acquitted of the crime. (978-1-62639-203-8)

An American Queer: The Amazon Trail by Lee Lynch. Lee Lynch's heartening and heart-rending history of gay life from the turbulence of the late 1900s to the triumphs of the early 2000s are recorded in this selection of her columns. (978-1-62639-204-5)

Stick McLaughlin: The Prohibition Years by CF Frizzell. Corruption in 1918 cost Stick her lover, her freedom, and her identity, but a very special flapper and the family bond of her own gang could help win them back—even if it means outwitting the Boston Mob. (978-1-62639-205-2)

Edge of Awareness by C.A. Popovich. When Maria, a woman in the middle of her third divorce, meets Dana, an out lesbian, awareness of her feelings brings up reservations about the teachings of her church. (978-1-62639-188-8)

Taken by Storm by Kim Baldwin. Lives depend on two women when a train derails high in the remote Alps, but an unforgiving mountain, avalanches, crevasses, and other perils stand between them and safety. (978-1-62639-189-5)

The Common Thread by Jaime Maddox. Dr. Nicole Coussart's life is falling apart, but fortunately, DEA Attorney Rae Rhodes is there to pick up the pieces and help Nic put them back together. (978-1-62639-190-1)

Jolt by Kris Bryant. Mystery writer Bethany Lange wasn't prepared for the twisting emotions that left her breathless the moment she laid eyes on folk singer sensation Ali Hart. (978-1-62639-191-8)

Searching For Forever by Emily Smith. Dr. Natalie Jenner's life has always been about saving others, until young paramedic Charlie Thompson comes along and shows her maybe she's the one who needs saving. (978-1-62639-186-4)

A Queer Sort of Justice: Prison Tales Across Time by Rebecca S. Buck. When liberty is only a memory, and all seems lost, what freedoms and hopes can be found within us? (978-1-62639-195-6E)

Blue Water Dreams by Dena Hankins. Lania Marchiol keeps her wary sailor's gaze trained on the horizon until Oly Rassmussen, a wickedly handsome trans man, sends her trusty compass spinning off course. (978-1-62639-192-5)

Rest Home Runaways by Clifford Henderson. Baby boomer Morgan Ronzio's troubled marriage is the least of her worries when she gets the call that her addled, eighty-six-year-old, half-blind dad has escaped the rest home. (978-1-62639-169-7)

Charm City by Mason Dixon. Raq Overstreet's loyalty to her drug kingpin boss is put to the test when she begins to fall for Bathsheba Morris, the undercover cop assigned to bring him down. (978-1-62639-198-7)

Let the Lover Be by Sheree Greer. Kiana Lewis, a functional alcoholic on the verge of destruction, finally faces the demons of her past while finding love and earning redemption in New Orleans. (978-1-62639-077-5)

Blindsided by Karis Walsh. Blindsided by love, guide dog trainer Lenae McIntyre and media personality Cara Bradley learn to trust what they see with their hearts. (978-1-62639-078-2)

About Face by VK Powell. Forensic artist Macy Sheridan and Detective Leigh Monroe work on a case that has troubled them both for years, but they're hampered by the past and their unlikely yet undeniable attraction. (978-1-62639-079-9)

Blackstone by Shea Godfrey. For Darry and Jessa, their chance at a life of freedom is stolen by the arrival of war and an ancient prophecy that just might destroy their love. (978-1-62639-080-5)

Out of This World by Maggie Morton. Iris decided to cross an ocean to get over her ex. But instead, she ends up traveling much farther, all the way to another world. Once there, only a mysterious, sexy, and magical woman can help her return home. (978-1-62639-083-6)

Kiss The Girl by Melissa Brayden. Sleeping with the enemy has never been so complicated. Brooklyn Campbell and Jessica Lennox face off in love and advertising in fast-paced New York City. (978-1-62639-071-3)

Taking Fire: A First Responders Novel by Radclyffe. Hunted by extremists and under siege by nature's most virulent weapons, Navy medic Max de Milles and Red Cross worker Rachel Winslow join forces to survive and discover something far more lasting. (978-1-62639-072-0)

First Tango in Paris by Shelley Thrasher. When French law student Eva Laroche meets American call girl Brigitte Green in 1970s Paris, they have no idea how their pasts and futures will intersect. (978-1-62639-073-7)

The War Within by Yolanda Wallace. Army nurse Meredith Moser went to Vietnam in 1967 looking to help those in need; she didn't expect to meet the love of her life along the way. (978-1-62639-074-4)

Escapades by MJ Williamz. Two women, afraid to love again, must overcome their fears to find the happiness that awaits them. (978-1-62639-182-6)

Desire at Dawn by Fiona Zedde. For Kylie, love had always come armed with sharp teeth and claws. But with the human, Olivia, she bares her vampire heart for the very first time, sharing passion, lust, and a tenderness she'd never dared dream of before. (978-1-62639-064-5)

Visions by Larkin Rose. Sometimes the mysteries of love reveal themselves when you least expect it. Other times they hide behind a black satin mask. Can Paige unveil her masked stranger this time? (978-1-62639-065-2)

All In by Nell Stark. Internet poker champion Annie Navarro loses everything when the Feds shut down online gambling, and she turns to experienced casino host Vesper Blake for advice—but can Nova convince Vesper to take a gamble on romance? (978-1-62639-066-9)

Vermilion Justice by Sheri Lewis Wohl. What's a vampire to do when Dracula is no longer just a character in a novel? (978-1-62639-067-6)

Switchblade by Carsen Taite. Lines were meant to be crossed. Third in the Luca Bennett Bounty Hunter Series. (978-1-62639-058-4)

Nightingale by Andrea Bramhall. Culture, faith, and duty conspire to tear two young lovers apart, yet fate seems to have different plans for them both. (978-1-62639-059-1)

No Boundaries by Donna K. Ford. A chance meeting and a nightmare from the past threaten more than Andi Massey's solitude as she and Gwen Palmer struggle to understand the complexity of love without boundaries. (978-1-62639-060-7)